JUN 2 0

Hard Cash Valley

Hard Cash Valley

BRIAN PANOWICH

MINOTAUR
BOOKS
NEW YORK

First published in the United States by Minotaur Books,
an imprint of St. Martin's Publishing Group

HARD CASH VALLEY. Copyright © 2020 by Brian Panowich. All rights reserved.
Printed in the United States of America. For information, address St. Martin's
Publishing Group, 120 Broadway, New York, NY 10271.

www.minotaurbooks.com

"Love Sonnet XVI": From 100 LOVE SONNETS: CIEN SONETOS
DE AMOR by Pablo Neruda, translated by Stephen Tapscott,
Copyright © Pablo Neruda 1959 and Fundacion Pablo Neruda,
Copyright © 1986 by the University of Texas Press.
By permission of the University of Texas Press.

The Library of Congress Cataloging-in-Publication Data
is available upon request.

ISBN 978-1-250-20692-3 (hardcover)
ISBN 978-1-250-20693-0 (ebook)

Our books may be purchased in bulk for promotional, educational,
or business use. Please contact your local bookseller or the Macmillan
Corporate and Premium Sales Department at 1-800-221-7945, extension 5442,
or by email at MacmillanSpecialMarkets@macmillan.com.

First Edition: May 2020

10 9 8 7 6 5 4 3 2 1

For Wyatt

If people bring so much courage to this world the world has to kill them to break them, so of course it kills them. The world breaks every one and afterward many are strong at the broken places. But those that will not break it kills. It kills the very good and the very gentle and the very brave impartially. If you are none of these you can be sure it will kill you too but there will be no special hurry.

—Ernest Hemingway, *A Farewell to Arms*

They say it makes you stronger, but first you gotta survive
What didn't kill you, will make you wish you died . . .
You call that a scar, a bruise, a tear, pillow marks, souvenirs

—Cory Branan, "Survivor Blues (The After Hours)"

Hard Cash Valley

CHAPTER ONE

Arnie Blackwell was sweating bullets.

He'd sweat so bad on the plane, he felt like he'd just stepped out of a shower fully dressed. When he'd boarded the plane in Atlanta, he'd had no idea that the suitcase he'd used to pack up the cash would be too big for him to carry on, and now Arnie was standing in front of the baggage-claim carousel on the bottom floor of the Jacksonville airport, shoulder to shoulder with all the other passengers, waiting on a little more than five hundred grand to magically appear on the conveyor belt.

He couldn't breathe. Every time a suitcase that wasn't his slid out from behind the black rubber curtain, his heart thundered in his rib cage hard enough to hurt. The baggage-claim area was massive and Arnie was surrounded by hundreds of people—every one of them he was sure knew something wasn't right with him—but as each new unfamiliar piece of luggage came into sight, the blue and gray concrete walls of the wide-open expanse moved in closer and tighter until it began to feel less like an airport and more like another prison cell. He began to feel claustrophobic. When his phone rang it nearly sent Arnie into cardiac arrest. He flinched hard enough to bump both of the travelers flanking him as they waited for their own bags. One man, a big, tough-looking joker in a Carhartt sweatshirt, actually pushed him back. Normally, Arnie wouldn't take that kind of shit from anyone—regardless of their size—but he kept himself in check. There was too much riding on his keeping his composure. He ignored the big redneck. Right now, he just wanted that light brown tweed suitcase with the Moosejaw bumper sticker plastered across the lid to appear on the conveyor so he could collect his payday and possibly get his hands to stop shaking. He fumbled the phone out of the pocket of his Adidas windbreaker and read the name on the display—*Bobby Turo*. Arnie wiped a sweaty palm on his pants and then held the phone to his ear.

"Bobby? Is everything all good? Did you get back safe?"

"Yeah, man. Smooth sailing."

"Is William okay?"

"Yeah, we went right where you asked me to."

Arnie's heart slowed a beat. "And you walked him in, right? You gotta walk him in. And you gotta stay there with him, Bobby. Don't you fucking leave him. You can't just break him from his routine. He'll freak out."

"Sounds more like you're the one freaking out. Take it easy. He's fine. He knew more about what he was doing than I did. Calm down, bro."

Arnie's head started throbbing with a sudden rush of blood. His voice suddenly quiet. "Are you high right now?"

"Dude. Arnie. Relax. We did it. We're home free and the kid is fine. We went over it a hundred times. I promise. It's all good."

"It better be *all good*, Bobby. If we lose that kid we lose even bigger scores." Arnie glanced around him and kept his voice hushed. "Two hours. You stay put for two hours. Right where I told you to go, and then take him where I said to take him—right? Bobby? Are you listening to me?"

"Arnie, Jesus, will you chill out. Randy says wassup."

"No, I won't *chill out*, you fucking idiot, and why is Randy with you?"

"He's not—he just texted me."

Arnie shook it off. "Bobby, I just want to know my little brother is where he's supposed to be."

"Well, he is. Okay."

Arnie took a deep breath. "Good. All right. Now try to pay attention, you pothead. I'm at the airport in Jacksonville. I just landed. I had a problem with my luggage. They wouldn't let me carry it on—you should've checked into that before you gave me the damn thing to use—but as soon as I get it in my hands, I'm going to pick up the other package. You did send the other package, right?"

"Yes. Days ago. I told you that."

"To PO Box 213. On Gaston Street."

"Jesus, Arnie, yes—to PO Box 213 on Gaston Street."

"Good. After I check into the motel and get a few hours' sleep, I have to set everything up down here for me and William long term. When I'm done, I'll be back for him, but you and I aren't going to talk for a while after that—clear? *Do not* call me under any circumstances. It's too dangerous—unless there's a problem with my brother. And there better not be a problem with my brother, Bobby."

"Just handle your business, Arnie. I got this."

"You fucking better."

Arnie heard the double beep of another call coming in on the line. He looked at the display again to see William's name. He lifted the phone back to his ear. "That's Willie calling me on the other line. I swear to God, Bobby, if you fucked this up. If he's alone right now and you're lying to me. If he's in trouble—"

"I said he's fine, man. You need to calm down." Stoned or not, Bobby was getting tired of being scolded like a child. He got defensive. "Maybe you should remember who bankrolled this little adventure, Arnie. Without me there would be no—"

Arnie ended the call in mid-sentence. *Little adventure?* If that hippie had been standing in front of him right that second, he'd have knocked his fronts out. He couldn't see what Bernadette saw in that idiot. He calmed himself and answered the other line. "William?"

"Yes."

"Where are you?"

"I'm hungry."

Arnie switched the phone to his other ear. "What?" His hands were shaking so bad that he dropped his claim ticket in the process of moving the phone. He nearly dropped the phone, too, as he frantically tried to pick up the slip of paper as if he'd just dropped a winning lottery ticket, which was not far off. He bumped the man to his left again. This time the big boy acted even less pleased and shoved Arnie harder than he had the first time. Arnie barely noticed the nudge as his eyes followed the claim ticket to the floor. He bent over and snatched it up before it had even settled and managed to bump the big man a third time as he straightened back up.

"You got a problem, buddy?"

Arnie dropped the phone down by his side and squeezed it tight enough to turn his knuckles white. "Maybe. Maybe I got a big fucking problem. Maybe I'm just one mouthy asshole away from losing my shit."

"Is that right?" Carhartt puffed his chest out, but his voice was timid. He couldn't get a read on Arnie's degree of crazy, and the lack of confidence made him sound weak. Arnie could smell the blood in the water. The big boy was soft.

"Yeah, that's right. And if you put your fat hands on me again, I'll shove this phone straight down your throat." Arnie was still sweating like he'd been sitting in a sauna for the last six hours, and this time Carhartt could read every bit of the crazy in his eyes, so the big boy quickly found another place to stand. The small victory made Arnie feel a little better. He swiftly forgot about the man and shifted his focus back to the carousel. A security guard in a gray uniform stood several feet over to Arnie's left. He'd been watching Arnie since he walked in—or maybe he wasn't. Arnie's paranoia made everyone around him suspect, but Arnie tried to avoid eye contact with the airport cop all the same. An Asian man pushed his way into the space vacated by the Carhartt redneck and made room for a young girl—his daughter, most likely—eleven or so— William's age. Arnie smiled at her, but after one look at Arnie, the girl's father immediately sheltered her and stood between them. Arnie couldn't blame him. He was soaking wet. His clothes were sticking to him and he smelled like spoiled lunch meat. He was also shaking like a dope fiend. The Asian man grabbed a sleek black suitcase from the conveyor and quickly hustled away. Arnie was freaking out. Where was his fucking suitcase? How could he be so stupid to let this happen? *Goddamn TSA.*

The security guard was moving in closer. At least, Arnie thought he was. His heart was pounding so hard he was sure everyone around him could hear it. He felt like the old man from "The Tell-Tale Heart," except there wasn't a body behind that steel wall. There was a box of money. It was Arnie's first real lucky break, and, he hoped, the last he'd ever need.

Fuck. Fuck. Fuck. Fuck. Fuck. Where is my damn bag? Arnie thought his head might spin right off his shoulders. *Please, God, just let me have this one thing—just this one thing.*

And then, like an answered prayer, there it was. The top of the tweed case slowly emerged through the curtain of thick rubber strips and inched into view until Arnie could see the red sticker his brother had stuck across the lid. William loved stickers. Arnie shoved his way past several other people, saying "Excuse me" all the way. He snaked his wiry frame through the crowd toward his luggage. "Excuse me. Sorry. Excuse me." An older woman mumbled something as he pushed past her, but Arnie ignored her. He didn't even see her. He stopped seeing people altogether, or security guards, or crushing prison cell walls. All he could see was that suitcase, and now he was only a few feet away. He nudged his way closer until he could get a grip on the leather handle and hoisted it off the conveyor belt with a renewed vigor. The act of lifting the bag made him feel stronger. He felt whole somehow, as if he'd just reconnected to a lost limb. As he turned to walk away, he could feel the excitement set in. He could feel the anxiety begin to melt away and he finally stopped sweating. Arnie homed in on the massive set of double doors leading outside. He navigated his way through the crowd and toward those doors with tunnel vision. All he could see was the sunshine on the other side of the sliding glass. He picked up the pace and slammed right into the airport security guard who may or may not have been standing there the whole time.

"Whoa—slow it down there, sir."

"Sorry." Arnie regrouped and kept walking. The young airport cop reached out for Arnie's suitcase, but Arnie snatched it away and held it up to his chest.

"I'm going to need to see that, sir."

Arnie just stared at the slim mocha face of the young man, unable to form any words. He tried to move to the left, but the guard sidestepped him and blocked his way. His voice stayed calm and smooth. "Sir, is everything all right?"

"What?" Arnie wasn't sure what was happening. Stars were bursting in his peripheral vision. He felt sick, as if he might throw up.

"I said, is everything all right?" The guard's eyes narrowed slightly with suspicion, but Arnie had trouble keeping eye contact. He couldn't focus. The walls of the airport baggage claim began to breathe and warp.

"Yeah. Everything is fine." Arnie struggled to stay in the moment—to focus. "What?" he said. "What do you want?" He stood as still as he could while he tried to form the right words but Arnie's gut instinct was to run—to just bolt for the doors. He probably would have, too, but he couldn't get his feet to move.

"I need to see your claim ticket?"

"My what?"

The young guard's voice sounded like a distant, untuned car radio.

"Your claim ticket, sir. For your luggage." That time Arnie made out the request through the static in his head. He relaxed a little—barely—and looked down at his hand. He was still holding the crumpled slip of paper—and his phone. He hadn't ended the last call. William was still waiting on the line. That grounded Arnie in reality.

Why hadn't the little weirdo hung up?

Still fighting the voice in his head telling him to just cut loose and run, but better equipped now to move his limbs, Arnie set the suitcase down at his feet, handed the airport security guard the claim ticket, and held the phone to his ear.

"Willie, are you still there?"

"Yes."

"I gotta go. I'm going to hang up now. Just stay put. When you're done there, go with Bobby and wait. I'll call you back."

"I'm hungry, Arnie."

"Well, eat something, then—shit," Arnie blurted into the phone, before ending the call and slipping it into his back pocket. William might've been his meal ticket, but he drove Arnie crazy with all his weird shit. Arnie looked at the young black man in the uniform with all the disgust he felt for his little brother and Bobby. He was feeling better, his paranoia subsiding, leaving his body like an apparition. He even smiled a little. "Are we good here or what?"

The security guard carefully inspected the sweat-soaked ticket and matched it to the sticker on the handle of Arnie's suitcase. He handed the ticket back to him. His eyes were bright green. Arnie wasn't sure why he noticed that.

"How about it, Smokey? Can I go now?"

That crack didn't sit well with the young guard, but he was used to stupid white people at the airport. He took a slow breath and answered almost robotically. "Yes. You're free to go. Is there anything I can help you with? Do you need directions to the cab stand or the car-rental area?"

Arnie ignored him and grabbed the suitcase. He was already making for the sliding glass doors leading to the sunlit outside world. Out of the corner of his eye, he thought he saw the guard talking into his radio—or maybe he didn't. He didn't care. All Arnie Blackwell knew was that he wanted the hell out of that place—and now he was.

Arnie didn't fully relax during the entire cab ride—even when he made a quick stop by the post office on Gaston Road to get the package Bobby had mailed to their prearranged PO box.

At least that pothead sack of shit didn't screw that up.

Arnie's anxiety melted away even further, like a layer of liquefied fat, once he tore open the package marked up with Bobby's handwriting and saw the five disassembled pieces of the Sig Sauer—each component bundled neatly in bubble wrap and all perfectly surrounded by a small sea of foam packing peanuts. *Potheads*, he thought. *Everything they do is like a high school science project.* Arnie let loose a small giggle thinking about Bobby carefully premeasuring the tape, wrapping each piece, and tucking each one into the box along with one magazine and individually wrapped bullets. Arnie shook his head. He pictured Bobby standing at the counter of the post office carefully tapping NO to the questions listed on the keypad for the clerk.

Anything liquid, fragile, or combustible?

"Nope."

Any lithium batteries?

"Nope."

And then walking out of the post office with his sunglasses pushed close to his face to hide his bloodshot eyes, smiling that dopey smile of his. "Good job, Bobby," Arnie whispered to himself, and eased back into the seat of the cab. The tension in his muscles had loosened but allowed a fresh new ache to set in, like a runner would experience after a 10k race, and despite the feeling of safety that having a gun gave him, Arnie was still so spun out from the airport that his leg wouldn't stop bouncing up and down in the back of the yellow Corolla. He discreetly unwrapped each piece and put the gun together down low behind the side passenger seat, using the speed loader Bobby had included to fill the magazine with

9mm hollow points. If the Iranian cab driver saw him do any of it, he was either accustomed to having people with guns in the back of his car or he didn't care. When the cab finally pulled in at the Days Inn, Arnie had already stuffed the gun in his pants and handed the driver two twenties for the eighteen-dollar ride. Arnie was finally feeling good. This was how he was going to be living from now on—large and in charge. The driver wanted to get chatty due to the big tip, but Arnie slipped out of the car, holding the suitcase tight against his chest, and bumped the car door shut with his hip while the driver was still talking. He left the open cardboard box filled with packing foam and bubble wrap on the floorboard of the car for someone else to clean up. He was done cleaning up messes. By the time he'd entered the lobby of the motel, he couldn't have even remembered what the man driving the cab looked like, or if it was even a man. He only knew he had gotten away with it. He did it. He finally did it. It was easy-peasy from here on out—nothing but high-dollar bourbon and uptown pussy from this day forward. First class all the way. The receptionist behind the counter, however, was quick to stick a pin in Arnie's inflated ego balloon.

"I'm sorry, Mr. Blackwell, your room is still being cleaned. Check-in isn't until four o'clock." The receptionist was a redhead who wore too much makeup to cover up her acne scars, and her monotone speech conveyed a clear hatred for her job—maybe people in general. Arnie couldn't be sure. He looked at the clock on the wall behind the desk. He liked redheads, and this one wasn't that bad-looking either, aside from the craters in her face. She was the kind of flawed tail Arnie would throw some game at under normal circumstances. But these weren't normal circumstances—so he was an asshole. "It's fucking three thirty."

The redhead stiffened in her chair as the stick up her ass expanded to its full length. "Yes, it is, sir, and like I said, check-in is at four o'clock." She pointed a rigid finger to a plastic gold-colored sign on the counter reiterating that point. Arnie read it and then read her name tag. Again, this is where his charm should've kicked in to help him get his way, but Arnie didn't need charm—not anymore. He had cash. Money talks. Everybody knows that.

"Look, Abby?" He said her name like a question. "I'll give you a hundred bucks on top of what I owe for the reservation—right here, right now—if you just take one of those key cards and swipe the damn thing so I can get myself settled in my room."

Abby just stared at him blankly. The room itself was only eighty dollars.

"Seriously," he said. "A hundred bucks. Cash. Just for you."

"We're not allowed to accept tips, sir."

Arnie leaned on the counter, never letting the suitcase touch the floor, and took a deep breath through his nose. If he didn't get himself behind a locked door with a fat joint soon, he felt like he might literally explode. He reached into his windbreaker and pulled out a wad of cash. He counted out two hundred dollars in twenties with his thumb and laid it on the counter. "I know you've got cameras on you right now. I know you don't want to lose your job, but there's a way around that. Trust me. We can make it look like I'm just paying for the room. Take the extra out later when you're counting your drawer down. It'll be the easiest hundred and twenty bucks you've ever made. Just please, break the rule and let me check in to my room. Please."

Abby stared at the money for what seemed like forever before she picked up the motel phone. Arnie's heart sank, and he suddenly became aware of the gun tucked into the waistband of his track pants.

If this bitch calls the cops, I'm screwed. Stop being a dick, Arnie. You can hold out in the lobby for thirty minutes. Don't blow everything now over a motel room.

He started backpedaling. "Look, Abby. I'm sorry. I'm not trying to be a prick here. I'm just really tired from my flight and need to lie down. I'm running on fumes here."

Abby ignored him and pressed some buttons on the phone.

Arnie reached around to the small of his back. "C'mon, Abby. I said I was sorry."

"Mario?" Abby said into the phone. "Is room 1108 ready yet?"

Arnie took his hand off the grip of the gun. He hadn't even realized he was going for it.

"I have a guest in the lobby that would like an early check-in."

Arnie mouthed the words "Bless you."

Abby nodded and offered him a *whatever* half smile. Arnie smiled back and tipped his chin. He thought he might even invite her up to his room later. When she saw his bankroll, she must've started to understand she was dealing with a baller—*a baller, baby*. After Mario finished talking, she held the phone against her chest. "He says the room is clean but he hasn't had a chance to restock the towels."

"Not a problem. I'll take it. Bring the towels whenever. I can drip dry."

"Um, okay." Abby held the phone back to her ear. "He said that's fine. You can bring them up later."

Arnie blew out another deep breath as Abby hung up the phone. She laid out some paperwork on the counter and Arnie grabbed a pen with a huge plastic daisy duct-taped to it out of a jar. He filled out the papers as best he could with one hand, still refusing to put down the case, and then handed over his Georgia ID. The state had taken his driver's license after his fourth DUI in 2010, so the state-issued ID was all he had. Abby took it, raised an eyebrow at him, and typed something into her computer. It took her forever. Long enough for Arnie to start thinking again about shooting her.

"All right, Mr. Blackwell. You're all done." She handed him back his ID. "You're in room 1108. That's right outside the doors you came in and to the left around the building." She tucked a set of key cards and his receipt in an envelope and laid it next to the cash. It felt to Arnie as if she was moving underwater.

"Bottom floor?"

"Yes. That's on the bottom floor. Out the door to the left."

"Thanks."

"What part of Atlanta are you from?" Abby said, suddenly friendly. "I've got a friend who lives in Midtown. It's not really the middle of the city so I don't know why they call it that. It's more north than anything else." Arnie looked at her, confused. He could feel his inner dickhead beginning to surface but decided instead to just ignore her. He blew through his nose and snatched up the envelope, and Abby with the friend in Midtown ceased to exist. He made for the front door.

After stopping at a vending machine to buy a can of Dr Pepper, Arnie soon found himself inside a locked double room, sitting on the bed, crumbling one of the fat green buds he'd pulled from one of Bobby's "special travel bags" he'd stuffed into the liner of the suitcase. Bobby promised the bags kept anything in them "undetectable, dude." And fuckin' A, he was right. Bobby was rarely wrong when it came to weed or weed-related accessories. He had that going for him at least. Arnie rolled the sticky kush in a torn-out page of a Gideon Bible he found in the end-table drawer. He'd make a proper pipe out of the Dr Pepper can when he was done drinking it. When Mario finally knocked on the door with the towels, he slid the case under the bed, feeling no pain and grinning like a damn fool. Maybe he'd get Mario high. The guy's name was Mario. He had to partake. He had to. And, man, a shower was going to feel damn good after the past three days of dust and grime at the farm, but on the upside, this was the last shitty motel room he'd ever stay in. He'd be laying down the rent on something oceanside by this time tomorrow. Arnie had already stripped out of his sweaty tracksuit and unlocked the door wearing nothing but a pair of boxers and a T-shirt.

He still had the makeshift joint burning between his teeth when he opened the door, swinging it wide without so much as a glance through the peephole. He quickly lost his grin. Pot might make you feel good but it also made you dumb. The joint fell from his mouth and burned his chin before it hit the floor.

"Hello, Arnold." A short Filipino man with a stiff wave of black hair and a shiny electric blue suit pushed his way past Arnie and entered the room. He wasn't alone. Another man—another Filipino bruiser about twice the first man's size with a similar spiked haircut—followed the shorter man in.

"What the hell—Smoke?" Arnie's mind raced as he smacked at the fresh burn on his chin. He quickly—well, as quickly as his freshly stoned brain would let him—shifted gears to remember where he'd put the gun. The gun he and Bobby had taken such a huge risk for him to have in case something like this happened. Arnie didn't even know where he'd put it. Again, pot—it made you dumb. His mind started to twist around the absurdity of it. Maybe he was imagining them. He shook his head and blinked a few times. No, they were real, and they were here—in Florida—with him. Arnie's heart nearly stopped again as the smaller Filipino man cased the room, taking it in as if he'd never seen the inside of a cheap motel before. He looked at the lousy mass-produced painting of a boardwalk-lined beach on the wall and then poked his head into the bathroom. He was pleased to see it vacant. He nodded to his partner, who nodded back, and then reached through the bathroom door and produced Arnie's gun.

That's where it was, Arnie thought almost matter-of-factly, but then nearly collapsed under his own weight right there.

"Nice piece, Arnold." The small man ejected the magazine from the Sig Sauer and tucked it into the pocket of his suit. "I bet you wish you hadn't left this sitting in the bathroom right about now, huh?" He pulled back the slide. A single bullet popped out of the chamber and landed on the floor, and then the man in the flashy suit laid the empty gun on the bed. The small man looked pensive. "How did you get a gun, Arnold? Is this what was in the package? At the post office?" Smoke laughed. The other man did not.

Arnie stared at the useless weapon. *Jesus*, he thought. How had they tailed him so fast? He'd been careful. Maybe they were guessing. He tried to turn on the charm, but really had none to offer. "Shit, Smoke. I got ways, you know? A man can't be too careful, if you know what I'm saying. But it's not like I had it for someone like you or nothing. I mean, look where I left it. I saw you out there before I let you in. Um, I mean, I'm a little surprised to see you, but we're all friends here, right?" He looked at the beast next to him. The giant man hadn't missed a workout in decades and looked as if he'd been raised on raw meat and gunpowder. The veins in his exposed biceps looked like they were about to burst. When Arnie followed the length of the man's massive arms down to his hands he noticed the Kali baston for the first time. The brute had flipped it out from behind his girth like a magic trick and only now allowed Arnie to see it. A baston was nothing more than a length of oiled bamboo about three feet long, but Arnie had seen one before. He'd seen how, in the right hands, it could be used to tear a man to pieces. This man obviously had the right hands. The sight of the weapon diminished the small amount of confidence Arnie had in his voice. He began to sound like a child. "What's going on here, Smoke? Buddy. I mean, like, what are y'all doing here?" Arnie's eyes were glued to the baston.

Smoke held a finger to Arnie's lips as if to hush the child Arnie had suddenly become and spoke to him as if he were one. "No—no, Arnold. We are not *buddies*. We are not *friends* like you say."

"But Smoke, I . . ."

Smoke pressed his finger harder into Arnie's lips, contorting his entire mouth. He hushed Arnie again. Arnie shut up.

"Do you want to know why we are not friends, Arnold?"

Arnie tried to step away from Smoke, but the giant man with the baston snaked in behind him, grabbed his shoulder, and held him in place. Arnie tried to spin some more bullshit about not understanding what was happening, but Smoke hushed him a third time and answered his own question. "Because friends don't steal from each other. That's why. We come to this country to have fun. We come here to make money, not lose it. And you—you ruined our fun. You stole our money, Arnold. You stole a lot of people's money, and we want it back. I want it back. Then do you know what I want, Arnold? Can you guess? Or do I need to explain that to you, too?"

Arnie said nothing. Smoke looked disappointed.

"I want to know who else was involved and I want to know how you did it."

Arnie still said nothing. He couldn't take his eyes off the length of bamboo. The edge was sharpened. He'd never seen that before.

Smoke finally took his hand away from Arnie's face and snapped his fingers. He raised his voice to get Arnie's attention and his eyes back on him and off the bruiser to his left. "Did you hear me, you hillbilly?"

Arnie was too scared to speak. He looked back and forth from Smoke to the huge hand still holding on to his shoulder, as if he needed to be released to answer. Smoke nodded at his partner, and the man let Arnie go. Arnie slid away from both Smoke and the big man but made no sudden moves. He didn't want to give that mean-looking bastard another reason to put his hands on him. "C'mon, Smoke. It's not like that. I didn't steal anything. I just won is all. I got lucky, man. It happens like that sometimes, you know?"

Smoke dropped his head and shook it. He motioned to his companion again. This time the silent man didn't use his hand to make contact. He drew back and cracked Arnie in the face with the blunt end of the baston.

The hit spun Arnie in a complete circle before he eventually collided with a small table. He and the table both slammed into the wall. He slid down into a heap on the carpet, drenched in the open Dr Pepper that had been sitting on the table. Arnie threw up on the carpet and then sat there in a daze, sticky and wet, as he struggled to keep from blacking out. The silent man with the bamboo stick crossed his arms and went back to his place in front of the door.

Smoke gave himself a once-over to make sure none of the soda had splashed on his expensive suit, then started to search the room. He slid open the folding doors of the closet and then closed them. "Don't treat me like I'm stupid, Arnold." He opened the bathroom door again and pulled back the shower curtain. "I'm not stupid, and you are not lucky. Finding a wallet with fifty dollars in it is lucky." He opened and closed all the drawers in the dresser. "Not catching crabs after fucking your mother—that is lucky." He checked the nightstand. "But what you did? That is not lucky. No one is that lucky. That is called stupid. It is also called stealing. So, like I said already, me and the people you stole that money from want it back." Smoke looked at the bed and then at Arnie. He lifted a manicured eyebrow and pointed under the bed. Arnie wiped a trickle of blood off his chin, oozing from the freshly split lip, and let his head drop.

Smoke smiled and then motioned to his enforcer. "Move this, Fenn." Smoke got out of the way and the man Smoke had just called Fenn used one arm to slide the entire queen-sized bed across the floor. It sat diagonally in the center of the room to reveal the tweed suitcase that had been tucked underneath. Smoke smiled wider and his sharklike grin matched the sheen of his sharkskin suit. It was an effect that made him seem otherworldly to Arnie—something other than human—or maybe that was just the weed. More blood poured down his broken fat lip as he watched Smoke pick up the suitcase and set it on the bed. He shook it to hear the contents. "This sounds like progress, Arnold."

Arnie began to beg. "C'mon, Smoke, please. I won. I didn't do whatever you think I did. I swear to God, man. This time I really just won."

Fenn moved toward him, and Arnie held up his hands to cover his face. Smoke snapped his fingers and Fenn stopped. Arnie slowly lowered his arms and opened his eyes. Smoke was sitting on the bed next to the case.

"I believe you, Arnold." Smoke used his thumbs to work the latches on the case. "I didn't say you were lying. I didn't call you a liar. I called you a thief—a stupid thief." He lifted the lid on the case and his grin evaporated. He saw the bundles of cash inside—tens, twenties, hundreds—all US currency, but he didn't see all of what he wanted to see. He estimated the amount in the case to be about half of the 1.2 million he was expecting to find. Still, the sight of that much money was hypnotic. Fenn even broke from his blank indifference to glance over at the contents of the case. It was a lot of money, even if it wasn't all of it. And Smoke *did* want to see all of it. His recovery wasn't yet complete. That meant there would be angry people back home. That meant more time in this stupid country. He closed his eyes and let out a long, whistling exhale.

Arnie started to cry.

Smoke closed the lid of the case and fastened the latches. He walked calmly across the room to where Arnie was sprawled on the floor. He picked up the small table and set it upright where it belonged, then lifted at his pants legs and crouched down to face Arnie. He reached out and Arnie flinched, but Smoke merely wiped at the tears on Arnie's cheek with his thumbs.

"Don't cry, stupid American. Not yet. Let me tell you something that will make you laugh instead. A joke, I suppose. Is that okay, Arnold? To tell you a joke? Shake your head okay, Arnold."

Arnie did.

"Do you know how Fenn and I found you so quickly?"

Arnie didn't say anything. He didn't even look up to meet Smoke's eyes.

"We never even had to look, dummy. We never lost you. All the way from that farm. There were other people on you, too. Some Mexicans. More Americans. Everybody angry. But you lost them all by the time you got to the airport. Not us, though. And get this, Arnie. We were sitting behind you on the plane, too. All the way from Atlanta. Isn't that funny?"

Arnie looked up and used the back of his hand to wipe at his eyes.

"Yes, that's right. We planned to kill you in the airport parking lot, but there were too many people around, so we followed you inside. You'd already checked the suitcase before we could scoop you up, so we had to buy shitty tickets on the same shitty plane you did so we could wait for you to claim the bag here in the Sunshine State." Smoke looked up at

Fenn. "We thought you were going to run away when that guard stopped you at the airport, didn't we, Fenn?"

"Yes, we did," Fenn said with a calm and almost feminine-sounding voice.

"You gave us a pretty good scare there, Arnold, but you did good. We were proud of you. Right, Fenn?"

"Yes. Real proud."

"So here we are, giving you a good scare, too. You know, to even things out. Are you scared, Arnold?"

Arnie didn't move. Smoke grabbed his face and squeezed his jaw. Blood leaked from the broken lip and stained the neck of the white T-shirt. "I asked you a question, Arnold. Are you scared?"

"Yes."

"Good. So now we are almost done here, and everything is as it should be. You are scared and stupid and I am smart and lucky. You see the difference, now?" Arnie cradled his head in his hands. He did see the difference. He'd been seeing it his whole life.

Smoke let go of Arnie and stood up. "Now tell me who else has the rest of our money."

Arnie was barely aware of the question. All he knew was that everything he'd done had been in vain. The whole year. All the practice. The escape route to the airport. All the small details. All the months of planning. All the risks. Mailing himself a gun. It was all for nothing. It always was. This was never going to end up any other way than this. Just like everything else he'd ever done in his whole miserable life. He should've known better.

"If you don't start answering my questions the first time I ask you, Arnold, I'm going to let Fenn start asking them. Is that what you want?"

Arnie looked up at the thick Filipino man behind Smoke. "Please, Smoke, I'll do whatever you want. Take the money. Just please don't hurt me. Don't hurt my friends. I'm begging you."

Smoke rubbed at his baby-smooth, hairless chin as if he was seriously taking the request under consideration. "That's a good start, Arnold." He narrowed his eyes at Arnie. "Be clear and precise with your next words, Arnold. If you are honest with me, no lies, then I give you my word that no one else needs to get hurt. Are you ready to be honest with me, Arnold?"

"Yes," Arnie said, but he knew Smoke was lying. Arnie knew this man's word meant nothing. In this game involving life-changing amounts of money, no one's did. They were going to kill him. He'd already said they were going to kill him at the airport back home. They'd kill Bobby, too. Arnie knew that. He hoped it would be quick, but he knew that was a fantasy, too. He's seen what a baston could do. He knew it wouldn't be a quick or painless death for either of them, but he also knew they didn't know anything about William and he wasn't going to give him up. He'd at least get that much right. He offered up one last defiant stare at Smoke as the small Asian man repeated himself for a final time. "Where is my damn money?"

Arnie opened his mouth to speak right before he was interrupted by the sound of Billy Idol singing "Rebel Yell" from somewhere behind them. All three men looked toward the bathroom. It was Arnie's cell phone. His favorite song played as its ringtone. "Ooh," Smoke said, almost giddy, as he crossed the room and entered the bathroom again. "Maybe I don't need your help, Arnold. Maybe I can simply ask whoever this is for the information I need. Now," he said as he scooped up the phone from the counter. "Who could this be?" He looked at the display, grinned, and then held it out for Arnie to see. "William Blackwell?" Smoke said with mild surprise. That is your last name, too, yes, Arnold? Is this your family calling? Is the rest of my money with someone who shares your blood? Maybe this William doesn't share your stupid as well."

Arnie's heart raced as he found enough of a second wind to sit up and beg again. "He's my little brother, Smoke. He's not involved. He's just a kid—and he's retarded, too. He doesn't know shit about any of this. I swear to you."

"Oh, yeah?" Smoke tapped the phone and held it to his ear. "Hello? William?"

There was a brief pause as Smoke listened to the voice of a child ask for his brother. "No," Smoke said. "I'm a friend of Arnie's. He can't come to the phone right now." He squatted back down to face Arnie. The left side of Arnie's face was now all swollen and puffy, matching his lip, from the hit he'd taken. Vomit mixed in with the blood and formed an elastic string from his broken mouth to his belly. He pleaded in a whisper. "Please, Smoke, just hang it up. He's a kid. He won't understand."

Smoke nodded but ignored him. "Yes," he said into the phone. "Your brother is here, William. It is William, right? Good. Now tell me where you are and I'll come get you. I'll bring you to your brother. Yes—that is what he wants you to do."

Arnie squeezed his eyes shut and straightened up against the wall. He knew he'd be punished for what he was about to do, but he had no choice. It was William. He wouldn't sell out the kid—*but Bobby would*, Arnie thought in a panic. If he gave them Bobby, then they would get to William. Unless he did something right now. Arnie yelled. He yelled loud enough for his brother to hear him clearly through the phone in Smoke's hand. "Hang up, Willie! He's lying! Hang up right now, and go to our safe place. Forget what I told you before and get out of there. Wait at our safe place. You hang up right this minute and wait—" That was all he was able to get out before Fenn swung the bamboo baston and hit Arnie hard enough to almost disconnect his jaw completely from his skull.

Arnie saw nothing but white bursts of light—fireworks in his peripheral vision—just seconds before the pain set in, and when the force of the blow did begin to manifest as pain, he nearly blacked out again. He didn't try to stop it. He invited it. He wanted everything to go black before the next hit came. His lower jaw gaped open and hung from the right of his face only by the skin of his cheek. Bright red blood filled his mouth and poured down his throat like a river of salted motor oil. The choking kept him awake. Blood splattered onto the carpet, speckling the pool of vomit with shiny red pearls. Arnie's blood peppered Smoke's face as well, leaving him covered with red freckles, but the sudden burst of blood didn't bother him at all. He barely reacted to it, as if having another man's blood hitting his face was part of his daily routine—like brushing his teeth. Smoke only seemed to show disappointment when he took the phone away from his ear and realized that Arnie's brother had heard the outburst and ended the call. That bothered him, and his annoyance turned to a slow-burning rage as he tucked the phone in his pocket and glared up at Fenn. "You broke his jaw. How is he supposed to talk now, you idiot?"

Fenn just shrugged, his eyes glazed over with pitch-black indifference. Smoke redirected the heat of his stare at Arnie. This was all about to come to an end and Arnie knew it, but his brother was safe. At least his little brother had a chance—he hoped. Someone would find him. Someone would help him. More tears streaked his ruined face. Smoke shook his head as if flies had begun to swarm around him. "That was very stupid, Arnold. Very stupid. Now you have just killed your own family. You know this, because you know me. I will find this boy and I will kill him. I will kill him with no mercy. I'll also keep him alive to feel all of it. I want you to know that. He will die like an animal and it will be your fault—yours."

Arnie fought through the pain in his face and turned his head slightly to look at the side table next to the bed. Smoke kept ranting. "You have killed your own family today, Arnold—not me—you. I offered you hope and you spit it back in my face." He wiped at some of the blood on his cheek and rubbed it between his fingers. "I want you to remember that and take it with you wherever you go from here. Let that be your final thought. You killed them all. This is all your fault."

Arnie had almost no strength in him, but he lifted his arm and pointed to the end table. He was barely conscious as he listened to Smoke drone on, but he kept his hand in the air and continued to point at the table. Smoke finally stopped talking and took notice. He stood up. "What, Arnold? Is there something over there you want me to see?" Smoke walked over to the side table and pointed to the drawer. "In here?"

Arnie tried to nod but he couldn't. His head just hung against his chest as if the only thing holding it to his body was an invisible length of string. He curled his fingers a few times in a *give me* gesture before letting his arm collapse back down to his side. Smoke studied the table, seeing nothing on it but the laminated TV channel guide and the motel's green binder of amenities. He looked at Arnie, who couldn't look back, and then slid open the side table's drawer. Inside he saw a green Bible embossed with gold lettering across the cover. At first he wanted to laugh, thinking that Arnie was asking for help from his American Jesus, but then he saw what he thought Arnie was asking for—a small unlined notepad of stationery with the motel logo printed at the top of each page and a matching ink pen. Smoke removed the notepad from the drawer. "This, Arnold? Is this what you want?"

Arnie still couldn't move his head to confirm, but he tapped his fingers on the carpet as a response. Smoke slid the notepad under Arnie's hand. He removed the pen and allowed Arnie to take it. It took some doing, but Arnie was able to write on the top page.

Dont hurt Willie
Please

Smoke read it and asked calmly for a third time. "I will not hurt the child if you tell me where my money is."
Arnie wrote again.

Your word

"Yes. Yes, of course, Arnold. You have my word. Unless you lie. Then the child dies."
Arnie wrote one more thing on the page. The sting of betrayal should've been something he was used to by now, considering all the people he'd sold out throughout the years, but it wasn't. It felt like the claws of a stray cat scratching down his spine as he wrote the name and address of his friend and condemned him to death.

Bobby Turo
313 Regan Drive GA

Arnie laid the pen down on the carpet. Smoke picked up the notepad. He studied Arnie's eyes for any sign of a lie and saw nothing but blank shame. He stood and slipped the entire notepad into the inner pocket of his suit jacket, then lifted the suitcase holding Arnie's take of the money—over five hundred thousand dollars in cash—and walked to the door. "You can finish him now, Fenn. Take as long as you want, but keep in mind that we have a long ride ahead of us. You will drive."
Fenn nodded. First, he removed a small plastic bottle of lighter fluid and a Zippo from a baggy pocket on his left thigh. He tossed them on the bed. "For later," he said, seemingly to himself in his unusual high tenor, and with his back still turned to Arnie, he twirled the baston like

a propeller between both hands. When he turned to face the broken man on the floor, it was the first time Fenn had let any real emotion play out across his face. He looked pleased. The talking was over. The screaming would begin.

Smoke turned to leave and opened the motel door. He didn't flinch or show any reaction at all when he found himself standing face to face with a young Cuban kid in a janitorial uniform. His nametag said MARIO, and he stood there holding a stack of fresh towels in one hand and a fist still held up in front of him mid-knock. Without any hesitation at all, Smoke lifted a towel from the top of the stack and used it to wipe the spatter of Arnie's blood off his face. "Thank you—Mario," he said, as if he'd called for the towel service himself. The young custodian dropped the rest of the towels on the cement and burst into a full sprint. Smoke stepped out of the room and onto the sidewalk. He watched Mario disappear around the corner of the building and then, using the towel in his hands, he eased the motel-room door closed behind him to quell some of the sickening sounds coming from inside. Fenn would not be happy about having to work faster, but Smoke didn't care as long as Fenn made sure to burn it clean. Smoke tossed the suitcase into the trunk of the stolen car, climbed into the passenger side, and waited impatiently. The drive would be long and they had more stupid to deal with.

"Fucking Americans."

CHAPTER TWO

Dane stared out across the rushing water of Bear Creek. His head was all over the place this morning, but still it remained stuffed full of ghosts. Soon enough he was talking to himself again. Or, rather, talking to her. "I love you, Mrs. Kirby."

The wind answered him. It always did. After all these years, he'd still never forgotten the sound of her voice. "I love you back, Chief Kirby."

Dane closed his eyes and let the rich smell of moist dirt and grass take him back to his favorite memory. "Whoa," Dane said, this time in his mind. "Don't jinx it. I'm not wearing the white helmet yet."

Gwen smirked. He smiled wider. He knew he had the job. The commission had already told him so. He was just waiting on the vote to be ratified—a formality. Gwen knew it, too. That's why she'd asked him to meet her out here at the same park where he'd proposed a few years back—to celebrate this new chapter in their life. He lay back on a huge chunk of rock and allowed himself to soak in the memory of his wife. The way she lay in the green grassy ocean of Noble Park. The warm sunlight dancing off her skin and how she glowed. She wore a sleeveless yellow sundress with a paisley lace print on it that day. The one she wore at her sister's wedding. Dane loved that dress and she knew it. She really poured it on that day to make it a special one for him and it was fair to say that in that moment, lying in that great wide open, Dane Kirby felt like the luckiest man alive. He finally had the job he wanted. He had good friends—real friends. He lived in the place he'd grown up—the place he loved. But even without all that—he had the girl. Not just *a* girl, but *the* girl. Gwen was, at that moment, as she always had been since high school, the most beautiful woman he'd ever seen. He was in awe of her. He was even more in awe of the fact that she had chosen him to spend the rest of her life with. He thought about a Rod Stewart song he'd always hated, but it fit the moment. The lyrics rushed his brain.

You're right, Rod, Dane thought to himself and nodded. *Some guys do have all the luck.*

Gwen had brought a picnic basket with her to the park and it sat in the grass above their heads. When she reached up to open the wicker lid, Dane took his index finger and poked her lightly, right above the dimple in her hip.

"Stop," she said with a coy smile, drawing her arm back. "That tickles."

"I can't help it. Your freckles are out today like crazy and they're killing me." Gwen's shoulders and back were covered in light sun spots that Dane read his future in every night, like old mystics would do with tea leaves. Gwen loved astrology. Dane thought it was all a bunch of nonsense, but those freckles—those freckles were as close as he'd ever gotten to the stars. Those freckles were Dane's own private constellations and he couldn't imagine his life without being able to see them—to touch them—so he did, every chance he could. He was positive that The Beatles wrote "Across The Universe" about those freckles.

"Well, keep your hands to yourself for just a minute, please." Gwen reached over to the basket for a second time and pulled out a bottle of wine and a corkscrew.

"Baby," Dane said, and sat up abruptly. He looked around the park. There was no one in the field other than them. But it was midday, and although he wasn't on duty, he was in his McFalls County Fire Department uniform. "I can't drink that. I'm wearing my badge. Are you trying to get me fired before my first day as chief?"

She ignored him, pulled off the silver foil covering the cork, tossed it in the grass next to the basket, and then used the corkscrew to open the bottle. "Hand me those cups in the basket," she said.

"I'm serious, Gwen. I'm not going to kill a bottle of vino with you in the middle of the day while I'm wearing my uniform."

"Suit yourself." She reached into the basket and pulled out two red Solo cups. She sat one in the grass next to the curl of foil and poured two fingers of red wine into the other. She recorked the bottle, took a long sip, and lay back down, careful not to spill. Dane had to laugh. This woman did whatever she wanted, *whenever* she wanted to do it—and it drove him absolutely crazy. In fact, everything about his wife made him crazy. She lit him up like a firefly in a jar. Her hair, so brown it could be black if not for the highlights that spilled like streams of honey onto the grass. That made him crazy. The way she smelled like honeysuckle and fresh-cut sugarcane at all times of day. That made him crazy. The way she'd been setting his senses on fire since the first day they met. That made him crazy. He had to physically force himself to break his high-school lovestruck stare from the curves of her yellow dress so he could lay back down in the grass next to her and hope no one gave them any static about having an open bottle of wine in public. Hell, he honestly didn't care. Noble Park was far enough from town. It wasn't a big deal. He reached over and felt for her hand. When he found it, she took it and squeezed. She spoke to Dane while they both looked straight up at the spun-cotton cloud formations. "You can't see it right now, but we are lying directly under Orion, the hunter. We'll be able to see it tonight. It's supposed to be really clear."

He turned his head to her. "Do you plan on lying here in the middle of this park long enough for the sun to go down?"

She turned to look at him now. Their faces were close enough for their noses to touch, their cheeks itchy from the grass. Dane didn't look away. He could feel himself fall even deeper into her eyes. Eyes so dark he could never see her pupils. But he could today. Her irises seemed lighter. As if someone had added cream to black coffee. Maybe it was the sun. After all, it was a beautiful day.

"If you lie here with me, I will."

"I'm not going anywhere, woman."

"You better not."

Dane remembered the way he kissed her that day. The way he just couldn't help himself. Gwen closed her eyes and kissed him back— hard—and her tongue found the back of his throat as if the fate of the world depended on it. He could taste the wine on her lips, sweet and waxy like lip gloss. When he found the courage to finally break away from her, he reached for the empty cup in the grass beside him. It was what she wanted him to do—and she'd always been able to get him to do what she wanted—so he decided he didn't care about the consequences of her little wine in the park scenario.

Well, maybe he cared a little. He was about to be sworn in as the new fire chief, so he lifted his head slightly and gave the park a good once-over. Still not seeing a soul, he caved in to her—like always. "Okay," he said. "Pour me some. Just a sip."

Gwen got giddy and sat up on her elbows. She took the bottle and poured a small nip of wine into Dane's cup. They toasted to freckles they could see and stars they couldn't. Dane lifted the cup to his lips, swirled the red wine around in his mouth, and almost spit it back out. "Gwen?" he said with a gag, then forced himself to swallow. "Um—I think this wine is corked or something. It's horrible. How are you drinking that?"

She returned the bottle to the basket and then lay back down, flat in the grass. She stared directly into the sun through a break in the clouds. "It's the best I could do—for something nonalcoholic, anyway."

"What?" Dane perched himself on one arm and stared at her as she lay there, her eyes closed now, a sly smile on her thin lips. He'd never known his wife to drink anything nonalcoholic—ever. In fact, he'd never seen her go without a cigarette this long, either. Something was off. And he hadn't noticed until right then. Her sense of calm was palpable. "Gwen?" Dane spoke her name as a question.

She kept her eyes closed and said, "Did you know that right now is the Year of the Rooster according to the Chinese zodiac?"

Dane didn't give one damn about the zodiac. He sat straight up and repeated her name with a little more intensity. His heart began to race. He stared at her, feeling completely confused. Gwen couldn't look any more content or relaxed if she tried as she lay there in the thick blanket of grass of the most secluded park in town. The rush of what she wasn't saying hit Dane like a wrecking ball. He felt winded. He was suddenly aware of the Georgia sun heating the back of his neck. The glow she had—her eyes—it wasn't just the sunlight.

"The Chinese," she said, "say that children born during the Year of the Rooster bring great intelligence and great joy to the world."

"Gwen," Dane said a third time, in a more subdued choke of a whisper. She opened her eyes slowly and caught his stare. "Yes, Dane?"

"Are you—are we—" He stumbled over his words.

"Yes," she said. "We are." And she rubbed his free hand over the flat surface of her belly. "Does that make you happy?" She already knew the answer by the tears lining his cheeks and that ridiculous grin on his face that only she was capable of bringing out of him. They held each other for a long time. Her wine spilled onto the grass. Dane hoped she'd never let go.

"I love you, Mrs. Kirby."

"I know," she said. "And I love you right back."

Dane wanted to remember this moment forever. He never wanted to forget. How perfect it all could've been, but somewhere in the thick of this moment Dane knew what was coming next. He could never just remember the good parts. He had to remember everything that came after. Just like he'd never been able to forget Gwen's voice, he also couldn't forget the sound of that shot. It sounded like a .30-30. He didn't want to, but like always, his mind drifted to the accident, to the blood. So much of it. Blood, cold and congealed, sticking to his clothes and his face. Blood mixing in with his tears, causing a slick, watery film to smear over his face. This is the part where he wants to scream.

So he did. Dane opened his eyes and screamed out over the water as the bright sun violently attacked his vision. For a moment Dane couldn't see, and he was grateful for the temporary blindness. The bursts of white replacing the pools of red. Dane looked down at the rock he was sitting on. Not just to avoid the sunlight, but because he no longer possessed the ability to look at the sky. He just couldn't do it. There wasn't anything up there for him to see anyway. Not anymore. Just cold fire and a host of raging stars camouflaged by the brightest blue. The sun shining down through the trees cast a spider web of shadows across Dane's cargo pants, boots, and skin. He focused on the patterns as his vision returned. He didn't look at the treetops anymore, either. They only held thoughts of carrion birds, more blood, and the broken bones of children. Dane could feel a chill rush through him although he'd been sitting in the warm morning sun for hours. The lab report papers from Dr. McKenzie's office, which Dane had spread out on the flat rock beside him before he dozed off, caught the breeze and started to lift into the air. Dane scrambled before he lost them to the wind and refolded them all, stuffed them back into the tattered envelope, and then pushed the whole mess deep into the utility pocket of his pants. He looked down at his leg and laughed a humorless laugh. It didn't matter where he looked—up, down—it just didn't matter. His future wasn't written in the stars the way Gwen had always said. It was written in faded printer ink on those goddamn papers—right there in black and white. He decided to stare straight ahead instead, out at the roaring water of Bear Creek. The creek itself reminded him of nothing. *Nothing* was something he could handle. *Nothing* was good. After a while, he closed his eyes again and filled his lungs the best he could with the fishy smell of dirt and wild water. It helped. He didn't want to come out here just to get lost in the black parts of his memory, or the big neon parts that refused to go away. He just wanted to catch a damn fish. Or maybe, for once, remember something good, something pure, something that pushed the stars and treetops and paperwork out of his brain, if only for a while. He leaned farther back and rested his head on the massive rock just in time to feel a buzzing on his leg. He reached into his pocket and yanked out the phone only to drop it. It slid down the smooth rock into the dirt. Unbalanced, Dane tried to grab for it and slid right down after it. He landed hard on his shoulder and left hip. He lay there in the grass and mossy earth until the pain subsided and he sat up slowly and looked for his phone. One missed call from a number he didn't recognize. The phone chirped in his hand—voicemail. He held the phone to his ear and listened to a message from the new sheriff of McFalls County. There'd been a killing up the mountain. The sheriff was asking for his assistance. "Thank God," Dane said. "Something to do."

CHAPTER THREE

It took Dane twenty minutes to get his old Ford close enough to the winding dirt path that led to the cabin the new sheriff of McFalls County had called him out to. He passed the young sheriff's county vehicle back by the main road, where he must have had to leave it and walk the rest of the way in. Dane figured the newly minted sheriff, Darby Ellis, didn't yet know the steep terrain well enough to know how to get his two-wheel-drive county-issued Crown Victoria this deep into the woods without getting stuck. The new sheriff was trying to play by the rule book, but Dane knew he'd be rolling over this mountain in a four-wheel drive as soon as he got sick of having to hike to every call.

For Dane, on the other hand, there wasn't a trail or pig path in North Georgia that he couldn't navigate with his eyes closed, no matter the vehicle. He'd learned every nook and cranny of every county from Fannin to McFalls to Rabun as a kid pitching dirt clods with his friends, from kindergarten through high school. He'd driven every road and trail out there in his Deddy's old Ford. The same old Ford he'd just climbed out of. What he hadn't found out about the area out here as a young man looking for the best place to take girls or sip whiskey his father kept in the truck's old rusted tool box, he had gone on to discover over an eight-year tenure as the fire chief and arson investigator of McFalls and a brief stint as sheriff for Fannin County—the next county over—a job he'd only recently vacated after two years. The former sheriff of McFalls, Clayton Burroughs, had taken his leave as well, and his abrupt retirement left this new guy, Ellis, ready and willing to take up the mantle. The locals around here half expected Dane to take Burroughs's job himself, but Dane had walked away for a reason. He enjoyed his retirement.

He decided to vouch for Ellis instead. He liked him, and Dane felt like the county needed younger blood behind the badge after almost two decades of Clayton Burroughs calling the shots. He liked Burroughs, although he'd been born to one of the biggest and meanest families of outlaws in the state. He'd done his part to keep them in check but some people thought he was planted in the office to turn a blind eye to his family's operations. Dane wasn't one of those people. He believed Burroughs to be a good man, but he believed Ellis to be an even better one.

Besides, Dane had been offered a much better gig to leave his post in Fannin. He now worked part-time for the Georgia Bureau of Investigation. He was in his first year with the Bureau now and it still felt a little strange to think about. Dane had never been all that fond of the police when he was coming up in the fire service, even during his short stint as sheriff, but now he was Agent Kirby. He laughed to himself every time he had to say that out loud. He was more of a consultant than anything else, and his new job kept him busy mostly deciding which side of the desk to stack the endless piles of useless paperwork on. He'd traded the wide-open spaces of his country home for a small box of an office. He did get to shoot a lot of darts, though, and midday naps had taken on an important role in Dane's life, so life was good. Fighting fire and running into burning buildings was a young man's game. The fire service was work, plain and simple, and Dane was enjoying the lack thereof that his new job afforded him. It paid a lot better, too. The state benefits were something he couldn't go without, even with his county pension, and a nice comfortable leather chair was much more appealing these days than constantly being on his feet in ravines like the one he was hiking into now.

He stopped and looked around the forest. He did have to admit, as easy as he had it now, he sometimes missed his old life. The pine-rich northern air and the feeling of authority that came with wearing a badge and a uniform were things he'd grown accustomed to, and it felt good to be back out on his old stomping ground, even if it was at the behest of the new sheriff. It made Dane feel relevant again and less like the paper pusher he'd become. The move to the Bureau was a good fit for him physically—Dane had just turned thirty-seven—but it wasn't much of a challenge for the investigator side of him. He'd never say it out loud to anyone, but he was excited to get Sheriff Ellis's call.

Dane stopped the truck about sixty yards from the old cabin. The place belonged to a recluse named Tom Clifford, who had been living there since before there were roads or trails to get to it. Tom had become a fixture in the Blue Ridge foothills, and his home, a town landmark. Dane hadn't run into him much during his time with the county. In fact, he only vaguely remembered meeting the old man once or twice as an up-and-comer. Clifford had been a friend of his father's and Dane remembered his being old as dirt even back then. Dane imagined the geezer had been born old. Clifford was also one of the last of the old guard living up here, and like most of the old-timers, he didn't care much for the company of other people. Dane couldn't much blame him for it, either. He wasn't a big fan of people himself, and from what Ellis had said when he called, the old man had been right to keep to himself. Because by the looks of things, one of those people Tom had gone out of his way to avoid had shot and killed him dead.

Sheriff Ellis was standing by the front porch of the solid cedar-framed cottage in a nicely pressed tan uniform. A second man wearing a matching outfit was hovering by the front door inspecting the doorjamb. Dane never remembered the former sheriff, Burroughs, wearing anything but a loose-fitting county-issued shirt with his silver star pinned to it, tucked into a pair of blue jeans, but this Ellis fella was all-in—pressed and starched from head to toe. Dane liked that. This mountain could use a few more just like him.

Four other men in Realtree camouflage jumpers and blaze-orange vests stood huddled by the left corner of the house spitting tobacco into Styrofoam cups. They were hunters—locals, Dane thought—and unfamiliar. All four of the men held rifles of different calibers. Dane chuckled as he held his balance on a sturdy yellow pine. Only in small counties like McFalls were civilian participants of an active crime scene allowed to keep their firearms on them. Dane had debated grabbing his Redhawk from the glove box in the truck, so he wouldn't feel so naked in present company, but had decided against it. This weekend had been his first real stretch of time off since he took the job at the Bureau and he was supposed to be fishing. Fishing didn't require a firearm and he had no intention of taking part in anything that did. This was Ellis's show. Dane was simply an invited spectator.

The sheriff waved Dane over and whistled at him as if Dane hadn't already seen him or wasn't already on his way. Dane smirked and held a hand up in response. He knew he was a little slower these days, but it was teaching him patience, something the rest of the world didn't seem to want to learn with him. He cleared away a clump of thorny brush and low-hanging birch branches as he carefully crept his way down through the woods. He stopped only once on his way down to the house to examine some ATV tracks that crisscrossed over the path. Some of the tracks were fresh, but most of them were old and crusted over in the clay. He wasn't surprised to see them. Four-wheelers were the best and most common method of transportation this deep in the woods. The fire department even used them sometimes to rescue hikers who wandered a little too far out of their depth. The diamond pattern of off-road tread indentations most likely meant nothing in this case, but the investigator instinct in Dane made him take notice regardless. Old habits die hard. He took wide steps, careful not to disturb the rest of the tracks. This was, after all, a crime scene.

But it's Ellis's crime scene, Dane. You need to remember that. There's no fire, and even if there was, you're retired. You're a desk jockey now, enjoying the weekend. You're just looking to catch a few fat brookies in Bear Creek. That's it. Now get over there and say hello.

"Down here," Ellis shouted.

"I'm coming. Just hold up a minute." As Dane got closer he could see a sheet draped over the front steps, and the closer he got to the sheet, the more the shape underneath it began to take the form of a body—old man Clifford's body.

"Thanks for coming, sir." Ellis held out a firm hand and Dane shook it. "I didn't know if you could hear my message when I called or not. Reception is for shit out here."

Dane knew that. He grew up here, too. He'd never heard a county sheriff call him sir before, either, but he figured Ellis was just playing up to his new role. Ellis seemed like a good fit for the sheriff's seat in McFalls County. Dane could read people pretty well, and he could also see Ellis's genuine love for the job. His neatly pressed uniform and regulation haircut were evidence of that. He was going to make a good sheriff—a great one, even, Dane thought as he turned and looked up the ravine at the main road—as soon as he learned what to drive, anyway.

Dane pushed his ball cap up on his forehead and leaned against the porch railing.

"Yeah, I got your message, Sheriff, but you don't need to call me sir. You're the one calling the shots out here. I didn't even have jurisdiction over this area when I was sheriff in Fannin. This section of the mountain falls square in McFalls. That's you, my friend." Dane didn't envy Darby's job, especially because Bull Mountain also fell under McFalls County jurisdiction, and no one ever wanted to be involved with the kind of shit that happened up there. They both knew that. An awkward silence began to creep in, so the sheriff went back to playing the role.

"Well, regardless, the last time I checked, GBI had jurisdiction over county law enforcement, so that still makes you sir to me, whether you like it or not."

Dane scratched at the three-day stubble on his face and looked past Darby at the other man in uniform. He was a deputy Dane had never seen before, who, as of yet, hadn't paid Dane any mind, and seemed to be fascinated with the crumbling paint on the open front door. Dane kept scratching at his chin and didn't bother to ask for an introduction. Instead, he stared down at the porch. "Fair enough, Sheriff. So tell me why I'm out here looking at this poor fella instead of casting flies in the river? I don't see any signs of fire."

Sheriff Ellis took a step up to the landing and squatted down by the covered body. "Well, you're right. I know this is a little outside your wheelhouse, and to be honest, this—"

Dane cut him off. "Hold up a minute, Sheriff." He was watching the young deputy again, who was now kneeling at the front door. He'd taken out a pair of latex gloves and a small black box and had begun feathering the doorknob with what looked like one of Dane's wife's makeup brushes. Dane had to know. "Who's that?" he whispered.

Ellis whispered, too. "He's my deputy, Woody. Woody Squire. His name's Woodson, but we all call him Woody. He's part-time and the county pays him next to nothing, but he's a good kid, and between me and you, I don't think he ever goes home. He heard this call go out and damn near beat me here."

"He looks like he's still in high school."

"Graduated last year."

"Right—and what's he doing?"

"I'm pretty sure he's dusting for fingerprints."

Dane stared blankly at the sheriff. "Really? He does know he's in the country, right?"

"I hope so."

"Aren't the forensic guys from Rabun on their way here with the coroner?"

"Yes, sir. I called them right after I got here—right after I called you."

Dane smiled as the kid worked the brush lightly over the cracked and peeling paint. Ellis shrugged. "What can I say? He says he wants to be federal someday." The sheriff leaned in and spoke even more softly than they already were. "You know, he pulled out all that crime-scene stuff right after I told him I'd called you out here. I think he's trying to impress you. You are kind of a legend around here."

Dane smiled a little wider and shook his head. "Well, I like him already." He shifted focus. "They find the body?" Dane motioned over at the hunters, who were now gathered around a spray-painted matte black ATV. He thought about the tracks he'd seen in the woods—same pattern on the tires.

"Yeah, they called it in on a sat phone. They said they found him just like that."

"What brought them out this way?"

"They said they heard a couple of shots from a handgun that spooked a buck they were walking down, and they made their way over here to see who fired."

"They said they knew it was a handgun? Not a rifle or shotgun?"

"Yep. Even called the caliber. These guys live for that kind of thing."

"And you believe them?"

"Yep. Well, I mean, they've been drinking a little, but hell, you know how it is out here, everyone in these woods normally is. I'd be surprised if they *weren't* drinking."

Dane's smile turned to one of pride. *The young man is catching on.*

"That being said, sir, I don't think they know much more than they're letting on. They all seemed genuinely upset that this old fella was dead. People up here liked this old coot."

"Yeah." Dane's smile vanished. "They did."

Dane let the sheriff's opinion be the final word on the hunters and gave his attention to the dead body at his feet. "Well, I'm not sure what I can do to help, but let's have a look at what you got." He kneeled down slowly and pulled back the sheet that covered the old man. The body lay facedown on the porch, flat on his belly, but it was Tom Clifford, all right. The skin that showed on the back of his neck was as old and leathery as dried jerky. Out of habit, Dane felt the old man's neck for a pulse—nothing, just hard, dry leather. The body was rigid and cold to the touch, but he certainly didn't look like a victim of any violence. On the contrary, he actually looked pretty peaceful. Other than a bit of dried blood on the porch next to the old man's head and the awkward position in which his face was pressed into the wooden slats, he looked like he had just fallen asleep there. He lay lengthwise over the five feet of porch with his boots just over the threshold of the doorway, as if he had tripped and fallen and just decided to stay there. Dane felt a twinge of doubt, or maybe hope, and pressed two fingers down hard on the old man's carotid artery again.

"He's dead, sir," Ellis said. "Two in the back."

Dane pulled the sheet back farther to see twin bullet holes in the man's puffy orange vest. Two perfect little circles in the fabric surrounded by loose down feathers. He pulled the vest up to see the wounds more clearly. "Yup, I suppose that would do it." Dane reached across the body to roll him over. "Give me a hand with him, Sheriff."

Ellis hesitated. "This isn't really what I—"

"Just give me a hand, Darby. I'm not going to compromise your scene. I just want to take a look at him."

The sheriff didn't argue. He was still green to this kind of work and this was Dane's old territory, so he grabbed Tom's shoulder and helped roll him onto his side. The body stayed in the same flattened position, stiff from rigor, with strings of congealed blood connecting bits of the old man's clothing to the wooden slats of the porch. They turned him over enough for Dane to see the not-so-perfect exit wounds in Tom's chest. There was nothing peaceful looking about that. Dane could finally see Tom's face and leaned in to get a closer look. He sighed. Death was always hard to look at up close. It lingered in the eyes as a cloudy reminder of how easily life could be stolen from a man. Dane and the sheriff eased Tom's stiff body back down onto its belly the way it had been before, and Dane stood up. "Well, Sheriff. It looks like you caught yourself a real whodunit right here."

The sheriff looked pensive and sagged a little in the shoulders. For the first time Dane felt like Ellis had been holding something back. In fact, the Sheriff had seemed unsettled ever since Dane asked him to help roll Tom's body over. Dane kept his tone gentle. "If I'm out of line, here, Sheriff, I promise you, I didn't mean any disrespect."

Ellis chewed his lip as if he was making an attempt to swallow his reply. "That ain't it, sir."

Dane was genuinely confused. He didn't just stumble upon this mess. He was called into it, so he pushed. "Listen, Sheriff, maybe a sweep of the cabin will turn up an answer or two as to what happened out here, but it'd be best to wait on them boys from Rabun before you try to start unraveling this little mystery."

Ellis still seemed uneasy. He removed his hat and pushed his thick blond hair back in a sweaty wave over his head. He kept chewing his bottom lip. Dane thought he might just chew it off.

"Are you okay, Darby? Is there something you're not telling me here?"

Sheriff Ellis pushed himself up from the porch with one hand and stood. It was the first time Dane took notice of just how tall and fit Darby Ellis was. He stood well over six feet—almost a full head taller than Dane. His broad, V-shaped shoulders were wide enough to put a strain on his uniform shirt. When he put his hat back on, Dane actually felt a bit intimidated. Sheriff Ellis hooked his thumbs into the sides of his patent-leather gun belt. "We'll sweep the cabin, sir, as part of my investigation, but truthfully, that isn't why I called you out here. I mean, I appreciate the help and all, but there is no mystery to solve."

Dane was confused by the sheriff's shift in demeanor. "Okay, Sheriff. If this corpse isn't the reason you called me, then what exactly am I doing out here?"

The Sheriff looked down at the body at his feet and let out a long, slow exhale. "Professional courtesy, I suppose."

Now Dane was really confused. "I don't understand."

Sheriff Ellis looked up and caught Dane's eyes. "I delayed the coroner by a few minutes because the perp said he was a friend of yours."

"What perp? Who is a friend of mine?" Dane watched the sheriff stroke at his clean-shaven chin.

Deputy Squire supplied the answer. "I think the Sheriff is trying to find an easy way to tell you that we wouldn't have bothered you at all with this ugliness, Agent Kirby—the murder part, anyway—if you didn't already know the man who shot him."

Dane swiveled his head from Ellis to the young deputy. "I do?"

"According to the shooter, you do—sir."

"Well, would somebody mind telling me who that is?"

"Him." Darby pointed across a clearing to the left side of the cabin, opposite the hunters and the ATV. At the tree line, where the dirt and saw grass turned to woods, a man Dane could barely make out sat propped up against a cluster of sweet-gum trees about twenty-five yards away. The man was far enough from the scene that Dane hadn't noticed him sitting there until that very moment. The man hadn't made a sound or done anything else to bring attention to himself since Dane had arrived. He sat with his back against the trees in a T-shirt, covered from the waist down with a sheet identical to the one that covered Clifford's dead body, but this man's sheet was covered with leaves and dirt from the forest floor and no longer had the pristine white glow that Clifford's had. Dane wondered at first how he could've missed him, but the truth was he hadn't been looking. He'd stopped to examine some useless ATV tracks, but missed a half-naked man against a tree within shouting distance from where he was now standing. That fact only reinforced his belief that he no longer had any business being out in the woods playing big shot. He took off his ball cap and scratched at his head with the brim of it before taking a step off the porch and straining his eyes to get a better look at the mystery man. Then recognition set in. "You have got to be kidding me," Dane said. He sounded winded when he spoke. The sheriff took the single step down off the porch to stand next to Dane.

"Lemon—he said his name was Ned Lemon."

Dane didn't say a word. He didn't look like he could.

"I'm guessing by the look on your face, it's fair to say you *do* know him."

"Son of a bitch," Dane said to himself, and slapped his hat back on. "Yeah, I know him."

"He asked for you by name. He said the two of you were close. He's the reason I got you out here. I hope it wasn't the wrong call." The sheriff turned and stood where Dane could see his face. His expression had softened a bit. "Was it? The right call?"

Dane dropped his chin to his chest. "I don't know yet, Sheriff, but maybe you and me should start over. What the hell happened out here?"

CHAPTER FOUR

"Ned."

"Chief."

"I'm not the Chief anymore, Ned."

"Uh-huh. And I'm supposed to believe that dipshit over there is a sheriff? He doesn't even look old enough to have hair around his pecker yet."

"Yes. He's the new sheriff of McFalls County, and he's definitely not a dipshit. He's a good man. I vouched for him."

"He's a dipshit. He's wearing slacks in the woods."

Dane raised an eyebrow at the dirty sheet covering Ned's lower half. "Ned, you're not wearing *any* pants in the woods." Dane had a point. Ned let it go. "Ned, what happened?"

"I don't know."

"Where are your pants?"

"I don't know that, either."

"This don't look good, Ned."

"That I do know."

"Well, that's a start." Dane sat down in the grass in front of Ned—a man he used to call his best friend; a man he hadn't seen in almost a decade—and helped keep the sheet gathered in the right place to make sure he stayed covered. Ned cleared a space for Dane to sit. After a long, awkward moment, Dane broached the next uncomfortable subject. "Is this yours?" He held up the gallon-size evidence bag Sheriff Ellis had handed him a few minutes ago—a bag containing an old but solid blued-steel .38 caliber revolver, a six-shooter with two empty chambers.

Ned barely looked at it before he responded. "No." He stared down at the sheet. Dane pointed back toward the group of locals by the house. "Well, those boys over there are saying that when they came upon you, you were sleeping off a drunk—right here—holding this in your hand."

Ned looked at the hunters, and then back down at his lap. He didn't take a second look at the gun. "I don't doubt that."

"Sheriff Ellis also corroborates that story. He says he took this from you before they woke you up. Do you remember any of that?"

"No."

"No, you don't remember having the gun, or no, you don't remember the sheriff waking you up?"

"All I remember is that tow-headed prick poking me with a rifle. That ain't no way to rouse a man from his sleep, Dane. He's lucky he took that damn gun away from me before I shot his ass with it. No telling what could've happened. You don't go poking at a man in his sleep, like some kind of dead dog on the side of the road. It ain't right."

Dane tucked the plastic bag with the antique gun into his coat pocket and took off his hat. He rubbed at his shaggy brown hair and could feel the sting of fresh sunburn on his scalp. "Well, Ned, in most cases, I'd tend to agree with you on that, but right now you gotta try and look at it from his point of view. The man gets a call that there's been a shooting up here, and when he shows up, he finds Tom—a fella well loved around here—shot to death on his front porch. He looks around and sees you over here passed out, free-balling against a tree and holding a recently discharged firearm. All things considered, I'd say he was just being careful."

Ned reached down under the dirty sheet and readjusted whatever was down there. "I suppose you're right."

"He also called me out here to talk to you like you asked him to when he could've just as easily arrested you and hauled you down to county lockup, so maybe you should cut him a little slack."

"I just asked him to get someone I knew is all. Someone who knew me."

"That's not what he told me. He said you asked for me by name."

"Well, maybe I did, then. I don't know."

"You know I don't even work for the county anymore, right? Did you know that?"

"I heard, but you're here, ain't you?"

Dane tried to catch Ned's eyes, but couldn't. Ned seemed to be pur-posely avoiding Dane's stare. "Yeah, I am—and that's all the more rea-son to cooperate with the sheriff, Ned. Seeing as he did what you asked him to despite you being an asshole and all." Dane scanned the woods and took in his surroundings. Sheriff Ellis said he could have five minutes alone with Ned before they hauled him in. "Is there anything else you want to tell me about any of this—seeing that it's just me and you right now? It may be the last chance we get to talk—alone, I mean."

Dane finally caught Ned's eye for the first time. He gave the impres-sion that he didn't need to talk. He seemed confident, as if Dane already knew everything he needed to know. "Nothing else to tell."

"Are you sure, Ned?"

"I'm sure, Dane. Tom is my friend. You know that. He was one of the only people that stuck by me after what happened."

"Was," Dane said. "He *was* your friend. Until somebody shot him, and I'm betting this gun in my pocket—the one you were holding—is going to match the holes in his back, which puts you in an awkward position."

"I didn't shoot him, Dane. You know I didn't."

"I didn't say you did, Ned." Dane kicked at an empty mason jar by his foot. "But by the looks of things, you were hitting the old man's shine pretty hard, and sometimes when you're drunk—"

"I didn't shoot him," Ned repeated. "I told you he was my friend. Why the hell did you come out here if you weren't going to help me?"

"I am helping you, Ned, and I'm your friend, too. Tom wasn't the only one who stuck by you back then."

"Yeah, man. Thanks for the commissary money. It was a big help."

"That's not fair, man." Dane felt a soft buzzing on his leg and reached into his pocket to grab his phone. The number on the display belonged to Charles Finnegan. Charles was Dane's friend and immediate supervi-sor at the Bureau. "Hang on a minute, Ned." He tapped ACCEPT on the phone. "Hey, Charles. Listen, I'm going to need to call you back. I've got a situation over here."

"Have you fallen and you can't get up?"

"Funny. No, but I am out here in the sticks right now. The sheriff up here caught himself a murder and things have . . ." Dane thought about how to put it. "Well, things have gotten a little hinky."

"Hinky?"

"It's complicated. I'll have to call you back."

"Dane, you're supposed to be taking some time off. Time off that you need. I shouldn't even be calling you right now, but I expected you to be fishing. You should be out by Bear Creek, not poking around meth labs up on Bull Mountain. I'm sure the sheriff up there can handle whatever he's got going on. You work for me now."

"You're right, Charles, but this ain't just some backwoods lab explosion. Wait a minute—how did you know I was at Bear Creek?"

"Because I know everything, Dane. That's why. And I don't condone freelancing. Especially in your condition."

"I'm not in any *condition*. Don't do that. And I'm not freelancing, either. It's just that this Sheriff—Ellis—he's a little new to all this, and like I told you, he just caught a real-deal murder—and it's a weird one at that."

"I don't care, Kirby. You need to be taking it easy, and besides, I—"

"I am taking it easy. Stop worrying."

"I'll worry if I damn well please, and like I said, I called you for a reason—"

"Well, give me a few minutes and I'll call you back. The victim up here is pretty well-known, and not only did he get gunned down on his own front porch, but as a bonus, a buddy of mine from back at McFalls County FD is involved." Dane looked at Ned and covered the phone. "You sure there's nothing else you want to tell me? This guy is good people."

"No," Ned said. He closed his eyes and leaned his head back against the tree. Dane put the phone back to his ear. "Anyway, the reception is for shit out here and the sheriff is getting antsy. I can hit you back and tell you all about it when I leave here."

"Hold on—Dane, I—"

Dane tapped his phone off and slid it back into his pocket. "Sorry about that, Ned. Now back to what I was saying. This looks bad, and we've only got another minute or so together without anyone else around, so if there's anything you want to tell me, now's the time."

Ned didn't hesitate to spit out another "No."

"Was there anyone else out here with you and Tom before you blacked out?"

"No," Ned said again, but this time there was a slight hint of hesitation in his voice. He looked down at his covered feet when he said it. Dane had known this man a long time. For more than thirty-five years. He also knew Ned could never look someone in the face when he was lying. But it had been almost ten years since Dane had seen him. People change. Ned kicked the sheet off his bare foot and rubbed his heel in the dirt to relieve an itch—or to keep Dane from thinking about any more questions to ask.

"Ned, I can't help you if you don't tell me everything you know."

"I don't know anything else."

"C'mon, Ned—"

"Trust me, Dane. I don't know any more than you do."

"Trust you? Ned, I haven't seen you in over what—nine years? Now all of a sudden, out of the blue, you call me out to—to this?"

Ned shuffled under the tree and scratched his back against the crumbling bark. "I'm telling you everything I know, Dane. I came over here a few nights ago to drink with Tom. I got lit up last night. I blacked out and woke up out here with that blond-headed jackass over there poking me with a rifle. I asked for you because the last I heard, you were wearing the sheriff's badge in Fannin, and I wasn't interested in pleading my case to a kid."

"I gave that sheriff thing up a while ago. It was a bad fit. And it doesn't sound like you're pleading anything to me but guilty."

Ned scratched his back on the tree some more. "If that's how you're taking it, then I guess I am, because other than what I told you, that's what happened and I haven't moved from this tree since. That's it. All of it. I got nothing else to tell. I wish I did."

"Right." Dane wasn't happy with the nutshell response, but he didn't press it—not yet. There was no time. "Well, Sheriff Ellis was kind enough to let us have this conversation, but he's going to have to do his job now. I can assume you're not going to give him any more grief, right?"

"There's not much grief I can give as long as I'm wearing a toga."

"I'm glad you recognize that. I'm going to tell him that cuffs aren't necessary, but he doesn't have to listen to me. He's still gonna have to bring you down to the station, so it's his decision."

"You mean he needs to arrest me?"

"Yes, Ned, he does. No way around it, but don't get all worked up about it. I'm going to ride down to the station, too, and take a look at all this." Both men sat in the grass and studied each other. It had been a long time. Dane stood up. He listened to both his knees pop and groaned. "I'll follow y'all down to the station and we can try to figure out what's what from there."

Ned picked up another empty jar of shine, shook it a bit, and set it back down on the ground. "You got a smoke?"

"I sure don't. I'm eight years quit."

Ned's eyes glazed back over. "Well, good for you, man. That shit will kill you."

Dane almost laughed, but he didn't. He and Ned just shared another moment of uncomfortable silence. Their faces had aged over the years, but the sadness they'd both carried around since they were young men was still as fresh as it had ever been. "You said you told me everything."

"I did."

"You said the last you heard I was wearing the sheriff's badge over in Fannin. So you must've been home for some time now."

Ned lowered his head. "About a year or so."

Dane felt the sting of that admission. "You've been home that long and you didn't think to call me until you found yourself in trouble?"

"I thought I was doing you a favor."

"By calling me out to this shit?"

"By not calling you at all."

"So where have you been staying all this time?"

"Here and there. Why does it matter? I didn't want to see anyone." Ned picked at the grass growing high under his palms and tossed clumps of it rooted to chunks of red dirt across the ground as if he were skipping stones over a lake.

"You know, I spent a long time worried about you, Ned. We all did. A postcard while you were gone would've been nice, or a phone call once you got back. I could've used you around, you know."

"I'm sorry about that, Dane. I never said I was a great friend."

Dane cocked his head. "Yeah, you kinda did."

"Well, add that to my endless list of disappointments."

Dane sighed and tucked his hands down deep into his cargo pants.

"All right. I suppose now ain't the time to talk about it anyway. How about I stop by Pollard's on the way to the station and pick you up some smokes?"

"That would be grand."

"You still a Camel man?"

"I'm a 'whatever I can get' man."

"All right, then." Dane pushed himself off the tree he was leaning on and let out a little grunt.

"Are you okay, Dane?"

"Yeah, I'm fine."

"You don't seem fine to me." Ned held a hand over his eyes to block the sun in his face until Dane stood directly in the light. It backlit him and Dane's face went full dark like some sort of phantom.

"I saw you come in," Ned said. "You were moving like a sixty-year-old. What *condition* were you taking about just now—on the phone—with that guy, Charles? You said you were taking it easy. Why should you be taking it easy?"

Dane seated his ball cap down low on his head. He looked less like a phantom now and more like the man Ned used to call his friend. "Why don't we worry about you right now, Ned, and not me," Dane said, avoiding the question. "I'll see you back at the station." He started back toward Sheriff Ellis and his deputy without saying anything else that would conjure up any more memories either of them would rather not deal with at the moment. He didn't say goodbye. It felt like the worst thing to do. The last time he said goodbye to Ned Lemon, he didn't see him again until just now. Dane's phone buzzed again, and he pulled it from his pocket. It was Charles again. He was about to answer when Ned called out.

"Hey, Dane."

"Yeah?" Dane sent the call to voicemail.

"Maybe I did kill him."

"Kill who, Ned? Tom?"

"Yeah. I didn't pull the trigger like that high-school kid over there thinks I did, but I'm sure I'm the reason he's dead all the same—you know that, don't you?"

Dane's phone started buzzing again almost immediately. "How do you mean, Ned?"

"I mean people die around me, Dane. Everybody knows that. That's who I am."

Dane just stared at his friend and had absolutely nothing to say that would bring him any solace. He knew exactly how that felt. Maybe he even agreed.

He kept walking, tapped ACCEPT on his phone, and held it to his ear. "Damn, Charles, I said I'd call you back."

"Number one, don't you 'Damn, Charles' me. I'm your boss. Number two, don't you ever hang up on me again if you like having me as a boss, and number three, tell your man Ellis over there that you're done playing hayseed cop. You're being called up."

"Called up? What the hell does that mean?"

"It means you've just been requested by name to fly to Jacksonville, Florida, by the big dogs. That's what I was calling you about in the first place before you hung up on me."

"What? Why?"

"You'll be briefed on the ride down here. You need to get to McFalls Memorial ASAP."

"Seriously, Charles, why?"

"Because it's the closest helipad to where you're at and I need you to meet the team they put together at the chopper."

"The team *who* put together?"

"Damn, Dane, you are slow. The FBI is who. Now get to that hospital, get on that bird, and get your ass to Jacksonville. Call me after you land."

Dane could feel his head swimming. He'd never heard Charles talk to him with such hostility. This was serious if it had Charles Finnegan riled up. "What the hell is going on in Florida?"

"Listen to me, Kirby. The assistant director of the FBI asked me personally to find and send you to him, so that's what I'm doing. I don't ask questions. I do as I'm told. You should try it. It's called chain of command. At the very least you should just do it because I damn well said so and that's good enough."

"Yeah, but—"

"No buts. I tried coddling your ass and I got hung up on. Now get it in gear and go do what I tell you."

Dane shot a stunned look at Ellis and his deputy, whose name he'd already forgotten. He handed off the bagged .38 to Ellis and watched both men move toward Ned. They struggled a little to keep Ned's lower half covered as they raised him to his feet. "Yeah, Charles. Okay, I'm going now."

"Good, and I expect a sit-rep once you're on the ground." GBI Deputy Director Finnegan ended the call, and Dane stared at his phone as if he'd forgotten what it was. He tucked the phone into his pocket and started the slow ascent back up the ravine to the main road. As he fought to keep his footing in the clay and pushed back the endless vines of kudzu and thorny brush, one thought played over and over in Dane's head like a record on repeat.

What the hell just happened?

CHAPTER FIVE

Dane had never been in a helicopter before. It wasn't as glamorous as he thought it would be. First of all, it was loud as hell, and the two young-buck agents in matching dark gray suits who had been sent to be Dane's escorts to the city just stared at him the entire time like he was a monkey about to perform a trick. He nearly lost his hat out the wide-open side hatch of the chopper several times, and the seat belt felt more like a sad joke than a safety precaution. Dane Kirby was about a mile and a half above his comfort zone in a Plexiglas bubble, and it was fair to say he didn't like it.

"Is someone going to tell me what is going on?" Dane felt like an idiot, having to yell above the noise of the whirling chopper blades, and even more so for having to ask the question in the first place, since Charles had told him he'd be briefed on the ride, but once they were in the air, neither of the agents, the Latino one nor the white one, said a word. One of the two men, identically dressed down to the matching sets of mirrored aviator sunglasses, put a finger to his lips and then to his ear. Dane assumed that meant he didn't want to talk over the noise. That made him feel even dumber, being condescended to like that, so he went back to gripping his hat like a rolled-up magazine and being judged by two arrogant FBI pricks.

By the time the chopper landed on the helipad at Jacksonville International Airport, Dane couldn't get out of the gravity-defying death machine fast enough. The same agent who'd given him the hush finger on the flight over got out first and offered him a hand. Dane ignored him and hopped out unassisted. He hit the tarmac a little harder than he wanted to, but he ignored the lightning bolt of pain that shot all the way from his heel up to his armpit. It was bad enough that he felt inferior to these stooges for being in the dark about why he was there, but he'd be damned if he was going to look like he couldn't handle a four-foot jump. The jolt to his knees made his eyes water, but he slid his hat on and pulled it down low to shield the swelling tear before anyone could see it.

The second agent dismounted from the chopper smoothly behind them by keeping a hand on the grip by the door that Dane had failed to see. "Keep your head down," he said as he hustled by his partner and Dane, as if all of a sudden he was in a huge hurry. Dane wanted to smack him, but he followed at a slower pace and did keep his head down. He couldn't hide the limp and decided he didn't care; he knew his limits, and the hell with what these guys thought.

The three of them made their way through the covered skyway to the other side of the glass enclosure, where an unmarked black Chevy Tahoe was waiting in a private lot to pick them up. All of the Bureau's government rides were Chevys. That should've been a hint right there that Dane had made the wrong decision about which job to take when he retired, but not everyone understood the magic of driving a Ford. He chalked it up to inexperienced youths cutting the checks in the governor's office. The bigger of the two agents held open the rear passenger-side door, while his partner and Dane got in. Once they were settled, the driver pushed the big black SUV into traffic and yet another agent, riding in the front seat directly in front of Dane, turned to face him. His face was familiar. Dane thought he recognized the guy as one of the higher-ups in the Federal Bureau. The FBI sometimes worked in conjunction with Dane's office in Georgia and they were easy to recognize from their pretentious manner. They thought their shit didn't stink. This guy was someone who wouldn't be talking to Dane at all unless he had to and, judging by the blatant irritation on his face, clearly that was the case right now. It was easy to tell that the agent was abnormally tall, even sitting down, and looked uncomfortably cramped even in the spacious cab of the vehicle. He looked older than Dane by at least a few years, with a high widow's peak of thinning, slicked-back hair with hints of silver that shone in the sunlight. The agent took off his sunglasses and reached a reluctant hand over the seat for Dane to shake. Dane tried to remember his name. It was something creepy.

"Welcome to the fray, Agent Kirby. I'm Special Agent Geoff Dahmer with the Federal Bureau of Investigation."

"That's right," Dane said and shook the man's hand. His palm felt clammy and his fingers were as abnormally long as the rest of him. "Man, that's a shit roll of the dice getting saddled with that name. I bet you caught a lot of hell as a kid."

"I didn't," he said dryly. "There is no relation, I can assure you." Dahmer spoke without a hint of humor in his voice. He had a mechanical sense about him that would've made Dane uneasy even if he didn't have a man-eating serial killer's name. Dane broke the dead-fish hand-shake and expected Dahmer to finally fill him in on what he was doing there, but the agent just turned around to face forward and said nothing. Dane looked at everyone in the car. They were all staring straight ahead, as if the whole interior of the SUV had been sucked clean of any form of personality. Dane felt like he was sitting in yet another vacuum—the first one, a plastic flying bubble, void of any comfort, and now this *Men in Black* piece-of-shit Chevy, void of any emotion. He was tempted to crack a cannibal joke but decided against it. Now wasn't the time. He doubted this guy Dahmer would even get it. These guys took themselves seriously, and since the Feds had gone through all the trouble of laying out the red-carpet treatment to get him there, Dane figured he probably should, too. And besides, this guy, Dahmer, would most likely take it out on Charles, and Dane didn't need that kind of ass-chewing when he got home from—whatever this was.

All the secrecy had begun to make Dane anxious. He thought about Ned, and how he had promised to bring him some cigarettes. He hadn't seen the man in years, and already Dane had fed him a lie about being right behind him on the way to the station. He rubbed his sweaty palms across his shirt and pulled at a loose thread on the pocket. He'd managed to poke a hole in it. He yanked the piece of thread and twirled it between his fingers as he thought about Ned and a time that seemed like a hundred years ago. It took roughly another ten minutes of riding in silence before Dahmer finally started to lay it out.

"Agent Kirby, my men and I have been instructed by Assistant

Director of Law Enforcement August O'Barr to personally escort you to the upcoming location." He glanced over his glasses at the truck's GPS. "ETA—five minutes."

"Okay. I got that. But what exactly is this upcoming location?"

"A motel, a Days Inn to be specific. It's the scene of an active homicide investigation that the local PD pulled us in on."

Dane's nerves still rattled. Nothing about this sounded right. "Any idea why this August guy wants me here, Agent Dahmer?"

"It's Special Agent Dahmer, if you don't mind, and in my presence, it's also Assistant Director O'Barr, not August."

Dane held his tongue. Instead he answered slowly. "Right. My bad." He waited for Dahmer to continue. The senior agent turned around to face Dane and removed his glasses. Dahmer's eyes were a cold, icy blue. Dane felt increasingly uneasy. At first, Dahmer didn't say anything. He just seemed to be sizing Dane up. Dane understood. He was still decked out in his civilian fishing gear—tan Wrangler cargos and a light blue Hanes pocket tee with a big hole in the pocket. Dane raised his eyebrows and took another look at all the silent stone faces flanking him in the Scooby-Doo Mystery Machine. He was starting to get pissed.

"Look, *Special* Agent Dahmer, my boss, Charles—excuse me— Deputy Director Finnegan told me on the phone that someone would tell me what the hell is going on here before we got to where *here* is, and so far, no one has told me anything." Dane looked over the seat at the GPS himself. "And now there's a two-minute ETA. So do you think maybe you could stop with the eye-fucking, and tell the guy with no jurisdiction in the state of Florida—the guy who *your* boss asked you to go get—just what the hell I'm doing here?" Dane held his hands up and addressed the whole crew. "Or is this how y'all treat everybody that doesn't shop at Men's Wearhouse?" Dane thought he heard a faint chuckle out of Twee-dledee on his right, but if he did, the blank look of obedience on the big Latino man's face didn't give him away. Dahmer eased himself further around in his seat.

"Eye-fucking," he said, tasting the words. "I've never heard that phrase."

"Well, I'd be happy to keep adding to your hillbilly vernacular, but seriously, what's the deal?"

"I'll let you see for yourself. We are almost there."

"That's it? That's all I get?"

"Assistant Director O'Barr mentioned that he believes that your presence here can benefit this investigation and possibly lead to a swift resolution."

"Well, Assistant Director O'Barr is wrong."

Dahmer tilted his head and narrowed his eyes at Dane. "About your presence being required here? Because I believe he's wrong as well."

Dane thought about it. He wasn't sure what to believe. He wasn't sure about anything, except that Dahmer was an asshole. Dane settled back into the leather seat and crossed his arms. "This is bullshit."

Dahmer's patience was being tested. It amused Dane. "Do I have to remind you, Kirby, that I am your superior?"

"No man is my superior, Dahmer, but if you mean you got me in rank, then go ahead and write me up or do whatever it is y'all do. Knock yourself out. I don't work for you. I've been a criminal investigator my whole adult life, and if this *August* fella called me out here, then it's for a damn good reason. So maybe you should cut the shit, and remember who's driving who, here." The cab of the SUV went dead silent, and that time Dane was positive he got a smile out of Tweedledee. The driver took another left off the main road and pulled into the entrance of the Days Inn motel.

"We'll continue this conversation soon, Kirby."

"Can't wait, *Geoff*." The SUV circled the lot and came to a stop just outside the yellow plastic caution tape cordoning off a small portion of the first floor of the motel. Dane gnawed his lip and waited for Tweedledee to get out first, and then slid out of the truck behind him. He saw a thin older man, in a brown suit that hung off him the way it would a coat hanger, lift himself off the hood of an '89 Oldsmobile, and despite his light weight, the car looked like it rose up a few inches under him when he stood.

August O'Barr was clearly in his sixties and looked every bit of it. He was tall and thin as a zipper on a pair of Levi's. He kept his hair bristle-short in a military-style cut that had most likely gone gray ages ago, but O'Barr dyed it brown, and apparently dyed it himself, so it had an unnatural faux-auburn color to it that made him look a bit ridiculous. Dane assumed he was too far up the food chain for anyone to ever bring it up to his face and that his subordinates probably laughed at him behind his back. O'Barr stuck a finger in his mouth and whistled, then motioned for Dane to join him at the car. Dane headed toward him, but Tweedledee grabbed his arm to stop him.

"That was good stuff back there, with Dahmer. He's an asshole." He held out his hand for Dane to shake.

Dane took it. "Thanks," he said.

"Not a problem, sir," the young agent said. He nodded, stuck his hands in his pockets, and walked back toward the SUV. Dane heard August whistle again and started toward him. "I'm coming," he said under his labored breathing. "I'm coming."

"Special Agent Kirby. Glad to meet you. I see you're already making friends."

"Everywhere I go, Assistant Director O'Barr."

"Please. Call me August."

"All right then, August it is." Dane looked back and tipped his hat to Dahmer, who had quickly stormed off toward a group of forensic technicians examining what looked like a pile of towels on the sidewalk outside the motel-room door. Dane shook August's hand. He was wearing a suit like all the other guys wore, but he'd removed his tie, and his shirt collar hung open around the loose skin of his neck. August reached into his pocket and pulled out a pack of menthols. He lit one up and offered the pack to Dane, who declined. "No thanks. Eight years quit."

"Good for you." O'Barr lit up. "How's Charles treating you up there, Kirby? You like working for the GBI?" he asked through a mouthful of smoke.

"I like it okay. I'd like it more if I knew why they sent me somewhere I have zero authority."

"They didn't send you here. I sent for you."

"An even bigger question."

"Fair enough. We'll get there. So, how'd you like that fancy helicopter shit. Pretty cool, right?"

"I can't say I enjoyed it, August. I'm not a big fan of flying."

"What? That's too bad." It was clear he didn't give a shit what Dane was a big fan of. "Moving on," he said. August put an arm around Dane like they were old friends catching up and began to walk him toward the motel. "I'm sure that big Lurch-looking joker over there has already told you why you're here." August nodded toward Dahmer.

"No, actually, he didn't, and he was kind of a dick, too."

"Well, that's understandable."

"Why is that understandable?"

August beamed a big toothy grin at Dane as another agent in a suit joined them. These guys were getting really hard to tell apart. They were like rabbits multiplying in the dark, but this new one stuck out from the bunch. She was the first female he'd encountered.

August made the introductions. "Dane, I'd like you to meet Special Agent Roselita Velasquez. She's one of mine. Rosey, this is Dane Kirby. He's a consultant with the Georgia Bureau." Roselita nodded but made no attempt to shake Dane's hand. Dane was actually thankful for it. He'd shaken more hands in the past few hours than he had in the past few years. He'd begun to feel like a politician and he didn't like it. Roselita was slim and fit and wore a dark pantsuit over a bright white shirt, but this woman didn't shop off the rack. Her clothes were expensive and tailored. Velasquez's shoes alone looked like they might cost more than everything Dane had on. Her dark hair was short and cropped around her face and looked like it had been trimmed and styled less than ten minutes ago. If she wore makeup, Dane couldn't tell, and there was something in her dark eyes that suggested she wasn't all that happy about something.

August kept talking. "Rosey, I'm putting together a multi-organizational task force for this case and Kirby here is going to help you take point." Dane and Roselita shared a stunned expression. August steamrolled on. "So, if you wouldn't mind catching him up on everything we know so far, I'd really appreciate it."

Roselita struggled but she kept her composure. "I'm sorry, sir, what?"

"No need to apologize, Rose. What part of what I said did you not understand?"

"I thought Dahmer was the lead investigator on this."

"He was, right up until Dane got here. Now he's not."

"Can I ask why?"

"Sure you can." August stood and waited, until Agent Velasquez actually asked.

"Okay. Why?"

"Reasons," August said, and slapped Dane on the back. "Now, you kids go to work."

Dane—and his new *partner*—watched August walk away, rubbing at the back of his neck, without another word of explanation. They turned to give each other a good once-over. Dane could only imagine what this pretty but hard-nosed young agent with the expensive suit and perfect hair was thinking. Dane was a middle-aged desk agent, with zero field experience, wearing a pair of dirty Wranglers and a Georgia Southern baseball cap—and this was Florida. Not only did he look wrong for the job O'Barr had just dropped in his lap, but Dane felt wrong about it, too. It was obvious from the look of utter disappointment in Velasquez's eyes that she felt the same. Dane smiled at her. He had nothing else to offer. "Wait here a sec, Rose."

Dane caught up with O'Barr just before he slipped behind the wheel of the Oldsmobile. "Hang on, sir, I'm not sure what's happening here. I—"

"Need a proper walk-through, I know. That's what Agent Velasquez is about to give you. Sorry about Dahmer. He was supposed to brief you, but he's an asshole. Always has been, but he'll get over it. Don't worry about it. Once you see the contents of that room, you'll understand why I brought you into this."

"August, I'm out of my jurisdiction over here. You have to know that, right?"

"You let me worry about that. You'll receive all the proper clearance from all the right channels within the hour. Right now, I've got to get over to the airport. Once you get your take on the scene, brief me directly on what you find, and let me know what you need. I'll make sure you have it."

"August, you're not listening."

Agent Velasquez joined them at the car and everyone began to speak at once until August held up a finger and took a call on his cell phone. No one else had heard it ring, but Dane and Roselita went silent anyway, like third graders hushed by their teacher. August held the phone to his ear and finished settling into the car. He mouthed the word "Go" and waved them both out of the way so he could close the door. He slammed it shut and cranked the engine. Once he'd rolled up the window, he dropped the cell phone on the seat, half-assed a salute, and wheeled the Oldsmobile out of the lot.

"What the hell just happened?" Dane asked himself for the second time that day.

Agent Velasquez turned toward the motel, unable to give a response. "Well, come on then," she said. "We're wasting daylight." She crossed the parking lot, carefully stepping over a puddle of fresh vomit on the asphalt, and held up the plastic yellow caution tape. Dane avoided the puddle as well and leaned down to slip underneath Velasquez's arm. A burned comforter lay in a heap by the curb. It stank of ash and burnt nylon and had been drenched with water. "Is that related to this case?" Dane pointed at the blanket.

"Yes, but it's not important right now. Just follow me."

Dane took off his hat just to put it back on. "Listen, Rose. It's Rose, right?"

"No, actually, it's Roselita. Nobody calls me Rose or Rosey except my mother and O'Barr, and he gets away with it because he's the boss. Oh, and this thing that just happened? This thing about you and me working together? It's temporary at best. You're not even cleared for federal-level cases, so I'd prefer it if you stuck with Roselita, or better yet, Special Agent Velasquez, until this circus lets out."

"Um, okay." Dane lost his train of thought. He was beginning to think being an asshole was a prerequisite of both men and women working in the field. Roselita kept walking. Dane followed.

"Great, let's get to work. We've wasted enough time already, and losing Dahmer is a huge setback for all of us."

"It figures you two would be buddies," Dane mumbled.

Roselita slowed her step and then came to a complete stop. She dug both hands into the pockets of her tailored pants and stared down at her expensive Italian leather flats for a moment before pivoting slowly to face Dane. "He's not my *buddy*, Agent Kirby. He's my partner—my *real* partner, going on four years now. He's saved my life more times than I can count and he's like family to me. He's also one of the finest detectives I've ever worked with, so seeing him get kicked in the balls like this and replaced with someone who isn't even cleared to work with Florida law enforcement, without any kind of explanation as to why, is slightly insulting to both of us."

Dane stopped walking as well, and for the first time that afternoon, he felt like he deserved the scolding he'd just received. Roselita was right. Dane would feel the same way if the situation had been reversed. He nodded his head. "Fair enough, Agent Velasquez. I can understand that. No disrespect intended."

"None taken. Now let's just get to it. Like I said already, we're just wasting time out here."

"Okay, show me what you've got, so I can figure out why I'm here." Dane looked over at the wet blanket on the curb. He caught a whiff of it, and it smelled like a house fire. Roselita stepped up onto the breezeway, grabbed a couple pairs of blue nitrile gloves from one of the forensic techs, and handed one set to Dane. He put them on, then used his elbow to ease open the door to room 1108.

"After you, *partner.*"

Dane stepped inside, and Roselita followed. "Agent Kirby, meet Arnold Blackwell."

CHAPTER SIX

The wave of stink hit Dane so hard it nearly bowled him over. He immediately recognized the familiar scent of smoke, burnt meat, and singed hair, but the musty copper smell underneath, like an old forgotten jar of pennies, combined with urine and human feces, caused him to dry heave as soon as he entered the room. An unaffected Special Agent Velasquez stepped over the charred, lifeless body on the floor, careful to avoid the congealed and caking pools of blood and vomit as she yawned. She looked at her watch while she waited for Dane to acclimate.

The moment Dane saw Blackwell's burned body, his assumption as to why August had called him in on the investigation was confirmed—murder by fire—but he still didn't understand why they didn't call in one of their own. He scanned the rest of the room before he took another step. He'd seen his share of death over the years. He knew what death felt like up close—to hold it in his hands—to be surrounded by it—covered in it, but even he'd never seen anything like this. And up until that moment, he'd thought he'd seen it all. Normally the victims of a fire died of asphyxiation long before the flame itself ever touched them, but that wasn't the case here. His initial assessment had been wrong. Less than a minute after he'd entered room 1108 it became obvious that smoke and fire weren't responsible for this horror show. The body on the floor had been gutted before it had been burned—sliced open from groin to sternum. Everything that made a person work—the gears of the human machine—was spilled out in a pile next to the charred corpse. The smaller bits—the pieces of him that weren't still connected to him in some way—were strewn about and scattered all over the carpet. Blood was everywhere. It covered everything in huge arch-shaped patterns that seeped down the walls and dripped from the ceiling. The bed had been sprayed dark red. Even the small lampshade on the telescoping light fixture above the nightstand had been speckled with it. Everything in the room had been tainted in some way by the insides of the hollowed-out man on the floor. The fire that eventually ate away his hair and skin had only been a quick flashover.

Dane covered his nose and mouth and leaned down to look into the dead man's eyes. They were open by default because his eyelids had burned away, but the white marbles resting in his sockets were bright and glossy. Dane reached down to touch the man's jaw. It was completely broken loose from the rest of his skull. Only the ruined skin of his jowls kept it in place. Dane barely had to touch it for it to fall and gape wide open. Now the dead man looked like he was screaming. Dane imagined that's exactly what he looked like before he died. He wondered if screams alone could cause enough force to break a man's jaw like that. He bent down a little further in order to see down the man's throat. It appeared intact. His tongue was still fleshy and pink, like a wad of bubble gum stuffed behind his yellowed teeth, and Dane couldn't see any swelling or constriction in his throat. That meant he wasn't breathing when the fire was lit. He'd been burned postmortem—dead before the first match was struck. Dane assumed the man who did this to him only used the fire to cover his tracks.

The man who did this? Dane repeated in his mind, and shook his head. *No—a man didn't do this. No man could ever do this to another person—not to another human being. Whoever—whatever did this—wasn't any man at all.*

Dane fought to keep looking. He'd seen this type of disembowelment done before, but to whitetail deer or wild boar after a hunt. He'd seen all kinds of animals strung up to trees and cut open like this to be bled out before being taken home and processed. Hell, back home, fathers taught their sons to disconnect from the horror of actually doing the killing, and considered it a rite of passage. But even then, the cuts were made with a practical purpose, and they almost always followed a quick and clean death. There was nothing quick or clean about what had happened in this room, and Dane was convinced by the expression of agony still on the ruined and peeling face of Arnold Blackwell that he had been alive to feel most of what had been done to him. Dane didn't try to hide his own expression of shock and disgust as he straightened himself out. He finally had to look away. A fresh wave of stomach acid began to churn in the back of his throat and he gagged on it again.

"You gonna be okay?" Roselita asked, more out of obligation than concern.

"Jesus Christ, Velasquez." Dane struggled to find a place to give his eyes a rest, his head in a constant swivel. "What the hell happened in here?"

"That's what we were in the process of trying to find out when we were told to stand down and wait for you."

Dane spoke through his hand. "What do you know so far?"

Roselita pulled out a small notebook from a pocket in her jacket and read aloud. Her voice was monotone. Her irritation was obvious. Dane knew she'd rather be working the scene and not playing catch-up for the new guy. "His name is Arnold Matthew Blackwell. Twenty-eight years old, according to his ID. We found his wallet on the counter over there in the bathroom." Roselita pulled the ID from the pocket-sized notebook and held it out for Dane.

"So you recovered his wallet?"

"Isn't that what I just said?"

Dane ignored the snarky remark and took the ID with his free hand. It was a Georgia issue. That answered another question about why he was there. He flipped it over and examined both sides. "Just a state ID? No license?"

"No, our boy likes to drink and drive. The state revoked his license in 2010."

Dane looked back down at the plastic card. "Is the address current?"

"We've got local PD up in Cobb County sitting on it until our people can get out there. The GBI is heading that up. I figured you'd know that. And before you ask, that same wallet had nearly six hundred dollars in it—cash. It's bagged and tagged already if you want to see it."

"No, I don't need to see it, but you're assuming that means this wasn't a robbery."

"I never assume anything, Kirby. It just means that if he was robbed, all this had to be for something a lot more valuable than the fat wad of cash in his wallet."

Dane handed the ID back to Roselita. "Is there a reason to think there *was* something more valuable in his possession?"

"The girl who works up front believes so." Roselita checked the notebook again. "Abigail Boardman. She's the one who called it in after the fire set off the smoke detector. She's also the one who checked him in. She told the first officers on the scene that the deceased had a suitcase with him when he showed up this afternoon in the office. She said he seemed pretty protective of it. He didn't even want to set it down when he paid for the room."

"And I'm guessing there's no suitcase to be found anywhere in here?"

"Nope."

"Where is the girl now?"

"EMTs took her and another employee, a Cuban illegal named Mario Cruz, over to Northside Hospital."

"Were they hurt as well?"

"Not like this." She motioned to the body on the floor. "The girl was burned. She tried to put out the fire with that blanket you saw outside. She did a good job, too, but she took a few second-degree burns to her hands and wrists. Nothing too bad, but enough to get her checked out, and both kids were pretty shook up. The Mario kid especially."

"How does he fit into this?"

"He claims to have seen one of the dirtbags who did this. Got a good look, too—up close. And yes, there's a sketch artist at the hospital to get a description."

"*One* of the dirt bags? As in plural killers?"

"Yeah, the kid said he was ninety-nine percent sure there was another man in the room, but he didn't get a look at that one at all."

"So how does he know?"

"The screaming." Roselita stuck her notebook back into her jacket. "He heard the screaming. So unless Blackwell was in here doing *this* to himself, I think it's safe to assume there was someone else in here carving him up while the kid was getting in some face time with the other one."

"So what did the kid actually see?"

Roselita pulled in a deep breath, holding the air in her cheeks, and then slowly let it out.

"An Asian man, short, about five two, in his midthirties, with dark hair. The kid said, and I quote, 'Dude's hair was cut in one of those spiky punk-rock eighties dos.'"

"That's it?"

"That's it—oh, and he said the guy was wearing, and again I quote, 'a butt-ugly homo-looking blue suit.'"

"Homo-looking?"

Roselita shrugged. "His words, not mine. Listen, the way the kid tells it, he was supposed to deliver some towels to the room for Blackwell and right before he could knock on the door, Long Duk Dong popped out. He said the guy looked right at him and took a towel out of his hands to wipe blood off his face. That's when the kid heard the screaming inside. Oh, and get this, the guy even thanked him for the towel before the kid turned and hauled ass outta here."

"So you are dealing with a polite Asian psychopath with a flair for the eighties?"

"Apparently. But that's we."

"Huh?"

"*We* are dealing with a polite Asian psychopath with a flair for the eighties. You're in this, too, now."

"Right." Dane did not want any part of this. But Velasquez was right. He had to be here for a reason, so he stuck to what he knew and said, "But there were no signs of fire or smoke in the room before the kid took off?"

"No. He said he was positive about that. I think the fire was an afterthought just to cover up the mess."

"So do I. That's why they didn't torch the whole room. Just the body."

"How do you know they didn't intend on burning the whole place?"

"Because they used an accelerant, and only used it on the body." Dane pointed at the scorch marks on the carpet. "See those? See how the burns go all the way down to the carpet pad right next to the body but they taper off around it?"

Roselita bent over and leaned on her knees to get a better look at the carpet.

"That means whatever they poured on this guy burned fast and hot. Lighter fluid maybe, but you're right. It was only insurance. If anything, they did it just to slow us down. It would have gotten out of control eventually, but look"—Dane pointed at the ceiling—"the sprinklers weren't triggered, so this fire barely lasted a minute or so at the most before it was contained."

"The girl did a good job."

"Yeah, but it's hard to believe a receptionist risked her life to come in here and put it out."

"Well, she didn't know she was trying to put out a burning disemboweled body at the time. If she did, she might not have been so quick to jump in."

"She didn't know?"

"Not until the smoke cleared. That's when she ran, too. That was her vomit we stepped over outside."

Dane wanted to scratch his nose, but he stopped himself. He had blood on his gloves. The nitrile was beginning to make his hands sweat, too. He wanted to take the gloves off, but he couldn't do that, either. This was the FBI. There were people watching. The rules weren't as easy to bend as they were back home. He carefully stepped over something wet and black—something still connected to Arnie's flayed abdomen. He walked the room with surgical precision. He didn't want to be the one to upset anything that might be vital to the investigation, but it was practically impossible to take a step in any direction without coming into contact with something that used to be alive.

Dane looked around the room at the blank faces of the forensic techs as they worked. He thought about everyone he'd met since he'd gotten into that helicopter back at McFalls Memorial. No one—not one person— seemed to find any of this shocking. He wondered if all of these other people had just become accustomed to dealing with nightmares for a living. Not one of them looked horrified or sick about it. Was it possible to grow so callous that this kind of thing was just another day at work? Dane felt sorry for all of them. Especially that August guy. His flippant attitude and apparent numbness to this bloodshed wasn't something Dane envied, and it definitely wasn't what Dane signed on with the GBI to become. He was way outside his element here. Seeing dead people came with the job. He knew that. Hell, he'd just seen one earlier that morning, but this was an entirely different beast. He could never get used to this. He didn't want to. He was ready to get the hell out of that room and let that August O'Barr asshole, with his cheap menthol cigarettes and shitty Oldsmobile, know he'd made a mistake bringing him there. Dahmer and Velasquez were right. Dane *shouldn't* be there.

"Kirby? You okay? You need some air?"

"I'm fine," Dane lied, and leaned down on his knees. "What else do we know about this guy?"

"Let me help you." Roselita held out a hand to help Dane maneuver back toward the door without disturbing anything.

He felt like an idiot but took Roselita's hand. "Thanks," he said.

"No problem." She let go of Dane's hand and he stood up straight. "As far as what else we know about Blackwell, we know he's a sack of shit, but that's about it. He's from your neck of the woods. He's been in and out of Gwinnett and Cobb County lockup in Atlanta enough to have a private room at both. And up until right now, I thought you might know him. Maybe thought that was the reason you're here."

Dane thought about it. "No. Never heard of him. You said he's been in lockup a lot. What's his vice?"

"Gambling, mostly."

"Really?"

"Yeah, stupid shit."

"Has he done any time?"

"The longest stint he pulled was a year down in"—she had to look at her notebook again—"Augusta, Georgia, at a Phinizy Road Jail—something to do with illegal poker machines. He got arrested at a gas station that didn't have a permit to pay out, and since his machine hit for over five hundred bucks, he caught a felony charge. The guy had zero luck. Even when he won, he lost."

Some people were just built out of bad luck. It filled their bones instead of marrow. Dane knew folks like that back home, and this Arnold Blackwell fella was definitely one of those people. The guy wins a fat payday in some convenience store somewhere and before he even gets to spend a nickel of it, he spends a year in prison for it. That was telling. "Maybe this is just another payday gone sideways."

"Maybe." Roselita squatted down by the door and used a ballpoint pen to pick up a Dr Pepper can. She motioned for one of the techs to mark the spot with a placard and then bagged the can.

Another technician, an attractive female with white-blond hair pulled back into an ultratight ponytail, stopped examining Blackwell's body, stood up, and tucked something else into an evidence bag. Dane couldn't make out what it was. "Excuse me," he said. "What is that? Part of a blade?"

"No, sir." She held it up. "It appears to be a sliver of wood. Bamboo, maybe."

Roselita slipped her pen back into her jacket. "Bamboo? You mean this guy was chopped up with a stick?" Roselita stared at the shard of wood in the bag.

"It's hard to determine at this point, ma'am, especially with the body being burned, but the wounds on the victim don't seem to be consistent with any sort of conventional blade, so it's a possibility."

"A fucking stick?" Roselita repeated, confused by the notion of it.

"Not just any stick," August said over Dane's shoulder from the door-way. Dane swung his head around hard enough for the bones in his neck to pop. Roselita looked back, too, but didn't look surprised to see her boss standing there. She was still trying to wrap her head around the idea of a bamboo stick doing this kind of damage to a man.

"I thought you were flying somewhere," Dane said.

"I said I was going to the airport. I didn't say I was getting on a plane." August held out a white paper sack. "I went to Checkers, too. Anybody hungry? I got a sack full of Big Bufords with cheese."

Everyone just stared at him. August shook the sack. "No takers?" He shrugged and rolled up the top of the bag. "Suit yourselves."

Dane felt his stomach churning again. He pointed to a small glob of mustard O'Barr had on the corner of his mouth, dangling from the edge of his mustache. "You've got a little something on your face." O'Barr touched at it, and then used his arm to wipe it away, leaving a smear of yellow down the sleeve of his brown suit jacket.

"Thanks."

"No problem. So about the airport?"

"Right, the airport. I met with the airport manager and a few folks from Delta to find out where our boy was coming from. I mean, he had checked into an airport motel, so I figured he had to be either coming or going."

"Well, which was it?"

"Coming. It appears our boy just flew in from Atlanta on a round-trip ticket and was headed back the day after tomorrow."

"So that's why I'm here?"

"That's part of it, Kirby." O'Barr leaned on the doorjamb with a wry smile on his face.

"Was he traveling alone?" Roselita asked.

"According to the flight manifest he was, but we ran the credit card you found in his wallet and saw that he made two more transactions to the same travel site, cheapflights.com, for two one-way tickets from Atlanta back to here three days from now. So I'm thinking his plan was to fly here, handle some business, go back, pick someone else up, and fly back. Both purchases were for the same amount at the same time—for the same flight from Atlanta back here, like I said, one way. Both in his name, but he opted for transferable tickets."

"So he bought two tickets?"

"It appears so."

"So he was planning on taking someone with him on his next flight."

"You are quite the detective, Agent Kirby."

Again, Dane ignored Velasquez's insult. "Okay, but why would he do it like that? Why not just put the name of the other passenger on the second ticket?"

"Because he was protecting someone," Velasquez said.

"Maybe," August said, and shrugged.

"Why not just stay here and let the other person fly out here to meet him. I mean, why go back?"

Another shrug from August. Dane stepped outside onto the breezeway, next to Assistant Director O'Barr. He spoke softly. "August, listen, man. Whatever this is, whatever you think this is, I promise you, I'm not the guy for it. I'm not doing anything here that Velasquez or even that guy Dahmer couldn't do better. This is outside my skill set."

"I agree," Roselita said, coming up behind them.

"See?" Dane made room for Velasquez in the doorway. "I'm just going to get in the way here. I know that. She knows that. The fire-related activity in this case isn't something you need me for. It's barely relevant. Velasquez had already put that together before I even got here."

Roselita nodded. "He's right, August. No offense, Kirby."

"None taken. I don't mind telling you both that I'm way out of my depth on this. Urban homicide is not something I have a long history with and I'll be honest"—Dane peeled off the light blue nitrile gloves and finally let his sweaty hands breathe—"I'm worried I may even fuck this case up for everyone."

August fumbled with the sack of hamburgers for a second before he tipped his chin at the blond tech holding the recovered sliver of bamboo. "Can I see that, hon?"

Dane and Roselita turned to look at her as she stepped to the door and handed the bag to Assistant Director O'Barr. "You're not here because of the fire, Kirby. You're here because of this." He handed Dane the evidence bag.

"What is it?" Dane and Roselita said in unison.

"My girlfriend here was spot on." O'Barr winked at the young forensic technician. It clearly made her uncomfortable and she excused herself to walk back into the room.

August stared at her backside all the way through the door. "Damn, boys, if I was thirty years younger."

Roselita had reached her limit. "No disrespect," she said, "but can we please stay on task here?"

August's face tightened and he gave Roselita his full attention. He never broke his smile, but something hot flickered behind his dark brown eyes that made everyone uneasy. Dane had been wrong. O'Barr wasn't flippant. He was just good at keeping the horror show hidden behind that carefree persona of his, and Roselita had just scraped back enough of that top layer to let some of that ugliness bleed through. It made the hair on the back of Dane's neck prickle. He wanted to go home.

"I'm sorry, Rosey," August said in a tone that was all business. "Allow me to skip right to it then. It's a piece of a stick, like the young lady said, but not just any stick. This is a splinter from a baston."

"And what is a baston?"

"It's a weapon—a deadly one when used by someone trained with it.

They are normally part of a set, and made from bamboo. More importantly, bastons are traditionally used by martial artists and overall bad motherfuckers mainly from the Philippines."

"So you're saying this guy was gutted by a Filipino martial artist?"

"Gold star for Kirby. He's beginning to get it."

"No, August, I'm not." Dane shook his head and took in a big chestful of the warm late afternoon air. He was getting tired. August dug into the paper bag and pulled out a burger wrapped in greasy wax paper as a 747 passenger jet pushed off the tarmac at the airport and roared into the distance. Dane stood and watched the plane lift into the sky as they all waited for the noise to subside. He really wanted to go home. Roselita stood with her hands in her pockets and watched August stuff the burger into his mouth with the same disgust Dane was feeling. At least they were on the same page about something. Dane stood on the curb, focused on the airplane lifting itself higher and higher into the tangerine sky until it was too small to make out and eventually it disappeared into the clouds. He pulled at the loose thread on the pocket of his T-shirt and wheels in his head began to spin. "The Philippines," he said to no one in particular.

"What?" Roselita said, and sidestepped Dane onto the parking lot.

Dane laughed. "Goddamnit."

"He *is* getting it," August said. "Finally."

"That guy in there." Dane pointed at room 1108. "He's got a Cobb County address."

"Yup."

"And he just flew in from Atlanta."

"Yup."

"And he was killed by a couple of Filipinos who just flew into the country a few days ago, right?"

"Four days ago, to be specific."

Dane looked back at the door of room 1108. "That guy is a cockfighter, isn't he?"

"Another gold star," August said in an enthusiastic tone.

"And he just hit it big at the Slasher, didn't he?"

August grinned. "And that makes three. That should also inform you, Special Agent Kirby of the GBI, as to why you are here." O'Barr stepped off the curb and chewed at a second bite of the greasy burger. He spoke with his mouth full. "Sorry for being so vague, but I had to be sure, and I wasn't until just now."

"He did, didn't he?" Dane pressed, but he already knew the answer.

"Yes, he did. I may not look like it, but I follow these things. Call it a hobby. His name was all over the Internet, but I had to make sure it was the same guy. It's a common name. It was, and not only was he there, but he won."

"How much?"

"All of it. He took the whole damn thing."

"That's impossible."

"Not anymore."

"What's a Slasher?" Roselita asked. Neither Dane nor August bothered to answer her. Dane just kept shaking his head and gnawed at his lip.

"And the Slasher was hosted this year in McFalls County. My home. Run by a guy you think I might know. So you had me flown down here to school your boys in how to survive in outlaw country."

"Yes I did," August said and chewed his burger.

Dane shook his head. "Son of a bitch."

August stuffed the wax-paper wrapper back into the paper bag and rolled it up tight. "Kirby, when I first got a hunch about who Blackwell was, I immediately called my man in the Georgia office, Charles Finnegan. He told me about a guy he had wasting away behind a desk who knew the area like no one else did, who would be thrilled to help me close this horrible murder. That guy was you. So here you are—a highly recommended detective with ties and deep connections to the notorious *Farm*. The same Farm that two Filipino high rollers just flew into for the biggest game in town. Filipino high rollers with a reputation for using bamboo bastons to get their point across if shit doesn't go their way—no pun intended."

"What the hell is a Slasher?" Roselita asked again. She was getting angry enough for the small V-shaped vein in her forehead to protrude between her neatly trimmed eyebrows. August and Dane might as well have been speaking Greek and Roselita might as well have been invisible. "Somebody needs to tell me what is happening here," Roselita said. "I'm serious."

Dane ignored her a second time—to his detriment. She lowered her head and scuffed one foot across the asphalt like a bull about to charge a flag. Dane tipped his hat back on his head and stuck his hands down deep in his pockets. For the first time in years, and despite his recent news, he wanted a cigarette. Roselita, at full tilt, pushed her way in between him and August and waved her arms in the air. "Hello? Is somebody going to fill me in here?"

"Just calm down a second, Rose."

"Don't call me Rose," she snapped. "And forgive me, Kirby, but I'm not going to calm down. This is total bullshit. I'm the one working this case, and before I can even begin to do my job, my partner is sidelined, your hillbilly ass gets brought in with zero experience in the field—in a state you have no jurisdiction in—and now the two of you are talking about fucking chickens, for God's sake. You both are clearly keeping me in the dark about something while whoever sliced open that guy in there and set him on fire gets farther and farther away. So no, I'm not going to calm down, but what I will do is go above this whole boys' club thing you two have going on and report the way this is being handled."

Dane let the moment sit a little longer before speaking. The breeze was salty. He wasn't sure if that was just how Florida smelled or because of all the blood in the air. "Okay, Roselita," he said. "I'm out here because your dead guy in there just got back from something called the Slasher. It's the biggest cockfighting tournament in the US. The name is stolen from the big tournament held annually in the Philippines, where it's legal. It's bigger than the Super Bowl over there. Here, it's held in secret, in different parts of Georgia, Tennessee, and sometimes North Carolina depending on who puts in the lowest bid. This year it was held in McFalls County, up in North Georgia, where I'm from."

"And it's illegal."

"Yes."

"Yet you not only know about it, but when and where it happens."

"Yes."

"And you—both of you—allow it?"

"It's complicated," Dane said. August pulled a swig of Sprite through a pinstriped straw. Roselita waited for a real answer, decided she wasn't going to get one, and moved on. "So. Cockfighting?"

"Yes," Dane said, and took a deep breath. He knew how it must sound to a cop like Velasquez in a city like Jacksonville, and her reaction was typical and anticipated.

"Are you fucking kidding me?" she said. "This is why you're here? That's why Geoff got sidelined? Because you're the GBI's resident cock-fighting expert?"

"I wouldn't say I'm an expert."

Roselita turned away and ran her hands through her hair. It fell right back into place as if it hadn't been touched. "This cannot really be happening."

"Calm down, Velasquez." Dane could understand her frustration, so he tried to soften the blow. "Look at it this way. The good news is you and your partner shouldn't be insulted that O'Barr called me in to help out on this. It's definitely not because of my skill as an investigator."

August faked a frown. "Now, that's not entirely true, Kirby. I think you're a fine investigator."

"Just stop the bullshit, *sir*." Dane turned to Roselita. "We were right about what happened in there. This is another payday gone sideways. And that's why you Feds are here taking over in the first place. Because the Slasher's payout is federal-sized money, right?"

August nodded. "We do love a big pile of tax-free cash."

Roselita stopped pacing. "So, okay, hold on. I want to try and get my head around this. Let's imagine that this guy was gambling like you say—on chickens no less—and scored big. It's ridiculous, but let's go with it. What could possibly be so big in the world of *cockfighting* that it warranted what they did to him?"

"He didn't just score big," August said. "He won the whole thing—all of it—the whole enchilada, every fight, every round."

Dane could've sworn August almost sounded impressed as he said that. Velasquez still didn't understand. "And still I say—so?"

"And so." Dane took his hat off and rubbed his head. "It's impossible. Or at least it was until now."

"You're saying no one has ever won this Slasher thing before?"

"Never a single man—not once. It isn't a winner-take-all sport."

Roselita's frustration was back. "I can't even believe I'm standing out here talking about cockfighting with a redneck who actually refers to it as a sport. This is insane."

"I'm going to keep ignoring your insults, Velasquez, for the sake of getting me home sooner, but please just shut up and listen for a minute."

Roselita stopped pacing, crossed her arms, cocked a hip, and waited to be enlightened.

"Without overloading your brain with the rules and regulations of how cockfighting works," Dane said, "if what August is saying is true, and Blackwell won the entire tournament—then he cheated. It shouldn't even be possible." He rolled his hat in his hands like a magazine. "It would be like walking into the MGM Grand in Vegas and clearing out the house of every dollar in one night, sitting at the same table. It just can't be done. It's logistically impossible."

"And so what kind of money are we talking about, then?"

Dane and Roselita both looked at August.

"He took them for a million two in cash, all clean, tax-exempt US dollars."

Dane watched that number hit Roselita in just the right place. This wasn't a joke or a hillbilly circus like she originally thought. This was big. That was the kind of money that could explain what attracted the wolves to room 1108 of the Days Inn in Jacksonville. "That's what was in the missing suitcase," Dane said. "That's why they didn't think twice about leaving the six hundred bucks in his wallet." Dane pinched at the bridge of his nose. "Jesus Christ, how did Blackwell think those guys wouldn't kill him for doing something like this?"

"There's a word for it," August said. They all knew what that word was, but no one said it out of respect for the dead.

Roselita shuffled the pieces of information around in her head. She still wasn't satisfied. "Okay, so Blackwell goes to the backwoods of Georgia and wins some chicken contest."

"That's a little bit of an oversimplification," Dane said, but Roselita held out a slim finger and kept talking.

"Whatever you people call it, I don't care. He cheated and the people who lost the chicken fight followed him back here, killed him, and took their money back."

"That appears to be the theory."

"Okay, so we ground every flight out of the States headed back to the Philippines and we nab these fuckers. If they aren't already gone."

"That's already in the works," August said.

Dane shook his head. "But I still don't understand why they did this guy the way they did him. I mean, why go through all the trouble of torturing the guy like that if they got back what they wanted? Even if he did cheat them and they wanted to make an example of him, a quiet bullet in the back of the head would've done the trick. This seems excessive, to say the least, doesn't it?"

"Unless they didn't get what they wanted," August said. He snapped his fingers at a patrol man and the uniformed cop lit one of O'Barr's cigarettes for him. He pulled in the smoke and let it drift up over his mustache. "I'm guessing they tortured him because he didn't have *everything* they wanted. We know he was working with someone because of the two plane tickets, so maybe only half the cash was in the suitcase and the rest went off with whoever his partner is. Maybe our killers are still searching for it."

"That means we've still got a chance to catch these bastards on the ground," Roselita said.

August pulled in another drag. "There's something else."

"What?"

August wiped at the sweaty fold of skin under his chin. "Kirby just laid it out a minute ago. Blackwell did something at the Slasher that had never been done before—ever. So think about it. What else could they want from him?"

Roselita looked back at the door to the motel and than beamed her dark, impatient eyes at August.

He asked the question another way. "What would a bunch of vicious pricks, who never lose, want from a guy who clearly cheated them out of all their money, other than their money back? What could be even more valuable than the money?"

Roselita quit pacing and stopped cold in front of August's car as the light in her brain popped on. "They want to know how he did it."

"Exactly," August said. "Blackwell had a system, and by the looks of what they did to him, he didn't want to give that information up. Now both of you pay attention, because this part is important. No one, and I repeat, no one who fits the description of the man the Cuban kid saw, or anyone of Filipino descent period, is scheduled to fly out of that airport anytime soon." August looked toward the airport. "I've also got every field agent I can afford scouring private airfields all over both states, so if that changes, I'll know it. If it doesn't, it means I'm right, and these animals aren't going home until they find what they're looking for. And until they do, I can almost guarantee there will be more of these." August pointed at the motel room. Roselita's phone buzzed in her pocket and she excused herself to take the call.

"Dane, you know what I'm asking from you, right?"

"Yeah, August. I know. You need a tour guide. I got it."

O'Barr didn't even try to deny it. "I appreciate your help with this. The Bureau will be in your debt. You might even find yourself looking at a future on a federal level."

Dane thought about the paperwork in his pocket from his doctor. The paperwork he'd kept on his person for over a week so his girlfriend back at the house wouldn't see it. The same paperwork that promised him a future far different from one of a celebrated FBI agent. He felt like pulling it out to give August a more detailed look at what his future really looked like, but he left the papers where they were and nodded his head. He felt tired again—exhausted, really.

O'Barr tossed the greasy paper bag into the Oldsmobile and Roselita rejoined them just as August was sliding behind the wheel.

Dane squeezed at his sore neck. "Listen, I know you guys are raring to go on this, but I need to go home for a few hours. My girlfriend just moved in with me and thinks I'm knee-deep in a creek an hour away from home right now."

"Fine. I'll have a chopper ready to bring you back to McFalls."

"I'll get myself there," Roselita said. "I've got some things to follow up on myself."

"Fine, the two of you do whatever you have to do, but track these bastards down before they find anyone else to shred into pieces." August slammed the long door on the Oldsmobile and cranked the engine. He rolled the window down. "Oh, and find the money, too." He gave an animated wink as the glass slid back up.

August pulled the car out of the lot and Dane waited until he was completely gone before saying another word. When the Oldsmobile had left his line of sight, he headed back toward the motel room. "Roselita, come with me." He crossed the lot, leaned down under the yellow tape, and stepped back up on the curb. He stood in front of room 1108 but didn't go in. Roselita had taken out her phone and began to tap in a text message. Dane wasn't a fan of that method of communication. Texting lacked inflection and it was easy to be misconstrued. He preferred talking. He guessed that made him old. He eased the door open and pointed down to the threshold. "Put your phone away, Velasquez, and look at that."

Roselita tapped her phone off and looked down at a dark smudge on the carpet just inside the door. She pulled at the legs of her pants and crouched down to get a better look. Dane didn't need one. He knew what it was.

"So what about it, Kirby? An ember drifted over here from the body."

Dane shook his head. "No. That's not from the same fire."

"I don't follow."

"You don't have to follow me, Velasquez. But you might want to follow the weed."

"Follow the what?"

Dane leaned against the wall, balanced himself, and squatted down to the threshold. He lightly rubbed his finger into the small scorch mark that Arnold Blackwell's joint had left on the carpet just before he was ambushed. Dane held his finger to Roselita's nose. "Follow the weed," he repeated. "No one could smell that over the stink in there, not even me, but you can smell it now, can't you? Blackwell must've been getting high in here when he was interrupted, and I know it may sound like a weak lead, maybe he has it on him all the time, but maybe, just maybe, he picked it up in Atlanta before he boarded the flight. Maybe you can trace it back to whoever he was working with or whoever the second ticket is for before our killers do."

Roselita agreed that it was indeed a weak lead. "He could've gotten it from anywhere."

"Look, Blackwell didn't have a pot to piss in, right?"

"Yeah, so?"

"Well, I know for a fact that you need ten grand in cash to buy in to the Slasher. That's what builds the pot. Where did he get the money? And once he had more, maybe he bought some weed with it. It's just a hunch."

"You're telling me Blackwell made a pit stop somewhere between this Slasher tournament and the Atlanta airport to pick up some pot and smuggled it via airplane across the state line with a suitcase stuffed full of cash?"

"Well, we've already established that this guy wasn't the brightest bulb in the box, and besides, where else can we start looking?"

Roselita rubbed at the mark on the carpet herself. She smelled her own fingers. "Maybe this burn was already here before he checked in."

"No. Trust me. This is fresh."

"And you think the men who did this are hunting the dealer right now?"

"They are hunting someone. And the interesting thing is that they took the joint. Why? It's not here, is it? Is there any evidence of drug use in the room?"

"No."

"Because they didn't want us to know it was there. Because *they* are following the weed. It's as good a place to start as any."

Roselita stood up and brushed the wrinkles from her pants. "Or you're completely full of shit."

"Maybe, but regardless, this is a piece of the puzzle, and maybe it's where you need to be on this case. Just see where it takes you."

Roselita sniffed her fingers again, and looked down at Dane. "How did you even see that, Kirby? And why didn't you tell August any of this?"

"Listen, Velasquez, you're good at what you do, I can tell. But I'm good at what I do. I've been investigating fires my whole adult life. That mark was one of the first things I noticed when I got here. I figured someone would've gotten around to telling me about it, or showed me the joint that made the mark, but no one ever did. That means someone took it—someone who didn't want us to know about it. I didn't tell August, because I don't want anything to do with this. I'm not the guy for this. You are, the girl, I mean, the woman—"

"I get the drift, Kirby, just keep going."

"Right. Well, this"—Dane rubbed the ash between his fingertips—"will prove it, so I'm telling you, follow the weed, beat those monsters to wherever it came from. Find the money. Find the killers. And maybe you crack this case wide open. You take the bust and I'll fade quietly back into the basement I crawled out of. Everyone goes home happy."

Dane could tell Roselita was still skeptical by the way she chewed at the corner of her bottom lip, but he could also see she was ready to make that deal a reality. "Okay," she said. "I'll keep you in the loop." She hopped off the curb, crossed back over the parking lot without a word of goodbye, and had her phone to her ear before Dane could even manage to pull himself upright.

"Hold up, sir," Tweedledee said. The stout young agent from the helicopter appeared as if he'd never left. He bent over and helped Dane to his feet.

"Thanks."

"No problem. The helicopter is ready, sir."

Dane sighed. "Great. Can't wait."

CHAPTER SEVEN

William put the brand-new cell phone his brother had bought him back in his rucksack. He sat inside the bus station although he wanted to go back outside where it was cool. The air inside the station smelled like body odor, the way Arnie smelled after he disappeared for a few days and came home all twitchy and upset. It made William want to throw up. Arnold was in trouble. Whoever answered the phone didn't sound very nice, and with Arnie yelling like that in the background, he knew it meant his brother had made someone else angry. Arnie was always making people angry. Their father used to sit up at night and talk to himself in the dark about the things Arnie used to do when they were younger. The thought of his dad put William in a bad place, but you wouldn't know it to look at him. He pushed it away. He pushed Arnie's angry voice away. He stared straight ahead at the huge map of Atlanta mounted on the wall behind a scratched-up sheet of Plexiglas. The different colored lines on the map represented the different train routes the MARTA took through the city. The darker black lines broken by the white circles were the buses and the bus stops. He couldn't read the legend of places, or the listing of numbers that ran down the left side of the huge map, but he didn't have to. It took him twenty minutes to memorize the map. He wanted to take the train back to the zoo where Bobby had dropped him off. It was hard walking in by himself, but he did it. He loved trains and he loved the zoo. He knew the exact route to take to get back there, but Arnie had told him on the phone to go to their safe place. They discussed that before they went up north to the pretty lady's farm. He called it a safe place because he couldn't say what it was in front of whoever had his phone. William understood that. He understood a lot more than Arnie thought he did. He was also okay with leaving the zoo to go there. He liked their safe place, too. It could be a lot of fun if Arnie wasn't in a bad mood. William had never been there by himself before. He hoped it would still be fun even with no one to talk to. He knew it would be. The birds talked to each other and William loved to just listen. Most people never just listened. They were always talking.

William looked at the time displayed on the cell phone. It would take a while to get all the way there. He thought about Bobby and how he had said he would be there to pick him up at the zoo at six o'clock, but he guessed Arnie would tell him not to now. Bobby was probably in trouble, too. He was another one who never stopped talking. Now William needed to go where he was told. He looked at it like another adventure, like the contest at the big farm. Maybe Arnie would let him take the train back to the airport one more time before they moved to the beach. They were moving to the beach because now Arnie had money. Arnie was really happy about that. William knew he'd helped Arnie and his friend make a lot of money at the big farm. Even with what happened to some of the birds, it was worth it to make Arnie happy, and money always made Arnie happy. William just wished his brother had the ability to hold on to some of it. He was bad with numbers. William was good with numbers and that's why they made a good team. That's what Arnie said, anyway. Maybe now that Arnie had a lot of money, he would stay happy longer— maybe forever. William wanted to believe that, but it didn't sound that way on the phone. It hadn't lasted very long at all.

William counted the slats in the bench and then moved on to the linoleum tiles on the floor. Six hundred and forty-eight. He moved his eyes up the wall, counting the painted cement blocks until he caught a glimpse of something that didn't belong. He fixated on the top left corner of the ceiling—a light brown pile of what looked like clay and grass constructed over time on one of the steel girders. As soon as he noticed it, he recognized it for what it was and began to scan the station for its owner. It didn't take long. The small speckled barn swallow had been perched on another steel beam, returning William's curious stare. William smiled. He wondered how long the small bird had been watching him—sizing him up—timing his movements—evaluating the threat. The clay mound was the swallow's nest—its home. And although William couldn't see them from the bench, he knew it was full of fledglings, hence their mother's watchful eye. William slowly reached into his rucksack and pulled out the last pack of Lance crackers Arnie had packed for him. He had told Arnie several times that he didn't like them. But he never listened. He was always talking instead. Eventually, William had stopped protesting and pretended to eat them by throwing them away in outside trash cans Arnie would never see. Now William peeled open the cellophane, pulled out one of the unnaturally orange peanut butter–filled squares, and crushed it in his hand, letting the bits and crumbs scatter on the bench beside him. He whistled a soft, low-pitched sound that mimicked the sound of a barn swallow perfectly. He could do all kinds of bird calls. He'd memorized the sound of nearly every bird indigenous to the state. The swallow chirped back and twitched its head. William smiled again and then stood up cautiously to make his way to the other side of the station. He crossed twenty-eight floor tiles and took a seat on another bench opposite where he'd been. He sat, watched, and waited. It took less than a minute for the swallow to swoop down to the cracker crumbs and peck away and digest its family's dinner. Every few seconds in between filling its beak, it glanced over at William, who had begun to crumble another cracker on the second bench. He nodded at the mother bird right before it flew up, circled the ceiling a few times, and landed in the makeshift nest. William imagined the bird nodding back at him with some kind of unspoken appreciation. He knew that wasn't the case. He knew the birds didn't have the same kind of brain capacity humans did. He wasn't an idiot. But he liked to think it anyway. He was helping a family in need live through another night and it made him feel good.

A line of buses began to pull forward and William took his eyes off the now frantically circling bird to look for bus number 422. It was the second one back from the doors to the station. He stood, picked up his rucksack, and gave a silent goodbye to the swallow. He pulled the plastic card Arnie had given him from the front pocket of his bag, hoisted the rucksack onto his shoulder, and waited in front of the bus door until the driver finally opened it up. William stepped into the bus and held the card up to a man with a thick black beard and handlebar mustache behind the wheel. William liked the man's facial hair. It looked cool. It reminded him of a chimney sweep. He'd read about them in a book once and pictured them looking just like this man driving bus 422. The driver pointed to a scanner and William held his card under the red light until it beeped. The driver looked at a screen William couldn't see behind the scanner. "Thank you," William said.

"You're welcome," the driver with the cool mustache said, and looked past William out into the empty station. "You riding alone, kid?"

"Yes, sir."

"Your parents aren't with you?"

"My parents are dead. They died in a car accident. I live with my brother, but he's rich now and we're moving to the beach."

The driver's expression never changed from the blank look of a city worker who'd heard it all. "Oh, yeah?" he said.

"Yes, sir," William said, as if he'd just given directions to a Waffle House and not a recap of his tragic family history. The driver stared at William, trying to gauge how old he was, but decided that it didn't matter. "You know this bus doesn't go to the beach, right?"

"Of course I do."

The driver took a second but finally dismissed him. "Okay, kid. Go have a seat."

"Thank you," William said for a second time. He put the plastic bus pass away and counted down four rows and over two seats before sitting down next to a window, hoping to see the barn swallow again. He couldn't. He settled into the high-backed seat, put on his seatbelt, and sat his rucksack in his lap. He took out a set of small earbuds that came with his new phone and stuck them in his ears just to block out the ambient sound around him. He pulled a ragged paperback book out of his rucksack—*Tarzan of the Apes*, by Edgar Rice Burroughs. It was one of his favorites. It had belonged to his dad. His dad loved pulp fiction novels. They used to search thrift shops and bookstores for them all the time before he died. Stories about Tarzan and Doc Savage were his dad's favorites. They were William's favorites, too. He'd read this particular book so many times the spine was beginning to give way and pages were starting to fall out. He was careful as he flipped to the playing card he was using as a bookmark and began to read.

The bus driver continued to watch William in the large rearview mirror in between scanning in a few other travelers and tearing some paper tickets. Once the six other people taking this trip boarded the bus, the driver got up from his captain's chair and walked four rows back to William's seat. "Excuse me, son."

William took out one of the headphones but didn't look up. "Yes, sir?"

"You know this bus doesn't go directly to your destination, right? You'll need to change buses in Columbus."

William looked straight ahead, directly into the back of the seat in front of him. "Bus four twenty-two goes one hundred and eight miles to Columbus, Georgia, and then bus forty-nine leaves at six ten and goes another eighty-nine miles to Black Mountain. It's going to take four hours and eighteen minutes by bus, but only two hours and twelve minutes if we were traveling by train. But no trains go there. I wish they did. I won't fall asleep and miss my stop, sir."

"Well, okay then," the bus driver said, and twirled at his chimney sweep mustache. His concern about the kid sitting in seat 4D vanished as William put his earbud back in and picked up his book. The driver walked back to his seat behind the wheel and finished prepping for the drive. "Weird kid," he whispered. William heard him since there wasn't any music playing in his headphones, but rested his head against the cool glass of the window. He was used to hearing it. Everyone said it. He really wished he was on the train.

CHAPTER EIGHT

The chopper ride back to Waymore hadn't been as tense as earlier, but it was just as uncomfortable. Dane had made an impression on his new courier by twisting the stick Agent Dahmer had firmly implanted up his ass, and now it seemed he'd made a friend. While Dane spent forty-five minutes in the flying plastic bubble with his new friend's chatter, he began to yearn for the strained and awkward silence of the last ride. During the time Dane was a captive audience, he learned more about the young agent's personal life than he cared to know. He smiled a lot and nodded, adding in the occasional "I hear you" as Agent Eric Talbott filled Dane in on all the juicy details about his wife's infidelity with a dental hygienist. He talked about how "that cheatin' bitch" had stolen his dignity—his manhood—and if that wasn't enough, now she was coming after his bankroll. He also told Dane about the whole Facebook thing he had with his "ex."

"It was nothing, man—nothing to make such a big deal about, anyway—but she's telling me she's got screenshots. She's saying her lawyer's got me by the balls."

Dane thought about the possibility of hurling himself out of the helicopter as the young man kept talking. "The system is rigged, man. Chicks bat their eyelashes for the judge and bam—we're the assholes. Nothing else matters, you know?"

"I hear you, man."

"You want to know how I caught them?"

Dane did not, but he knew he was going to hear about it anyway.

"The commode, man. I tell you, Dane—it is Dane, right? Can I call you Dane?"

Dane didn't answer. He didn't care. Talbott took his silence as a yes.

"Cool. So how stupid is this bitch, Dane? I come home from work a couple weeks back. Slow night. My stomach ain't doing that great. Bad sushi. I don't know. Anyway, I get home and head straight to the john— you know, to drop a deuce, right? You with me, Dane?"

"I'm with you, Eric."

"Okay, so the wife is downstairs cooking dinner. Nothing out of the ordinary there. She's doing her wifely duties. It's just another day in the neighborhood."

Dane held up a hand. "Her wifely duties?"

"Yeah." Clearly Eric wasn't sure why Dane wanted to repeat that. Dane just shook his head and looked out the glass window at the swirl of treetops below him.

"Right, anyway, I'm in there about twenty minutes or so, I don't know, maybe longer, and I hear the bitch call me down. She says, 'Baby—come and eat.' I mean, she calls me baby—like it's just another fucking day."

Dane was fading. He could feel his eyelids getting heavy.

"So I flush and the damn commode gets plugged up. I know what you're thinking. Bad sushi, right? I must've plugged it up. I did it. I thought so, too, at first, so I'm like, oh shit, and grab the plunger, before the damn thing starts to overflow and there's shit water all over the place." He paused as if Dane would be able to put the rest of the story together on his own. Dane remained silent and stared out the window.

"Jimmy hats," Talbott finally said. "Freaking condoms, man. Tied in knots at that. Little spunk balloons were choking up *my* john. And they wasn't mine, brother. Can you believe that shit?"

Dane could believe it. He could also see the approaching hospital helipad from the air, the only one in McFalls County, and couldn't wait to get his feet back on solid ground. The sound of Talbott's voice became a drone that blended in with the whirl of the chopper blades until the bird landed. Talbott was still in the middle of his story when Dane turned to cut him off. "Give her everything," Dane said. "The house. The car. The money. Everything. Just sign the papers and wish her the best, because at the end of the day, Agent Talbott, none of that stuff matters.

None of it. Life is too short. Just be done with it all, and then go out and find yourself a woman you could never bring yourself to ever call a bitch, because *that* woman—the one out there waiting on you to find her—ain't never gonna be found, as long as you're still giving all your attention to a woman who—let's face it, man—fucked your dentist."

Talbott went blank. Immediately, Dane wished he'd just left it alone and said nothing.

"He's a dental hygienist, Dane. He's not even a real dentist."

"Does it matter, Eric?"

"You're damn right it matters. That's the point. You know?"

Dane didn't know. He just sighed. "I hear you, man," he said, and scrambled out of his seat and then looked for and found the small fiber-glass handle that would help him down out of the chopper.

"Wait a second, man," Talbott said, and grabbed Dane by the shoulder. He scribbled his name and number down on the back of a Walmart receipt from his wallet and handed it to Dane through the open Plexiglas door. "Call me, brother. We can go out and pound a few beers sometime. I'm in Hotlanta all the time."

Dane took the slip of paper and smiled to himself. "Sure, man. Anytime."

Once Dane got back to his truck, he wheeled the old '65 Ford F100 out onto State Route 60 and drove a forty-seven-mile winding strip of blacktop with unpaved shoulders into Fannin County before taking a left onto an unpaved road without a street sign. He drove another mile or so until he saw the white mailbox at the head of a gravel drive with his last name on it. He pulled off into the grass just short of the box and came to a stop. He cut the engine and the lights and decided to walk up the drive. He popped the door and eased himself out into the moonlight. He checked the mailbox, but it was empty, so he started walking toward the house and became aware again of the fold of papers he'd been carrying around with him for the past few days, still pressed against his leg in the pocket of his cargo pants. He left them right where they were as he stared up the long driveway to his house. He didn't want to think about that right now. All of the death he'd just witnessed had kept his mind free of it, and it was a welcome break for his brain. He felt a chill. The night wasn't cold, but it was cool out, and he'd never walked the expanse of his property at night before. This time it wasn't his own problems or the temperature outside that caused the gooseflesh to cross his neck but the still-fresh image of what he'd seen back at that motel.

Jesus. That poor bastard.

The picture of that burnt and gutted corpse helped the night breeze run its fingers deep into the collar of Dane's jacket as he walked up between the twin ditches of weeds and pea gravel that served as the driveway to his house. The porch light was on and it lit up the front door of the modest ranch-style house. Dane had painted that door fire-engine red the very day he moved in. It was the only thing he'd added to the house decor. The rest was all recent—and it was all Misty. She loved to decorate. She lived for it. Dane didn't give one damn. Even the house didn't matter to him when he bought it. He just loved the land. He'd live in a trailer as long as the land it was on kept him at least a mile away from the closest neighbor. The house was only as important as the people who lived in it. Otherwise it was just a box. Dane had just pointlessly tried to explain that to the young agent who'd escorted him home, but he knew it didn't stick. He'd been the same way at that age.

Dane had started dating Misty about a year before he'd decided to leave McFalls County and relocate to Fannin. The drive back and forth to see each other had been taxing for both of them, so after the first few times she'd brought it up, he'd finally agreed to let her move in. He wasn't sure it was a good idea then and he still wasn't now, but it wasn't like she didn't practically live here already, only now it was official. And it made her happy. Dane rarely had that effect on people, so he rolled with it. And after so many years alone with no one but ghosts in his head to talk to, it was kind of nice to have a real person around when he got home.

As he got closer to the house, he could make out one of Misty's handmade wreaths hanging on the door and he shook his head. It was made of burlap and brown ribbon with a huge *K* made of green wire in the center. She loved to make those things and, honestly, Dane didn't mind seeing them. It was something else that made her happy, and for a moment, the wreath made the details of room 1108 fade. He'd deal with those later. He would never forget what he'd seen back there, but it had no place in his home. In fact, the closer he got to the house, the warmer he felt. The night pulled its fingers off his neck. The darkness outside was apparently no match for Misty's love of the craft store. It was things like that—the things that went unnoticed by so many—that made all the difference, and if there was one thing Dane knew to be true, it was that for all the cruelty and violence the world had to offer, none of it stood a chance against the unassuming power of a man's porch light being left on to welcome him home. Dane managed a smile for the first time all day as he slowly made his way up the steps. He ran his fingers over the folds of wire and burlap on the wreath, right before he fished his keys out of his pocket and unlocked the bright red door.

Dane was about to drop his keys into a coaster-sized ceramic turtle bowl on the small table against the wall in the foyer but picked it up instead. It always looked to Dane more like a warped oak leaf than a turtle, but he never argued the point. Dane's daughter, Joy, had made that turtle in kindergarten, and it had sat right inside the door of the old house they'd lived in every day since she'd brought it home. Now it was here. He ran his thumb over the jagged edges. He'd broken it several times over the years but superglued it together every time. It was more glue and cracked purple ceramic chips now than it was oak leaf or turtle, but he loved it. He loved that damn turtle. Dane thought about how upset Misty had gotten the first time she'd come over and seen it there. She said he was just torturing himself. Maybe she was right, but he put it there anyway. Some things were worth the torture. Some things he didn't want to feel distant from. That turtle-blob-thing made this house feel more like a home—his home. The turtle stayed.

He had no sooner picked it up before he felt the vise-grip hug of a little girl with long hair, wispy and blond and in need of a good brushing, crushing his leg. He'd expected it. He also knew it wasn't real. The little blond girl let go and vanished around the corner. Dane said nothing as he followed her into the house. He poked his head sheepishly around the corner and looked over the living room into the kitchen. He saw what he always saw.

Gwen.

He knew she would be there, too. He also knew she wasn't real, either, but there she was—waiting on him—almost every day. She was standing in the kitchen facing away from him, her dark cocoa hair tied in a loose, shiny knot behind her neck, falling down her back. She wore a simple wrap dress painted an autumn floral and bunched up at her hips, stopping a quarter way down her thighs—her swaying thighs. Her hips moved in time to The Bangles' "Manic Monday"—

OH-ooh-OH, Dane hummed to himself.

She acknowledged Dane's presence with a quick glance over her shoulder that said, "You can go back to looking at my ass now," before lip-syncing Susanna Hoffs into her wooden-spoon microphone. She stayed that way, dancing like a teenager in a movie, while she worked the pans on the range like a game of three-card monte for a crowd of invisible spectators.

Dane felt the familiar ache in his chest beginning to burn its way out like kerosene in the back of his throat. He closed his eyes and pinched the bridge of his nose. He stayed like that for a long moment. That move had become ritual for warning off his ghosts. When he opened his eyes, he was still in the foyer holding the purple turtle and the house was silent. He set it back down on the table and emptied his pockets into it—about two bucks in loose change, a tied fly he'd begun to make at the creek, and a mushroomed .30-30 bullet he'd been carrying around for years.

He announced himself and kicked off his boots as he walked past the stairs into the living room, and this time, grounded in reality, he stared into the empty kitchen. He made his entry loud in case Misty was in the shower or busy upstairs. He wanted to surprise his girl, but not scare a woman who knew her way around the Colt 1911 Dane kept in the safe by the bed. It took him nearly a full minute to notice her nephew, Jackson, sitting on the carpet in front of a muted TV to his right in the den. He had to do a double take and he blinked a few times just to make sure this boy was real and not another apparition. But the boy was real, and Dane suddenly wasn't surprised to see him there. Misty kept her little sister's boy more often than his own mother did. Dane knew Misty hadn't gotten used to being alone in the strange house for any length of time yet, so she must've volunteered to take Jackson for the weekend just to keep her company. Dane liked her nephew just fine, but the kid wasn't exactly the person he had hoped to come home to. The romantic surprise idea was a bust. He'd parked by the street and walked the drive for no reason.

Jackson sat cross-legged on the floor, surrounded by sheets of paper he'd taken from the printer in Dane's office. A spilled box of crayons littered the carpet in a circle around him. The boy looked up to acknowledge Dane's presence, but that was it—just a casual glance—before going right back to work on his Crayola masterpiece.

Dane took a seat on the ottoman in front of the sofa. "Hey, buddy, I didn't know you were staying with us." He said it like a question but didn't get any response, so he tried again. "Hey, bud, when did you get here?" He ran a hand through the boy's hair, a thick tangle of brown curls that matched Misty's and her sister's both. Dane thought the kid needed a haircut. Jackson drew away from Dane's hand. He didn't like to be touched. Dane was familiar with that quirk in the kid's personality, but it didn't stop him from doing it anyway. He picked up one of the drawings from the floor. "Whatcha working on, buddy?"

The child said nothing as he tossed a crayon back into the pile and searched for a better shade of green.

"Jack? Bud?"

"I don't like that," the boy finally said, pushing his kid-sized plastic-rimmed glasses up on the bridge of his nose.

"What, the crayon or the picture?" Dane looked at the drawing of what he assumed was some kind of dragon. "I don't know, buddy, I think that's a pretty cool dragon."

"It's not a dragon. It's a pterodactyl. It can fly. I like those."

"Then what don't you like?"

"He doesn't like it when you call him buddy," Misty said from the stairs. "Right, Jackson?"

"Right, Aunt Misty."

Misty was wearing a Killers: Sam's Town T-shirt that showed off all the right curves—no bra—and a pair of soft pants that hung low around her hips, giving Dane just a sliver of skin to look at around her waist. The sight of her immediately erased the thoughts of his nephew. He loved his woman's after-hours look and he allowed himself a smile for the second time that night. Dane held his arms out. "I'm home."

"I can see that." Misty took the last step and tripped on one of Dane's boots. He'd left them in the middle of the floor again.

Strike one.

"Ow, shit," she said, closed her eyes, and braced herself against the wall to keep from falling over. Dane quickly jumped up and pushed his boots to the corner. Misty balanced on one foot and rubbed at her toe while Dane held her steady. That was not the way he'd wanted this homecoming to go, either.

"Sorry, babe. Are you okay?"

"I'm good," she said through her teeth. "I'm fine."

"Are you okay, Aunt Misty?"

"I'm fine, Jackson. Your uncle"—Dane wasn't comfortable being called the boy's uncle, but he never corrected her—"on the other hand, is going to be a long way from fine if he leaves his boots in the middle of the floor one more time."

"Never again," Dane said. "I swear." He held a hand over his heart, but it didn't mean much. He'd said it before, and he'd most likely say it again.

"Don't swear." She let go of the wall and he let go of her. "Anyway, what's up? Why are you back so early?" She finally put her foot down and came in for the hug Dane had been waiting for.

"I'll tell you after you-know-who goes to bed."

"I know you're talking about me, Uncle Dane."

"I know you know, buddy."

"I just told you he doesn't like that."

Dane grunted. It wasn't that he didn't care, he just didn't—well—he didn't care. He nuzzled his face into the crook of Misty's neck right behind her ear. Her hair was all driftwood and sage—and still damp, too, from her bath. He touched the small of her back and ran his hand under her T-shirt and up the curve of her skin. Her back was still damp, too. He pulled her in tight and she let him. Jackson stood up and hugged Misty's leg. Dane thought of the phantom hug he'd received from Joy when he got home, but let the thought drift and tried to stay in the moment. "Looks like everybody wants a little love from you."

"Can you blame him?"

"No, ma'am, I cannot," Dane said, then kissed her, and her lips were soft and perfect. He slid his hand down from her back to grab a handful of her butt, but she playfully arched back out of his reach. "Not in front of you-know-who."

"He knows you're talking about him. Right, Jack?"

Jackson didn't answer. He just sat down on the carpet and went back to work. Dane lifted an eyebrow at Misty. "See? I might as well be invisible around you."

"Stop being so sensitive, Dane." Misty pulled herself all the way out of the hug. "And for real, what are you doing back here? I thought you'd be gone until tomorrow night. I haven't hung the new drapes I bought yet and it's why I told Jenn I'd take Jackson. I didn't even hear your truck."

Dane plopped down on the sofa. "Yeah, well, my weekend didn't quite go as planned—and I parked the truck down by the mailbox."

"Why?"

"I wanted to surprise you."

"Aw, how sweet." She leaned over and kissed his ear. "So what happened to the fishing trip?"

"I told you. It's a story for upstairs."

"Did you even get to fish?"

"I got a few hours in this morning, but I didn't catch shit."

"Language."

"Right." Dane thought about her saying that exact same word when she stubbed her toe. He rubbed at his temples. "Anyway, then things got crazy. First Sheriff Ellis called me, and then Charles called me in to look at a case the FBI is working in Jacksonville. They even flew me to Florida and back on a helicopter."

"Ooh, a helicopter. Fancy."

"It's not as cool as it sounds. Anyway, I've seen enough terrible shit—"

"Stuff."

"Right. Stuff. I've seen enough terrible *stuff* today to last me a lifetime, and all I want to do is take a shower, get off my feet, and get into bed with you. Oh, and you're not going to believe who's back in town."

"Well, you can tell me and do all of that as soon as you help me get this kiddo's teeth brushed and get him ready for bed."

Dane nodded. Again, that was not the response he was looking for. Misty bent over and scooped Jackson off the floor. "C'mon, big guy. Let's go brush them chompers."

"So *big guy* is good," Dane said, "but *buddy* is not. Got it."

"Uncle Dane went on a helicopter? Did he fly? Like a pterodactyl?"

Misty leaned Jackson out from her hip. "Maybe you should ask him."

The boy pushed his glasses up again and considered it, before pulling himself back in to Misty's stomach. They started up the stairs, Misty holding Jackson tight under her arm. "You gotta take it easy on your uncle, Jackson. He's sensitive."

"Okay, I will."

Dane actually did feel invisible, standing there watching Misty dig her face into the boy's neck and give him all the kisses Dane had been looking to get himself. Jackson squirmed and giggled. "You coming?" Misty asked from halfway up the stairs.

"Yeah. I'll be right up." Dane faked a grin and watched them disappear around the landing. By the time he heard them upstairs in the hall bathroom, his smile had faded completely. More often than not, he'd felt like a spectator in the background of his own life. He thought after he'd bought this house it would different. It wasn't. He thought after he'd let Misty move in that things might change. He could have some semblance of a normal life. He was wrong. Most of the time he felt as hollow and lifeless as the ghosts he spent all his time with. He patted at the paperwork in the pocket on his leg. *And now this.*

He took off his hat and tossed it onto the coffee table. He leaned his head back on the sofa and pulled the paperwork from his pocket. The Walmart receipt with Agent Talbott's phone number on it fell onto the cushion beside him. He left it there and took the thick stack of paper, stapled in the corner, out of the worn and ragged envelope. He looked at the computer printout of numbers and abbreviations for maybe the fiftieth time. He still didn't understand any of it, but he didn't have to. He knew what it meant. That had been spelled out for him very clearly last week when he picked it up. Maybe tonight would be the night he'd tell Misty. He'd known for a while now, and every day he continued to keep it from her made him feel like a bigger and bigger thief. She loved him. She didn't deserve to be kept in the dark. He heard laughing upstairs and looked in their direction.

Nope. Not tonight.

He refolded the lab results, picked up the crumpled receipt from the sofa, and tucked it all back in the envelope. He tossed it on the table with his hat. It landed next to a framed photo of Dane and Misty—taken by her sister out by Toccoa Falls. Dane hadn't seen the photo before except on Misty's phone. He hadn't seen all the squat candles on the table or the throw pillows on the sofa, either. She was definitely settling in. He sighed and stared at the photo for a good while. It was a good picture. He looked into the empty kitchen again before using the edge of the table to push himself upright. He tucked the envelope back in his pocket, grabbed his hat, walked around the table, and cleaned up the pile of drawings and crayons Jackson had left scattered on the floor. "She's right, you know, *Uncle Dane*," he whispered to himself. "You are sensitive."

Dane set a cold can of Diet Coke from the fridge downstairs on his nightstand. He tossed the boots he'd carried up from the hallway over to the far corner of his room, as far out of stepping-on distance as possible, and then he took a long shower. He knew Misty had just gotten out, but he hoped she'd join him anyway. She didn't.

Strike two.

When he was finished, he slipped on a pair of boxers and a clean T-shirt and climbed onto his side of the bed. After Misty finished setting Jackson up in the guest room, Dane caught her up on the events of the past twelve hours. She listened without saying much as she finished folding a load of laundry she'd dumped on her side of the bed. By the time he'd finished, Misty had everything folded and she'd slipped out of her flannel pajama pants and eased her way under the heavy goose-down comforter. She didn't lie down or curl up in the crook of Dane's arm as she normally would. Instead, she sat up straight, Indian-style, using the comforter just to cover her bare legs. Dane could already tell by her expression that she didn't quite know what question she wanted to ask him first. She started exactly where he thought she would.

"Ned Lemon is back in Waymore?"

Strike three.

Dane knew he'd walked the driveway in vain for sure now. He didn't really want it, but he turned and took a sip of the Coke so she wouldn't see him roll his eyes. He knew she'd start with Ned, because that would eventually segue into her asking about Gwen. Dane swallowed the soda, rested his head on his pillow, and just let it happen. He should be used to it by now, but he wasn't. He tried to turn it around.

"Yeah, he is. I couldn't believe it, either. Darby Ellis, the new sheriff, called me out to Clifford's place and there he was, just sitting under a tree talking to me like he'd seen me every day for the past eight years."

"The sheriff called you because Ned asked him to?"

"Yup."

"And he wasn't wearing any pants?"

"Nope."

"How did Ned even know you'd be there?"

"No idea."

"Did he tell you why?"

"No. I told you, I didn't get to talk to him for that long. I told you, Charles called as soon as I got out there and I was in Jacksonville an hour later."

"So Ned didn't ask how you've been? He didn't want to catch up?"

Here it comes, Dane thought. "Babe, I just told you, I didn't get to talk to him that long, and what we did talk about had everything to do with it looking like he killed somebody. I wasn't out there reminiscing about old times."

"Did you tell him about me?"

Dane tried, but did a terrible job, of hiding his distaste for where this conversation was headed. "I think you're missing the point here, Misty. He was in trouble—*accused of murder* trouble. It kind of took precedence over any small talk."

"You're saying he didn't say anything about—I don't know—how you've been?"

"Like what?"

"I just said, about how you've been doing."

Dane was sitting up now, too. He didn't want to do this. Why did she always want to do this? "He didn't say a thing about it, Misty."

"I find that hard to believe."

Dane squeezed his eyes shut and pressed at his temples again. The sides of his head were getting red and raw from the constant rubbing. Dane took Misty's hand. It was warm despite her cold demeanor. "The man had something a little more important on his plate. So, no—*she* didn't come up—at all."

"You act like it's not a legitimate question, Dane. Ned left after the accident. It's only natural that he'd say something to you about it. I'm only asking."

"Yeah, Misty, you're only asking. You're only asking about something I try every day to forget—and maybe I could if you didn't find a reason to bring it up all the time." Dane's words were harder than he intended but he didn't apologize. It wasn't true, either, but Misty started to shut down. That's what she did whenever Dane's temper flared. "After everything I told you about today, all you want to talk to me about is Gwen?"

Misty shut him out completely with that. She still burned whenever Dane used his dead wife's actual name. It was okay when he said *her* or *she*, but using her name made her real, and it stung Misty every time. Dane leaned over and took another sip from the warming soda. He stared down at his boots against the wall and then stood up. This was not what he wanted to be doing, but it was happening anyway. He turned back around to face her, but she'd already settled into the bed with her back to him. "I don't understand why you always feel the need to bring her up, and I can't for the life of me understand why you continue to get mad. I'm with you, now, Misty. I love you."

"I love you, too, Dane. And I'm not mad. I'm just tired. I'm sorry. It's been a long day, and I just want to go to sleep."

Dane walked over to stand in the doorway of the bathroom. He hated the "I'm tired" excuse as a reason for them not to talk about the things that really mattered in their life. Misty turned to face him when she repeated her apology. "I said I'm sorry, Dane. It's just hard for me."

It's hard for her?

It infuriated him to hear Misty say that more than the "I'm tired" line—and she said it a lot. He knew compassion was the only real way through these mini-wars of theirs, but he still hadn't learned the lesson. Dane walked into the bathroom and stood at the counter. He looked at himself in the mirror and saw the anger in his reflection when he desperately wanted to see sympathy. He wasn't proud of it, but his shame and his understanding of his own actions weren't enough to stop his mouth from fueling the fire. He spoke calmly, but the quiet intensity was just as bad as yelling. He spoke to his own face in the mirror. "It's been twelve years, Misty—twelve years."

"I know that, Dane, but it—"

"She's dead, Misty." Dane swung the weight of that sentence like a hammer. He wanted it to hurt her, but it hurt him, too. It always did. He might as well have been swinging that hammer at himself. He knew he should've stopped there, but he was angry, so he kept swinging like an idiot. "Sometimes I wonder if you even remember that. She's not an ex-girlfriend who can threaten you. She's dead. And she wasn't the only one who died that day." He felt the tears welling up. He fought them back, but they came and went like dry heaves. He thought about the broken ceramic turtle on the table by the front door.

Misty is the one not letting us move past it? You're an idiot, Dane, and that's enough.

He slammed the bathroom door shut. He knew what he'd just done, and he regretted it already.

Proud of yourself now?

He held his head in his hands. Blame could be a bitch when there was no one to lay it on. It just sat in your belly and festered until it spewed out at the first available target. After twelve years of trying to come to terms with it, Dane figured by now he'd be all out of tears. He was wrong. He was always wrong. He looked back at the mirror. For a moment he thought he saw a small piece of tape. Gwen was always sticking little poems and notecards to the mirror back in the day. It was her thing. Dane's heart raced. He wiped at the tape residue, but it was only a smudge of dried mouthwash or something. Jesus, would he ever stop seeing things? Was something like tape residue on a mirror going to capsize his ship like this for whatever was left of his life? He knew the answer to that. Yes. Yes, it would.

He rubbed his fingers together and ran the water in the sink before he sat on the edge of the tub and cried for over an hour.

When he finally came out of the bathroom, Misty was asleep. She had turned off all the lights. He didn't go into his closet and pull out the old shoebox of photos, birthday cards from Gwen, concert ticket stubs and anniversary dinner receipts, his personal box of scars that held trinkets and snapshots of a life that might've been. He gently closed the closet door instead. He couldn't do it—not tonight. He slowly made his way over to his side of the bed and lay down. He stared at the curve of Misty's neck and shoulder in the moonlight. He studied the bones in her back—spending time examining each one as if they were the stations of the cross. He thought about saying something, but knew he would fumble his words and make it worse. He felt the urge—the guilt—to apologize, but he decided to leave it be, to let her sleep. There was no point in trying to turn it around. She had already put up the wall and Dane was too tired to try and climb it again tonight. Besides, somewhere in the back of his mind, he'd known this was going to happen. From the moment he heard Ned's name that morning, he knew. And all day, despite the positive outlook he tried to keep when he got home, he knew this would be the inevitable outcome. Everything always came back to Gwen. Truthfully, he'd been dreading telling Misty about the events of the day, and this was why. They were from a small town where everyone knew everyone. Misty used to see Dane and Gwen together. She also saw Dane crawl into a hole for years after the accident. She saw him finally emerge from that hole a changed man, a cautious man. Uninterested in ever starting over. It took her nearly ten years, but Misty finally got through to him. She also knew when she got involved with him that she was agreeing to spend her life with this damaged version of Dane, a broken version of the real thing. She knew he was a good man—a faithful, honorable man—but she also knew going in that she would always feel second fiddle to a ghost. Dane did his best to keep her shielded from that feeling, but no matter what he did—what he said—it would never be enough. The damage was a part of him. It lived inside him waiting for opportunities to show itself, and tonight was just another example of that. He could've comforted Misty instead of sitting in the bathroom alone, crying, waiting for her to fall asleep, but he didn't. It was an unwinnable battle. He'd thought about not telling her anything, but he was keeping enough from her already, and he'd said it before—she deserved better than that.

If honesty is the best policy, then somebody needs to start thinking about revising the rule book.

He rolled over onto his back and stared up at the ceiling. He was scared to death of closing his eyes. He knew where he'd be in his dreams. He knew who'd be waiting on him there. So he turned to stare at Misty's shoulder again in the moonlight. She was beautiful, and he knew he loved her, at least to the best of his ability. Maybe it was just his selfish loneliness, but he reached out to touch her anyway. He stopped just shy of her skin. Instead of stroking her hair, or running a finger down the curve of her neck, he hovered that finger over her shoulder and outlined a daisy, right where Gwen's tattoo used to be.

He was almost asleep when his phone rang. Misty faked being asleep as Dane reached down to grab at his pants on the floor. He searched the tangle of canvas until he found the right pocket and tapped the phone. "Kirby."

"Dane, this is August O'Barr."

"What's up, August?"

"I am—and it's late, and I don't like it. I pay people to make these calls so I don't have to, so I don't like the fact that I'm the one making this one."

"Well then, how about we just get to something you do like, August." Dane clicked on the lamp and slid himself up the headboard.

"Okay, well, for one, you and Rosey need to learn how to play nice because I don't plan on being the go-between for you two past tonight."

"She doesn't like to be called Rosey."

There was a silence on the line and Dane thought about how he felt when Misty told him Jackson didn't like to be called buddy. He wished he hadn't said it. "I've got no problems working with Agent Velasquez, sir. You have my word."

"Good, because you and that tamale have got to get together on this faster than I imagined."

Dane wanted to tell him that if Agent Velasquez didn't like being called Rosey, being called a tamale would most definitely earn him a smack in the mouth, but he didn't mention it. "Did we learn more about the case, sir?"

"We did. We've got intel on the next of kin for Blackwell."

"That's good news."

"No, it ain't."

"What do you mean?"

"Both of his parents were killed in a car accident a year ago. The only family he had left is a younger sibling—an eleven-year-old brother named William."

"A kid?"

Misty turned around in the bed to face Dane. She'd been crying. He hadn't noticed. He put a hand on her shoulder.

"Yeah, when the Blackwells bought it, our boy Arnold was named his brother's legal guardian."

"You're right. That's terrible. How did he take it?"

"Who?"

"The kid."

"He didn't take anything. The kid is MIA, and no one has been able to find him. Velasquez is over there turning out the shithole apartment they were living in over in Cobb County and there's no sign of him, and I'm still waiting to hear back from the airline. It's possible that the other ticket Blackwell purchased was for the boy, but as of right now no one knows where he could be."

Dane switched the phone from one ear to the other. Misty was sitting up now, too.

"Well, an eleven-year-old kid shouldn't be that hard to find."

"No, he shouldn't, so let me know when you do."

"Wait a minute. I thought—"

"Stop thinking, Kirby, and listen. I need you to drop everything else I told you to do and put this William Blackwell kid on the top of your priority list."

"August, listen—"

"No, Dane, you listen. I'm not done. There's more. This kid, William, he also has a condition."

"What kind of condition?"

"According to the social worker who set up the guardianship, he's been diagnosed with Asperger's syndrome. I don't pretend to know anything about it except it's a form of autism that apparently no one seems to know jack shit about."

"The boy is autistic?"

Misty tugged on Dane's arm. "What's going on?"

Dane switched ears again and reached over to hold her hand. She let him.

"Pay attention, Kirby. I said it's a form of autism. But regardless, his condition, or whatever you want to call it, puts this kid in harm's way just by being out there alone. The social worker I spoke to said, and I quote, 'William isn't able to function properly in an open-world environment,' and without some kind of guidance, he could end up being hurt or hurting someone else, so finding this boy is now our top priority."

Dane tried to say something, but August didn't let him.

"That being said, I'm not going to just need you as a tour guide through chicken country anymore. I need you on this missing-kid thing, Kirby—all of you. This is the kind of thing that can make or break a career and I'm not letting this one break mine. Do you understand me?"

"Yes, sir, I hear you."

"Arnold Blackwell stepped in a huge pile of shit. You happen to be a doorway into that shithouse, and now it's not just about clearing a murder off the board or finding a suitcase full of money. Missing kids make headlines. I hate headlines. So I'm not asking you. I'm telling you. If big Blackwell was fighting roosters out there in Hard Cash, at the Farm, then you know right where to start looking for the little Blackwell, and I need to see some results—fast. Are we clear on this?"

Dane looked at Misty. "Yes, sir. We're clear."

"Good. I hope you got some sleep and kissed your girl already, because *Rosey*"—August leaned heavy on the woman's name—"will be there to pick you up in a couple of hours."

"All right. I'll be waiting."

"And FYI, I put someone on the pot dealer."

Dane eased his head back and closed his eyes. "Shit."

"Yeah, your partner, *Rosey*, told me about the lead you gave her as soon as you told her, and the reason I'm not dropping paper in your jacket for withholding evidence from your supervisor is the same reason I'm putting you on this missing kid—because if you could sniff out a smudge on a motel carpet like that, you can sniff out a kid lost in the sticks. That being said, though, if you keep anything from me again, your redneck ass will be looking at obstruction charges. I'll even have your boy Charles Finnegan demoted for mentioning your name to me. Are we clear on that, too?"

"Crystal."

"Good. Now is there anything else you need to tell me before I hang up this phone and pound a coffee mug full of scotch?"

"Just the name and address of the social worker you talked to. We can start there."

"Rosey's already got it. Her name is Clementine Richland, and she'll be expecting you first thing in the morning."

"Okay, August. I'm on it."

"That's what I like to hear. Compliance. Check in daily."

"I will."

"And Kirby?"

"Yes, sir?"

"As long as my door says Assistant Director of Law Enforcement for the Federal Bureau of Investigation, I'll call Special Agent Velasquez Rose, Tulip, Violet, or Fuck and Suck Sally if I want to. Is that understood?"

"Yes, sir."

August ended the call as Dane wondered how August could see inside his head like that. He set his phone on his nightstand.

"You called him sir like over six times," Misty said.

"Yeah."

"The lead you gave the other agent—it bit you in the ass, didn't it?"

Dane smiled. Misty was still holding his hand. "Yeah, it did. You know me well."

She kissed his hand. "Yes, I do," she said, and rolled back over. "I'm sorry, Dane."

"For what?"

"For being shitty earlier."

"It's okay, baby, I get it." He didn't, but Dane cut out the light and wrapped his arm around her anyway. He kissed her shoulder and tried his best to sleep until sunup.

CHAPTER NINE

Bernadette had been sitting on the toilet long enough for her legs to fall asleep. She didn't know how men did it—sitting on an uncomfortable rim of hard plastic for hours at a time. Somebody needed to invent an ergonomic shitter, like all those fancy office chairs Bobby kept bringing home from Goodwill to put around the dining-room table. Maybe she'd invent one and make a million bucks.

A million bucks. Right. Not in this lifetime, girl.

She shifted her butt on the edge of the seat, but she knew she would be stuck there now for at least a few more minutes until the feeling in her lower extremities returned. Truthfully, though, she didn't care. She was thankful for the quiet. She'd been ready for all the people Bobby had in her living room to go home. He'd given her the money to pay the mortgage out of the blue. She didn't ask him where he suddenly got all the money to pay it, but she didn't care. She was just happy to be out from underneath the house note for one more month. Regardless, now all of those assholes out there crowding up her sofa, acting like they lived there, were smoking her and Bobby's personal stash, and they needed to get the hell out. Maybe her disappearance into the bathroom for the past half hour would offer Bobby up a clue. She shook her head. No, it wouldn't. If anything, one of those mooches would be banging on her bedroom door any minute now needing another pint of blood. She was surprised they'd let her have this much time to herself already. She could hear Bobby now.

"Bernie, the boys need something to eat. Bernie, we can't find the remote.

Bernie, we're done smoking up all your weed for free and now we're going to break something by accident because we all have our heads shoved directly up our asses."

She rubbed at the corner of her eye. It was dry and itchy—an inconvenient by-product of her favorite vice. Pot made her dull gray eyes bright green, but it made them itchy, too. It didn't make her stupid, though. She wondered why it had that effect on Bobby and all their friends. She smoked out every single day, but still managed to work a full-time job at the IGA, pay the bills, and keep her shit together like a normal person. She was still hot as a firecracker, too, in her opinion, but Bobby? He was getting fat—and lazy as hell. Every time she walked in the door of her own house, it was like clocking in at a second job—being mother hen for "Big Bobby" and all his idiot buddies. It was like wrangling an entire kindergarten class of stoned five-year-olds. It made her crazy. If she could keep a job and still function as an adult when she was baked, why couldn't everyone else? In fact, Bernie felt more comfortable with the idea of *being* an adult when she was lit up, but not Bobby and them.

Fucking morons. All of them.

She leaned her freckled forearms down on her numb freckled thighs and huffed at the springs of curly red bangs that fell across her face. The rust-colored coils blew straight up and then fell right back to where they were. She repeated that useless action three more times before finally tucking the bulk of it behind her ear.

"My legs are asleep," she said into her phone. She had it on speaker so she could hold the thin plastic testing strip while she sat and talked to her sister, Jessica.

"Are you in the bathroom talking to me again?"

"Yeah, so?"

"Nothing. It's just nice to know that the only time you think of me is when you're taking a shit."

"I'm not taking a shit, Jess. I just had to pee, and the reason I always call you from the bathroom is because it's the only time I can get a moment's peace around here."

"Bobby being an asshole again?"

"No. He's fine. He's just on my nerves. He just got back after being gone for a few days and already I needed to get away from his band of merry men for a minute. They're out there celebrating something. Maybe one of their lame asses got a job. But they're being especially obnoxious tonight." Bernadette's hair sprang back into her face, so she set her phone down on the ledge beside her and used an elastic hair tie to pull it all back into a fat, fuzzy knot. "But I've been sitting here so long, I think my legs are going to fall off."

"Well, move your butt around. You gotta get your blood to circulate."

Bernadette slid around on the seat again, peered down between her legs, and repeated her sister's advice out loud. The words had an entirely different meaning when she said them. "I wish my blood would circulate, Jess. I swear to God, if I'm pregnant with that idiot's kid, I'm going to kill myself." She held the pregnancy test strip under her stream.

"Don't say things like that, Bern. Bobby loves you. And a baby wouldn't be the worst thing in the world to happen to you guys."

Bernadette smirked at the phone. What an idiotic thing to say. "First of all, Jess, a baby wouldn't be happening to *us*, it would be happening to *me*. Bobby's practically an infant himself, so it would really mean I'd have two kids to raise. And second of all, yes, it would be the worst thing in the world to happen to me. I'm twenty-six and I haven't started school yet. I'm still working at the fucking IGA, for Christ's sake. This is not the way I pictured my life turning out." She sank her head deeper into her slumped position.

"C'mon, Bern. I had Peanut when I was twenty-six and my life didn't turn out that bad."

"You also had your degree already—and Steve has a job. Have you seen my life lately?"

"Maybe it's time to think about getting your act together, then. Stop smoking pot every day. You're only enabling Bobby anyway."

Bernadette closed her eyes and leaned her head back. Her sister's voice was beginning to have that tone that grated on her. She was slipping into mom mode. She hated mom mode. The banging on the bedroom door came right on cue. "Jesus, here we go."

"I'm not starting on you, Bern. I just—"

"No, not you. Bobby's at the door. Hold on." She looked at the small blue lines forming on the tip of the plastic testing strip and wanted to scream. "What?" she yelled loudly enough to be heard through both the bathroom and bedroom doors. She heard a voice, but couldn't make out the words. "I'm taking a piss," she yelled even louder.

"Classy, sis."

"Shut up, Jess." She tapped the phone, taking it off speaker. The voice on the other side of her bedroom door rose to match her own yelling.

"I said there's somebody here, Bern."

"Well, who is it?" Bernadette said, and reached for the toilet paper only to spin the bare brown cardboard roll Bobby had left on the holder. "Goddamnit." She held the phone to her ear. "Let me call you back. There's someone here—no, I don't know—yeah, I brought a test home from work. I'll call you back tonight after I know for sure. I love you, too. Bye." She held the plastic strip up and already knew that two blue lines meant positive. "Fuck," she whispered as her eyes got wet.

"I don't know, baby," Bobby yelled from the door. "I think it may be the cops."

Bernadette sat up straight at the mention of that word.

Cops?

She set her phone on the floor and tossed the positive test in the trash. She tried to stand up, but her legs were still asleep and she almost collapsed onto the linoleum. "Shit. Shit. Shit." She tried to hike her sweatpants and panties up over her knees, but her legs were so sensitive from the rush of blood reviving them that she had to stop moving altogether.

"They might be cops, babe, but I'm not sure. Do you want me to let them in?"

"I want you to stop yelling about cops across the house," she said, as thousands of tiny pins and needles began to swarm her skin from her thighs down. Bernadette pushed herself off the commode and caught her balance on the bathroom counter. She opened the cabinet for a fresh roll of toilet paper, as if that was the most important thing to worry about at the moment, but she was high, and she couldn't walk, and she was confused. Seeing the empty cabinet, which she knew she'd stocked the day before, confused her more. "Where's all the fucking toilet paper?"

"What, baby?" Bobby knocked again. "You okay in there?"

Why the fuck was he knocking, anyway? He knew how to unlock the door. Why was she still looking for toilet paper? She knew she'd left at least a quarter ounce of dope on the living room table in plain sight and there was no telling what else Bobby had stashed around the place that she wasn't aware of, so if cops were at the door, a wet spot in her panties was the least of her problems. She hiked her sweatpants up and shook her legs back to life one at a time.

"Bobby, don't you let a soul in this house. I'll be out in a minute." She couldn't believe she even had to tell him that. She unlocked the bathroom door and took a careful step over the mountain of dirty laundry on the floor in front of the threshold.

"I don't know, baby. These guys don't look like—" A thunderclap drowned out the rest of what Bobby had to say.

The sound caused Bernadette to jump. She flinched so hard she knocked over a jewelry armoire by the closet, and a cascade of cheap gold chains, tiny ring boxes, and multicolored costume jewels spilled all over the carpet.

Was that a gunshot? Oh, my god, that was a gunshot.

She began to hear yelling that quickly turned to screaming. Her heart sped up and pounded in her chest like a hummingbird in a box. Without thinking, she yelled out for Bobby and immediately regretted it. She was answered with another gunshot and more yelling—frantic yelling. Something fell over somewhere in the house. She thought she heard the sound of glass shattering, but had no idea what it could've been. She moved into the closet, her legs still not fully cooperative, and sank down onto all fours. The sudden eruption of more gunfire and chaos in the next room had her head spinning with sensory overload, but her hands had already begun clearing the floor before the rest of her even knew why. A fourth and fifth gunshot clarified the moment before everything went silent. She yelled for Bobby, but there was no answer. The yelling had stopped, too.

She knew where Bobby kept his gun—in the same place she kept her weed in case of a raid, in the floor of the closet. She slid another pile of dirty jeans and shoes she never wore across the cluttered hardwood floor to clear the space in the corner. The boards were loose there when she bought the house, and one night, while she and Arnie Blackwell were blasted on some killer shit Bobby had brought home from a hiking trip in Colorado, they'd decided to build a small hidden compartment under the slats. It took them two straight days. Bobby kept a handgun in there, even though none of them knew how to shoot it. Her hands were shaking so bad she wasn't sure if she'd be able to figure out how, either, but she had to try.

The house had gone completely quiet beyond the room—even the stereo had stopped playing—and Bernadette sat there on the floor, quivering. Gun smoke had seeped in under the bedroom door and filled the room with a soft blue haze. The rancid smell of cordite stung her nose and her eyes watered. They itched so badly. She couldn't keep a clear thought in her head. There was a brief moment when she thought that maybe whoever was out there had done what he came to do and left, but that glimmer of hope vanished when someone rattled the doorknob on the bedroom door. She used the side of her fist to bang on the end of the rectangular piece of wood at her knees and lifted it up by the edge. She tossed the lid of the hideaway hole on top of the pile of clothes and immediately thought she was going crazy.

"What the fuck?" She could hardly breathe and felt herself spiraling into something other than reality. Bricks of cash wrapped in plastic wrap and rubber bands were crammed in the homemade hole. More money than she'd ever seen. Nothing made any sense. Her entire world stopped working correctly at that moment. Everything went Picasso. She sat completely still and stared into the hole until someone knocked on the door again. She jumped. "What?" she screamed, and she started to cry. "What do you want?" She knew it wasn't Bobby this time. Whoever it was out there was rapping his knuckles against the wooden door to a tune. It was maddening. It was like the sound of a child tapping out a secret knock asking for permission to enter a private clubhouse. She didn't care about where all the money in the floor came from as she dug into it and flung it all aside. She didn't even stop to think about how much it was. It had to be thousands—hundreds of thousands—but she just kept pulling out the stacks a handful at a time, hoping, praying that Bobby's stupid gun was still in there buried underneath.

It wasn't.

When she'd gotten to the bottom of the hiding space and scraped her fingernails around all four edges of the empty hole, she pushed herself up straight and slid her back up against the wall. Nothing made sense. Up felt down. Down felt up. She wiped at her face with the back of her hand, still squeezing one of the wads of cash.

What the hell is happening?

She thought about Arnie. He and Bobby had been gone for days and then all of a sudden Bobby comes home smelling like a goat, talking about buying a Harley. Bernadette just assumed they had been out being boys. A low-rent score. No big deal. Jesus. It was a big deal. She looked down at the bundles of money.

"Oh, my god, Bobby. What did you do?"

The bedroom door exploded with another gunshot and Bernadette screamed. She pressed herself tighter against the wall in the closet as splintered pieces of wood and molding rained over the room. Bernadette covered her ears and squeezed her eyes shut, too. She heard footsteps outside the closet door.

Bobby said it was the cops. Please, God, let it be the cops.

When she finally opened her eyes, a short Asian man in a bright blue sharkskin suit was standing in the doorway—smiling—and holding Bobby's gun.

Fenn dragged Bernadette out of the closet by a fistful of her hair, while Smoke collected the cash from the floor. He tossed it all into a small wicker hamper—brick by brick—and acted as if he didn't hear Bernadette screaming all the way down the hall to the living room that had been painted with fresh blood. Neither of the men who'd just murdered the six people in her house, including Bernadette's unborn child's father, had spoken a word until Smoke finished gathering up the money and joined them in the front room with the basket of cash.

Fenn had pushed Bernadette up next to the sofa, propping her up so that she sat between the dead bodies of Matt Conklin and Mike Goode—two friends of Bobby's that now sat completely still, staring out of glassy eyes, both of them with fresh bullet holes in their foreheads. From the few brief seconds Bernadette had opened her eyes, while Fenn dragged her through the house, she saw Bobby's two other friends sitting exactly as they'd been before she disappeared into the back of the house earlier, but now their goofy smiles had been replaced with slack jaws and half-frozen expressions of surprise. If not for the spray of blood and bone behind them that covered the sofa cushions and the floral wallpaper, Bernadette would not even have guessed they were dead—just simply frozen, trapped in time. Chris Kutcher and another man who Bernadette only knew as Randy—he'd been new to Bobby's crew—must have made a run for it. Both men lay in crumpled heaps on the rug in front of her like marionettes whose strings had been cut midperformance. The white shag of the rug was mostly pink now, with swatches of red and black still growing larger under the bodies.

The blue-gray smoke had begun to dissipate and Bernadette let her hands fall away from her face to get a look at the man who'd dragged her in there. He stood by the front-room window as still as the dead men next to her, and his eyes were as black and glazed over as his victims'. He was huge. He was a monster. He was holding a long shaft of bamboo, sharpened and stained black on the end. Bernadette saw nothing on this man's blank and emotionless face that resembled a human being. She covered her face again with both hands to block out the sight of him— and to block out the bloody dollhouse her home had just become. Maybe it would all disappear. Maybe there was PCP or something in the weed she'd been smoking and all this was some big head trip. Maybe if she just caught her breath and counted to three it would all go away. She'd hear Bobby's voice again from the bedroom door. She prayed to hear Bobby's voice. Maybe it wasn't his body this monster had dragged her past in the hallway. Maybe it wasn't her Bobby lying out there missing most of his face and left arm. Her crying had gone from a frightened sob to a maniacal heaving sound that hurt her abdomen.

The shorter man in the suit began to speak. His words—his voice— drove away any thoughts Bernadette had of waking up from the worst dream of her life. This was real. These men were real. They had killed her boyfriend. They had killed her friends. They were going to kill her, too, and it was because of Bobby and Arnie Blackwell. She was sure of it.

"Did you even know my money was here?"

Bernadette didn't answer. She couldn't. She took her hands away from her face and looked at the man in the suit clearly for the first time. He'd set the gun on the table next to the basket. Bernadette looked at that, too, and said only one word. "Bobby?" It was most likely part of a longer sentence like "What did you do to Bobby?" or "How did you get Bobby's gun?" but her brain would only allow one word to pass her lips. "Bobby."

Smoke looked at the gun, and Bernadette thought he started to laugh. But just as her brain would not allow her to speak in complete sentences, it also wouldn't allow her to process the sound of laughter. The room went silent as if the entire house had just entered a vacuum and begun to hurl aimlessly through space. The Asian man in the suit was holding his belly and Bernadette thought of how strange it was that without sound, his laughing looked so much like crying. The other man—the monster—still stood by the window, completely content inside the void. Bernadette thought—no, she knew—that this was how madness felt. She would be her own witness as she lost her mind.

The short man waved a hand in front of her face. He was talking to her and his words were slowly forming over the drone of space. "I'm very sorry for all this," he said. "I can see by the look on your face that Arnold told me the truth. You really had no idea you had my money. Is that your gun, too? Did he take your gun without your permission?" Smoke shook his head. He looked like a disappointed father. "I'm sorry I laughed. It really isn't funny for you. I know that. It's very unfortunate for everyone, really." Smoke looked around the room at all the people he'd let his pet monster turn into rag dolls, but there was no real compassion in his words. There was no real remorse. It was the exact opposite. In the same way that Bernadette felt a palpable indifference to the violence resonating off the bigger man, the smaller one practically beamed with pride in what they'd done.

Bernadette felt her stomach churning and did nothing to stop herself from throwing up. A stomach full of Hot Pockets and bile bubbled over her chin and spilled down the front of her button-up IGA work smock. She didn't even make an attempt to wipe it away. Her brain wouldn't let her. She was systematically shutting down, and the man in the suit could see it happening in her eyes. Now he looked the way he really felt. He was disgusted with her and he backed away. He leaned over and picked up the gun from the coffee table.

"Fenn, you don't want to fuck this nasty bitch, do you? You'll need to clean her up first if you do." He looked at the big man and lifted both his hands in the air as if to say, *Well?*

"No," Fenn said. That was it. Just one syllable from this man and the strange sound of him made Bernadette throw up again. This time everything left in her stomach was now down the front of her. Smoke looked even more disgusted with her. He raised the gun and pointed it at her. She just stared at the barrel, still lost in the warped reality of the last few minutes of her life. Everything from the first gunshot going off to this man in a suit pointing Bobby's gun at her played out in her head all at once. She thought about her sister. She couldn't remember if she had told her she loved her or not. The muscles in Bernadette's face were loose and sagged. "Love—Jess," she said in short bursts.

"Oh, how sweet you are. It's a shame to kill such a sweet girl. We could have had a little fun first, but oh well."

"Wait," Bernadette said. Another word escaped past the gate of her traumatized mind, and then another one followed. "Pregnant."

Smoke smiled and uttered another syllable that made Bernadette's abdomen seize. "So?"

She stared at the man and accepted it. She waited to die.

A sharp whistling sound came from behind her in the kitchen. Bernadette thought it was her imagination at first, but she saw the man in the suit shift his attention past her and look at where the sound came from. He heard it, too. He looked surprised, but before he could do anything— say anything—another shot rang out so close to her that it robbed Bernadette of her hearing for real this time. She screamed again but could only hear it in her head.

The man in the suit still stood there before a second shot rang out and put him down. The monster by the window lunged toward her. She kept screaming, but two more shots rang out through the droning in her head, and the bigger man fell forward onto the coffee table, smashing it to pieces. Bernadette kept screaming as the short man's blood oozed out of him and the slick pool inched its way closer to her. She was barely aware of the third man walking out of the kitchen behind her, a man with no face, a figure composed completely of shadows. He sat beside her and made a noise she couldn't make out. Her ears were still ringing. She was still screaming. He was holding her hands now. He wore gloves and he was handing her something. He was handing her a gun. He was saying something. His words began to cut through. He was telling her it was okay—that she was safe now. He kept repeating it in her ear as he sat with her.

He kept saying "It's okay" and "You're safe now" until the mantras finally quieted her. She was holding a gun now, and then the dark man was standing up. He crossed in front of her and leaned down to touch the first man he'd just killed. He moved like liquid—smooth and relaxed. He was touching his neck. He was feeling for a pulse. Bernadette's world was beginning to come back into focus and she could make out the details. She screamed and the man removed his hand from the small dead man and moved closer to her.

This man wasn't made of shadows at all. He was just dressed in black and wore a mask. His clothing was tactical—military, maybe. His pants were covered in Velcro-fastened pockets and he wore a tight black fleece hoodie, zipped up to the top of the collar covering his neck. Not a bit of skin showed on the man from head to toe. Bernadette avoided the man's eyes. She couldn't bear to see another pair of eyes like those of the other two men who had invaded her home. She sat against the sofa surrounded by dead people and held the small gun the man in black had given her. She kept it pointed at him, but he didn't seem to mind. She watched him pick up the gun her attacker had been holding and do something to it so the part holding the bullets ejected into his gloved hand. "Bernadette," he said. He knew her name. She squeezed the grip of the gun, unaware or unable to do anything else with it. "Bernadette," he said again, and held the two parts of the dismantled gun out in front of him for her to see. It was a calming gesture. The third time he spoke her name she answered.

"Please," she said. "Please—don't—hurt—me." Her voice came out in short, suffocated bursts of sound. The gun she held outstretched in front of her shook under its own weight, but she didn't let it lower.

"I'm not going to hurt you," he said. "The men who did this are dead. You're safe. Just breathe."

"Who—are—you?"

"That doesn't matter right now. The only thing that matters is that you're safe now. Just breathe and try to calm down. The police are on their way."

"The police?"

"Yes, the police, but I need you to focus. Just breathe and focus." He spoke softly with a soothing tone, and soon Bernadette began to do what he said. She took in a deep breath and let it out slowly.

."That's good. Very good."

She pulled in more of the rancid, copper-tinged air and heaved it back out.

"All right," he said. "Now listen to me carefully, okay?"

Bernadette nodded and let the gun lower a few inches. Her arms burned and she wanted so badly to just let it drop to her lap.

"The person who gave Bobby this money, a man named Arnie Black-well—"

"He's not here." Bernadette had regained her bearings and her voice. It was easier to speak. "I didn't even know the money was there."

The man stood silent and Bernadette wished she'd said nothing. He moved toward the front window and then back to where the bodies were on the floor. He took short, deliberate steps as if he was measuring the distance with his footsteps. He faced her again and Bernadette immediately looked down at his chest to avoid eye contact. "But you do know the man I'm talking about, right? Arnold. Arnold Blackwell."

"Yes," she said.

"Okay, so he didn't tell you about the money?"

"No."

"And you don't know who these people are?" He kicked at the smaller Asian's lifeless body at his feet.

"No."

"You're sure?"

Bernadette looked at the dead men but didn't have to in order to answer.

"No. I've never seen either of them before in my life."

"Okay, Bernadette. I believe you, but I need to ask you one more question, and I need you to be very sure of your answer, all right? It's very important. Do you understand?"

She nodded again. "Yes."

"Do you know where I can find Arnold's little brother?"

The question almost didn't register. It was a strange question and Bernadette felt like she was slipping back into that place between real and not real. "What?" she said.

"You do know that Arnold has a brother, yes?"

"Yes. Yes, of course. William, but what do you want with him? He's only a kid. He's eleven. He likes fish sticks." Neither of them knew why that random detail had come to the surface.

"Bernadette, we are running out of time. You can do this. Focus and just answer the question."

Bernadette didn't understand why they were running out of time. He said the police were coming. She let the gun in her hands fall even closer into her lap. The man in black took a step closer and squatted down in front of her. "Your boyfriend and Arnold did something very stupid and these men killed them for it."

"Bobby is dead?" she asked, but she already knew the answer.

"Yes. He's dead. Arnold is, too, and the same people who killed him— bad people like this—are now looking for William, too."

"But he's—"

"A little kid. I know, but thanks to his brother, he's a little kid in a lot of trouble. I need to find him before any more of these bad people do, so I can protect him. I need you to help me find him. So please, Bernadette. Think real hard and tell me where I can find the boy before it's too late."

"I—I—" Bernadette fumbled for the words, but again she didn't know why. She already knew her answer. "I have no idea. Arnold only brought him here once. Having a kid here made Bobby nervous. Oh, God, Bobby. Is he really—"

"Stay with me, Bernadette. The kid. Where is the kid?"

"I told you. I don't know. I don't even know where they live now. Arnie moved right after his parents died. I swear. I don't know what else you want me to say."

"Bernadette, look at me." The man's voice hardened. She didn't want to look at him. Something in the pit of her stomach told her that if she did, it would be the end of her. He repeated himself, and she knew from his tone she had no choice. She let the small-caliber gun fall completely into the lap of her sweatpants and she raised her head to meet the man's eyes. They were a swirl of storm clouds with hints of ice—nothing like the glassy black stones of the men who had murdered her Bobby and her friends. They were sad eyes—desperate eyes.

"I'm sorry," she said. "I can't help you. I would if I could, but I honestly don't know."

He studied her face for the lie. He didn't stare at her so much as through her, like someone trained to recognize what others couldn't. He saw nothing—no twitches or involuntary shifts—no signs of betrayal. She was telling the truth, but the man's own eyes revealed no sign of rancor at that discovery. They held no anger or rage—only disappointment. He stood and began to walk with the same calculated footsteps back over to the space in front of the window. He placed his feet in exactly the same spot the monster had stood.

"I believe you," he said. Only then did Bernadette realize that her savior in black tactical clothing was still holding Bobby's dismantled gun. She watched him shove the magazine back into the handle and rack the slide. He still had that look of disappointment in his eyes as he aimed the pistol and shot Bernadette in the belly. His decision to shoot her in the gut was deliberate. He clearly knew how to stage a scene.

She stared at her killer as she held her hands to her belly. Blood oozed out between her fingers, and she watched the man who shot her put Bobby's gun back into Smoke's hand. He pressed the dead man's fingers tightly onto the grip and trigger just in case his own gloves had wiped it clean. Bernadette watched him carefully shift the details so the room told the story he wanted it to. She watched her killer turn her into a murderer, too. When he was done, he sat with her. He held her stare without remorse, but with that same disappointed look. His sad blue eyes were the last thing she saw before her own eyes glossed over and she faded from this world to the next.

The man felt her neck for a pulse, then removed his balaclava. He crouched down next to her and lifted her freckled hand. It was still holding the small-caliber unregistered handgun he'd given her. He aimed her hand at the wall and pressed her finger on the trigger to fire another round. He shifted her arm and fired again, making sure to cover her hands and chest with the gunshot residue she'd be tested for.

He laid her hand back in her lap, careful to avoid the blood still draining from her abdomen, but made sure her fingers stayed curled around the grip. He stood and looked around to take it all in before carefully stuffing the cash into a trash bag from the kitchen. He laid it on the kitchen counter, then returned the wicker basket to the closet in the bed-room and reset the hideaway in the floor to look untouched. He made his way back into the kitchen and rifled through the fridge for a Coke or a cold beer. There was nothing in the refrigerator but a two-liter bottle of flat Mountain Dew, so he passed on any refreshments. He shut the fridge and went to pick up the bag of cash, but it wasn't there. He froze for a second before spinning around with his gun out. He surveyed the room. It was quiet. Everyone was still dead, but the big man—the one he had put down himself—was gone—and so was the money.

"Damn."

He cased the entire house, busting into every room. The place was empty. He left the way he had come.

CHAPTER TEN

The small DFCS office in Cobb County was nothing to speak of and nowhere Dane wanted to be. He reckoned no one ever did. The large sterile environment of the Children's Services waiting room, along with the rest of the run-down government complex, felt completely devoid of joy. Places like this were built with the intention of providing a service that, by any measure of human evolution, shouldn't have to be provided at all, but still did. The air itself gave off a thick, stale feeling of resentment that reminded Dane of a song he'd heard once called "Happiness Is Not a Place." If anything, this was a place happiness came to die, or at least get the shit kicked out of it before limping home.

Several rows of conjoined navy blue hard-plastic seats ran down the center of the spacious lobby with fake mahogany endcaps covered by parenting magazines and brochures that covered nearly every tragic life track in existence.

"How to spot physical and mental abuse." "The myths concerning childhood vaccinations." "A guide to becoming a foster family."

The building's decor did its best to disguise what it was, but it still felt like a probation office dressed up to look like a kindergarten classroom. Puzzles made of wire with sliding wooden beads, old toys, and some ragged Dr. Seuss books littered a large, colorful floor mat that took up most of the left side of the room, opposite the wire-enforced, plate-glass-protected office windows lining the right. Two heavily secured doors bookended the windows. One led into a labyrinth of cubicles where the

fates of children born into circumstances beyond their control were decided by burned-out twelve-dollar-an-hour employees, and the other, a
unisex family restroom clearly marked by the stick-figure signs of both a
man and a woman on a bright blue placard labeled FAMILY. Cobb County
had a foothold in progressive thinking.

An attractive middle-aged Haitian woman holding a squirming tod-
dler sat in the front row of seats. She wore a purple taffeta wrap with
flip-flops, and the kid had on a pair of pink leggings with dirty feet, no
shoes, and a *Little Miss Sunshine* T-shirt. Another woman, a bowling-
pin-shaped blonde dressed for a day at a gym she'd never get to, sat uncomfortably behind Dane with a teenage girl who favored her mother
right down to her look of disgust and boredom. Dane turned and smiled.
The smile was not returned. No one was happy to be there, including
Roselita, who paced the lobby like a caged animal. They'd only been
waiting a few minutes, but the icy monotone greeting they'd received
from the receptionist had already tested her patience. She stomped from
one side of the room to the other, refusing to sit or even touch anything,
as if she might contract something horrible if she did. She also hadn't removed her sunglasses since entering the building. Dane hated that shit. It
was so pretentious. But Roselita liked to advertise that she was important,
and the sunglasses helped her do that.

Dane imagined it must be tough for a woman in her position—
surrounded by so much male posturing—but he also imagined Velasquez was the type to already come aboard wound up. The chip on her
shoulder was already firmly in place before she ever attended Quan-
tico. Her pacing the room like a lion, however, was giving off enough
nervous energy to make everyone in the room uncomfortable. "Sit
down, Velasquez," Dane whispered as he stretched out his legs under
the seats in front of him. Roselita grunted at him and continued to
pace the lobby until a petite blond woman, wearing red lipstick so
bright it washed out the rest of her facial features, appeared through
one of two doorways, holding a clipboard. "Special Agents Kirby and
Velasquez?"

Dane put a hand in the air. "That would be us."

The woman smiled. "Sorry to keep y'all waiting. I'm Clem Richland.

Come on back." She propped the door with her foot, but Roselita was already inside.

"Sorry, folks. Have a seat."

Dane and Roselita sat down in two plush office chairs facing Richland's desk. The cubicle was small but cozy. Pictures of Richland's family cluttered her desk, and it was clear from all the UGA paraphernalia scattered among the walls and bookshelves that she was a Bulldogs fan. She sank into her own chair behind her desk. "I pulled an all-nighter. I didn't even have time to get home and shower before I had to be here to meet you guys. I'm running on fumes. Another one of these"—Richland picked up a coffee mug from her desk that read ALL THE POWER. HALF THE PAY and drained half the contents—"and maybe I'll be able to be coherent enough to help you this morning."

"An all-nighter?" Dane said.

"Yes. We had to go pick up this poor kid from an RV park over on Moreland. His mother and her latest loser boyfriend were cooking crystal over one of those portable propane camping ovens right out behind the trailer—stinking up the whole park. Like someone wasn't going to call in that complaint?" Clem Richland stopped talking abruptly and addressed Roselita. "I'm sorry, Agent Velasquez, right?"

"Correct."

"Could you please take your sunglasses off. I have trouble talking to someone when I can't see their eyes."

"Of course," Roselita said, and tucked her aviators into the outer pocket of her jacket. "Please, continue."

Richland did. "Well, the police got there, arrested both of the so-called adults, and found the kid covered up in a mound of dirty laundry. He was using it for a bed, and eating dry cornflakes out of a baseball cap—a friggin' baseball cap. Can you believe that? The kid is nine years old. He'd been taking care of himself and getting himself to school for months from living conditions like that and not a single one of his teachers thought to let us know. He was filthy. Hadn't taken a shower in weeks. It's like no one cares anymore. It happens so often that no one pays it any attention. It breaks my heart."

"It breaks mine just hearing about it," Dane said.

"And can you believe, when they finally called us out there to get him, he didn't even want to come. He didn't want to leave his mom. He said he wanted to go to jail with her and not with us. It's unbelievable."

"Not really, Mrs. Richland. That's family."

"Please, call me Clem. My name is Clementine. I don't know what my parents were thinking, but I go by Clem."

"Okay, Clem."

"You were saying?"

"I was saying, that kid. His mother is his family. Kids who get raised in that kind of environment don't know any better, so taking him away from the only family he knows is always going to make you look like the bad guy. I've seen it a hundred times over up in McFalls County."

Richland finished the coffee in her cup and nodded. "You're absolutely right, Agent Kirby, but it doesn't make it any easier for us to deal with."

"What's going to happen to the kid?"

"Well, he's going to spend a few days at one of our halfway houses while we try and find a foster family to take him in. If we come up empty, he'll go into the system and stay at the halfway house until mommy of the year is cut loose and then the whole cycle starts over again. I swear to you, Agent Kirby—"

"It's Dane."

"Dane." She nodded. "By the time that kid is sixteen, he'll be the one cooking the crank, just like his mama, and we'll be fishing *his* baby out of the laundry. Every time I come to work it's like going to war—and there's more of them than there are of us." Richland held up her mug and whistled at someone down the hall. A few seconds later, a big bruiser with midnight skin and arms like redwood trees walked into the cubicle. He wore a short-sleeved button-up shirt, two sizes too small, and an equally tight argyle sweater-vest. Clem handed the man her mug.

"Thanks, Hank."

"Half a pound of sugar, no cream?"

"You know me too well."

Once Hank gave Agent Velasquez a once-over that clearly turned her stomach, then disappeared, Richland sat as far back in her chair as possible and stretched her arms above her head. She was cut and toned like a runner, with thick, natural blond hair that hadn't seen a brush in at least twelve hours. Her facial features were sharp and pronounced. She wore no makeup except for the ruby-red lipstick, but she didn't need any. She was a natural beauty and Dane didn't understand the need for the cherry-red lips, but he guessed it wasn't for him to understand. He also guessed she couldn't have been a day over twenty-five.

"Okay," she said. "Enough about that. Your boss, a friendly old man named O'Barr, is that right?"

"That's right."

"Right, O'Barr. That's it. He asked me to get everything I could on William Blackwell, so here it is." She slid a file as thick as the Monday edition of the *Atlanta Journal-Constitution* across the desk and Dane picked it up.

"This it?"

"That's it."

"Was he one of your cases? I mean you handled him personally?"

"He was, and I did. And to be honest, he was one of the better ones."

"What do you mean?"

"I mean there was no sign of abuse of any kind. It was a refreshing change of pace. Up until last year, William was a pretty well-adjusted kid living with two well-adjusted parents. You can see there in the file what happened to end all that. Both his parents, Matthew and Nadine Blackwell, were killed in a car accident on the two eighty-five bypass. They were sideswiped by a tractor-trailer."

"Drunk driver?"

"No, actually. The driver was a long hauler. The truck drifted. He barely tapped the Blackwells' SUV, but it was enough for them to lose control of the vehicle. They ended up rolling the truck doing about seventy, and both of them were killed. The truck driver didn't even realize there had been an accident until he heard it on his CB. He turned around immediately but there wasn't much he could do. Him or anyone. Accidents happen."

Dane felt his skin go cool and moist. For a moment he thought he might be sick. He muscled through it before anyone could notice but still looked uncomfortable in his chair.

Clem cocked her head at him. "Can I get you some water, Dane?"

"No, thanks. I'm fine. Please, continue."

"Well, of course, the family had no papers drawn up. No will. No power of attorney. No preparations at all in place for what would happen to William in the event of their sudden demise. So that's how I ended up with him. He was given to me, and we did what we do. We located his next of kin—the older brother, a real piece of work named Arnold. The guy is a total degenerate. I knew that William was going to end up back here, or worse, as soon as I met the brother."

"Why was that?"

"I've been doing this long enough to know when people are a lost cause. This guy, Arnold, was exactly that. He'd just lost both his parents in a horrible accident, and all he seemed to care about was if it were possible to sue the trucking company and William's disability check."

"He received a check?"

"Yes. William's condition made him a candidate for government assistance. It wasn't much, but it was enough to convince that worthless brother to sign the papers. I didn't like it. Nobody did. But, despite his record of arrest, the brother had no history of violence or drug abuse, so we had to release William to his custody. That's the law. So even though William was one of the kids who actually might've benefited from the state foster program, we had no choice. It is what it is. And despite what I thought about Arnold, William seemed to genuinely love his big brother and wanted to be with him. It's like you said earlier—family—sometimes it's all you got. In William's case, Arnold was the hand he got dealt."

"Tell us more about William's condition," Dane said, still staring at the papers in his lap.

"William has Asperger's."

"So I've been told. Tell me about it."

"I'm not a doctor, but I know it's a distinct form of autism that affects each person diagnosed with it differently. Sometimes it can be misdiagnosed as extreme OCD, or present as severe social anxiety, but in all cases, routine and patience is paramount in maintaining a somewhat normal life. Without it everything can quickly become chaos."

"If it affects people differently, then tell us how it affected him, based on your personal experiences with the boy."

"He's a follower. He needs direction, or he begins to spin aimlessly.

Not physically, but internally. For example, if he knows he's supposed to do the dishes at three thirty in the afternoon, and there are no dishes to do, and there's no one there to tell him otherwise, then he'll shut down. He doesn't know how to process what to do with that allotted time frame in his head, so he struggles to get through it. He's not incapable of doing something else. He just needs to be told what that something else is. I don't know if this is making sense, but that's the best way for me to describe it."

"So he's dependent on some type of leader figure to guide his day-to-day actions?"

"Sort of. Yes."

"And in this case, that figure was Arnold."

"Yes."

"So without him, what will happen?"

"I don't know. I told you, I'm not a doctor, but like I told your boss last night, the fact that William is out there by himself could be dangerous to both himself and anyone he comes into contact with."

"What do you mean? He is violent?"

"No, not at all. Just the opposite. His brain doesn't interpret conflict or process violence like you or I would. Violence for most of us is an emotional response to some type of stimulus. William doesn't think in terms of emotion. At least, not outwardly. He's more like a machine calculating a problem, and that's how he responds to that type of stimulus. It can make him appear cold at times. It frustrated me to no end until I found out it's not his fault. It's just his wiring. It's hard to explain. Shit. It's been a long night. I'm sorry."

Dane closed the folder. "Try."

Clem cocked her head again as if she'd forgotten what they were talking about. "Try?" she asked.

"To explain," Dane said.

Clem eased back in her chair and blew two big cheekfuls of tired air from her lungs. "Well, for one, he's brilliant."

"Define brilliant."

"I mean brilliant, intellectually. It's like he thinks in math. It's how he sees the world, in numbers and puzzles that are meant to be solved, but that's not all. The best way to describe how William sees things is to say he sees the negative space in things."

"I don't understand," Dane said.

Richland leaned forward. "Okay, look. A pebble bounces off the highway and cracks your windshield. We—you or me—see the crack it makes. We get angry because we know we need to get it fixed and deal with insurance companies and yadda yadda, but William doesn't see the crack. He doesn't get caught up in the aggravation like we do."

"What does he see?"

"He sees the two new shapes made in the glass. He sees the reaction to the rest of the windshield and not the crack." She leaned back and scratched a pencil against the back of her neck. "I don't know. I told you. It's hard to explain."

"So how is that dangerous to others?"

"Okay. Think about it like this," she said, and wriggled around in her seat. She held both hands out in front of her as if she were physically framing an image for them to see. The caffeine must've been working on her because she was coming to life behind her desk. Her blue eyes were getting softer and wider as she spoke, and Dane could hear the genuine excitement in her voice as she talked about William. Her job hadn't devoured her entire sense of hope, not yet, anyway. She still cared for the children in her charge—especially the Blackwell boy. Dane also noticed that the cold feeling of despair from the lobby wasn't present in Clem Richland's small section of the building. He wanted some of that coffee Clem was drinking but didn't want to interrupt her to ask.

"He was almost eleven when he was given to me, and at that age, he could perform advanced mathematics in his head that I couldn't do with pen and paper. It was amazing to watch. His IQ is off the charts—genius level—but he isn't capable of picking out clothes for himself that match, or driving a car."

Roselita repeated Dane's question. "So, still, how does that make him a danger to others?"

Dane answered for her. "She's saying what if he did decide to drive a car?"

"Exactly. Listen, the longer he's alone, the bigger the chance is of something terrible happening, and I'm telling you, something *will* happen. The worst part is that it won't be his fault. Asperger's is a relatively newly identified condition. There isn't a lot of research yet on how to treat it other than maintaining a healthy daily routine. Without help, he could end up in a system a lot worse than this—like juvie—and a kid like William can't survive in those conditions. It's impossible." Richland sank her head into her hands and ran her fingers back over her skull.

Dane imagined it must be tough for her. She rarely got to hear a happy ending in her line of work, and to find out one of the kids she was most fond of was in this kind of trouble had to be heartbreaking. Dane didn't envy her job. He thumbed through the file again, scanning for the newspaper article concerning the car accident. "Was William in the car with his parents when the accident occurred?"

"Heavens, no, and thank God," she said. "He was at school. The Blackwells had him enrolled at a school in Decatur for children with special needs. His parents were incredibly dedicated to helping him. They spent a lot of time and money finding the right resources to help him adjust to normal life."

"What's the name of the school?"

"Morningside."

"Did Arnold maintain William's attendance there once he'd been granted guardianship?"

"He was supposed to. The disability money wasn't enough to cover the school's cost, but even if it was, I knew Arnold had no intention of using the money for its intended purpose. I'm telling you, if there wasn't a monthly payday attached, I doubt the guy would even have showed up here when we called about William in the first place."

"So can you tell us any place William liked to frequent? Somewhere he'd hide if he were scared? Anything at all you think might be useful."

"You've already searched the last known address?"

"The apartment here in Cobb is a dead end," Roselita said. "We came up empty, and we still know nothing about this kid or where he'd be likely to go."

"He would be wherever he was told to be," Richland said. She sounded much more alert and concerned now despite her lack of sleep.

"You said he followed a routine. If one fell through, would he try to fall back into another? Meaning, could he have gone back to the school?"

"No. It doesn't work like that, and if he'd turned up at Morningside, they would've contacted us the minute he showed up."

"Could you possibly reach out to them anyway? We could use all their information as well."

"I've already done that. There is a problem with the phone lines over there this morning, but all the contact information on Morningside that I have is in that file already. We don't have a lot of dealings with places like that. William was a special case."

Roselita took the file from Dane and flipped through it until she found a card clipped to some type of invoice from the school. "This it?" She held up the card.

"Yes. That's all I've got."

She handed the file back to Dane. "Anywhere else, then? Somewhere off the grid that Arnold might've mentioned during one of his visits to this office? It doesn't matter how far-fetched. Anything he may have told you could help."

"Agent Velasquez, I just filled out the paperwork. Arnold was a scumbag. I never talked to the man at length about anything if I didn't have to. If something stuck out, I'd tell you. Believe me."

Dane pieced through the file in his lap. He didn't look up when he spoke. "When William was released to his brother's care, was it a requirement for him to keep your office in the loop? To check in with you?"

"We encourage it, but no, it isn't a requirement. It is with foster families, but not with blood relatives."

"So he didn't?"

"Not officially, but I made a few unofficial visits to their apartment on my own time. I told you, I liked the kid, so I kept hoping I'd find a reason to take him out of his brother's care. I never did. I eventually stopped."

"And that's the only contact you've had with either of them since?"

"Yes. When a child is placed with a blood relative, even one as messed up as Arnold Blackwell, the rules are far more lenient. We are basically at the mercy of the law. If someone calls us to report abuse or neglect, then we can act, but generally, this office views having a member of his immediate family take him in as a win. What happens after that is out of our hands. I had no choice but to let it go."

The big man in the sweater-vest who Richland had called Hank returned to the cubicle with her coffee and set it on her desk.

Roselita looked up at the man. "How about you? Did you know this William Blackwell kid?"

Hank leaned his hip onto Richland's desk. "Yeah, I know William. He's a good kid. I hated letting him leave with that loser brother of his. I knew this would happen. I knew it."

"But you let it happen anyway."

Hank straightened back up and glared down at Roselita. Agent Velasquez sat completely at ease. "Why don't you go find him instead of judging the people that work in this office. We did our job, darlin'. Maybe you should do yours."

"Maybe if you'd have done your job right, we wouldn't even be here. And if you call me darling again, I'll kneecap your black ass."

Hank looked both appalled and aroused. "Who do you think you are, coming in here, talking to me like that. I could report you."

"Oh," Roselita said, sitting up slightly in her seat. "You get to be sexist, but I can't be racist. Why don't you go fetch me a cup of coffee, too."

"All right, all right," Dane said, putting his hands up. "That's enough. I apologize, Mrs. Richland. My partner hasn't had much sleep, either. I'm sure you understand that."

Clem glared at Roselita, who glared right back as if the woman behind the desk were a fresh log of dog shit that a stray had just laid on the carpet, before turning her stare back on Hank. Everyone just sat in awkward silence while Roselita and Hank sized each other up. Dane finally spoke, putting an end to it. "Is there anything else you can tell us about the boy, Clem?"

"No. I think we're done here."

Dane looked up at the big black man. "How about you, Hank? Anything you remember about him? No matter how insignificant."

It took Hank a few beats to answer but he did speak. "He likes to read," he said, keeping his stare directed at Roselita. "When he was in our care, he was always reading something—anything from comic books to medical textbooks. Whatever he could find lying around. He's like a sponge when it comes to soaking up information. And he really likes birds, too. Talked about them all the time. He could tell you the mating habits of a brown thrasher down to the sounds they make. He'd get excited talking about it, too. I learned a lot from that kid. I really hope he's okay."

"We're going to find him, Hank. Thank you for the insight. Anything else?"

Hank shook his head. Richland thought about it for a moment longer before shaking her head as well. "That's really all I know, other than he detests chocolate."

"Really?"

Hank finally stopped eyeballing Roselita. "Yeah, that's true," he said. "The day I brought William in, I tried to give him some M&M's and he practically threw them back at me."

"Maybe it wasn't the chocolate he detested."

"Wow." Richland glared at Roselita. "Where did you find her, Agent Kirby?"

Hank took a step toward the door and Roselita unbuttoned her suit jacket. Her gun didn't show, but the tanned leather of her shoulder holster did. It was enough to remind the big man who he was talking to. "You damn Feds. You think you know everything."

"Relax, Hank," Dane said. "We're all on the same side here." Dane gave his partner a hard stare. "Agent Velasquez and I are on our way out anyway."

Richland helped Dane try to defuse the tension in her cubicle. She flipped through a Rolodex on her desk. She found the card she was looking for and copied a number down on a legal pad with a Sharpie. She tore off the number and handed it to the big man. "Do me a favor, Hank. Keep trying to call Morningside until you reach someone. When you do raise somebody, check to see if William Blackwell has been seen anywhere around there within the past twenty-four hours."

Hank didn't take his eyes off Roselita, who only sat back and smiled a pearly white smile. "Of course, Clem. I can do that."

"Thank you."

Hank turned to leave, and Roselita buttoned her jacket as she stood. Dane stood up and tucked the thick file folder under his arm. He removed his hat. "Just one more question, Clem. If you don't mind."

"Not at all," she said with an impatient huff. She clearly wanted Roselita Velasquez out of her office.

"During your unofficial visits to see William, did he ever mention a place called the Farm? Or did he ever talk about a farm of any kind?"

Richland thought on it. "Yes. He did say something about going to a farm. He also mentioned a safari."

"A what?" Roselita said.

"A safari. He said that Arnold took him on safaris all the time. I had no idea what he was talking about and never did get a chance to find out; Arnold would cut him off after he brought it up every time. He acted weird about it. I didn't think much about it then, but it was strange now that I think about it. Do you know what that means?"

Dane ignored the question, put his hat on, and pulled it down low over his brow. He stayed on his own line of questioning. "Listen, I know it was a while ago, but try and remember. Did he say he was going to *a* farm or *the* Farm?"

"I honestly don't remember, but what's *the Farm* mean?"

"Maybe nothing," Dane said. "Come on, Velasquez." Velasquez smoothed down the front of her pants.

"If you can think of anything else, Clem, anything at all that might be of any help, please call us—day or night." Dane took a card from his pocket and laid it on her desk.

"I suppose that means you're not going to tell me? What the Farm is?"

Dane smiled at her. "Have a good day," he said as he left the cubicle. Richland didn't pick up the card until after the buzzer on the lobby door sounded and clicked shut.

CHAPTER ELEVEN

The Georgia sun had busted the afternoon wide open by the time Dane and Roselita finished up with Clementine Richland, and both of them groaned as soon as they opened the door and were hit with the blast of sticky heat. Dane was used to the weather that went along with being a Georgia native, but the heat in the city was an entirely different beast than the heat just a few hours north. In the city, the sun bounced off the steel and glass like a racquetball, getting meaner and more intense as the day went on. It soaked into the asphalt of parking lots like the one they were standing in now, waiting to leap out and beat the living shit out of any person who dared to walk across it. It was a humid, miserable feeling. Up north in places like McFalls County, people at least had shade trees to defuse the swelter. There was also a constant breeze swirling down from the mountains. That breeze didn't exist in the city. Living here meant accepting that there was no natural escape from the sucker punch of summer. The only relief came from finding somewhere to hide—somewhere air-conditioned, like a car, or an office, or a box. That's what Dane's life in Atlanta felt like—a daily series of jumps from one box to another until he finally made it back to the one he owned. Roselita, used to the constant salt breeze of Florida, had already removed her jacket. A dark stain of sweat had begun to form along the open neckline of her silk shirt. Dane tried not to linger. She hit a button on her keys and her Infiniti chirped.

"Hurry up, Kirby. It's fuckin' hot." Roselita had the engine cranked and the AC blasting long before Dane even opened the door and slid into his seat. He settled into the small bucket seat and shut the door. "Where you from, Velasquez? It ain't Florida. Too much drawl in you for a native of that place. So where?"

"Alabama. Roll Tide. Where we headed?"

"What part?"

"What part of what?"

"What part of Alabama?"

"You writing a book about me, Kirby?"

"Maybe?"

Roselita shook her head and laughed a little. Her brain pictured them on the interstate already. She didn't want to have a Q and A with the good ol' boy, but she played along. "Mobile, by the Bay. Happy? Now, can we get a plan together and on the road before we start with the small talk?"

Dane settled deeper into his seat and pulled down his seat belt. He clicked it in place and put on a pair of Wayfarers. He was hanging with the FBI. He wanted to fit in. He nodded at Roselita and almost got a smile out of her—almost. Velasquez just waited for an answer.

"Let's go to Blackwell's apartment in Cobb."

"I've already swept the place. There's nothing there. Nothing that's going to move us forward, anyway. What is the Farm?"

"I want to see it anyway."

"Do you not trust me, Kirby?"

Dane took his sunglasses off. "Yes, Velasquez, I do. But what I'm hearing is that you don't trust me. You asked. I answered. We're still not moving."

Roselita hard shifted into drive and pulled out of the lot.

"Were you police in Mobile?"

"No."

"What did you do there?"

Roselita sped through a yellow light, shifted into third, pulled off Fairground Street, and made her way onto the interstate. "Why?" she said, as she weaved from lane to lane through the dense midday traffic.

"I'm just curious as to where your fearlessness comes from."

Roselita cut off a late-model Ford Explorer and the driver, a woman, lay on the horn. "Explain," she said, not paying the other driver any attention at all. Dane began to wonder if Velasquez drove like this through the night to be here, but he stayed on subject.

"That guy back there at DFCS. The big dude. You know he's a handler, right? He wasn't just some meathead paper pusher. They get some pretty bad shit in there. Inner-city gang shit. Hence the buzz-in locks and all the security. He was most likely law enforcement, too, to some degree. Maybe the same training as you."

"And your point is?"

"My point is that you looked ready to draw down on the man. How do you know he wasn't armed as well?"

Roselita took her eye off the road for just a second to see if Dane was serious, and then went back to cutting I-75 to pieces. "First of all, the man was a pig and he *was* carrying. Small caliber. Concealable. Most likely a .380 or a .22. Slight lump on his left hip. And a big boy like that? Working with juvies? He probably had a taser stashed somewhere under that Old Navy sweater-vest as well." Roselita looked at Dane again, somewhat disappointed. "I'm curious as to why you didn't know that, too?"

Dane scratched at his newly forming beard. "Then how did you know he'd back down like that?"

"I didn't. But I don't like pigs, and it was his job to protect that kid. He failed. I don't have a tolerance for that kind of thing. So are you going to give me shit about how I handle myself in the field or are you going to tell me about this Farm now?"

Dane put his hands up in surrender. "It's where we're going when we get finished at Blackwell's apartment."

Roselita didn't argue or even acknowledge Dane's answer. She just kept burning down the interstate as if there were no such thing as Georgia state troopers, with Dane holding tight to the armrest. Roselita finally pulled off onto the exit 83 ramp and rolled to a stop at the red light at the bottom of the hill. She waited out the light impatiently and for the adjacent light to turn yellow, then punched the gas, launching the car left hard enough to press Dane into the window beside him. Dane straightened his sunglasses and shook his head.

The building that the late Arnie Blackwell called home was one of the many old stick-built houses that stood elbow to elbow with one another, lining both sides of South Greene Street. All the houses were nearly identical, with real wood siding and decades-old paint that had peeled so badly over the years it looked as if the entire neighborhood caught leprosy, every wall covered in scales that curled up in thin rolls. Like a lot of the old houses in this area of the city, this one had been chopped up and rebuilt to accommodate several tenants. The house had been built in the early fifties by American union carpenters, but the original owners had long since vacated, fleeing urban decay. The renovations that followed were cheap and hastily done, and it was always easy to rent out to tenants with bad credit or to low-income families who couldn't afford nicer complexes.

This area of Cobb County was one of the oldest residential zones in central Atlanta. It was even called Old Towne—always with an *e* on the end of Towne. The old English spelling did nothing for the neighborhood's appearance, but looked good on the sign leading in and allowed the homeowners and management companies to charge a few dollars more a month on account of the vintage, historic feel. It didn't change the fact that the entire neighborhood was a thug-infested shithole.

The Blackwell brothers rented the bottom half of the dilapidated house, and their apartment consisted of two bedrooms, a small kitchen–dining room, an even smaller living area, and a single bathroom that couldn't be occupied by two people at once. Most of the stuff Arnold had left behind was already on the curb for the vultures to pick through. A few locals scattered from the trash heap as the Infiniti pulled to the curb. The pungent smell of cop had that effect in places like this. Dane got out of the car and peeked into one of the heavy plastic trash cans filled with paper, broken pieces of particleboard, and beer bottles. The house's owners had wasted no time in getting a dead man's home move-in ready for a new tenant.

Dane picked through the trash bin and found nothing of interest, so he climbed the crumbling brick steps onto the primer-gray porch. The door was unlocked, so he turned the knob and inched it open. "You coming?" he shouted over to Roselita, who'd gotten out of the car but stopped short of the dry brown grass out front.

"Nah, I told you. I've seen it. There's nothing in there. Knock yourself out."

"Right."

Dane pushed the door all the way open. He instinctively ran his hand over the Redhawk clipped to his belt before walking in. He felt relatively sure that he wouldn't have a need for it, but the cool brushed steel of the .45 tight against his hip still felt reassuring. The living space was cleared out of any furniture that may have been there, leaving the hardwood floors dusty and unswept. Bits of trash and a few dust bunnies were the only things left in the room to prove anyone had ever lived here. There wasn't any furniture on the curb next to the trash bins, so the owners must've found some other use for it, or maybe Arnold had gotten rid of it before he left to get himself killed. That meant he had no intention of ever coming back here. That also meant that Roselita was probably right about this being a waste of time. Still, Dane preferred his mistakes to be his own. An ancient window-unit air conditioner hung in the window directly across from the door. A pigtail of electrical cord hung free beneath it. The closest wall socket was over ten feet away by the kitchen, so Blackwell must've been using an extension cord to run it—to cool the box. Dane thought about how he and Ned used to hunt down details like that in the aftermath of a house fire. Ned was like a bloodhound at a fire scene. One of the best Dane had ever known.

Ned.

It was the first time Dane had thought about his friend all day. The last thing he said to him was that he'd be right behind him. He'd bring him some cigarettes. A pang of guilt shot through Dane for standing Ned up like that, but there was plenty of time to sort that out. Dane had a plan for Ned, and even after all the time that had passed between them, he was sure Ned knew it.

The apartment had a shotgun layout. That meant the only way to get from the front door to the back door was to walk through every room, so Dane moved slowly over the creaky floorboards until he got to the kitchen. It was as bare as the living room, except for an old microwave that looked like it was built the same year as the window unit, a dirty plastic coffee maker missing the carafe, and some old newspaper. Coffee had spilled and dried on the countertop, and Dane touched at it. There was a fine layer of dust over the spill and the rest of the counter, so it wasn't recent. He picked up the newspaper dated weeks prior and set it back down. Half of it stayed stuck to the Formica in the dried spill.

Probably the reason it's still there, Dane thought, and wiped the dust from his hand onto his cargos. He opened the fridge to nothing but an empty pizza box and the stench of old food. The light came on, so the electric hadn't been cut off. He opened the cabinets one by one—all empty. No glassware. No plates. Nothing. He kept walking and opened the next door, which led to the bigger of the two bedrooms. This room had the bathroom and a small closet with accordion-style doors. He slid one side of the closet door open with the back of his hand—nothing but wire coat hangers and more dust. A queen-sized bed with paper-thin sheets took up most of the room, along with an empty dresser with nothing on top but an ashtray overstuffed with Doral cigarette butts—all burned to the filter. The room reeked of cigarette smoke. A few centerfolds from crude porn magazines were tacked to the walls, and Dane wondered if the shitbirds who owned the place left them hanging there as some warped selling point. The girls in the pictures looked barely old enough to be out of high school. Dane felt his heart double its weight. *What happened to these women?* he thought. *Where were their fathers? Could their parents have stopped them?* Dane felt acid burn the back of his throat. These were questions he would never get answers to. He thought about his daughter and felt stiff fingers squeeze his already-heavy heart. His palms moistened to a clammy white and he reached into his pocket and ran his fingers over the deformed metal bullet there. He closed his eyes and focused on his breathing for a full minute as the panic attack faded.

When he opened his eyes, he felt weak and was thankful Velasquez had stayed outside and not been witness to it. Dane put his head back in the game. He lifted the two-page centerfolds up by the bottom edges as if he might find something written on the wall behind them, or maybe an undiscovered hole in the Sheetrock like in *The Shawshank Redemption*, but the walls were blank and intact. Dane felt silly for thinking they wouldn't be.

The bathroom hadn't been cleaned in years, and the smell alone convinced Dane to skip that tiny room altogether. He opened the door that led into what must've been William's room. Hanging above the bed was one poster of a rock band that read INTRODUCING THE BLACK CROWES across the feet of Chris Robinson and the boys. The bed in this room was a twin, pushed flush against the wall, with nothing on the bare mattress and box spring but a stuffed penguin and navy blue quilt. Dane picked up the quilt to find it wasn't a quilt at all. It was a moving blanket—a goddamn moving blanket—the kind you rent from U-Haul to protect furniture. *This miserable piece of shit, Blackwell, didn't even bother to get his kid brother a proper blanket.* Dane shook his head. And tossed the stiff blanket back on the bed. The closet was no more than two feet deep, and it was as empty as the other one. There wasn't a chest of drawers in this room, but there were two makeshift bookcases made from two-by-six pine boards, held together with ten-penny nails. Not master carpentry, but sturdy and difficult to move. That was most likely why they were still there.

One of the bookcases was tall, rectangular, and completely bare except for a five-by-seven family photo of the Blackwells. It was the first time Dane had seen what the boy looked like outside of the mug shot–style picture in the file he got from Clem Richland. In this photo, the shaggy-haired boy had a smile that took up his whole face, but his eyes had the same far-off stare as the mug shot, as if he'd been told to smile and this was his go-to picture face. The father in the photo looked like an older version of the boy with slicked-over, thinning hair and glasses, and the mother was a thin, pretty woman with sad eyes. Despite the everyday flaws, they looked like a happy family. Arnold wasn't in the photo. Maybe he'd been the one to take it. Or maybe his absence was the reason they looked happy. Either way, Dane knew for sure that the older son was responsible for the sadness in his mother's eyes.

Dane stuck the photo in his pocket and ran a finger over the rest of the shelves, and it came up dust-free. The bookcase, he figured, had been used to hold the kid's clothes in folded stacks because there was no dresser, but the other shelf, the one that ran the length of the far wall, had been used for its intended purpose. It stood waist-high and still had a few books and magazines scattered across its shelves. Dane picked up the stuffed penguin from the bed and squeezed at it as he leaned down to examine what had been left behind. Several drawings of chickens, sketched accurately and well done, were stacked on the wood. Each sketch included the type of bird it was with numbers listed in a column down the left side of each sheet of paper. Dane didn't understand any of it. There were at least twenty drawings. He flipped through them slowly and then set them back down. He saw a heavy hardcover encyclopedia of birds indigenous to Georgia on the shelf, a veterinary medicine textbook, and a few comic books. He also found at least twenty to thirty sudoku books, the kind of thin, magazine-style puzzle books you can pick up at any Family Dollar or Walmart. He took one of them off the shelf and flipped through the pages. Every puzzle had been filled in. He picked up another one and it was filled in as well. All of them were. In all, there were hundreds of number puzzles, and every single one of them had been solved. Not one of them had any rewritten numbers or eraser marks—not one.

He set the books back down and flipped through the comics. He didn't know comics that well but he liked Batman. It looked like William did, too. He stood. He was still holding the stuffed penguin under his arm, so he sat it back on the bed. He rubbed at his rough beard. He stood in the middle of the room for a few more minutes, taking in all the random interests of an eleven-year-old kid, until he noticed the back door. It was slightly open. As he got closer he could see that it had been forced open. The wood around the lock had been splintered and pried back. Dane set his hand on the grip of the Redhawk and unsnapped the holster. He'd just walked the entire house. He'd seen every inch of it. There couldn't be anyone in there, but he kept his hand on the grip of his gun anyway. He pushed open the back door and saw nothing but a patch of dirt for a yard, stretching out no more than twelve feet from the cinder-block stoop he stood on. The back of another run-down house directly behind this one had a toolshed in the yard and was separated from this one by a rusted length of chain-link fence. He stepped out and looked around at nothing. When he looked down at the cinder blocks at his feet he saw the blood.

Blood?

He crouched down and tapped at what looked like a single drop of blood. Unlike the coffee stain in the kitchen, this time his finger came away sticky and red. The drop of blood was fresh. He stood up and examined the floor of the bedroom a little more carefully.

Nothing.

He walked with one hand on his gun into the next room. There it was. Another drop. He bent over to feel that one, too, and it was as fresh as the first. He looked around until he saw another drop in front of the bathroom door. He had skipped that room because of the smell.

Stupid, Dane. Stupid.

He drew the Redhawk and thumbed back the hammer. The bathroom door was open, but there wasn't a window, so the room was dark. The shower curtain had a blue floral print muddled by mildew stains. Dane exhaled when he realized he'd been holding his breath. He thought about walking out the front door. At least getting Velasquez in here with him. His gun hand was actually shaking.

There's no one behind the curtain, Dane. Get a hold of yourself.

"My name is Dane Kirby," he said out loud. "I'm with the Georgia Bureau of Investigation. I'm armed and have other agents outside. If there is someone in there, I'd advise you to come out—slowly, with your hands up."

No response.

He remembered the fridge light, so he reached a hand inside the doorway and felt for a switch. He flipped on the light. He still couldn't see or hear anything behind the curtain, but the blood was more abundant on the tiled floor. Not much, but enough to know it hadn't come from someone cutting himself shaving. He moved in closer and could see more blood in the sink. He announced himself again to the blue plastic curtain and again got no response.

"Ah, fuck it." He slid the curtain back on the rod.

Empty.

Dane let out a breath of relief and leaned back on the wall. He holstered his gun and almost laughed.

"What the hell are you doing?" Roselita said.

Dane flinched and knocked his head against a steel towel rod. It broke off the wall and fell to the floor. It banged against the tile and bounced up to pop Dane in the shin. "Jesus Christ, Rose. You scared the shit out of me."

"My bad. Who are you talking to in here?"

"Nobody. There's nobody here." His heart was racing.

Roselita picked up the towel rod and surveyed the blood. "Did you hurt yourself?"

"No, I'm fine. It's not my blood."

Roselita unbuttoned her jacket and put a hand on the hilt of her gun.

"There's nobody here. I've searched the entire place, but I'm guessing that blood wasn't here when you came by last?"

Roselita had dropped the towel rod back to the floor and pulled her gun out. She swept the main bedroom and the next room anyway. "No, it wasn't. I'll call it in and get a tech out here. Don't touch anything."

Dane finally lifted himself off the wall. His heart rate was slowing down. He was thrilled he hadn't shot himself in the leg. He got his balance back as Roselita examined the broken wood and lock. "This is recent, too."

"So the door was intact last time you were here?"

"Yeah." Roselita slipped her Glock 17 back into the holster under her arm. "But it's not uncommon to see these places busted into after someone moves out. The people around here are like vultures on roadkill. Some punks probably broke in to see what got left behind and one of them hurt himself in the process. Serves them right." She took out her phone, held it to her ear, and began pacing the length of the room.

"Or someone was here looking for William. The same as us."

Roselita stopped pacing, held up a finger, and spoke into the phone. She gave the address and asked for a full forensic team. She repeated both her name and the address three times before ending the call. "Fucking idiots," she said, and slipped the phone back into her pocket. She looked at Dane for a long time before finally asking him, "Why? Why would anyone else be looking for this douchebag's brother?"

"Take a look at this." Dane picked up one of the sudoku books from the stack on the bookcase. He flipped through the pages to show Roselita the penciled-in pages. "Not a single mistake in any of these." He picked up another one. "Here." He handed the books one at a time to his partner. "Look for yourself."

Roselita flipped through the magazines, unimpressed or uninterested with what she was seeing. "You're going to have to give me more."

Dane handed her the stack of drawings with the renderings of different roosters and what appeared to be statistical information listed across the pages. "What do you make of this?"

Roselita didn't make anything of them. She handed them back to Dane almost immediately. "What are you trying to say, here, Dane? Seriously. This shit makes zero sense to me."

"Okay," Dane said. "I know what you're going to say, but hear me out. What if Arnold didn't create a system to beat the Slasher? What if it's his brother?"

"Okay, so you're saying he used the kid's big brain to create a system to cheat the other players?"

Dane shook his head dismissively. "No, I don't think he used the kid to *create* a system."

"Then what?"

"I think the kid *is* the system. Seriously. Think about it. He took his brother in under his care. He didn't give a shit about him before. He didn't even want him at first, but now he goes to great lengths to protect him. He buys separate airplane tickets. They fly separate. He stashes him so he won't get caught. I mean, why even take the kid with him in the first place if he didn't actually need him to be there? It can't be because all of a sudden he became brother of the year. It makes more sense that he went through all the extra trouble to protect his meal ticket."

"I don't know, Kirby."

Dane said it before Roselita could. "It's a stretch, I know, but if I'm right, and the kid was able to do what he did at the Slasher without a single person there able to pick up on how he was pulling it off, then imagine what he'd be worth to those people, or to anyone smarter than his idiot brother."

"That's an interesting theory, Kirby, but it doesn't answer the main question we're here to find out. Where the hell is he? That's what we need to know."

Dane leaned his weight into the doorjamb and rubbed at the scruff on his chin again. "I don't know yet, but I do know where we can start looking."

"The Farm?"

"The Farm."

CHAPTER TWELVE

Fenn was not inhuman. He felt pain just like anyone else. He didn't have any specialized training. He wasn't on any type of drug that altered his mind, enabling him to shut down all the same receptors in his brain that other people had, letting him know when he'd been hurt. He'd been shot. The pain was excruciating. He was badly hurt and he was well aware he was dying. The difference between Fenn and most people who found themselves in this position was his tolerance—his instinct to survive. It took discipline to endure pain. It took discipline and focus to work through it. Most people Fenn encountered lacked enough discipline to keep their emotions in check, to keep from acting out of impulse, much less the ability to move through pain and use it to their advantage.

This country was the worst. Americans were soft. It was a nation of children, spoiled and fat, who blindly followed leaders whose intent was clearly to keep them that way. That is why Fenn had been such an effective tool in the United States. But Fenn was not a tool. He was a soldier. Fenn had been a soldier his entire life but, unlike these fat and spoiled Americans, he followed no one blindly. Fenn had also been a prisoner once. His imprisonment at the camp in North Korea where he learned about discipline—where he learned about pain—had been a direct result of following leaders who didn't have his best interests in mind. He'd been subjected to some of the most intense and horrific torture imaginable, and although what he learned there was exactly why he was still alive right now, he knew then that it would be the last time he followed anyone. It's why he wore the vest, although Smoke had told him not to. Smoke said

Fenn was weak to take such precautions, but now Smoke was dead. Fenn would've been, too, if he had listened to Smoke—if he had followed.

The wound in his shoulder still throbbed and shot fire through his whole body with his every movement, but he moved anyway. It had taken everything he had to push himself off the floor back at the American woman's house. He had considered staying and ambushing the man who attacked him—the man who killed Smoke—but it wasn't important. He had what they'd come for. He'd taken the money and made it to the car. He was able to stay conscious all the way to the address he'd taken off the fool he killed at the airport motel in Florida. He thought perhaps he'd find the boy here, the second objective he'd been tasked with. He blacked out in the bathroom. He wasn't sure how long he'd been out, but he was able to get out before the other men arrived. He left through the back door before he was seen and made it back to the car. There were most likely American police in the house now. They were not with the man who killed Smoke. The man who attacked them last night was a professional killer.

Fenn was still bleeding, and the blood loss was making him too light-headed to drive anywhere else. Discipline was one thing, but science was another. He knew the limits of the human body, and he had reached his. The man with the baseball cap went back into the house, but the other one—the female in the nice clothes—remained outside in the yard. Fenn watched them carefully from the tiny car until the woman went inside, and then drove around the block to the next street over. He could not allow himself to be seen but couldn't afford to black out again. He was in no condition to take on anyone—even weak American police like the ones inside the house. Fenn stopped the car. He began slipping in and out of the blackness again. White light snapped and sparkled at the edges of his vision. Unless he took care of himself quickly, nothing else would matter. Dead was dead.

Fenn stayed as calm as possible as he unbuttoned his shirt and un-peeled the Velcro straps of the Kevlar vest. Fresh patches of dark yellow and eggplant-colored bruises covered his entire chest. He was sure a few ribs were broken, too, but none of that concerned him. It was the bullet wound from the hit he took in the shoulder that was going to cause him to bleed out all over the front seat of this silly car. Fenn had already carefully torn the sleeve off his shirt, starting at the rip where the bullet had hit him, and wrapped the material around the wound, but it was blood soaked and needed to be changed and redressed. He ripped another large piece of the plastic trash bag that held the money he'd taken from the redheaded woman's house and wadded it up to plug the leaking hole three inches up from his left bicep. He pushed the black plastic in deep and could feel himself passing out, but he didn't. He thought of Smoke instead. He thought of all Smoke's big talk and flashy suits. Smoke didn't like the way the thick Kevlar vest made him look under those expensive clothes, so he never wore it—vanity—stupid. Smoke might as well have been American himself. Fenn didn't care how he looked. He just wanted to take his money and find a way home. He pulled himself out of the car with his good arm, and slowly walked around to the trunk. He grabbed the shotgun Smoke had put back there and walked in between the houses and entered the toolshed out back.

"Lashawn!" Wanda stood at the backdoor and yelled for her son, who was upstairs playing video games.

"Yeah, Mom."

"How many times have I told you to shut the door to the shed when you and your friends are done out there? If someone steals the lawn mower, it's coming out of your allowance."

"I thought I did." Lashawn bent the blinds in his bedroom window and looked out into the backyard. "Sorry, Mom, I'll go do it now." Lashawn took the stairs two at a time.

"Don't run in the house."

"Sorry, Mom." He opened the door leading into the backyard and practically walked right into Fenn's bare and bloody chest, taking up the entirety of the doorway. The sight of the huge man rendered the young boy speechless. Fenn removed all traces of pain from his face and held a single finger to his lips. "Say nothing," he whispered to the boy, "and turn around very slowly."

Lashawn didn't hesitate. He did what he was told. When Wanda saw the man following her son into her house, she started to scream.

Fenn pressed the shotgun into the small of the boy's back and held that same finger up to his lips. "I will kill him if you open your mouth."

Wanda stifled her scream hard enough to choke on it.

"Do not speak," Fenn said, and pushed the boy further into the house. I will ask you questions. Just shake your heads to answer. No words. Do you understand?"

"Yes, just please don't hurt my son."

Fenn sighed. Americans were so stupid. "I will repeat only once. Do not speak. I will ask you questions. Just shake your heads to answer. No words. If you speak again, I will kill this boy. Do you understand?"

Wanda nodded.

"Good. Is there anyone else in this house? Do not lie. I will know."

Wanda shook her head no. There wasn't anyone else in the house. Fenn studied her. She was too afraid to lie. "That is good. Now sit—both of you. I will need you to surrender your phones. Bring them to me now."

Lashawn slowly reached into his back pocket and held out his cell phone.

"Set it on the counter, boy."

Lashawn did.

"Turn around."

Lashawn did that, too.

"You are a good boy. I can tell."

Wanda tried to keep from crying, but the tears streaked her face.

"I will need bandages, boy. Needle and thread, too. You will go get them. If you do anything else other than bring me what I ask for, I will kill her. She is your mother, yes?"

Lashawn nodded.

"I will also need food and water. I don't require anything else from you except a place to rest. Do you understand this?"

The woman and her son both nodded.

"Good."

With his bad arm, Fenn tossed the trash bag onto the counter next to the phone. Wanda backed up and Fenn lowered the gun to dig through the bag. "In exchange for this service, I will give you ten thousand dollars."

He pulled out a bound brick of cash and set it on the counter next to the bag. "Do we have a deal?"

Lashawn stared wide-eyed at the money, while his mother nodded in agreement a third time. "Okay then. Boy. Go."

Lashawn took the stairs headed up to the bathroom two at a time. His mother didn't ask him not to run in the house again. He came back down with a plastic container of medical supplies and his mother's sewing kit. He set them both on the couch and then joined his mother in the kitchen. She pulled him into her hard and fast.

Fenn removed the battery from the phone and broke it into several pieces. "You will be able to purchase another one after I leave." Both Wanda and her son nodded. Fenn leaned back into the sofa. "Can you make an American cheeseburger?"

Wanda almost said yes but stopped herself. She nodded again and began to pull the things she needed from the fridge. Lashawn brought Fenn a huge tumbler of cold water and set it down on the coffee table while Fenn patched himself up. He drank the water and ate the burger Wanda fixed him. Fenn slept upright on the couch for several hours. Neither Lashawn nor his mother tried to call for help or leave the room. They waited. The bloodied stack of bills on the counter. It was almost over. They'd done exactly as the man said. When Fenn awoke, he rubbed at his sutured wound and then his belly. The food had been good. He felt refreshed. He took no pleasure in slicing the boy's or his mother's throat with one of the kitchen knives before he left. He killed them in separate rooms, so they wouldn't have to watch each other die. That would have been cruel, and Fenn, after all, was not inhuman.

CHAPTER THIRTEEN

They hadn't reached the McFalls County seat before Roselita got the call. At first Dane thought it might have been from her husband or a boyfriend by the way she got quiet and evasive as she spoke, or by how she shielded the phone's display from Dane, but maybe that was Dane's paranoia brought on by his not knowing a thing about this woman—a woman he was about to allow into the darkest corners of his life. Dane didn't know if Roselita was married or not. She didn't wear a ring, but that didn't count for much these days. He didn't know if she had kids—nothing. In fact, he didn't know much about his new partner at all, other than she was quick-tempered, well-dressed, and from Alabama, and it was clear that she felt completely uncomfortable out in the country.

Dane had always assumed that if you were from the South, that meant you were southern, but that wasn't always the case. City folk were as city as any far-northerners he'd ever met. They didn't talk the same, act the same, or even smile the same as the people he'd known his whole life. They didn't carry themselves anything like the people Dane had been used to dealing with in the mountains. There was an easygoing nature to the people who lived in the foothills that didn't exist in central Georgia—or any metropolitan area. Everyone in the flatlands had somewhere to be and they needed to be there yesterday. Dane still had to get used to it.

He didn't even understand how they dressed. Roselita stopped at her hotel to change clothes before they headed out. Her suit, she guessed correctly, wasn't appropriate for a trip to a place called the Farm, but she'd walked back out to the car wearing a fresh pair of pressed khakis and a peach-colored polo shirt, tucked in and cinched off with a braided leather belt. She topped off the whole Kentucky Derby mess with a tweed Kate Spade pocketbook. Dane just didn't get it. He knew Roselita wasn't trying to look like an asshole. She just didn't know any better. She had even put on some fancy-ass pair of pink and tan hiking shoes that looked like she'd taken them out of the box for the first time that day. Dane just shook his head when she opened the driver's-side door and slid in.

"What?" she said. "You asked me to dress down. I dressed down."

"Yeah. I said to dress down. I didn't say to go get a job as a catalog model for L.L.Bean."

"Fuck you, Kirby." Roselita's response set the tone for yet another painfully long car ride north.

Dane continued to chew on a pinstriped straw from a Waffle House to-go cup of sweet tea when Roselita answered her phone. He looked out the window at the blur of pine trees and pretended not to be interested. Roselita kept the conversation brief, using one-word answers until she ended the call and tossed the phone into the console. Dane looked over and waited to hear if the call was relevant to the case. Dane hoped it wasn't, but the conversation had turned Roselita's tan skin pale, so he knew it was.

"What's the word, partner?"

"I'm not your partner."

"Okay, whatever. Are you going to tell me what that was about?"

Roselita drove another quarter mile before she answered.

"They found Blackwell's dealer."

"Dealer?" The term didn't register at first.

"The dealer," Roselita repeated. "Arnold Blackwell's partner. He was a midlevel pot dealer named Bobby Turo. C'mon, Dane, he's the guy you told us to find. Well, they found him." She sounded almost defensive before adding, "I should've been the one to find him instead of being out here with you."

"Why? That's great. Did they get anything out of him? Did they find anything that might lead us to William? Wait, you said he *was* a midlevel pot dealer?"

"Right. He's dead—along with seven other people, including a woman."

"What?"

"Those bastards who did Arnold got to them first—killed everyone in the room including a young woman named Bernadette Sellers. The house?" Agent Velasquez wiped at her face with the back of her hand. "Less than ten miles from Arnold's rattrap apartment. We were right there."

"Well, shit." Dane rubbed at his knee. "Hold on, Rose. We got our people there as fast as we could. It isn't our fault."

"No, it's not *our* fault. It's my fault. You gave me the lead. I should've acted on it right then, instead of—" Roselita pounded her fist against the steering wheel. "Goddamnit."

"Take it easy. It's not your fault. How do they even know if the two scenes are related?"

"They're related. August was right, but I didn't want to listen. Geoff said the house was attacked by the same two bastards that killed Blackwell."

"Geoff?"

"Yeah, Geoff—Dahmer. Remember? My partner."

"He's the one who tracked her down?"

"Yeah."

"Did he go alone?"

Roselita didn't care for Dane's tone. "I'm sure he didn't. That's not the way we do things, Kirby, but I should've been there instead of here. I could've—"

"You couldn't have done anything." Dane checked his own phone for any missed messages from August. There was nothing. "What else did he say?"

"Only that it had to be related."

"How does he know that?"

"The woman," he said. "She fought back. She killed one of them."

"And what makes Dahmer so sure it's one of the same assholes who killed Blackwell?"

Roselita reached over and popped the glove box. She pulled out an ancient-looking soft pack of Marlboro Ultra Lights with a BIC lighter tucked into the outside cellophane. Dane hadn't seen Roselita smoke before, and by the way she threw a fit half an hour back about Dane tossing his empty Waffle House cup onto the floorboard of her pristinely kept car, he was surprised to see her light up to smoke in it.

"Because the man she took down was Asian and they've got a positive ID from the Cuban kid at the motel. Long Duk Dong. It's the same guy."

Dane leaned back in his seat and massaged at his knee a little more. It was cramped inside the small sports coupe. Roselita took a long, deep pull from the Marlboro and tipped the ash out the window.

"They only found one?"

"Are you fucking deaf, Kirby? I said he told me the woman only shot one of them. Seven found dead, but only one murdering piece of shit. Goddamnit. I'm always repeating myself with you." The sudden anger surprised Dane nearly as much as the smoking, but he let it go. Roselita was clearly rattled about something more than she was letting on.

"Did they find the money?"

"No."

"Did he mention any sign of the kid being there?"

"He didn't say anything about the kid, Kirby. If there were any signs of the kid, don't you think I would've told you?"

That was enough. Dane turned in his seat. "Okay, what the hell is your problem, Velasquez? I'm only asking you questions anyone on this case would ask. What's with all the attitude?"

Roselita tossed the hot-boxed cigarette out the window. She held the steering wheel steady with her knee and immediately began to light another. Her hands were shaking. She pulled in another deep chestful of smoke and coughed it out. She wasn't a smoker, not anymore anyway, but that phone call had been enough to push her off the wagon. When the hacking fit settled, she held the pack out to Dane.

"No, thanks. Eight years quit. Those things will kill you."

Roselita tucked the pack into the glove box and took it easy on the second cigarette, not attacking it as she had the first. Dane stared at the glove box and debated the cigarette. It wasn't like it mattered now anyway, but he decided against it. Roselita tossed her second butt out the window. She was staring out at the road, but she was looking at something else as well, something that wasn't there. She was squeezing the steering wheel harder than she should've been, too. Dane had watched this woman stroll through Arnold Blackwell's guts the day prior without a second thought, but a phone call about a bunch of dead bodies shook her up this bad? It didn't make sense. "What aren't you telling me, Rose?"

"Stop calling me Rose."

"Goddamnit, Velasquez. For once, try not to be an asshole and just tell me what else is going on with you."

It took another few minutes of rolling blacktop before Roselita pulled the Infiniti into the parking lot of the McFalls County sheriff's office. She cut the engine, but she didn't open the door or try to get out. She just sat there, gripping the wheel, staring through the windshield at whatever that call had put inside her head. Dane sat there, too—still hoping for an answer.

Roselita let go of the wheel. She let go of the image in her mind, apparently, too, and dropped her eyes to look at the building in front of her. She focused on the bronze star mounted to the wall by the front door of the sheriff's office. "There were eight people killed at that woman's house."

"I thought you said there were seven."

Roselita took her hands off the wheel and dropped them to her lap. "The Sellers woman."

"What about her?"

"The forensics team found a test kit in the bathroom. They also did a blood test. She was—she—"

Dane understood immediately. "She was pregnant."

"Yes, the test was positive."

"Jesus."

"And the way she died. Gunshot to the belly."

Dane felt a knot form in his own gut and stared at Roselita, who sat looking down at shaking hands. She repeated herself as if Dane hadn't heard her.

"A gunshot to the belly."

Dane could feel his palms getting sweaty. He needed to focus. Now was not the time for another episode. He turned and stared at Roselita. Dane figured Roselita to be in her late twenties. Most of these agents were really just kids. They tried to be hard. The Bureau teaches them to be hard—to push their humanity down deep into a place no one can see it in order to do their job. That had always been bullshit in Dane's opinion.

He had experienced loss. He'd seen the worst kind of ugliness up close. He lived with a thing in his guts worse than guilt—worse than anything most people could ever even imagine—but he'd also allowed himself to feel every bit of it. Sometimes he needed to feel it. He thought that of all people. Pain needs to be processed or it will eat you alive from the inside out. He was lucky. He always had people who cared about him around to help get him through it. He'd had Ned. He had Misty. Folks like Roselita had been taught not to show any of that emotion. It was considered a sign of weakness. Double down on that for a woman. Dane had enough years behind him and not nearly enough ambition in front of him to know all that bravado shit could, and eventually would, do more harm than good.

He thought about leaving the conversation at that. Maybe Roselita needed to work it out for herself, but as usual, Dane couldn't keep his mouth shut. "Are you married, Roselita?"

It took a moment for her to answer, and she never looked at Dane, but eventually she did say softly, "Engaged."

"Do you and your fiancé have any kids?"

"Not yet."

"You're trying?"

Rose looked straight ahead at nothing. "She's pregnant. We're due in June."

It took a minute for Dane to process Roselita's response. "Oh," he said, failing miserably to mask his surprise. Roselita hardened up a bit and looked at him. "Is that okay with you, Kirby? Gay isn't contagious, you know."

Dane could feel himself blush and felt ashamed for being taken off guard. "What? No. I mean, yes." Dane stumbled. "It's fine. I don't care. Why would I?" Dane's inability to catch the softball of information introduced levity to the situation.

Roselita shook her head. "Right," she said. "Why would you?" Agent Velasquez honestly wasn't worried if Dane cared or not. She was used to the backpedaling whenever her sexual preference came up, but at least Dane's reaction didn't come from a place of judgment. He just obviously didn't know any better. It was kind of cute. She looked back down and kept talking. "We're having a girl," she said, a little softer now that her walls were crumbling to expose the human inside. "We're going to call her June, too. We thought it would be sweet, you know?" She turned to Dane with a look that almost asked for approval. "A girl named June born in June."

"Yeah," Dane said. "That's cool."

"We've talked about trying again right after she's born. We're hoping for a boy so we can name him Johnny. You know, like Johnny and June."

"Best love story ever, right there."

Roselita let out a small laugh. Somebody finally got it without her having to explain it. Dane reached over and put a hand on Roselita's shoulder. "Whenever you're ready, partner. I want to introduce you to a friend of mine."

Before Dane opened the door, he popped the glove box and took out the pack of cigarettes. "You mind if I take these?"

"I thought you didn't smoke. Eight years quit, remember?"

"I don't."

Roselita shrugged and wiped a finger under each eye in the rearview mirror. "Whatever. Go ahead."

"Thanks." Dane tucked them into the pocket of his T-shirt and slid out of the car. They both walked up the front steps of the sheriff's office. Roselita let Dane lead the way. He pushed open the front door and stepped in. Nothing much had changed inside the small lobby. The block walls were still painted white with long stripes of blue and gray that led to the county emblem mounted between two office doors. A squat mahogany reception desk was still in the same place behind the high-rise counter, but the ten-year-old PC and printer that used to sit on top of it had been replaced with all-new equipment.

"Damn, Velasquez, look at that," Dane said. "I tried to get the county to upgrade the computers in here for years." He reached around and unlatched the hideaway door cut into the counter and held it open for Roselita. Dane ran his hand along the dispatcher's desk, admiring the sleek black PC and updated radio system. Other than the large desk, a few filing cabinets, and a portable CD player on a folding card table, there was nothing else in the main area. The administrative office of the fire department now had its own location up Main Street, so the desk he used to use during his time here had been removed, leaving nothing in the far corner but an empty space and a coaxial cable curling out of a wall plate next to the door that said Sheriff Darby Ellis. Dane looked around at the rest of the building he'd reported to for work almost every day for twelve years and felt a rush of nostalgia.

"Is it usually this empty around here?" Roselita asked. "Any jackass off the street can walk in here."

"I suppose they can, since we just did."

"Funny. You good here, Kirby? You look a little out of it."

"Yeah, yeah. I'm fine. It's just strange to be back. I haven't been in here since I packed up my desk and moved to Fannin. It's a little overwhelming."

"I can understand why you'd miss it." Roselita picked up a Waylon Jennings CD from a stack on the card table, and then set it back down. "This place is a fucking palace."

"Have you seen my office at the Bureau, Rose? Believe me. This *is* a palace."

"Well, seriously. Where the hell is everyone? Is there a potluck somewhere? Or is the sheriff the mayor, too, and he's in the back changing his hat?"

Dane smiled. "Glad you're back to your normal self, Velasquez. I was worried about you for a minute there." Dane rapped his knuckles on the sheriff's door.

"Come on in. It's open."

Dane turned the knob and walked into the office. Now this room *was* different. Sheriff Burroughs had practically lived in here, and back then it was always a wreck. Boxes and boxes of case files, folders, and stacks of newspapers had been piled in every corner, and a sleeper sofa that stayed open and messy took up more space in the room than his desk. Ellis had definitely made the place his own. The office was now wall-to-wall bookshelves filled with pristine volumes of state penal code and bound copies of McFalls County SOP manuals. A nice leather sofa had replaced the ratty old sleeper.

Ellis sat at his desk in full uniform—all starched and crisp. He wore the wide-brimmed sheriff's hat that Dane had never seen him without, and he pushed it back out of his face when Dane and Roselita entered the room. His stormy eyes were bright blue and his smile was genuine.

"I like what you've done with the place, Darby." Dane picked up a framed photo from one of the bookcases—a picture of Darby and his girlfriend Cricket, pinning his badge on him at his induction ceremony. He faced the photo at Ellis. "How in holy hell did you manage to convince that woman to go out with you? She must've turned everyone else in the county down."

"I ask myself that question every day, Dane. I think it has something to do with the uniform. She's a sucker for a man in uniform." The sheriff stood and stuck his hand out for Roselita. "I don't believe we've met. Darby Ellis."

Roselita shook his hand. "Special Agent Roselita Velasquez," she said, and held the sheriff's grip. "So you're the guy that held a gun on Halford Burroughs and all his men in order to save your boss up on Bull Mountain a few years ago."

Ellis smiled and looked a little perplexed.

Roselita filled in the blanks for him. "I was part of the federal team that seized the mountain after Big Hal was taken off the board. While I was up there, I heard the Darby Ellis story maybe fifty times—those folks were mighty impressed."

Darby's fair-skinned cheeks reddened immediately. He let out a light, embarrassed chuckle. "All I did was hold a shaking gun. It was my boss, Clayton, who got us out of there alive."

"That's not the way I heard it."

"And maybe what you heard is a story for another day," Dane said, cutting in, and set the photo back on the bookcase. He quickly changed the subject. Talk of Clayton Burroughs and his family damn near always led a conversation down the wrong road. "What happened to that sleeper sofa that Burroughs kept in here?"

"That raggedy piece of trash? I had that thing hauled off and burned. It smelled like twenty years of Camel Lights, whiskey, and bad decisions."

Both men laughed. Roselita did not.

"Have a seat. Please."

Dane and Roselita opted for the two big leather chairs opposite the sheriff's desk and they all sat down.

"Dane, you didn't tell me much on the phone. How can I help you?"

"The man you arrested at the scene of Tom Clifford's murder. Ned Lemon? I was hoping I could borrow him for a little while. I know he's a person of interest in your case, but—"

"Whoa." Darby put his hand up. "Hold up a second. What do you mean *borrow* him?"

"I was hoping I could take him with me. We've got some business here in McFalls that will go a whole lot smoother if I've got Ned with me."

"What kind of business could possibly supersede a murder investigation?"

"I've got to go out to Hard Cash Valley. I need to talk to Rooster."

Ellis leaned back in his chair. He looked at Roselita and then back at Dane. "You're talking about Eddie Rockdale?"

"I am."

Ellis took off his hat and set it on his desk. Dane pulled his chair in closer to the desk. "We're working a missing person's case, Darby—an eleven-year-old kid. He's in trouble and we're pretty sure that we're not the only ones looking for him."

"And you think Eddie's got him?"

"I think Eddie might know what happened to him. Other than that, I don't know much more than the boy's in for a world of hurt if we don't find him soon."

"Are you sure you want to go down that road, Dane? Rockdale is about as mean as they come. My deputy and I can be suited up and ready—"

Dane cut him off. "No, I'm not even sure that showing up there in plain clothes with Ned as a buffer is a good idea, but the less police presence the better. Otherwise Rockdale is likely to shut down altogether and not give us anything. I could really use your help with this by loaning me your prisoner. Ned and Eddie are like brothers. I might be able to get him to talk to me, but I know he'll talk if I can bring Ned with me. Without him, it's possible that Eddie might not be that cooperative at all. You, of all people, know how it goes up here, Darby." Dane cocked his head sideways at Roselita. "They don't like cops and they can smell 'em comin'."

Roselita looked offended. "Hold up, Kirby. You say that like you're not a cop, too."

"That's my point, Rose. Eddie may not even talk to me, so it's going to be strained enough as it is. That's why I need Ned."

The sheriff crossed his arms and contorted his mouth as if he were licking at the back of his teeth to consider what Dane was saying. "Dane, Lemon isn't just a *person of interest* in this mess with old man Clifford. Not anymore. He's been arrested and charged with murder. I can't just let him go even if I wanted to."

"Last time I checked, Sheriff, it was your name on the door of this office. I reckon that means you can do anything in this county you damn well please."

"You're asking me to break the law, Dane."

Roselita leaned forward in her chair. "Sheriff, we've got nine dead bodies already—that we know of. Nine. We're just trying to keep that from going into double digits by adding a little kid to that list. We're not asking you not to do your job. We're just asking you to give us a little leeway so we can do ours."

Sheriff Ellis wasn't sure if he liked Roselita or not. The bloodhound behind his young, narrowed blue eyes was still sniffing her out, and Dane could see the conversation going sideways like it did back at Child Services in Atlanta. The sheriff's eyes got a little less young and bright, and more partly cloudy with a chance of cocky. This was not the place for Roselita to pull the "who's got the bigger gun" act. "Darby, I can tell you right now, Ned didn't shoot anyone."

Ellis stopped eyeballing Roselita. "You don't know that for sure, Dane."

"Was there any GSR on his hands or clothes?"

Darby looked uneasy. "Well, no."

"Did anyone actually see him pull the trigger?"

"No, but you already know that. You were there."

"Right. I was. So I know the only thing you have on him is circumstantial at best."

"I don't know, Dane."

"At least walk me back there and let me talk to him."

Sheriff Ellis picked up his hat and put it back on. He leaned down hard on his desk and pushed himself up. "Okay, Dane. I'll play ball, but I'll need authorization from your superiors, and something in writing that says that I strongly object to all of this in the event it all goes down the shitter."

"I can do all of that."

"Okay, then, get your boss on the phone."

Dane and Roselita waited outside in the parking lot for about ten minutes before Sheriff Ellis got off the phone with August O'Barr and stepped out of the front door. He held a small canvas zipper bag and a ring of keys that accessed McFalls County's lockup. They all walked around the side of the building. Ellis went through the motions of unlocking the outside gates and locking them back behind them. Once they were inside the jailhouse, they all stood silent in the hallway leading back toward the county's twin holding cells. They stayed quiet and walked directly behind Ellis until they reached the far cell. The Sheriff used another key on the ring to open the cell door and stepped to the side, allowing Dane to walk through. His appreciative nod at the sheriff wasn't returned. They might all be on the same side, but the sheriff didn't like having his jurisdiction tampered with. It was understandable. Dane leaned a hand against the bars and slid a chair into the cell opposite a steel-frame bed bolted to the floor. Ned lay across it with his hands behind his head. His eyes were closed. His feet were bare and crossed. He wasn't asleep, but he didn't move or bother to look at anyone, either. He seemed at home, as if he belonged there. He was wearing a bright orange jumpsuit with MCFALLS COUNTY printed in block letters down the leg. A pair of size-large jelly shoes were kicked off on the floor. Ned finally glanced over at Dane before turning his head back to stare at the ceiling. Ellis set the canvas bag on the cot next to him. "Here are your personal effects, Lemon."

Ned still didn't move.

"Can you give us a minute, fellas?"

"Sure, Dane. Take all the time you need. We'll be right outside. Hit the buzzer when you're ready to go."

"Thanks, Darby." Dane reached into his pocket and tossed the crumpled pack of Marlboro Ultra Lights from Roselita's glove box onto Ned's chest. Ned looked down at them and then finally sat up. He ignored the canvas bag and shook a smoke out of the pack. He slid the lighter out of the cellophane. "These are two days late, man."

"But I brought 'em."

"Ultra Lights?" Ned said as he lit up.

"You know the one about beggars and choosers?"

"You know the one about 'Hey, I'll meet you in an hour or so, and we'll sort all this out'? Your boy back there is ready to put me in front of a firing squad for this shit."

"You and I both know that's not gonna happen."

"Well, that's up for debate." Ned slipped into the jelly slippers. "Seriously, that guy has been planning the press conference for two days now, while you were out"—Ned looked at the pack of Marlboros in his hand—"fishing stale cigarettes out of a dumpster, apparently." He took in a deep drag and coughed it out. "Damn, Dane, I said I'd take anything I could get, but could you get anything worse?" He tossed the pack back to Dane, who caught it and tucked it back in his pocket with no intention of giving him another one.

"You really have become an asshole while you were gone. How about thanks for the get-out-of-jail-free card I just handed you? Or maybe just thanks for—"

"Okay. Okay. Stop. Thanks. Now tell me what exactly you did to pull this off. Why is Opie Taylor letting me go?"

"He's not letting you go. He's remanding you to me."

"You mean I'm your prisoner now?"

"Yup."

Ned laughed and took another drag. This time he knew what to expect and didn't cough it all out. "That's fucking rich."

"No, Ned, it's dangerously close to me being locked up in here with you."

"What do you mean?"

"It means what I just did to get you out of here puts me and a lot of other people in the position to lose their jobs—Opie Taylor included—but it just so happens that—" Dane stumbled a little, as if he were suddenly winded. Ned caught him by the elbow to keep him steady. "Dane?" he said, the cigarette clamped between his lips. "You okay?"

Dane shook his head and blinked his eyes a few times. "I'm fine." He pulled his arm away from Ned and stood up straight. "Just a long few days. Anyway, the point—like I was saying—I need your help."

"With what?"

"We'll talk about that once we get you out of here."

Ned dropped his smoke to the floor, stomped it out with a jelly slipper, and then stood up and stretched his back. Dane stood as well, but slowly. He felt weak and he leaned on the back of the chair for a moment to let the rush of blood return to his head before he stood all the way up. Ned turned to the commode and took a piss. "I'm sorry, Dane. I didn't know what else to do."

"Seriously, Ned, we'll talk about it later. Let's just get you out of here and somewhere we can talk."

"This was a mistake."

"Ned, stop."

"No, seriously, just forget about all this and let me take the rap for shooting Tom. If I don't fight it, then everybody wins. The case is closed. You stay clear. Blondie over there gets a feather in his cap, and I go somewhere I should've gone a long time ago. You and I both know I deserve it anyway."

Dane listened to the sound of Ned's piss hitting water and had the urge to just slam him into the wall. "That's bullshit, Ned. You didn't shoot anybody and we both know it. So please just shut up, and don't say another word until we are long gone from this place."

Ned didn't say anything else. He washed his hands in the sink and ran them through his collar-length hair before wiping them on his jumpsuit. His hair hadn't a lick of curl to it, and even wet, it fell flat and stringy. It looked like it hadn't been washed in weeks. He pushed it back behind his ears to keep it out of his face. "Okay, Dane, you're the boss."

Dane hit the buzzer. Ned reached over to pick up the flattened cigarette butt from the smear of ash on the floor and tossed it in the toilet. The sound of the outside door opening caused both men to look as Sheriff Ellis came back down the hall. He opened the cell door but kept his distance in the hall. It was hard to believe Dane had even seen any color in his eyes earlier. They were sunk back into his skull and damn near impossible to see at all now, but Dane nodded and offered a silent thank-you.

Ellis crossed his arms. "Dane. I hope you know what you're doing."

"Thank you, Darby. I do, too."

CHAPTER FOURTEEN

William had to pee. He'd been holding it for hours. Ever since he got off the bus. Arnie said to go to their safe place, so he did, but Arnie was taking forever. William didn't want to pee in his pants, but he didn't want to not wait anymore. Arnie told him to wait. William knew where the bathroom was, but it was late now. He knew the fat man with all the keys would've locked it by now—and it was far from where he was. If Arnie came back and he wasn't there, Arnie would be upset. He'd scream. Arnie always screamed. William tried calling Arnie again to tell him he really had to go pee, but someone else answered—the same man from before who said he was a friend of Arnie's—but he was lying.

William broke the phone in half, the way Arnie had told him, after that call. He threw it in the bushes right before he jumped the fence when he got here. He wished he'd peed in those bushes. He wanted to go back to the Farm—to the pretty lady who lived there. William really liked the Farm. It was cool. William loved the birds there, but hated that the birds were used in their stupid game. That didn't make any sense. Why train the birds to listen and to take commands just to let them fight and kill each other? It was cruel, but thoughts of the bird game kept William's mind off his bladder for a while until taking a piss was all he could think about. He didn't want to just pee on the ground. That would be gross, and he definitely didn't want to pee near the trees. The birds lived in there. That wouldn't be cool at all. If there were nests nearby, the smell of urine would keep the mothers from coming back and feeding their babies. William wasn't about to be responsible for the death of even more birds. He'd done enough of that for Arnie already.

William was hungry, too. He had six dollars in his wallet but he was sure the fat man in the uniform had locked up all the places to eat, too. Him and the others, the loud kids with the matching blue T-shirts, shut all that down an hour ago—when they locked up the bathrooms. He was sure of it. He bounced his leg on the bench enough to bruise the heel of his foot even through his sneaker, to keep from pissing himself, but he had to do something. Finally, William made a decision. He'd have to leave—just for a minute—and find a suitable place to urinate. Arnie would have to be okay with that. He would have to understand. He hoped Arnie didn't show up and sound the way he did over the phone earlier. When they got on the plane after the big contest, Arnie was pretty excited. He was happier than William had ever seen him. William didn't understand how his brother could be so happy one minute and then so upset the next, but Arnie had always been like that—his whole life he'd been like that. Arnie would just have to understand. He couldn't hold it anymore.

William stood up and walked. He wasn't sure which way he should go, but the walking immediately helped him hold it in, so he just walked. He stayed off the sidewalks and kept in the shadows because he knew if anyone saw him, they wouldn't let him stay there. They wouldn't let him continue to wait where Arnie told him to, and he didn't want his brother to be any angrier than he already was. William didn't walk far before he saw the vending machine. He turned around and knew he'd be able to see the bench he'd been sitting on if he stepped out into the lighted breezeway, so Arnie couldn't get too mad at him for moving. He was technically still in the same place. He hustled over to the machine and unzipped his pants. There was already a small pool of something nasty on the concrete under the left side of the machine, so he wasn't affecting too much by adding to it. William peed on himself a little in anticipation, and with nowhere to wash his hands, he was mortified, but finally he relieved himself into the pool of sticky filth behind the vending machine. It felt so good. It also felt like it took forever, and he leaned his shoulder against the lit-up machine as the feeling of relief washed over him. He hoped Arnie hadn't come back yet. He couldn't hear anyone. He kept swiveling his

head from the puddle growing at his feet to the bench way back behind
him. He wondered how Arnie would even get in here now that everything was locked up. It was against the rules, but Arnie didn't care about
rules. William knew that. He peed and peed until he had nothing left.

When he was done he zipped himself up and almost started back toward the bench, but then he remembered the six dollar bills he had tucked
in his wallet. He stopped next to a tree and took the wallet out of his
pocket. He counted the bills over and over again several times and tucked
them back in the wallet before he approached the vending machine again
and studied the contents behind the Plexiglas. He scanned each row. Everything had chocolate on it. William hated chocolate. Arnie thought
that was weird. "All kids like chocolate," he'd say. William supposed his
brother was right, but William wasn't a kid. Why didn't Arnie understand that? Why didn't anyone understand that? When William spotted
the row of Paydays six rows down and nine rows over, he smiled. Paydays were the best. They were like Baby Ruths without all the chocolate
to ruin them. He immediately pulled the neatly creased fold of money
from out of the wallet again and counted the bills a few more times. Other
than those six one-dollar bills, the wallet was completely empty, so he
tossed it in the huge plastic trash can on the other side of the vending
machine. It served no purpose now, so why keep it?

He straightened out the bills as best he could, and one by one he fed all
six of them into the slot on the machine. In between each bill he lined up
and checked—and double-checked—the correct number, before mash-
ing the button—"F nine," he whispered out loud every time he hit it. By
the time he was done, the machine had dispensed six Paydays into the
collection container at the bottom of the machine. William pushed back
the plastic cover and grabbed them all, stuffing them into the front pocket
of his hoodie. He wanted to eat them right there, he was so hungry. He
wanted to shove them all into his mouth, but he knew he'd already taken
enough time for himself. He needed to get back. Arnie might already
be there. He was being selfish. William pulled his hood over his head,
tucked his hands into the pocket full of candy, and took the same dark-
ened route under the trees back to the bench. He'd made a promise to stay
put and he'd broken it. Arnie wasn't there. Maybe he'd come and gone.
Maybe since William didn't do what he said he'd do, Arnie left him there.

No, William knew Arnie would've yelled or screamed. He would have heard him. He wasn't that far away—but he wasn't sure. William sat back down and started to cry. "I'm sorry, Arnie," he said into the darkness. "I'm still here. I won't get up again." William didn't eat a single one of the candy bars in his pocket. He could wait. Arnie would be there soon. Everything would be okay. They would go to the city with all the lights and water and everything would be okay. Just like Arnie said. He wiped at the tears on his face with the back of his sleeve. Arnie was coming. He just knew it.

CHAPTER FIFTEEN

Winston Waymore Bell and his wife of forty-one years were lifetime residents of McFalls County. The main township at the foot of Bull Mountain had been named after his grandfather, James Waymore Bell, and the family owned just about every business in town. They started by opening the county's first and only bookstore back in the early sixties, just a few blocks over from the municipal building that at the time housed the sheriff's office, the jail, City Hall, the clerk of court, and the fire department. Over the next several years, the Bells invested in several other businesses around the small downtown area, and most of them were still owned and operated by the surviving members of the Bell family themselves. Some opened Waymore Valley's first and only coffee shop, adjacent to the old bookstore. Suzanna Bell, the couple's youngest daughter, ran a children's clothing consignment shop and a rustic-styled bakery and sandwich shop that boasted the best blackberry cobbler in the state. Burnside Bell, Suzanna's younger brother, once told Dane that the secret to his sister's award-winning cobbler wasn't in the locally farmed berries, but in the hefty dose of fresh butter that he churned himself every morning before sunup. The question of cobbler credit was always a hot point of contention between the siblings.

Although the sandwich shop was the most popular attraction McFalls County had to offer for travelers and tourists of the Blue Ridge foothills, by far the most lucrative Bell-owned operation was one they ran from behind the scenes. Lucky's Diner was the only bar in the county, and the Bells had made an arrangement with a couple of brothers from

New York—looking for, let's say, a less frantic life in the Georgia foothills—to run it for them. A bar was something the Bell family believed didn't suit their family-friendly reputation, but the money those two Yankee brothers generated from it on a nightly basis seemed to suit them just fine, so they remained silent partners and allowed Harold and Harvey Polanski, along with Harold's daughter Nicole, to be the public face for Lucky's, while the Bells put all that unsavory money into other ventures.

Burnside and Cynthia Bell's son, Keith, had worked at Lucky's as a barback almost every night since he was eighteen, and in return, his parents paid his bills, kept his bank account flush, and allowed him to live rent-free in the spacious loft directly above the diner. The Bells were rich and thought themselves to be of a higher stature then most of the residents of McFalls County, but they were still good people—good country people—especially Keith. He and Dane had known each other their whole lives. They'd grown up together. Same hospital. Same school. Same trouble. Same blues. They had one of those friendships that didn't need constant nurturing to maintain. Five days or five years might pass since they'd seen each other, and they could pick up a conversation from where it left off. Dane also knew if there was one place he could show up unannounced with a federal agent from Florida and a malnourished Ned Lemon in need of a hot shower and some clothes—it was Keith's. Dane also knew Keith was a creature of habit, so at this time of the morning, Keith would be home.

Keith finally woke up after the third knock, and he opened the door wearing only a pair of buffalo-plaid boxers. Keith was about six foot one and fit, outside of the small lump of belly that alcohol had built on his midriff. No expression at all crossed his boyish, handsome face when he saw Dane standing on the flimsy wrought-iron landing between the short, put-together build of Roselita and the tall, lanky frame of Ned. Keith just scratched at something behind his ear. No words passed. He rubbed the crumble of sleep from his eyes, then moved aside to make way for them all to come in.

"Sup, Dane," Keith said under a yawn as they entered the loft.

"Sup, Keith. Sorry to wake you."

"No, you're not. But it's cool. I'll make some coffee as soon as I put some pants on." The itch behind Keith's ear had moved to his ass, and he worked at it under his boxers as he disappeared behind an accordion-style divider wall that separated where he slept from the rest of the wide-open loft.

"You've got quite the roster of friends, Agent Kirby," Roselita said as she took off her sunglasses and cased the apartment.

"Well, I can't imagine you've got any, Agent Velasquez," Ned said as he pushed past her in the doorway. It was the first thing he'd said to Roselita since he'd come out of the holding cell.

Roselita didn't answer, and Dane smiled. "He's got a point there, Roselita." Dane passed her, too, and walked into the loft. Roselita followed and closed the door.

The loft looked more like a day room in a college frat house than a full-grown man's home. Sixties and seventies horror-film posters hung haphazardly on the walls with thumbtacks, and thrift-store bookshelves were filled with graphic novels, ragged and well-read pulp paperbacks, and VHS cassette tapes of even more old-school horror movies. The top shelf of a tall bookcase to the far right, close to the kitchen area, held a massive blown-glass hookah, green with specks of white and blue at the base. Six leather-wrapped pipes fell down the sides of the rectangular unit like the tendrils of an octopus. The steel grating on top of the liquid-filled pipe was pristine and shiny and looked unused. The loft smelled of incense and hippie. "Why are we here, Kirby?"

"I was fixing to ask you the same thing, Dane," Keith said as he appeared from behind the divider. He was now wearing a pair of loose-fitting Levi's and a *Day of the Dead* T-shirt that used to be black three hundred washings ago and was now more of a light gray.

"Keith, you remember this guy?"

Ned tipped his chin and cocked a half smile.

"Of course, man—Ned fuckin' Lemon. It's been a hot minute." They shook hands in a way that turned into a shoulder bump—a man hug. "I heard you were back, but I didn't believe it."

"Well, you can now. You got any real cigarettes?" Ned shot a sideways glance at Dane.

"Uh, no," Keith said. "I don't smoke. Not anymore. It's been almost three years now. Second-hardest thing I've ever done."

Ned scowled. "When did everyone in Waymore get so goddamn

healthy?" He walked toward the kitchen and opened the fridge as if it belonged to him, and Keith mouthed the words "What the hell?" at Dane.

Dane held out a palm as if to tell him that all would be revealed in due time. Keith nodded.

"This is Special Agent Roselita Velasquez with the FBI," Dane said. Roselita tipped her chin. Keith worked at the itch on his ass a little more. Neither of them spoke. Keith didn't have to be told Roselita was police. She reeked of it.

Dane sighed and began to explain. "Listen, Keith, Ned needs a shower and maybe some clean clothes. As bad as this may sound, his pants are now being held as evidence in a crime scene, and he can't be walking around in those sweats on loan from the sheriff's office."

Keith scratched and watched Ned close the fridge and lean heavily against the kitchen counter, letting his long, unwashed hair fall into his face.

"Yeah," Keith said. "Cool. Whatever y'all need."

"And that coffee you mentioned wouldn't be a bad idea, either, if you're still offering."

"Yeah, no worries." When Ned turned to face his friends, he looked exhausted and filthy. Keith pointed over to the divider. "Ned, the bathroom is over there on the other side of that wall and the bed."

Ned pushed himself off the counter, nodded as if it was a struggle just to keep his head up, and disappeared behind the portable wall without a word.

"There are clean towels under the sink, too," Keith shouted. "And as far as clothes go, grab whatever fits—mi casa, su casa. Oh, but don't take anything from the pile at the foot of the bed. That's all dirty. No telling what's in there. Otherwise, take whatever you need."

Ned still didn't answer—no thank-you, no okay, no nothing—but Keith didn't seem bothered by it. He gave the itch on his ass a break, walked into the kitchen, scooped some coffee from a can in the cabinet, filled the plastic machine with a tumbler of tap water, and flipped the switch on. It lit up, and he pulled out a chair to take a seat at the kitchen table, where Dane and Roselita had already settled in. Roselita nodded and Keith nodded back. He noticed Roselita staring at the hookah. "It's never been used. I just thought it looked cool."

"It does," Roselita said before adding, "and I don't care if it's been used. None of my business."

"Right on, then," Keith said. It was clear, though, that he felt uneasy around Dane's new friend.

Once they could all hear the water running in the shower, Keith broke the uncomfortable silence in a whisper. "Holy shit, Dane, where the hell did he come from?"

"I'm not quite sure yet. I just found out he was back the day before yesterday."

"Jenkins and Boner told me he was back, but I didn't believe it was him. They said they found him in the woods. They said you were there, too, and Darby Ellis had him locked up down at the station for shooting some old-timer up the mountain. Seriously, though, I didn't even think to call you or go down and ask Darby himself because I really didn't think it was him. And because, I mean, Jenkins and Boner are full of shit most of the time."

"Well, it's him."

"Did he really kill somebody?"

"No." Dane shook his head as if the notion of it were preposterous. "But I can't prove it one way or another—not yet, anyway."

"Dane—it's been what? Ten years since he disappeared?"

"Coming up on nine."

"And you don't believe he did it? Boner said he was stone-cold drunk, still holding the damn gun."

"It's circumstantial, Keith. You know Ned as well as I do. He would never shoot anybody. He doesn't have it in him."

"I don't know, Dane. He looks like shit. And people change, man. And who knows what the hell he's been up to since he left."

"You're right, Keith. People change, but not like that they don't, and not Ned. I don't believe it for a second. Neither should you. And once you hear everything other than what you heard from Jenkins and Boner you'll understand. Everything about it stinks; I just can't tell you why. He might've been set up."

Keith leaned back enough to tip the front two chair legs from the ground. "Who the hell would want to set up Ned Lemon for murder? As if the poor bastard hasn't been through enough already—and where's he been? Why did he come back?"

"I've got my suspicions, but to be honest, Ned's problem is not my main focus here. We're actually here running down a lead that could help us find a missing child—an eleven-year-old boy named William Blackwell. Does that name mean anything to you?"

Keith didn't hesitate with his answer. "No, but you think Ned knows something about him?"

"How about we wait on him to get out here so I don't have to tell this story twice."

Roselita's antsy leg bounced up and down under the table. She kept looking at her phone while Dane and Keith had their conversation. She felt like they were wasting time again, and now this Ned guy and his predicament seemed to be part of her new partner's angle. She didn't like it. She didn't like it at all. They had been tasked with finding a child, not with proving the innocence of one of Kirby's childhood buddies, and once again she was sitting in a chair instead of moving. She hated the whole idea of heading out to this damn farm with one lowlife to smooth over talking to another lowlife. And she wasn't happy about O'Barr allowing it to happen, either. The old man was taking too many liberties here, and lives were at stake. Lives had already been lost. Innocent lives. This was not at all what she'd signed up for. Roselita felt she'd be better off up here on her own, but for now she was going to keep her mouth shut and ride it out.

The coffee maker burped and Keith got up to pour three mismatched mugs of joe from the carafe. He set the mugs on the table along with a thin carton of milk that he sniffed at first before setting down. He retook his seat. "I knew you were working for the GBI now, Dane, but I thought you were a glorified secretary or something. I thought you didn't do shit like this anymore—you know, like real cop shit."

"He doesn't." Roselita blew at the steam coming off of her mug and then sipped her coffee. She scowled. "And I gotta ask. Did I hear you say you know a man named Boner? As in hard-on?"

Dane sighed and Keith sipped his coffee. "As in, that's his last name, yeah."

Roselita shook her head. "Wow."

"And who are you again, exactly?"

"Oh, allow me," Dane said. "Keith Bell, Agent Roselita—don't call her Rose—Velasquez here, as of yesterday, is my new partner."

"We are not partners."

"And as you can see, we're already besties."

Roselita shook her head and lifted her mug as a sarcastic toast to her and Dane's newfound partnership. Keith did the same. "Okay, then," he said, and then stuck out his hand. Roselita met it with a firm shake. Keith wasn't expecting it. His arms were cut and vascular, and cluttered with tattoos. He hadn't had all his work done at once, like a sleeve, but had big colorful pieces of old-school traditional art that looked like they came right off the wall of Sailor Jerry's tattoo parlor. On his left forearm, a blue anchor wrapped in a red and yellow ribbon that displayed the date 3-13-10 took up most of the bare skin. The piece was prominent, and Roselita assumed the date must've held some significance for Keith, but she didn't care enough to ask what it was. He also had some sort of branding or scarification on his upper biceps, but it was mostly covered by his T-shirt. Roselita was indifferent about tattoos. She herself didn't have any, but she did find two of Keith's worthy of her interest. They were matching circular symbols on the insides of both of his lower arms, right under the creases in his elbows. Both tattoos, each about the size of a half-dollar, were rings with triangles in the middle. She'd seen the symbols before.

"You're an alcoholic?" Roselita said, still keeping her grip on Keith's hand.

Dane's chin dropped to his chest. "C'mon, Velasquez. Do you have to be this charming everywhere we go?"

"No, Dane," Keith said. "It's cool. And it's a legit question. I'm not ashamed of it. But can I have my hand back first?" He looked down at his arms and Roselita let go of his hand. "Yeah, I am," he said. "But I've been sober five years this coming October."

Roselita leaned back and crossed her arms. "But Kirby told me on the way over here that you were the bartender for the place downstairs?"

"I'm the backup. Nicole is the main bartender. But yeah, I fill in sometimes. Mostly I do the books now that Harold is getting up there in age. His sight ain't so good anymore."

"And that's not a problem for you?"

"What?"

"Being around booze all the time."

"It actually helps, believe it or not." Keith smiled. He had a good one. "Keep your demons close, you know? Shit like that."

Roselita lost interest as quickly as she found it. "Whatever you say, buddy."

Keith rubbed at the circles tattooed on his arms and gave his attention back to Dane. "Is she always like this?"

"Oh, yeah, she's a real peach. She loves to be called darling, too. Try it out."

"Um, I'll pass," he said, and Roselita took a big swig from her coffee cup, nearly draining it. She set it back down on the table.

"Look, I'm not trying to be a bitch here. I'm glad to meet you, Keith. Congrats on your five-year chip. That's a long haul. My father was an alcoholic, abusive piece of shit who never made it through one of the twelve steps, so good on you. I'm not judging, but you have to forgive me. Me and your homeboy here are supposed to be working a multiple homicide and a missing person's case that might—and that's a strong might—have something to do with a place up here called the Farm."

"The Farm," Keith repeated, and looked at Dane. "You're heading out to the Farm?"

Dane said nothing and Roselita ignored the interruption. "So I'm sorry for being curt, but that's where we should be right now. Not playing nursemaid to a guy"—Roselita pointed a thumb over her shoulder toward the bathroom—"who may or may not have killed someone who has nothing to do with our case. We are nowhere close to the scene of any of the crimes under our charge, or out there interviewing people who might know something, or pursuing suspects involved, you know, real police work—instead we're here drinking stale Maxwell House above a bar in Mayberry four hours away from where our original dead body dropped, chasing down a lead that has something to do with chickens and boners."

Keith listened to Roselita rant, slightly impressed.

"So to sum up: People are dead. A lot of people. And more people are likely to end up dead while we sit here gabbing. And the longer this little high-school reunion takes, the less likely we are to find out who's responsible for any of it—or find this kid Kirby mentioned, if he isn't dead already. But it's cool. We can wait for that asshole to take a bath—and you have to admit, that guy *is* an asshole."

Keith leaned back even further in the unfinished pine chair and studied Roselita's tight, impatient expression. "She doesn't know, does she?" he asked Dane.

"No, I haven't told her anything. You got any sugar?"

"Yeah, it's in the cabinet above the coffee maker."

"Told me what?" Roselita said.

Dane got up and opened the cabinet. He took out the small sack of Dixie Crystal sugar and grabbed a spoon from the drawer beneath him. On a whim, he turned the can of coffee in the cabinet so he could see the logo—Maxwell House. He tipped the can to look at the date printed on the lid and it read: BEST IF USED BY APRIL 2010.

He closed the cabinet and smiled before returning to the table and refilling Roselita's cup of stale Maxwell House. "As you might've already guessed, Ned and I used to be pretty close—Keith, too, but Ned dropped off the radar coming up on a decade ago."

"I'm sorry to hear that. I can't imagine why."

"No, you can't. You see, Ned used to be the one guy everybody knew was going to amount to something. We were all a bunch of losers growing up in a small town that didn't leave a lot of options open for advancement, but Ned was smart, funny, driven, all that. He knew about computers and stuff like that before most of us even knew what the Internet was. He was college bound with an academic scholarship, and that doesn't happen all that often up here. You're born here. You stay here. You end up working in the granite quarries your whole life, you drink yourself to death, or you cook crank for the Burroughs up on Bull Mountain. But whatever road you take, it's normally a shit life and in the end, you die here. As an adult looking back, that isn't really true. In fact, being from a place like this is something you tend to be proud of once you get some sense about you, but when you're a dumbass kid, all you want to do is get high and get out. Ned was getting out, and we all knew it. He'd be the one to put Waymore on the map—North Georgia's first legal claim to fame. He was going to be the next Steve Jobs or some shit. Maybe the first Steve Jobs before Steve Jobs became Steve Jobs—or whatever. You hear what I'm saying."

Roselita still looked bored and antsy. "So, I'm guessing something terrible happened and all that changed?"

"Yeah. Something did," Keith said. "A few things did. The first one happened during our last year of high school. Dane and me were seniors. Ned was a year younger. There was a car wreck out by the Slater Street Bridge." Keith told the rest of the story while staring into his coffee cup. Roselita noticed Dane doing the same thing. "Some dumb kids were acting the fool, dropping cinder blocks off the bridge in front of cars. A woman died."

"Some dumbass kids, huh?"

"Yeah, but that's not the point. Ned was there, too. He didn't do anything, but he was there. He was trying to help. The deputies who arrived on the scene saw a longhaired kid trying to yank open a car door, and instead of trying to help him, they tossed him on the ground. When they searched him, he had an ounce of weed in his pocket. A woman died that night, but instead of trying to find out who did it, they focused on Ned—who got arrested. He ended up being charged as an adult for possession with intent to distribute and was sent to Tobacco Road Prison in Augusta. He did four years of a ten-year sentence. No one ever found out who really caused the accident or why, and since the case went cold, it seemed like the whole town turned on Ned just for being there. In a small town like this one, when no one is to blame, folks tend to start pointing fingers at whoever they want. In this case, Ned was painted as a drug dealer who was most likely responsible for the accident in some way when all he was trying to do that night was help. He got four years' hard time and a scarlet letter for his trouble."

"So Ned's fast track out of McFalls came to a screeching halt."

"Yeah, it did. He went to prison. He was seventeen, man. It's fair to say he has a right to be bitter."

"Tough break."

Keith was getting edgy, but Roselita didn't care. She'd heard these sad-sack stories her whole life. Most of the time the sucker in those stories was their own worst enemy. No one ever took accountability for their actions. He was holding. He got caught. The rest is superficial. She sipped her coffee. It still tasted like shit.

"Everything about that night—what happened, what happened to

Ned—was fucked. He had nothing to do with it, but he took the wrath of the county—all of it—all the same." Keith kept staring into his coffee cup. He rubbed at the circular tattoos on his arms.

Dane put a hand on Keith's shoulder and took over. "Anyway, after that, nothing was the same anymore. Ned eventually got out and started working in the quarries. Not quite the life he had imagined for himself." Dane sipped his coffee. "Anyway, fast-forward a few years. I had become a fireman and eventually the fire chief here. One of the first things I did after I got the job was call Ned. I told him to go down to Forsyth, Georgia, and get all the training he could so I could get him a job working for me—to help get his life back. I owed him that much."

"Why?"

"Why what?"

"Why did you owe him?" Dane stared at Roselita until she put it together on her own. "Because it was your weed he was holding, wasn't it?"

Dane just stared back into his coffee mug.

"His and mine," Keith said, not wanting Dane to carry the weight of his omission by himself.

Roselita shook her head dismissively. She didn't care but understood the guilt. "Okay. I'm tracking. So then what?"

"He did it," Dane said without looking up. "He went and got certified in Forsyth and came to work for me running the county fire department. We worked together every day and he did the job better than anyone I knew. He found a place not far from where we're sitting right now, and I think it's fair to say that he was pretty happy. It was a good time overall."

"And so then what happened? He started eating dickhead pills?"

"No," Dane said. "That's when the other shoe dropped."

Keith excused himself and stepped outside on the landing for some air. It was obvious that he'd heard this story enough not to want to hear it again.

Dane waited until Keith closed the door to start talking again. "Every year the county used to throw a big shindig on the Fourth of July. Keith's parents funded the fireworks show. They'd get this huge outfit over from South Carolina to come in and light the place up. Everyone alive and breathing from here to Fannin all the way to Gatlinburg, Tennessee, would come to downtown Waymore. It was a big deal. The Fourth around here was bigger than Christmas—no joke. It was something to see."

"You said *was*. What happened?"

Dane stared at his reflection in the coffee cup. Suddenly he didn't feel like talking.

"The last Fourth of July celebration in McFalls County was in 2010. We stopped doing it because of what happened. Too many people around here were opposed to it after that."

"Well, what happened?"

"Something went wrong—right from the start. Something in the mechanics of the machine that handled the fireworks malfunctioned. Two of our guys from the FD—two volunteers—and one of the guys from the Carolina outfit who owned the fireworks rig were burned really badly. All three of them died a few weeks later at the Burn Center in Augusta." Dane drank some coffee and Roselita could see the memory age Dane's face like a time lapse.

"That's terrible, Dane, really, but what's it got to do with Lemon?"

Dane slid his coffee cup away from him. "They were Ned's guys. He hired them. He trained them. He was supposed to be in charge of the whole operation. The kid who died was nineteen. When the whole thing happened, Ned took it pretty hard. He blamed himself."

"Accidents happen, Dane. That's life. People get hurt in that line of work. I can understand the concept of losing people under your command, but if I'm not mistaken, weren't you the head honcho around here? I mean, you were the Fire Chief, right?"

Dane's stare got a little more distant. "I was."

"Then don't take this the wrong way, but wouldn't that make all of that something that happened under your watch? No disrespect, but where were you?"

"I wasn't there."

Dane's phone buzzed in his pocket, but he just glared into his cup at nothing. It rang again. He still didn't move.

"Dane?" Roselita said. "Your phone? Could be August."

Dane stayed distant.

"Dane," Roselita said again. "Are you okay?"

Dane snapped back to the moment, reached into his pocket, and took out his phone. He tapped it to read the number on the display. "It's my girlfriend. I've got to take this." He actually didn't need to nor did he want to. But he didn't want to talk about the Fourth of July anymore, either. He stood and answered the phone. He walked out onto the landing and passed Keith on the way in.

"Hello?" Dane closed the door behind him. Keith poured himself another cup of coffee and sat back down at the table. Roselita wasn't positive, but she was pretty sure she'd just gotten blown off. "Keith, right? Listen. When we were back at Sheriff Ellis's office, Dane mentioned having to go see a fella named Eddie—"

"Eddie Rockdale?"

"Yeah," Roselita said, and leaned forward on the table. "And the sheriff got all bug-eyed about it, kind of like you just did a few minutes ago when I mentioned the Farm. Why all the trepidation about Dane going out to see this guy Eddie?"

"Why all the what?"

Roselita rolled her eyes and clarified. "What's the story with those two?"

Keith blew at his coffee, though it was already cold, and thought about the best way to put it. "That's his story to tell, Agent Velasquez. And if he hasn't told you, then I guess he doesn't want you to know. You're his partner; maybe you should ask him."

"Well, at least tell me why the Fourth of July is so hard for him to talk about. He was telling me about the malfunction and how Ned carried it like it was his fault, but what about Kirby? What happened to him?"

Keith took a long, slow breath before he answered. "Agent Velasquez, that was the day his whole family died."

CHAPTER SIXTEEN

"Dane, we need to talk."

"Hey babe, now's not the best time. I'm about to leave Keith's. We're heading out to the Farm."

"The Farm? As in Rockdale's Farm in Hard Cash?"

"Yeah."

"Why the hell are you going out there?"

"It's a longer story than I have time for right now, but don't worry. It's going to be fine. We can talk later when I get home."

"I'm not going to be home tonight."

That was good. Dane didn't think he would be, either, but now he didn't need to feel bad. He redirected the blame. "What? Why not?"

"Because I'm going to my sister's."

"That's great. I may be late getting in." Dane felt equal parts disappointment and relief. He didn't understand that feeling, but it always accompanied this situation. That wasn't true. He knew why. Misty was his woman now, but the idea of seeing her later left him unsettled. He knew he needed to tell her. He hated himself for not telling her already. He needed to tell her before she found out from—the thought froze in his brain and dread poured over him. His head began to spin. She said they needed to talk. What did she want to talk about?

The lab report.

He slapped at the empty pocket on his leg. Of course it was empty. He had left the paperwork from Dr. McKenzie in his other pants, lying on the floor in the bedroom. She could've found them this morning while she was cleaning up.

Stupid, Dane. Stupid. You've been laser focused on keeping that information close to your chest for over a week now, just so you could just leave it on the floor? Damnit.

The only thing he could do worse than waiting to tell her was letting her find out about it on her own. He looked through the window at Keith and Roselita staring back at him through the blinds. Roselita looked different. She looked—softer somehow. Dane knew that look well. It was sympathy. It was that sad look of sympathy he'd grown accustomed to. There was no doubt about it. He'd been enduring that look his whole adult life. That "poor bastard" look that he got from people when they first found out what happened—when they found out what he did. Now Roselita had been infected by that look. Keith must've told her. They were talking about the Fourth. Of course Keith told her. It wasn't a secret. It was public record that Dane was a murderer. He just enjoyed being around people who didn't feel like they had to walk on glass when he was around—people who didn't have to choose their words wisely before they spoke. "Shit," he said.

"Are you talking to me?"

"What? No, babe. I'm just—never mind—listen—" He was almost scared to ask. "So we can talk at Jenn's house, then—later?"

"I guess we'll have to."

"Misty—I'm sorry. It's just this case, and this kid, it's got me all tied up."

"It's fine, Dane. I'll see you at Jenn's when you're done. Be careful out there at Rockdale's. I hate that man."

"I know and I will."

Misty ended the call. Dane stared at the phone and looked out over the railing into the alley that ran between Lucky's and the post office. It was one of the spots where he and Gwen would sneak off to smoke cigarettes on nights out at the bar, or just to catch some shade from the heat while Dane was at work. There were so many places like that in this town. He was born and raised here, but when all was said and done, it was Gwen's town. In a way, she took it from him, and he felt selfish for thinking it since he'd taken everything from her. That's why he left and moved to

Fannin. Coming back here was like coming back to her. Maybe subconsciously, that's why he picked Bear Creek to go escape to when he first got the news. He wanted to share it with her first. He wanted to tell her he was coming home to her whether he wanted to or not.

He looked at the navy blue canopy across the street—above the bookstore Keith's great-grandparents built this town around—and could see the far corner of Noble Park. He could smell the cigarette smoke and hard candy on Gwen's breath mingling in the air. He could hear her laughing at the people coming in from out of town—the tourists and church groups with matching T-shirts. She didn't laugh like that often, but when she did, she laughed with a rumble from her belly and she smiled with her whole face. Jesus, he missed that laugh. He missed that smile—that face. He closed his eyes and asked her for a cigarette.

CHAPTER SEVENTEEN

"I remember the day I met you, Dane Kirby." Gwen's slim fingers inter-laced between Dane's on the wrought-iron handrail of the terrace outside Keith's loft. "You used to hate it that I smoked," she said.

"I never hated anything about you, Gwen." Dane looked back through the window at his friends. He wondered how crazy he looked talking to himself.

"Whatever you say, cowboy." Gwen shook a smoke out of a blue and white box and handed it to Dane.

Dane took the imaginary cigarette and let Gwen light it for him. He tried to remember how it felt to have that rush of hot smoke fill his broken lungs. Even now, knowing what he knew, he still missed it.

"You look handsome standing out here, Mr. Kirby."

"Thank you, Mrs. Kirby." Dane pointed down at the building across the street. "You remember that?" he asked.

"Of course I do."

"I miss stealing kisses from you under that awning."

"You never had to steal them, Dane. I was a willing participant." Gwen lit up a smoke of her own and blew the smoke out sideways, away from him, like she always did. Sliding his hand out from underneath hers, Dane turned and faced her. She was wearing a red skirt with a blue sleeveless sequined top that fit her like a second skin. A pattern of white stars danced across her chest. It was the outfit she was wearing that day. The day she died. The day Dane killed her. He could feel the tears swell-ing behind his eyes as he drank her in.

"You're thinking about that day again, aren't you?" Gwen asked, and brushed at his hair. "You always picture me wearing this when you think about that day." She pulled at the hem of her skirt. Dane said nothing. He looked down at her hips but he didn't close his eyes. He didn't want her to disappear, not yet. Gwen tilted his head up until he was looking directly into her black-coffee eyes. "It wasn't your fault, Dane."

The tears began to push their way out and Dane's eyes got wet.

"It was an accident," she said. "Accidents happen. How long are you going to do this to yourself?"

"I should never have let you and Joy ride in the back. I knew it was dangerous. I knew—I knew it was . . ."

"You didn't *let* me do anything, Dane. Seriously, when did I ever *let* you tell me what to do?" She took another drag and blew it out sideways. "I was a grown woman. I was capable of making my own decisions."

"But you don't know. You didn't see."

Gwen tossed her cigarette down over the terrace and they watched the sparks hit the street below.

"Dane, I live inside your head. I know everything that happened that day. Every time you drag yourself through it, I'm right there with you. I see and feel everything you do. You need to stop all this."

Dane's eyes glazed over. He didn't want to see it, but he knew he would. He didn't even know what they were out doing that day. That memory was lost. The rest was crystal clear. In that moment, they weren't standing on Keith's terrace anymore. They were loading up the truck on the Fourth of July.

"Hang on just a second," Dane said from the front seat of the truck. It was piled high with Dane's turnout gear. He'd stuck an extra SCBA air pack in there, too, and various other gear—a triage kit, an extra AED, and a whole med-pack still sealed with zip ties. "Shit." Dane popped the door of the Ford F-250 and tried to catch his helmet as it fell out. He missed and it hit the concrete at his feet.

Gwen picked it up. "Here." She handed it to him. "Leave all that stuff where it is. We can ride in the back."

Dane argued, but it was pointless; Gwen had already stepped up on the back tire and begun to pull herself over the fender well.

"Baby, I don't know. There are a lot of people on the road today. Just give me a second to clear all this out of here."

Gwen wasn't having it. She and Joy had ridden in the back of the big brush truck a dozen times before, so it was nothing new. The bed of the truck had a gas-powered pump and a huge plastic tank that carried two hundred gallons of water, along with fifty feet of folded yellow forestry hose. There was enough room for them to sit and plenty of things bolted to the truck bed to hold on to. And Joy liked to ride back there. Her little round face lit up. "Here—hand her to me," Gwen said, and reached over the side.

Dane stuffed his helmet back into the truck and held it in place while he slammed the door to keep the whole pile of Kevlar and medical equipment from spilling out. He bent over and lifted his five-year-old daughter up into the air. She barely weighed a whisper. She was petite like her mother. Joy had the lightest, finest blond hair Dane had ever seen. He could always spot her right away at a playground or at school because that hair practically glowed. She was the second-most beautiful girl he'd ever seen. He spun her above his head a complete three hundred and sixty degrees before setting her next to her mother on a stack of folded canvas tarps that smelled of ash and burnt wood. The tarps were used to overhaul, cover, and protect property from smoke or water damage during a fire. *Hardly the appropriate throne for a princess of Joy's caliber*, Dane thought, *but it would have to do*. He grabbed at Joy's soft, puffy cheeks and looked into her big green eyes. When the light hit them just right, he could see flecks of gold in them. "You hold on to Mommy now, okay? And don't touch any of the stuff on the pump. That's all Deddy's work stuff."

"I know, Deddy. You tell me every time."

"We're fine, Dane. Let's go." Gwen put an arm around the little girl and pulled her in snug.

Dane walked over to the driver's side and opened the door. "Hang on tight, ladies." Dane wheeled the truck out onto White Bluff Road. Dane remembered Nirvana's "Heart-Shaped Box" was playing on the stereo and Gwen was singing in the back. She was a terrible singer. It was possibly the only thing she wasn't good at. He remembered the sun sparkling off the blue sequins of her shirt in the rearview mirror and Joy's blond hair blowing back from her head in frantic strands like the streamers on the handlebars of a bicycle. He remembered his daughter smiling, her big green eyes open against the wind, but that was it.

He'd only made it about six miles down the road before he lost control of the truck. Dane hadn't heard the shot itself so much as the echo. It sounded like a .30-30. That was the reason he took his eyes off the road. The two-hundred-gallon tank of water in the bed of his truck caused it to be considerably top-heavy, so even at forty-five miles an hour—the speed the investigators concluded that Dane was going—the deer suddenly appearing in the road that made Dane yank the wheel to avoid it caused the vehicle to capsize.

He cracked his head against the back window and blacked out almost immediately, but not before seeing the deer's insides spatter over the windshield like a bucket of wet purple rags and red paint. There were pinches of hot white light in his vision and then nothing—just full black. He was informed of the rest later.

The truck had tumbled over at least twice, judging by the extent of the damage done to it and the road. The deer had just run right out in front of him. There was nothing Dane could've done. That's what everyone said. Nothing he could've done any differently to avoid what happened. But he never believed that. When he regained consciousness, the sun was going down, but from the way he was hanging, it looked more like it was coming up. The skyline was all wrong. He couldn't keep his head right. Nothing made any sense. He could feel the bits of glass embedded in his face and the blood in his eyes. They stung. He wiped at them but could hardly get his hands to work.

He fumbled at the latch on his seat belt, but when he finally clicked the lever, his full weight fell to the roof below him and pain shot from his neck to his knees. The pain was brilliant but clarifying. It allowed his brain to process what had just happened. He tried to say his wife's name. He tried to scream her name, but it came out a thick, wet wheeze that sprayed more blood over his chin and dripped onto the roof liner he was folded on. He kept trying to scream. Patches of Dane's memory were missing from those first few minutes of being awake. He couldn't remember getting out of the truck, but did remember stumbling in a puddle of mud and water from the tanker. He also remembered Gwen's red skirt flapping in the breeze. That piece of fabric was the only thing moving when he saw her. That's when he stopped calling her name. He knew from the unnatural way her body lay, still and broken, that there was no way she could answer him, and she never would again. Dane's silence turned to screams and cries for help, and he felt as if he were standing outside himself, watching another version of himself go mad. He sat there in the grass, sobbing and holding Gwen's limp body. There was another gap in his memory here, but he managed to drag her out of the tall grass, slick with both of their blood, and collapsed onto the shoulder of the road.

He blacked out again. A fire in the ravine began to burn its way into the woods as Dane lay still next to the body of his dead wife. When he opened his eyes, he reached over and took her hand. The modest oval diamond ring on her finger sparkled in the sun and the light of the fire. Dane screamed again and faded back into the darkness. Each time he returned to the moment he begged God to have mercy—to make it a dream—but it wasn't a dream. Dreams didn't hurt like this. He asked God to let him die instead. He begged.

Dane lay there as the day faded to a light purple, sticky and broken on the asphalt shoulder of White Bluff Road for nearly forty-five minutes before the first car approached and stopped just beyond the spreading fire in the woods. After that first car stopped, it only took another five minutes before the entire county knew what had happened. Fire crews took to the woods to contain the blaze and sheriff's deputies blocked off the road from rubberneckers. Dane was sedated and put in the back of an ambulance with several broken ribs and a mangled leg. Most of what happened next he had to be told by the people that arrived afterward. It was Ned who found Dane's daughter. He was the one who thought to start looking up instead of down as they canvased the woods. He spotted Joy's tiny, twisted body more than twenty feet up, in a cradle of broken branches and moss-covered limbs—in the arms of trees more than thirty yards from where the truck had crashed.

The tanker truck had obliterated the animal that ran into the road. Its carcass was strewn in chunks in the street. There was no way to tell if it had been wounded prior to running in front of the truck or not, but Dane had heard the shot, or at least the faint echo of it.

"It sounded like a .30-30," Dane said to himself, coming out of the memory.

"Dane," Gwen said, pulling him out completely. "How many more times are you going to put yourself through that?"

Dane looked down at the street, ignoring her question. "I'm riding out to Hard Cash. I'm going to find this boy. Maybe then I can—"

"Get yourself killed," Gwen finished his sentence. "I'm sorry, Dane. But I don't want to be around to see that."

"Wait," Dane said, and reached toward her, but she was gone. He gripped the wrought-iron railing with both hands until his knuckles went white. He could feel every set of eyes burning into his back through the window behind him, but he didn't care. Right then, in that moment, he didn't care about anything. He considered hopping the railing, but decided against it. It wouldn't be high enough to kill him anyway.

CHAPTER EIGHTEEN

The Farm was a seventeen-acre parcel of land nestled in the hay fields and soft red dirt of Hard Cash Valley, a community on the outskirts of the county, near the southern border. It had originally been a small dairy farm run by a couple named Manny and Belinda Sweetbriar. In the midsixties, the farm eventually failed, like a lot of other small farms in the South, and the bank foreclosed on the property. On the same day the bank put all the cows up for auction, Manny sat down in his favorite chair in the couple's modest single-wide trailer and shoved a rifle in his mouth. While Belinda was in the kitchen filling out paperwork with the loan officer, her husband blew out the back of his skull, allowing a young man by the name of Casper Rockdale to buy the land for a song. Casper had been a medic in Vietnam, and got himself disfigured when his helo went down over the Mekong Delta. He survived the crash and his injuries provided him with both a ticket home and a fat compensation check. After he bought the land from the bank, Casper had only a single aspiration—to grow pot on those seventeen acres and sell it out of the trailer whose inside walls had once been painted with Manny Sweetbriar's brains. It was a good plan, but there were two major flaws Casper hadn't seen coming. For one, the land was useless for farming, mostly rock and red clay. It might as well have been seventeen acres of blue steel. The seed wasn't going to take. Not that it mattered, because the second problem—an infinitely more dangerous problem—was the Burroughs family. They ran Bull Mountain, the same mountain that loomed down over Casper's newly acquired patch of rubble. The Burroughs also had a firm lock on the dope trade. No one dared to edge in on their dealings, and anyone stupid enough to try ended up as dead as Manny. Those boys were not to be trifled with, so Casper amended his plan. He'd given the US Army one of his eyes and a good chunk of the left side of his face, but he still felt that those six years in the jungle hadn't stolen nearly as much as they'd given. Killing gooks and farming weed weren't the only things Casper had learned overseas. He'd also spent a good bit of time in the underground Vietnamese cockfighting pens. He knew the kind of money they generated over there, and as far as he knew, those boys up on Bull Mountain didn't fool with game chickens. That racket was wide-open as long as he kicked them up a cut of his earnings.

He started with a stack of plywood he stole from a construction site outside of Rabun County and a roll of chicken wire he bought with his first disability check. Out behind that dump of a trailer, Casper built a small but sturdy row of chicken coops. He wasn't a carpenter by any means, but he built those boxes well enough to keep out the foxes and coons. A few months later, he traded a pound of Burroughs-grown marijuana to a Vietnamese breeder for a shoebox full of tiny, chirping, blue-headed chicks that had been smuggled stateside. Those humble pens Casper built in 1966, along with the birds that survived the initial trial-and-error period, lived to multiply and eventually became what everyone around Hard Cash simply referred to now as the Farm. Now, nearly half a century later, that slab of red clay in the middle of nowhere had become a premier breeding ground for champion roosters whose bloodlines could be traced all the way back to Casper's days in the war. Casper never had any children of his own, so when the time came to step down and let someone else run the show, his sister's boy, Eddie, became his apprentice and his eventual heir. The Rockdale Farm wasn't the biggest stretch of prairie land in McFalls County, but it was one of the most well known. It was now also one of the most infamous cockfighting scenes in the entire United States. Contenders and buyers from all over the country, as well as places like Mexico, Canada, Vietnam, Korea, and the Philippines, came to shop Rockdale's birds. They also came to *show*, as it was called, at one of Rockdale's seasonal blood sports—an event that most people didn't even believe existed. Cockfighting was something folks saw on TV in old

Sergio Leone films, not in the foothills of North Georgia, and on film it was definitely not treated with the same hardcore emotion shared by the competitors. Some people would go so far as to call it spiritual.

Dane was not one of those people. Ned, on the other hand, during his years working at the granite quarries, had become a fan. He'd taken solace in training gamecocks once he was released from prison. It was something he found he was good at—something all his own. He was twenty-two when he got out of prison, and he felt lost in a world he didn't recognize. Being out in the open air of the Farm working with the animals made sense to him. It helped him regain footing in his life. Eddie Rockdale, Rooster to his friends, had known Ned before he was arrested. They ran in the same circles, and Eddie courted a fair amount of trouble himself. He even ended up spending a few months in a cell next to Ned at Tobacco Road Prison, so he turned out to be one of the few locals who welcomed Ned home when he got out. Eddie never passed judgment. They were brothers with matching knuckle tattoos to prove it. Ned felt at ease on the Farm with Eddie. It was the only place in the county—the county he was born and raised in—that felt like home. Everyone else had either forgotten who he was, or worse—they remembered who he wasn't. Today the bond between them would be tested.

Dane borrowed Keith's Nissan Titan and drove it down State Road 515 until the forest broke open into massive fields of overgrown wheat and wildflowers. The landscape turned into a sea of violet, gold, and swaying rust. He slowly brought the truck to a stop at a sun-faded stop sign mounted to a petrified wooden post. Ned and Roselita just watched and waited as Dane looked both ways, scratched at his stubble. He shifted the truck into park and got out. He walked around to the front of the truck and crouched down. He rubbed his hands over the fresh indentations in the dirt. There were several tire tracks in the road, but only one set came from a compact car. It was unusual to see small tread like that out here. Cars that size had no business out here where the roads ended. That's why they'd borrowed Keith's truck and left the Infiniti at the station.

"What are you looking at?" Ned said from the window.

"Nothing." Dane rubbed at his chin again and got back in. He sat behind the wheel for a few beats before he pulled the shifter into drive and hung a right.

"You trying to earn your Eagle Scout pathfinder patch, Dane?"

"Shut up, Ned. It's just been a while since I've been out this way. Don't the roads out here turn to shit past this four-way?"

"Yeah, they get a little rough. Why?"

"Just keep your eyes peeled for something compact. A Volkswagen, maybe—something that doesn't belong."

"Why?" Roselita asked.

"Because cars like that don't fare well on roads out here. That's the reason we took this and not that hot rod of yours."

"It's not a hot rod."

"Whatever. I'm just saying that if someone drove a small car like that out here, they're likely not to be from around here, and they're likely to be stuck. Ned—which way am I going?"

"Just drive about a half mile down and pull off to the left after Tater's Rock."

Dane nodded as if it were coming back to him. "Right. I remember."

"Tater's Rock?" Roselita repeated like a question.

Ned explained. "Yeah, it's a big-ass chunk of limestone that looks like a fucking meteor crash landed. Nobody knows how it got there—kinda like those heads on Easter Island. It's a national treasure around here."

"Tater's Rock is a national treasure?" Roselita still couldn't believe August O'Barr had her out here running around with the Dukes of Hazzard.

"Yep. It should be, anyway."

"And why is it called Tater's Rock?"

Ned looked at Roselita as if that was the dumbest question he'd ever heard. "Because Tater named it."

"Who the hell is Tater?"

Dane shut down the banter. "It doesn't matter, Roselita. It's just a big rock. You'll recognize it when you see it. The high-school kids around here have been spray-painting shit on it since we were in school, so it should stick out like a sore thumb. We're almost there."

"Right," Roselita said, and began to recount out loud all the redneck shit she'd heard over the past few hours. "Tater—Boner—Rooster—everyone up here sounds like they were named after cartoons. Is there a Tweety Bird out here, too?"

Now Ned looked offended. "Watch your mouth, Velasquez. Tweety is good people. No reason to trash talk good folk."

Roselita wasn't sure if he was kidding. If he was, he didn't show it. Roselita rubbed at the bridge of her nose and Ned went back to hanging his head out the window like a dog. "It's right up there," he said. "On the left."

"I see it." Dane cut the truck to the left at the huge rock that had been painted green and white and said FUCK STATE FARM in detailed spray paint, and pulled the Nissan onto a road most people would've missed, just a set of twin ditches gnawed into the wheat grass by other big trucks like this one. Most of the roads out in this part of the county looked like this one—unmarked and unnamed. The few signs that were posted were handmade and put there by the families that lived out there. Soon enough, the truck's chassis was vibrating from hood to tailgate as Dane tried to keep it in the winding set of ditches. Every time the truck hit a stump or an exposed root, all three of them bounced an inch or two off the seat in the cab. At one point, Roselita's sunglasses were jarred off her face, but she caught them before they fell to the floorboard. "This is ridiculous, Kirby. You're going to break my neck driving like this."

"It ain't my driving. It's the road."

"C'mon, Kirby, are you sure you can even call this a road? It doesn't look like it's been driven on by anything with an engine—ever. I can feel my teeth rattle."

Dane adjusted the rearview mirror. "Relax, Roselita, we're almost there."

"Yeah, Rose, relax." Ned pulled the side mirror on the door inward and looked at his reflection. He rarely liked to look at his own face, but he didn't have to very long before they bounced again, hard enough to test the limits of the truck's shocks. Ned cracked his forehead against the window frame and Roselita caught her sunglasses a second time. She laughed as Ned rubbed his head. "That right there was the thumb of God, Lemon."

Dane revved the big-block V8 through the last stretch of ditch before the ground finally flattened out into red dirt. The ride smoothed out, and so did the conversation, until the talking stopped completely as Rockdale's house came into view. It was gorgeous. The two-story farmhouse looked like something ripped off the cover of *Southern Living*. The entire place was log built and trimmed with red brick. Perfectly pruned azalea bushes surrounded the house, with manicured flowerbeds surrounded by stone pavers underneath. The house was a far cry from the single-wide trailer Casper Rockdale had lived in all those years ago at the far edge of the property. The trailer was still there, and Dane could see it from where he stopped and parked the truck, but no one else mentioned it. No one looked toward the chicken coops or the row of X-shaped scarecrows made from wooden crossbeams that led back to the barn. All of them, including Roselita, who didn't expect to see a place anything like this, were out of the truck with their eyes now glued to the only thing more beautiful than the two-million-dollar home.

Her name was Lydia, and she was the lady of the house.

Lydia stood barefoot in the open doorway, leaning against the jamb as if she'd been expecting them. Dane was sure she had. Anyone in the house or down at the barn knew they were coming the second they turned off the main road back by Tater's Rock. Just because you couldn't see the security didn't mean it wasn't there. Two men with scatterguns weren't necessary anymore now that trail cams were so advanced. This place was well protected and for good reasons. Lydia was just one of them. The thin material of her cotton dress hugged her figure, showing off every curve exactly the way she wanted it to. The hem slapped against her thigh in the breeze to a rhythm that was almost hypnotic to watch. She pushed herself off the edge of the door and moved like river water across the porch to the steps. Dane took off his hat.

"Who the hell is that?" Roselita whispered to Dane. She sounded unsure of the question.

"That's Lydia," Dane said. "Eddie's wife." He smiled as he saw Roselita become speechless for the first time since they met. Lydia had that effect on people—men and women alike. Dane wasn't sure if Lydia and Eddie had ever been legally married, but it didn't matter. They'd been together longer than anyone could remember. Paperwork and court proceedings weren't necessary to enforce that fact. Eddie's reputation was enforcement enough.

Dane walked up to the steps first with his hat still in hand.

"Lydia."

"Well, hello there, Chief." She stared through Dane at the two people behind him.

"I'm not the chief anymore, Lydia. You know that, right?" Dane turned and followed her stare, but he knew she was just sniffing out Roselita. She was a stranger. She didn't belong. Lydia didn't bother to speak to her at all, but she smiled before she said hello to Ned. He nodded, looked down at nothing, and kicked at the dirt like a shy high-school kid.

"Sorry to hear about your Deddy passing," Dane said. "He was a good man."

"Thank you, Dane. He was. It would've been nice to see you at his funeral." Her voice was cold and distant.

"My new job—I know it sounds lame, but it makes it a little tougher to get back home as often as I'd like. But you're right. I should've been there. I'm sorry."

"I wasn't fishing for no apologies, Dane Kirby. Not tryin' to make you feel bad or nothin'. It's all right. I understand. I'm just saying that Deddy liked you. It would've been nice to see you, that's all."

"Thank you for saying that, Lydia. It means the world."

"So do you want to go ahead and tell me why you and Ned Lemon there are bringing city police to my house, or am I supposed to guess?"

Dane side-eyed Roselita and put his hat back on. "Lydia, you do know that I'm city police now, too, right?"

Lydia shook her hand out in front of her as if to dismiss what Dane said as heresy. "You may work for them, Dane—but you'll never be one of them." She drilled that last bit right into Roselita with a stare as hard as cast iron. Dane wasn't sure if Roselita would be insulted by that comment or quick to agree with it. Lydia didn't give her a chance to do either. "Well, since I'm having to guess and all, I'm guessing you're all here to talk to Eddie? Is that right?"

"That's right."

"Well then, bye, I suppose." Lydia tossed another glance over Dane's shoulder. "He's down at the barn. He lives in that damn barn." She spoke as if she preferred that he did and then added, "No one ever comes here to see me anymore." She disappeared into the house. The door closed behind her. Dane thought her words were curt. He didn't understand.

Roselita wiped at the sweat on her forehead. "You think that meant she was going to go let him know we're here, or are we just supposed to walk on down there?"

"Trust me, Roselita. He already knows we're here. Honestly, I'm surprised he even let her answer the door."

"Why? Because of her boyfriend here?" She nudged Ned with her elbow and nearly knocked the bone-thin Lemon off balance. Ned caught himself but looked pale and surprised.

"What?"

Roselita peeked over her sunglasses and a smug expression filled her round face. "C'mon, Lemon. I'm a detective, remember?"

Now Dane looked confused. "What are you talking about, Rose?"

"I thought you were good at this shit, Kirby. You saw the way that woman eye-fucked your buddy here, right? I mean, everyone I've met who's seen this guy acts like they've just seen a ghost, but her—she didn't have nothing but sugar for him. I would've guessed at first that she didn't know him, but she called him by his name, so now I'm guessing they've got a little history. That line about 'no one ever comes to see her anymore'? That was for your boy here. I'd bet my last dollar on it."

Ned became indignant. "You don't know what you're talking about, lady."

Roselita lifted her hands in the air and backed away. "Okay, Lemon. Whatever you say. It's none of my business anyway. Just an observation."

Dane wasn't sure what part of Roselita's theory he wanted to address first, so he opted to just shut it down instead. "Roselita, it ain't the time to go digging in a boneyard, and right now, we're standing smack-dab in the middle of one. Let's just do what we came out here to do. Keep your theories about what you think you know to yourself, before this whole thing turns into a huge waste of time."

Roselita shrugged and stuck her hands in her pockets. "Whatever you say, Kirby. And good lord, you people act like this guy Rockdale is some kind of Godfather or something. He's a chicken farmer, for Christ's sake. How scary can the guy be? I've been working this gig a long time and I've run down a lot of gangsters, and never have I had an *Eddie Rockdale* pop up on my radar. So I'm sorry, but the intimidation level from this guy is pretty low. Maybe the two of you need to dial down the fear factor a little and remember who's got the weight of the federal government on their side." She smirked at Ned. "Of course, you might have a little more reason to be afraid of the guy. If it was my old lady you were squeezing that lemon juice into, I'd be a little nervous, too."

"Dane"—Ned's balled-up fists were shaking—"I ain't never hit a woman before, but I'm telling you, your partner here needs to shut her mouth."

"I agree." Dane went to say something else, but he was interrupted by the click of the door latch.

It opened, and this time an old man whose age was impossible to determine appeared in the doorway. He had thin salt-and-pepper hair pulled back over his head tight in a frizzy ponytail, and he wore a white button-up shirt, open at the collar to expose an overflow of gray curly chest hair. Both of his sleeves were rolled up past his elbows, and veins in his arms showed through his paper-thin skin like faded tattoos. "Gentlemen," he said with a loud, drawn-out southern drawl as he made his way down the steps. "And lady," he added as he looked over Roselita from head to toe.

She was used to that sort of shit, and although it disgusted her, she let it go and stuck out her hand. "You must be Eddie," she said.

The old man smiled wide, showing off his pearly dentures, and shook Roselita's hand.

"I'm sorry for the intrusion," Roselita said. "But let me start off by saying you have a lovely home."

"Well, thank you, darlin'." The old man smiled even wider at Dane, who just stood quiet and watched Roselita eat another slice of condescension.

"You're welcome," Roselita said, and let go of the man's hand. "I believe you know my partner there." Roselita motioned at Dane. His chin had dropped to his chest.

"I do. I know that other fella behind you, too—but I don't believe I know you."

"Of course, my apologies again. I'm Special Agent Roselita Velasquez, with the Federal Bureau of Investigation, and my colleague, Agent Kirby over there, seems to believe you might be able to answer a few questions concerning an investigation we're working on."

The old man glanced over at Dane for a second, and then he smiled and narrowed his eyes on Roselita. "I'm sorry, darlin'. Who did you say you were, again?"

"Right," she said through gritted teeth. One more *darlin'* and this asshole was going to lose some more teeth. "Where are my manners?" she said, and reached into the pocket of her slacks to take out her ID. Dane didn't realize she was being baited until it was too late.

"I said my name is Roselita Velasquez, and—" A gunshot echoed out across the field and gravel popped and ricocheted off Roselita's shoes. Her whole body seized. When she realized what had just happened she jumped back, slammed into Ned, and dropped her credentials into the grass. She reached around to the small of her back. The old man didn't flinch at the shot.

"I'd leave that where it is, dear—leave your badge there on the ground, too. Tater's a wicked good shot, but he can't hear us and might not be able to tell from the scope on that M40 of his if that thing in the grass is a gun or not."

Roselita froze in place.

The old man kept talking. "Now you said your name is Velasquez. That right?"

Roselita's head moved in a swivel, looking for any sign of the shooter. She took occasional short glances at the old man's face and the other two men standing to her right. They all seemed unfazed by what had just happened. That's when Roselita noticed that the old man's left eye stared off, blank, in a slightly different direction from the other one, and his warped half smile caused most of the same side of his face to collapse and sag. Roselita began to feel the sting of her mistake. This old man wasn't Eddie Rockdale. He was Casper, Eddie's uncle. Dane had talked about him in the truck on the way there. He'd also warned her about talking—about being cocky. Roselita hadn't listened to any of it. "Dane," she said in an effort to defuse the heat or possibly gain an ally.

"Just ease it back and keep your hands out in plain sight, Rose."

"Velasquez," the old man chewed on the name. "I used to do business with a beaner named Velasquez." He took a step closer and gave Roselita a good once-over. "Now that I think about it, he mighta looked a little like you, too. Where you from, little lady?"

Roselita felt like she was going crazy. This old buzzard just had someone fire on two law-enforcement officials and now he was right back to being a sexist prick. "This racist son of a bitch just shot at me, Kirby, and you're asking me to ease it back?"

"Yes," Dane said. "Seriously. Show your hands so we can speed this along."

"Alabama," the old man said, and slapped at his jeans. "I bet you're Alabama born and raised."

"Casper, signal whoever you've got drawn down on us and let him know we ain't here for nothing but a conversation with Eddie."

Casper loomed over Roselita. "The stars don't glow all that bright over Alabama, do they, darlin'?"

"Call me darlin' again, and you'll find out just how bright they glow."

"Casper, I'm serious. Call 'em off."

"Well, Dane, I'm serious, too." Casper's tone changed. He stopped toying with Roselita and raised his voice a notch higher than Dane's. "You, of all people, oughta know better than to bring police out here without going through the proper channels. Much less lettin' them go diggin' around in their pockets like that."

"You're right, Casper, I do know better. It's my bad. I'm not even going to mention that you baited her. Now the woman is showing you her palms, so I'm asking you—one more time—call off your boy."

"Your bad," Casper mumbled as he stroked at the long, wiry whiskers of his gray goatee. Finally, the old man raised one hand up above his head long enough for the sunlight to catch the silver in one of his rings. He had one for every finger. When he lowered his arm, Dane and Ned both took a collective breath. The old man turned his attention back to a fuming but still-frozen Roselita Velasquez. "You can put your hands down now, and the name's Casper, not Eddie. Eddie is my sister's boy. But maybe the mistake was a good thing. Tater can be a bit more high-strung around him than me." Casper turned and walked toward the row of scarecrows.

"C'mon, Dane, Eddie's in the barn. He's sparring with a couple Mexicans and he's got a buncha money riding on it, so don't go taking food off the table. Keep it short, say yer piece, and keep Alabama there quiet."

"And that's it?" Roselita said. Her face was hot and red.

Dane held out a finger to hush her but didn't answer. "Good to see you, Casper."

"Yeah, yeah. Y'all come with me." The old man kept walking and Roselita picked up her badge from the grass. Everyone followed Casper down the path. Roselita did, too, but she kept looking back over both shoulders as she walked. She kept her eyes on everything she passed—a shed that looked like it might be an outhouse, a silver LPG tank that could hide a sniper.

"You're not going to see anyone," Dane said. "Tater's already back at the barn by now."

"Son of a bitch," Roselita said, and stopped.

"Seriously, Rose. Let it go." Dane watched as Roselita lifted her foot to inspect the bottom of her expensive hiking shoes.

"First I get shot at and no one seems to care, and then I have to wade through chicken shit—goddamnit."

Dane had to cover his face to hide the smirk as Roselita wiped her foot in the grass to get the shit off her shoe.

As they got closer to the barn they could hear the yelling. A small green Toyota Camry with a rusted-out side panel was parked in the grass beside a few big trucks outside the huge barn. "Does that car belong to the buyers?" Dane asked as Casper swung open one of the huge, rein-forced steel–framed doors.

"Yeah," Casper said. "You can fit fifty Mexicans into one of those things. It's like a goddamn clown car."

"Well, that's one mystery solved," Dane more or less mumbled to him-self, relieved as he thought about the tracks he'd spotted up at the main road. They walked in. Dane and Ned had seen this place before, but Roselita was getting her first look at what it was they did out there at the Farm. It could be impressive to an outsider. The barn was as big if not bigger than the main house and equally as well built. The inside of the building was separated down the middle by a neat dirt path, and both sides of the building were divided into six pits separated by waist-high walls of cedar planking, each one accessible by a set of hinged doors with rack-style locks. There were twenty or so of what looked like wooden lockers made of thick, hand-carved oak to the right of the show pits, shadow boxes that ran the length of the wall. Some of them were open and empty, but most of them were locked up tight with a variety of different padlocks.

Casper explained to Roselita, who looked as if she had a hundred questions to ask and didn't know where to start, how the birds were kept in the wooden boxes—locked up in the dark—until it came their time to fight. Keeping them isolated and in the dark kept them confused, angry, and more important—mean. Roselita felt like she'd just come out of one herself. The sound of birds cawing and pecking from the insides of the wooden boxes and the crowing from the pens outside were unnerving, but only Roselita felt it. Dane and Ned seemed to feel right at home. The yelling they'd heard outside the barn was coming from a group of men in the far-left corner. Several were speaking Spanish and they all were looking down at something none of the new arrivals could see yet. A tall black man with a mouth full of gold teeth was yelling louder than the rest. He was also the only one speaking English.

"All right, goddamnit. I told y'all before we came out here to knock off all that Spanish shit, so again—knock it off." The black man stood a good head taller than the rest of the group and he wore a bright white tank top that hugged his cut muscular torso.

Dane turned his head to Roselita. "That's Rooster." He nodded toward the man with all the gold in his mouth. "But don't call him that. You call him Eddie if anything, but I'd advise against saying anything at all. Let me and Ned handle it initially. Just stay back for now."

Roselita was taken aback and it played out across her face. She wasn't one to be easily surprised. "Eddie Rockdale is black?" she asked.

"Yeah, so?"

"So nothing. I just didn't expect—"

"Didn't expect what?" Casper said, interrupting the hushed conversation. "You got a problem with colored folk?"

Roselita stumbled over her words, backtracking. "No. I don't. I just thought—I mean I just didn't expect it is all. You said he was your sister's child. So I—"

"So I—so I—" Casper mocked. "My sister had a taste for dark meat, and contrary to popular belief, not all us southerners buy into all that racist shit you folks from Alabama do."

"I'm not racist."

"And I got two good eyes."

Ned snaked his way past Roselita and Casper. "Just hush, Velasquez. Seriously." He raised a hand to get Eddie's attention, and the tall black man in the tank top stopped talking. He stopped paying attention to what he had been doing as well. He glared at Ned.

"Y'all hold up a minute," he said to the group of Mexicans as he opened the plywood gate and stepped out into the dirt walkway. He didn't look at all pleased to see them—especially Ned. He approached them and they all felt the air in the barn thicken into pea soup.

This was not the greeting Dane expected to invoke by springing Ned from lockup and dragging him out here. Dane was confused.

Eddie stood about a foot in front of Ned, ignoring Dane and Roselita altogether. He looked down. Ned looked up. "Well, look at this motherfucker right here. I heard you was back. I heard you was back a while now, too." Rockdale cocked his head to the side and the bones in his neck popped. He licked at his teeth and the gold in his mouth shone.

All Ned said was "Sup, Rooster."

"Sup, Rooster, he says . . ." Rockdale repeated Ned's greeting like he was disgusted by it. He stared around at the rest of them and licked at his gleaming teeth again. He put his eyes back on Ned. "I was wondering when you'd get enough sack to make your way out here."

Roselita wanted to reach around to the small of her back again, but Dane must've known what she was thinking, because he shook his head just once and burned a "don't you fucking move" stare into his partner. Roselita didn't fucking move.

Ned didn't back off an inch, either. "The hell is your problem, Rooster? I've been busy, if you haven't heard."

"Oh, yeah. I heard. I heard all kinds of shit."

Ned stepped in closer and spread his legs in a boxer's stance, easing his left foot back for balance. Not a soul took a breath until Rockdale's grimace morphed into a huge golden smile that stretched across his face. His dark eyes softened. He leaned back and raised his arms out to his sides.

Ned eased his position and Rooster lifted Ned a good six inches off the ground in a bear hug that could've easily snapped his spine if he applied the right pressure. The entire group remembered how to breathe. Ned tapped on Rockdale's ribs. "All right, man," he wheezed. "Put me down before you break my back."

Rockdale let go, but held Ned out in front of him by his shoulders. "Damn, you done got skinny as hell, white boy. You lost some serious weight."

"Well," Ned said, and thumped Rockdale's abdomen. "You must've found it."

The two men hugged again but without all the bone-breaking bravado. Ned stayed on the ground this time.

"Damn, Ned. So when did you really get back?"

"A while ago. I should've come out sooner."

"But you had to go shoot somebody first is what I hear. That right? You shoot some old bastard up Bull Mountain?"

Ned didn't even squirm. "I ain't got the sack to shoot nobody, Eddie. You know that."

Eddie laughed. "Well, you damn right about that, but whatever. None of my business." He stared Ned up and down again. "Goddamn, it's good to see you, brother."

"You, too. Eddie. It's been a long time."

"Too long."

Eddie let him go completely and shifted his attention to Dane. "You just tagging along, Kirby, or are you out here on po-po business?"

"A little bit of both, Eddie." Dane seemed cautious and uneasy around the big man. The two of them shook hands, but the greeting lacked all the warmth Eddie had shown Ned. Dane introduced Roselita, and Eddie gave her the same once-over his uncle had. She shook her head and wondered why men thought it was okay to treat women like that.

"Damn, Dane. She don't look like no police I ever seen. No sir."

"I'm standing right here, Mr. Rockdale. If you have something to say, you can say it to me."

"Oh, snap. She's ice cold, too. I like that shit." He licked his teeth, crossed his arms, and stared right through her. "Sorry about that misunderstanding back at the house when you drew down on my uncle."

"I didn't draw on anyone. I—"

"Tater scared the shit out of you, didn't he?"

Roselita wasn't sure how to respond.

Eddie hollered across the barn. "Was she scared?" Everyone turned to see a tall, slender man in a T-shirt and overalls wiping down an M40 with a blue bandana. He was standing by the door they'd just come through. They'd walked right past him. He'd been a shadow until right that moment.

"I told you that you wouldn't see anyone," Dane whispered. The man with the rifle just nodded at Roselita, but neither of them said a word to the other. "There was no need to fire on us like that, Eddie. My partner was only letting your uncle know who she was."

"Water off a duck, Dane," Eddie said, as if Dane were asking forgiveness and not pointing out the federal crime Eddie and his silent friend had just committed. Rockdale must've remembered what he'd been doing before Dane and his crew walked in because he turned and looked back at the haggard Mexicans in the far pen and then back at Ned. "All right. Look here. I'm in the middle of something with these wetbacks right now, but if y'all can hold up a few and let me finish this up, we can conversate after."

"That's fine, Eddie. Do what you gotta do," Dane said.

"You're gonna have to be quick about it, too, Kirby. I've only got a few minutes before I gotta go meet with a few more potential buyers this afternoon."

"You negotiating a price with those fellas over there?" Ned asked.

"C'mon, Ned, you know me. I don't negotiate shit. If they want to buy the best, they need to pay the premium. I ain't haggling around here."

Ned let a sly smile slide over his face. And he pushed his bangs back behind his ear. "You want a little help with the incentive?"

Eddie licked his teeth and smiled again. "You think you still got it in you, white boy?"

Ned winked at him. "Never lost it, brother."

"Well c'mon then." Eddie walked back and stepped into the pen. Ned followed. Dane and Roselita did, too, but they stayed back behind the betting wall.

The four Mexicans seemed to be in a heated debate about something, but no one could understand Spanish. Eddie stuck a finger in his mouth and whistled them quiet. "Okay now, look, I ain't got all day to be out here dicking around with you motherfuckers. I got company and more business to handle, so we need to wrap this up. If y'all want these birds, then pay me, and Tater will set you up—end of story. If you want to see what else I got in a lower price range, then Tater over there will show you around the yard, but I was under the impression y'all wanted champions." Eddie bent over and picked up the big, muscular bird pacing the pen at his feet. The animal's powerful wings flapped, and a few loose feathers floated to the dirt. Eddie held the bird close to his chest until it calmed, and then he tucked the bird under his arm like a football. He stroked the animal's neck. Up close, it was a truly beautiful bird; blue and black feathers darted out from around its neck, reflecting the sunlight coming in through the huge window looking over the pen. "This here is a motherfucking champion," Rockdale said, still stroking the bird like a pet. "A pure-blood killer. I trained him myself." Rockdale spoke with genuine pride as he continued to rub at the bird's chest. "The bloodline is pure as snow and my time is money, so you boys need to shit or get off the pot."

The Mexicans began to argue again, but now Eddie was impatient. "I said English, motherfuckers. One more Mexican word gets spoke in this barn and it's going to be adios, amigos. Comprende?" He raised his eyebrow to the apparent leader of the crew. "I asked if you're reading me, Paco?" He tapped his wrist as if he were wearing a watch.

"Yes, Mr. Rockdale. We understand, but you ask for too much money."

"Bitch, you know who I am?"

"Yes, we know your reputation, but no one charges so much. These birds are untested. All we have is your word."

"And my word is all you need." Eddie licked his teeth, but the Mexican wasn't swayed. Rockdale tipped his chin at Ned. "How about we give Paco here a demonstration?"

"Sure, Rooster. Be happy to."

The whole group in the pen seemed pleased with that idea. Eddie pointed toward the blackout boxes. "Y'all head over there and pick any bird you want. I don't give a damn which one." He yelled over to Tater.

"Hey, take Paco and his buddies over there to the wall. Let them pick any number they want."

Tater nodded and slung the M40 over his shoulder.

"Here's the deal, Paco. If your pick wins, then you get to keep him—free and clear. I'll even throw in a few hens and a couple dozen eggs for your trouble. But if my baby right here wins—like I know he's gonna—then you stop yanking my dick and pay me what I want for him—*and* you cover my loss for the dead bird. We got a deal?"

The Mexican man agreed, and they all followed Tater to the wall of wooden boxes. Once they were out of earshot, Eddie whispered to Ned, "You sure you remember how to do this shit?"

"I got you, man."

"Well then, let's do this shit."

Tater whistled across the barn. "Eddie, they want number sixteen."

"Well, then open number sixteen and let's get this show on the road."

Tater pushed the rifle back further over his shoulder, fished a set of keys from his pocket, and unlocked the padlock on the box labeled 16. He set the keys down and slid on a pair of work gloves he had sticking out of the back pocket of his jeans. He carefully reached in and pulled out a mostly white rooster with a leather hood covering its head. It fought against him, flapped its wings in a frenzy, and tried to peck at everything as Tater carried it down the center aisle. He handed the bird over the wall to Ned. He unsnapped and peeled off the hood. The bird's yellow eyes were feral and made it look completely insane as they ticked left and right to adjust to the light. The damn thing looked mean as hell. The Mexicans all smiled, pleased with their choice. Some of them had even pulled out rolls of their own cash for a little internal betting. The Spanish started again, but Eddie didn't seem to mind this time. The Mexicans all cleared out of the pen and crowded around the outside wall as Ned calmed the white-hackle fowl in his hands. Eddie looked at Dane and licked his teeth again. "You got good timing, Kirby. Watch this shit."

Once the pen was clear, Ned held the bird across from Eddie, who still had the shiny black and blue one in his hands. Rockdale's uncle entered the pen to act as referee. "Ned, I don't need to tell you anything about how this works, do I?"

"Nah, I got this." The white gamecock wanted out of Ned's grip something fierce.

"You boys want to see where your money is going?" Eddie said. "This is why you came here and nowhere else. The Farm, baby."

Casper moved into the pen without being told to and held out an arm in the center before dropping it and moving to the side wall. Ned's and Eddie's faces went from mischievous to ominous without missing a beat as they squared off, each holding a bird out in front of him, first just a few inches from each other, and then from a few feet back.

Casper counted it down. "Three—two—one—"

Ned and Eddie dropped the birds into the dirt. Ned's rooster flapped his wings and looked gigantic, double its original size, as Eddie's bird stood seemingly uninterested in the whole affair. The two animals circled each other like boxers feeling out their opponents, but like a strike of dry lightning, it was nothing like boxing at all. It was savage and brutal, the way the birds went at each other, so fast that Dane and Roselita nearly missed the whole thing. The whole encounter only took a few seconds. The bird Eddie had been handling barely moved, but when it did, it struck the other so hard, so fast and precisely, that all anyone saw was the blood flashing red over the white feathers of Ned's bird. The Mexican's pick also showed a fresh break in its beak, but no one knew how it happened. The white bird sulked away, its gigantic wings dragging in the red dirt like a drunk. Eddie let out a howl. "You see that, you wetback motherfuckers? That right there is what you're paying for."

"Hell no," Ned said, "hang on a minute. We ain't done." He picked up the dazed white bird. Blood seeped from the feathers on its neck and began to drizzle from its beak and face. Without a second's hesitation, Ned stuffed the bird's entire head in his mouth. Eddie beamed a golden smile and the group of Mexicans cheered. Roselita watched, wide-eyed and disgusted, but Dane just leaned down heavy on the cedar wall. He'd gotten tired of standing. It was happening more and more often. He wished it was the heat, or the work, but he knew better. He knew what it was. He turned to look at Tater, who'd taken his place back by the door. He was looking directly at Dane and he still held firm to the M40. Dane winked at the silent marksman as Ned finished showing off.

Ned pulled the rooster's head out of his mouth and spit a mouthful of blood into the dirt. Uncle Casper, ever the vigilant master of ceremonies, held out a bottle of water he snatched from thin air and let Ned take a swig. Ned swished the water around in his mouth and spit another red stream across the cedar wall. "Round two, baby." His teeth were still slick and pink behind his grin when he spoke.

"Oh, okay. You think you still got it, white boy?" Eddie picked up his bird and the two of them went through the face-off again. "Turo tried that trick and still lost his ass, Casper, you remember? He was puking his guts out after."

The old man nodded.

"Lemon-head is going out the same way Bobby-boy did." Eddie howled and made a quivering motion that made his muscles ripple. "Count us down, Casper."

The old man held his arm out again. "Three—two—one—"

Both birds dropped to the dirt, but there was no circling this time. Blood had been drawn. They were in a frenzy from the jump. The white bird pecked with its broken beak, possessed by some renewed vigor, but it wasn't enough. Eddie's bird struck again and again until Ned's bird dropped under its own weight. Eddie didn't wait for the match to be called. He knew it was over. Everyone did. He snatched up his bird and held it high above his head. "What's my name, bitches?" Eddie kept the bird up high as he circled the pen. The Mexicans went back to speaking Spanish, but Eddie still didn't seem to care. He wasn't even thinking about the money. He was relishing his win. Ned squatted down to pick up his broken bird. It didn't seem to have any strength left in it at all. Ned gently picked it up and handed it over the four-foot wall to Casper, who took it, pulled in its wings, and walked out the open door on the other side of the barn.

Roselita leaned over to Dane, who'd taken a seat in a wooden chair he'd found propped against the wall. He hadn't seen what happened, but he'd seen enough of these things to know the outcome. "What happens to that one?" Roselita said. "The loser."

Dane just tipped his chin toward the back door. They both watched Casper twist and snap the bird's neck before he disappeared outside into the sunlight.

"He'll go toss it in the incinerator out back."

"Jesus."

"Yeah, fly fishing it ain't. There's a reason this shit ain't legal in Georgia."

"Yet here we are."

Dane slid his ball cap back on his forehead. "Yeah, here we are."

Ned came out of the barn after completely rinsing the taste of blood from his mouth with the rest of the bottle of water. He tossed the empty plastic container in a trash barrel and joined Dane and Roselita at a picnic table out by the incinerator. The smell of burnt feathers was a lot like the smell of burning hair, but the breeze cleared the stink away in no time, and now it smelled more like a Sunday afternoon barbecue. The sun was setting behind the mountain and it had begun to get a little cooler. Casper had gone inside, but not before taking a pitcher of iced tea from the main house and setting it on the table. Eddie was over the rush of his win and didn't look all that happy anymore, especially with Ned. His face conveyed annoyance, but something in his eyes was harder than that. He carried a meanness in them that made everyone uncomfortable. Once everyone uninvolved with the business at hand had departed, he spoke. "That stunt you pulled, sucking that bird's head clear like that. It could've gone the other way and ended up costing me money."

Ned put a hand on Eddie's shoulder and used him as a prop to slip himself down on the bench. "Yeah, but it didn't, did it? There's a lot to be said for showmanship."

"True that," Eddie said, and tucked the fat fold of cash he'd just taken from the Mexicans into his jeans. "Just don't expect a cut 'cause you swallowed a little blood."

"Wouldn't dream of it, Rooster."

"So, now that my business is concluded, how about somebody tell me what y'all are doing here?"

Dane spoke up. "What's your relationship with Arnold Blackwell?"

"Who?"

Dane didn't repeat himself. He wasn't feeling all that great. His stomach felt tight as a fist and the smell of the burning chicken behind him wasn't helping loosen it up. Eddie poured some tea and Roselita saw the action for what it was. He was stalling. Roselita read every detail on

Eddie's face during that moment of hesitation. The way his tense brow softened up as soon as Dane mentioned Blackwell, and the way his eyes shifted down and to the left just for a split second before he grabbed the pitcher, before his eyes went cold and hard again, cold and hard as stone. It told Roselita everything she needed to know about Eddie Rockdale. He was in the game. No matter what he claimed. Rockdale poured some tea into a mason jar for Dane and Ned as well. Dane didn't touch it. Ned drank it down to the bare ice.

"You asked what we are doing here, Mr. Rockdale. That's the answer. I'd think you'd appreciate Dane being direct."

Eddie stalled again. "And who exactly are you again?"

"You know who I am, Mr. Rockdale. There's no need to flex. It's a simple question. You do know Arnold Blackwell, do you not?"

"Yeah, of course I know him. Everybody knows him. He took the Slasher."

"The tournament you held out here at this farm last week?"

Eddie's smile returned and he shook his head. "Is that what you're here for, Kirby? Damn, man. You want to break my balls because I hosted this year?"

Dane shook his head. "No. That's not why we're here at all. We're—I'm—asking if you knew this Blackwell guy personally."

"He means how well did you know him?" Roselita said.

"I know what the motherfucker means." Eddie glared at Roselita and then turned back to Dane. "I knew him as well as any other white boy who comes out here looking to make some scratch. That's it. No more. No less. He got his birds from me. He's been coming up here for months. Wait—you said 'knew.'" Eddie leaned back. "Is he dead already?"

"Yes, he is," Dane said, looking at his pale skin in the fading sunlight, fighting back the memory of that motel room in Florida.

"That didn't take long—the flips kill him? They lost their ass. The Mexicans did, too, but those flip boys were fuming. Was it them?"

Roselita took the volley. "We're not at liberty to discuss the details of an ongoing murder investigation with you, Mr. Rockdale. We're out here hoping you could help us out with something else entirely."

"Really. And what would that be?"

Dane wiped at his forehead with his hat and then laid it on the table. "Did Arnold ever have anyone with him?"

"You mean the kid?"

Roselita sat up straight on the bench and Dane took out the photograph of William with his parents he'd lifted from the apartment back in Cobb County. He slid it across the pine table. "This kid? He had this kid out here with him?"

Eddie picked up the photograph and nodded. "Yeah, that's him. Don't tell me Blackwell kidnapped the little fucker. I can't be involved in any shit like that. I just sold the guy some birds. That's it."

"No," Dane said, a little alarmed that Eddie skipped over the possibility of the boy being related to Blackwell and made the jump to kidnapping. "It's nothing like that. This boy is Blackwell's brother and he's missing."

"Well, he ain't here."

"We didn't say he was, Eddie, but what, if anything, can you tell us about him?"

"Only that he's a weird little fucker. He was the reason Arnie got into the show. The kid made all Arnie's picks for him."

"What do you mean?"

"I mean, Arnie would just let the kid wander around the yard and stare at the birds for a while and whenever the kid pointed at one, Arnie would pay me for it. No haggling like you just saw. No bullshit. Just cash on the barrel. I thought he was a damn fool just picking out random birds like that. Hell, I thought the kid was retarded, too. I figured Blackwell was either an idiot tourist dabbling in shit he didn't know anything about, or he was with some Make-A-Wish Foundation shit or something. You know, like a camp for retards?"

Dane gnawed his lip. His blood got hot every time the word *retard* spilled from Rooster's lips. He wanted to smack him—in those obnoxious gold teeth.

Eddie continued. "But then I saw what the kid could do."

"What do you mean?" Roselita said. "What did he do? Where did you see him?" She was coming on too hot. Dane put a hand on her arm, but it was too late. Eddie remembered who he was talking to.

"Look, Rose, or whatever your name is, I'm not about to sit here and snitch out nobody. These two might be somewhat trustable. I got shit on both of 'em, but I don't know you, so I'm not saying jack."

"Eddie—look," Dane said, "we don't care about your business. That's not why we're here. We're just trying to find the boy."

"I don't give a damn why you're here, Dane. I'm not talking to the police about anything—period. You should know that."

"Mr. Rockdale, we could bust you right now for what we just witnessed. I could haul you and your buddy Tater in for discharging a firearm at us if we wanted to."

Eddie stood up. "Bitch, I'd like to see you try."

Ned stood up, too. "Y'all take it easy. No one is hauling anyone anywhere. The point Velasquez is doing a shitty job of trying to make is that they're not here for you, Rooster. No one is trying to backdoor you."

Eddie narrowed his eyes at Ned. "Right," he said. "And since when are you running with the po-po, Ned? I don't see you around here for years, and then all of a sudden you're out here at my place again hangin' with cops? I appreciate what you did in there with the spics, but maybe it's time for all y'all to hightail it off my property."

"Please, man—just tell Dane about the boy—that's it. If you can tell him anything that might be helpful, we'll call that thousand bucks I just helped you make a wash. You know you were only hoping to crack seven hundred, if that. Seriously, Rooster. I just sucked off a chicken for you."

Even Dane laughed at that, although it was evident to everyone that he wasn't feeling that great. His skin looked even paler now and sweat had broken out down his neck like a fever.

"Are you all right, Dane?"

"I'm fine, Rose. I'm fine." He held a hand out to the empty seat on the other side of the picnic table. "Please, Eddie. Ned's right. This is about a missing boy. That's it. You have my word."

Eddie licked at his teeth. It was a disgusting habit that was beginning to rub at Roselita's nerves. "Look," Eddie said, "all I know about those two is that they came looking to buy birds. Arnie didn't give a shit about the bloodline or the training—nothing. The kid would just point and Arnie would ask how much. That's it. He asked me how to get set up for big money, and I hooked him up with a handler. He ponied up the money to enter the Slasher and I took it. I had no idea he was going to do what he did. I didn't even think it was possible, but he proved me wrong. I'm not surprised he's dead. There was a shitload of pissed-off people around here when he dipped with the payout."

"But not you?" Roselita asked.

"Nah, I made my money as the host. He didn't take my chunk. Just the other fighters'."

"And you don't have any idea how he did it?"

"You mean how that weird little shit knew which birds would perform just by eyeballing them? Hell, no. If I did, I never would've let the kid off the farm. It was crazy. He could just tell by looking at them how they would react in the ring. It's like his eye was trained to see things a normal person couldn't. I've been around this shit my whole life, so I know which birds are winners and which ones ain't, but it's because I know the bloodline, or the training that goes into a certain bird. That weird-ass kid could tell the reaction times just by watching them walk or graze. It's damn near inhuman what he did. Shit, I'm telling y'all, that kid is a goddamn walking money machine."

"And you have no idea where the boy could be now? Did either of them ever mention anything to you about where they were staying when they'd come up here, or anything at all that might help us find him?"

"That dude never said shit other than how much and the kid never said a damn word to anyone but Arnie. I didn't even know the little dude's name until you just told me." Eddie picked up the photo, licked at his front teeth, and set it back down on the picnic table. "Hell," he said, "if the truth be known, after I saw what that dude did, I was glad I didn't know anything about either of 'em. I don't want any part of that shit. Those flip motherfuckers don't fuck around. Neither do those Mountain boys and they lost a pretty penny here, too. I don't need that kind of trouble—too dangerous. I don't even host fights out here anymore. The Slasher was a one-time deal. I just sell birds. I'm just a trainer now—a businessman. I'm glad I stayed clear of it."

"So which is it, Mr. Rockdale?"

Eddie cocked his head at Roselita. "Which is what, FBI Lady?"

"You said a minute ago that if you knew what the boy was capable of, you wouldn't have let him off your property. You called him a walking money machine. But just now you said you're glad you stayed clear. So which is it?"

"You fucking cops love to twist up a man's words."

"I'm just trying to sort out the truth, Mr. Rockdale."

"Are you calling me a liar?" Eddie stood up. "Are you sitting in my fucking backyard calling me a liar?"

Roselita looked around at the area around the barn. "This the back-yard?"

"Okay. We're done here. Kirby, get this bitch off my land, before I have Tater shoot *at* her instead of *near* her."

"Are you threatening me, Mr. Rockdale—again?"

Eddie leaned down hard on the wooden table. "Yes. Yes, I am. Fuck this. Your missing kid, your dead white boy, and their whole family-accident sob story. Ain't none of this got shit to do with me. So go on and get to steppin'."

"All right, Eddie." Dane stood up as well. "Calm down. We're leaving."

"Good, because I'm about a cunt hair away from smoking this bitch myself."

Roselita was on her feet now, too. "You mean you don't want to have some inbred sniper do it for you from behind a barn?"

Eddie jumped at the table. Ned stopped him by wrapping his thin arms around the big man in a sleeper hold. "Let me go, Ned. Let me go or I swear to God, you're next." Eddie struggled to free himself, but Ned had the reach. "Go, Dane. Get her out of here. Go now."

Tater came out of the barn and trained the M40 on Ned. "Let him go, Ned—now." It was the first time anyone had heard the man speak.

"You heard the man, Ned. Let me go before bodies start dropping."

Dane balanced himself on the edge of the table. He knew for all Eddie's bluster he wouldn't attack an FBI agent. "Let him go, Ned."

"Not a good idea, Dane."

"I said let him go." Ned did and backed way up. Eddie flexed once he was free, but his bluff had been called. "Get the fuck off my land." The threat sounded hollow. Tater lowered the rifle, too. "Sure thing, Eddie, but just one more thing before we head out."

"What?"

"You know a Bernadette Sellers?"

"Nah."

"How about a Bobby Turo. That name familiar to you?"

"Never heard it before in my life."

Dane nodded and put his hat on. "You hear about Ned's trouble over at Tom Clifford's cabin?"

"Yeah, I heard about it, but I knew it was bullshit. Ned ain't got it in him to be no killer."

"Yeah, I agree."

"So what's your point?"

"Where were you the morning Tom was shot?"

Eddie got quiet and backed away from the table. It was clear that the wheels in his head were spinning full tilt. "You need to leave," Eddie said in a near whisper, and stared hard into Dane's eyes. The tension that started in his jaw rippled though his whole body. "I got nothing else to say." He looked at Ned with the same intensity, but whatever passed through the two of them stayed silent, unexposed.

Dane pocketed the photo from the table. "We'll be back, Eddie."

"I hope so, motherfucker." His voice lacked the commanding tone he had prior to Dane's implication. Roselita had already started back to the truck. She'd gotten all she needed. Dane tipped his chin to Eddie and to Tater, who had let the rifle fall to his side, and followed.

"I'm sorry about all this, Rooster."

"Fuck you, Ned."

Ned nodded and slowly started down the dirt road toward his ride. A few minutes later, the three of them crammed into the cab of Keith's Nissan and Dane cranked the engine. He saw Lydia in the rearview mirror as he turned the truck around and headed out. She was standing in the doorway of the main house where she'd been when they arrived. Ned strained his neck to look back at her. Roselita sighed.

The stolen Subaru hatchback didn't handle the rough roads out in the country all that well, and he felt every bump in the road deep in his shoulder as if someone were gouging a thumb into the wound. He was pleased to finally be still, and off those godforsaken trails. He had refused to bring anyone with him. He didn't know anyone from the organization here personally, so despite his injuries, he felt safer working the rest of this job on his own. The last thing he needed out here was another idiot like Smoke to let his American-influenced ego get him killed.

Fenn watched from where he'd stashed the car behind a deep thicket of bushes as the same Americans he'd seen back at the apartment in Atlanta passed him in a bright red pickup truck. They had added one to their number, but he looked even less formidable than the other two. Fenn was not surprised to see them here. They were all seeking the same information. This farm belonged to the American who ran the games. It only made sense that this would be the place to start looking for the boy, but he was hoping to have already come and gone by the time the police arrived. He was planning on waiting until dark to approach the farmhouse, but now he had no choice. Maybe it was better this way. Maybe these American police arriving when they did would provide Fenn with an opportunity. He'd scouted the area thoroughly after he'd hidden the car and found only one man patrolling the property line—another man of no consequence hiding behind the false security of a long, high-caliber weapon. Fenn would make short work of him, but now it was possible that his death would be unnecessary. That man would surely be busy now with the police, making it easier for Fenn to approach the house undetected—possibly even to enter the house. The woman living there was beautiful, nothing like most American women—she was delicate and stately, a woman of Fenn's caliber. Maybe there would be time to see more of her. Maybe this trio of police in their fancy pickup truck had just made that introduction possible.

Fenn got out of the car, careful of his shoulder, and eased the door closed. He took his baston and a small canteen of water from the hatchback and looked at the suitcase and trash bag tucked down under the back seat that contained a small fortune. Fenn knew he'd be rewarded with a lot more if he could provide his people with the boy, so the idea of taking it for himself never entered his mind. Greed was American. Greed got you killed. He thought of Smoke, and slowly eased the hatch closed. His wound was still a slow-burning fire that spread down his arm, but he ignored it and flexed his fingers. Silently, he made his way through the woods toward the house. He wouldn't be able to get close enough to hear what they were saying, but he'd be able to see how many people he would need to kill if that's what it came to. He opened a small pill bottle he'd taken from the same house he'd stolen the car from, and chewed three of the small oval pills into a chalky paste that he washed down with water from the canteen. Within minutes he was feeling better. The throbbing in his shoulder had settled into a dull ache, and he nestled next to a tree and watched the thin man with the rifle fire at the police from the truck— the woman with the pink shirt talking to the old man on the porch. The woman did something of a dance and fell into the other man—the skinny one with the long hair. They all jerked about and bounced around the yard. The man with the rifle chambered another round but lowered the weapon. He had not intended to hit anyone, but fired just to show the old man's dominance over the visitors. Fenn smiled while he watched the havoc the rifleman had caused. He would've laughed if he could've afforded to break his silence or give away his position. Other than the man who drove the truck, who remained stoic, the movements of the others in front of the house reminded Fenn of an old silent movie he'd seen on American TV once as a boy. Fenn loved American TV. *Keystone Cops*, he recalled. Yes, that's what they looked like. The Keystone Cops. They were very funny.

CHAPTER NINETEEN

When Dane pulled the truck over to the side of the street near Lucky's, they got out and he tossed Keith's keys on the seat. They walked to the parking lot of the sheriff's station across the street. Dane and Ned slid into Dane's old Ford and Roselita stood at the door of her silver Infiniti. Dane rolled the window down. "Are you going to tell me what you're thinking, Rose? Or are you just going to leave without a word like you normally do?"

Roselita leaned down on the hood of her car. "I thought the reason I followed you out here was because you thought that asshole, Rockdale—who shot at me, by the way—could lead us to the Blackwell kid, but that ain't the truth, is it? I think we both know now that isn't the reason we went out there." She pointed a slim finger at Ned. "We didn't need a buffer out there, either. You wanted to bring your buddy out there to see if he could rattle your *Rooster's* cage because you think he killed the old man in the woods out there, and for whatever reason you think he set Ned up to take the fall. You went out there looking for a motive."

"Rose, wait—"

Roselita held her palms out. She sounded tired. "And you know what else? I don't give a shit. The only thing I know for sure is that we aren't any closer to finding this kid than we were before we went out there, so I guess you could say I'm thinking I got played for a sucker."

"That's not entirely true, Rose."

"Oh yeah, which part? About you being more interested in helping your buddy get off a murder rap, or me being a sucker?"

"He lied to us," Dane said. "Eddie. He lied to us about the boy."

"When?"

"He said he barely knew them, and I never said anything about William and Arnold's parents, but he sure as hell spit that out when you got him riled up. He knows them both—a lot better than he tried to lead us to believe. That means he's hiding something."

Roselita straightened her back, stretched, and crossed her arms. "Do you think he knows where he is?"

"No, but I think he's actively looking. Another thing. He said he didn't know Bobby Turo. That he never heard of him. But during the sparring match with Ned, he was all hopped up and running his mouth about a Bobby-boy Turo. He knows a lot more than he said, Rose. A lot more."

Roselita clicked her key fob and unlocked the Infiniti. "So what do you want to do? Sit on him and see if the kid or any bad guys show up? We still don't know anything."

"That's exactly what I want to do. I'm thinking he'll either lead us to William or to Arnold's killers. Either way, we now know for sure that Eddie is neck-deep in this."

Ned lit up one of Roselita's Ultra Lights on the passenger-side seat of Dane's truck as if he wasn't listening to their conversation.

"All right, Dane. I'll run all this up the flagpole with August and see about surveillance at the Farm." She still wasn't happy, and it was easy to see her trying to fit pieces together in her brain as she got into her car.

"Hold up, Rose."

Roselita cranked the car and rolled down the window.

"You said I went looking at Eddie for Tom Clifford's murder. What's his motive?"

Roselita looked forward through her windshield. "Dane, I've got two rules I live my life by. As long as you don't break either of those two rules, we may not ever be best friends, but we'll always get along."

"And what are those, Roselita?" Dane leaned over and adjusted the AC vent to blow Ned's smoke out of his face.

"Don't make a mojito with sour mix—and don't fuck my old lady."

"Well, I don't think there's ever going to be a problem with either of those."

Roselita leaned back in her seat and shifted the Infiniti into drive. She looked over the rim of her aviators, past Dane, at Ned. "I'm just saying that maybe Eddie Rockdale goes by the same set of rules."

"You're talking out of your ass, Velasquez," Ned said.

"Sure I am, Ned. Sure I am. But if I'm not, we both know you didn't make the man a mojito." Her cell phone rang and she put it to her ear. She told whoever it was to hang on and turned back to Dane. "I'll catch up with you once you return the sheriff's prisoner. Because that's what you're about to do, right? Return the sheriff's prisoner?"

"Of course."

"Okay. I'll let you know what August says once I check in. I'm going over there to rent a shitty room in that shitty motel."

"You know you're more than welcome to stay at my sister-in-law's trailer. It—"

Roselita held a hand out the window. "Stop right there. I'm good."

Dane watched Roselita wheel the silver coupe out of the lot and sat in the truck outside the station with Ned. They listened to Eric Church reminisce about summers and Bruce Springsteen on the radio, and watched a few kids across the street smoking cigarettes on the front steps of the bookstore. Dane reached over and turned the stereo up a little to hear George Strait give it away.

"I love that song," Ned said.

"Yeah, so do I."

Ned just stared out the window at the brick building. "I don't get to sit and listen to music that much anymore. Do you remember when that's all we did? Just trading out cassettes full of songs we recorded off the radio on that stupid boom box of yours?"

"It was Keith's boom box, but yeah, I remember."

"I miss those days, Dane."

"I do, too, Ned."

They sat there for another few minutes until George turned into Carrie Underwood. She was clearly upset about her man's infidelity and planned to take out her anger on his truck. Dane turned it down and then clicked it off. It was full dark out now, and Dane was feeling better. The night air felt good, and just sitting there with Ned made him think of better things—better days. Ned lit the last cigarette in the pack and blew the smoke out the window. Dane scratched at his chin. He'd put it off long enough. "Ned—"

"Yeah, man?"

"How long have you been fucking Eddie's wife?"

Ned didn't even try to get defensive. He just kept staring at the red-brick wall of the Sheriff's office. "It's not like that, Dane."

"Then tell me what it is like."

Ned took another drag and held the cigarette loose outside the window, as if now it mattered about smoking in Dane's truck. "You want me to get out of the truck with this?"

"I want you to answer my question, Ned. I think you owe me at least that much."

Ned laughed a little and took another drag.

"C'mon, Ned, I'm doing my best to help here. If I'm going to help you, then I need to know all of it. Just tell me. How long has it been going on?"

"Since always, man. Since we met."

"Are you serious?"

"Yeah. It was love at first sight." He took another pull of smoke and looked at Dane. "We were just two pieces of the same puzzle. We fit together. I know you can relate to that." Dane was stunned, but he did understand. "Like you and Gwen, man," Ned added for emphasis.

"Like me and Gwen," Dane repeated.

"Yeah."

Dane repeated it again in his head, *Like me and Gwen*, and looked in the side mirror of the truck. The kids across the street at Lucky's were gone. The steps were empty and the streetlights were on. *Like me and Gwen*, he thought again.

Dane loved hearing Gwen's name out loud and without apology like that. More often than not, when people brought her up in conversation around Dane, they drowned her name in sympathy. They coated it in a layer of sadness as thick and syrupy as that bullshit Carrie Underwood song he had to stop listening to a minute ago. Gwen's name made him feel good most of the time. It wasn't something he needed protection from. Ned knew that, and hearing him say it was like having her there in the truck with them, if only for just a split second. Ned had known her. He knew *them*—when there was a *them*—and then the moment was over. She was gone—again. Dane thought back over the timeline. "Ned, you met Lydia in high school. Before I even met Gwen. Are you telling me it's been going on that long?"

"Yep." Ned tossed the cigarette out the window. "You remember the night I got arrested? That night over by Slater Street Bridge?"

"How could I ever forget that, Ned?"

"Well, I was leaving Lydia's that night. She'd only been dating Eddie for a few months at that point. He wasn't even that into her. I'd been finding reasons to go see her. That night I scored y'all's weed from Casper. It was also the first time Lydia and I, well, you know. That's why I was coming home from that way, but I saw the wreck and just reacted. The rest is history."

Dane took off his hat and rubbed at the bridge of his nose. "Jesus, Ned."

"Look, Dane, you need to know. It wasn't just something cheap—Lydia and me—it was—is—real. I'm not just *fucking her.*"

"Okay, I get it."

"Anyway, that night at the bridge, what happened—happened." Ned crushed the empty pack of Marlboros into a balled-up wad of paper and cellophane. "By the time I got out, Eddie and I had a different kind of friendship. Our time at Tobacco Road had made us brothers. Lydia was also his woman—lock, stock, and barrel. He'd got out to become bigtime at the farm by that point, so I stayed away. I tried to ignore what Lydia and I had."

"But then you came back."

"Yeah, and that was a mistake, as you can see. I should never have come back here."

Ned's eyes were back to staring out the window at the sheriff's office. He wiped at his face. "I'm sorry I left, Dane. I'm sorry I left you here by yourself after what happened to Gwen and—" Ned couldn't even bring himself to say Joy's name. "You were my best friend, Dane. My brother. And I left you here alone because I was a selfish piece of shit, and now I've done dragged you into this, too."

Dane put a hand on Ned's shoulder. He didn't have any words, nothing worth saying that would make a difference. "Give me that," he said, and motioned for the crumpled-up pack of cigarettes. Ned looked down at his hands and then handed Dane the trash. "I dragged myself into this, and I promise you, I'll get us out. The real people responsible for what happened to Tom will go down. You have to trust me, but I need to return you to Ellis before I can do that. I don't want to, but I don't have a choice. You won't be in there long. I'm almost done here."

"I do trust you, Dane, but—" Ned stumbled on his words.

"But what, man?"

"If your partner is right. If you're looking at Eddie for what happened to Tom, you need to stop. He's innocent." Ned added, "Of that at least."

"How are you so sure about that?"

Ned's eyes hardened. "Because it was me. I did it, man."

The car went cold and silent. "Did what?"

Ned began to look ashamed, and his shoulders sagged even more than they already were. He looked as if he'd wilted.

"Ned, what the hell are you saying?"

"I'm saying that when I came back here, me and Lydia fell back into it. It's just not possible for us not to. I know you understand that, Dane."

Dane stared at Ned, slack-jawed. "Ned, tell me about Tom."

He sighed. "Tom was letting me crash there. He was never home. He took off for days at a time to hunt or fish or whatever. I was there by my-self most of the time, so that's where—"

"You and Lydia would meet."

"Yeah. She came to me. It's not like we could be seen anywhere. It was secluded. Perfect even."

"And?"

"And, well, Tom was supposed to be gone for a few days, so Lydia came over to spend the night. Tom must've forgot something because he came back the next morning. He saw us together in his house, in his bed, and he freaked out. He started talking about how if Rooster found out he'd kill all three of us. How I'd made him party to shit he didn't want no part of. He was screaming at Lydia. Called her a whore. Told me to pack my shit and get out. Dane, I pleaded with him, but he insisted that he was going to tell Rooster. It was a death sentence, Dane—for me and her." Ned shook his head and stared at the floorboards. "Jesus, man, I'm not really sure what happened next, but after he said he was going to tell

Rooster, he headed for the door and I tried to stop him but couldn't. I was drunk and somehow ended up holding Tom's gun. I don't even remember doing it, but I did. Lydia freaked out. I tried to calm her down, but Tom was dead. I couldn't do anything about that, but I wasn't going to let Lydia go to fucking prison, man, for something I did. Or worse, have Rooster find out why she was there."

"So you told her to run. And you what, got drunk?"

"I told her to run, yeah. I told her to run like hell, and I'd figure something out."

"And your figuring something out was passing out against a tree half naked with the murder weapon?"

Ned shrugged. "I didn't have time to think. As soon as she left, I chugged a jar of hooch, paced around the front yard, and I guess I just fell out." Ned let out a small laugh. "I didn't even think to put my pants on. I can't imagine what you must've been thinking when you got there."

Dane wasn't amused. "A man is dead, Ned. There's nothing funny about that."

Ned turned sharply in his seat. "Yeah, I know that. And if I could change that, I would, but I can't, so I'm just going to confess and be done with it. And listen to me, Dane. I won't tell anyone that Lydia was there. I'll deny telling you if I have to. If it was Gwen you'd do the same thing."

"Stop," Dane said. "Stop talking about Gwen."

Ned stopped. He just sat there melting even more into the seat. They both stared out the window at the wall to the county lockup before Dane downshifted the truck into reverse and backed out of the parking space. Ned looked confused. "Where are you going?"

Dane tossed the wadded-up plastic and paper cigarette pack onto the floorboard of the truck. "I promised to bring you back, but I didn't say when." He wheeled the truck out of the lot and onto Main Street. "I figure we've still got enough time to run by Pollard's and get you some proper smokes first if you plan on laying all this out to Darby."

Ned wiped at his face again. "Thanks, Dane."

"Yeah, Ned." They drove about half a mile before Dane asked, "Why did you ask for me? What was the point?"

"I don't know. Maybe I just wanted to see you again before I was sent away for good. It was stupid. I shouldn't have."

Dane didn't correct him. He drove a few more miles up the road to the local gas station and bait shop. He pulled into the gravel lot and shifted into park.

"And you're positive Eddie doesn't know—about you and Lydia, I mean?"

Ned studied Dane's face hard before unclicking the shoulder belt and opening the door. "No fucking way, man. He'd have killed us both already."

Dane nodded and handed him a twenty to pay for the smokes. "I want my change back." Ned got out and Dane watched him disappear through the front door of the store. He felt his leg buzz and pulled out his phone.

"Kirby."

Nothing.

"Hello? This is Dane Kirby."

Still nothing. Dane was about to end the call and redial the number when he heard a female voice cut in on the line.

"Hello? Can you hear me?" The voice sounded familiar. It didn't take long for Dane to recognize Clementine Richland from the Cobb County DFCS office.

"Yes, Mrs. Richland. I can hear you. I'm sorry. I'm up in North Georgia and the reception is awful."

"That's okay. I can hear you fine now. Listen, I hate to bother you, but you said to call if I found out anything useful about your case—about finding William."

"Of course, go ahead."

"It may be nothing, but I don't know."

"Please, Mrs. Richland, I'm listening."

"The school I mentioned when we met—Morningside. The special school that William attended before his brother pulled him out."

"Yes. What about it?" Dane switched the phone from one ear to the other.

"Well, I had them get in touch with me like you asked, and it took a while—most of the afternoon actually—because they were apparently dealing with their own situation this morning."

"What situation?"

"They were vandalized. Someone broke into the main offices last night and smashed up the place pretty good. They busted up the computers, knocked over filing cabinets, and broke all the phones. That's why they took so long to call me back."

"And you think the break-in had something to do with William?"

"Well, I don't know, but when I asked if they could send over all the files they had on William and his particular curriculum, they couldn't find them."

"Because the offices were in disarray, or because they're missing?"

"I don't know. All I know is that it's been several hours and I've spoken to several people over there and everything else seems to be intact—except a few files that are still missing—including William's."

Dane sat up in his seat and tried to get a better look through the glass door of the store for Ned. How long did it take to get a pack of smokes? "Mrs. Richland, did William have a special teacher? Someone who worked with him one-on-one. Or did he go to several classes like normal middle school students?"

"Oh, no, William had a specific teacher. That's how the school is set up. Her name is Dawn Jeffers and she specializes in kids with Asperger's. We actually work with her from time to time here at my office. She's a wonderful person. She's a doctor of child psychology."

Dane sat up straighter in his seat. "Would Ms. Jeffers's home address be listed with the missing paperwork you mentioned?"

"Um, I suppose it would. Do you think that she could be in some sort of danger?"

Dane cut the truck's engine and reached over to the glove box. "You said you worked with her from time to time in your office. Do you have her contact information there with you?"

"Yes, I think so. Agent Kirby, is she in danger?"

"Listen, Clem, I don't know, but I need to reach her ASAP, so please, if you have her contact—"

Clem recited the number over the phone and Dane used a Sharpie from the glove box to write it on his hand. He read the number back, and Clem confirmed. "Thank you, Mrs. Richland. Please let me know if you find out anything else." Clem began to answer him, but Dane quickly ended the call and tried the number written on his hand. It went directly to voice mail. He tried again—and again—before he dialed August. By the time he answered the phone, Dane was already out of the truck. He opened the door to Pollard's and scanned the small shop for Ned.

"What is it, Kirby?" he heard August say through the phone.

"August. I need you to get as many men as you can to the personal address of someone named Dawn Jeffers."

"Who?"

"Call the local PD down there. Again, her name is Jeffers—Dawn Jeffers."

"Who is that, Kirby?"

"She's someone in the crosshairs of this mess and I think she might be in danger—right now. I think our killer vandalized the school she teaches at to get her address in order to get to William." Dane walked each aisle of the small grocery, bait, and tackle shop frantically looking for Ned.

Where the hell did he go?

"What's this Dawn Jeffers's address?"

"I don't know, August. How many can there be? She's a doctor. Find her address and get some people out there—now—please."

"Okay, I'm on it."

Dane stuffed his phone in his pocket. He banged the bell on the counter by the register. It startled the kid on the floor stocking cigarettes under the counter.

"Damn, Chief, you scared me."

"Bailey, where's Ned?"

"Who?"

"Ned. Ned Lemon. He just walked in here five minutes ago to buy some cigarettes."

"Skinny dude—long hair?"

"Yeah."

"He bought a pack of Camel Lights, told me to keep the change, which was pretty sweet, and then told me to tell someone named Dane he was sorry."

"I'm Dane, Bailey. That's my name."

Bailey looked baffled. "Really," he said. "I ain't known you as nothing but Chief Kirby my whole life."

"Then what happened, Bailey?"

"Well, then he asked for the key to the john."

Dane leaned over the counter and looked behind the cigarette rack. Nothing else but a folding chair with an open copy of *Hustler* on the seat filled the small gap where Bailey stood. Dane leaned down heavily on the counter and squeezed his eyes shut, then walked over to the bathroom door. He pushed it open but knew it would be empty.

"What's the deal?" Bailey said. "Did I miss something?"

"Where's the back door?"

"Right there, but it's locked up tight, sir."

"Is the key to the back door on the same ring as the one to the bathroom?"

"Um," Bailey said. Dane made his way over to the back door and saw the twelve-inch sawed-off pool cue dangling from the key still stuck in the lock. "Goddamnit." He barely had to press the security bar for it to open. "Goddamnit," he said again.

"Well, I'll be damned," Bailey said over Dane's shoulder. "I'm glad he didn't steal the key. That's why I put that pool cue on there. I've had to replace those keys three times already out of my own pocket."

Dane just stared at him.

"I dodged a bullet there, huh, Chief?"

Dane didn't say anything. He marched back to the front door and nearly broke the glass pushing it out of his way.

Bailey followed him outside. "Hey, you want me to have him call you if he comes back in? You want to leave a number?"

Dane didn't answer. It took a few minutes before he was calm enough to drive.

CHAPTER TWENTY

The man in black set his gun down on the counter and peeled off his rubber gloves. He always wore gloves when he worked, but the thin powder-blue nitrile material had snagged on something as he was coming in the back door and ripped it, causing him to get blood on his left hand. He set the wadded-up gloves down next to the gun and gently lifted the handle to the faucet with his elbow. Once the stream of water was hot enough, he rubbed his hands together, letting the blood mix and swirl down the drain of the kitchen sink. He used his elbow again to mash the pump on the bottle of fancy hand soap.

Lilac, he thought. That smells nice. He finished scrubbing his hands and used his fingers to push the remaining soap suds down the drain before cutting off the water and shoving the ruined rubber gloves into his pocket. He was careful not to touch the counter with his bare hands and even more so when he lifted his gun and returned it to the shoulder holster hanging under his armpit. He slipped on a pair of black tactical gloves and opened the fridge next to the sink. He knew from the furnishings and the fancy soap that he'd find either a high-end bottle of wine or some hipster craft beer.

"Sweetwater. Georgia Brown. You have good taste, Dr. Jeffers."

The doctor didn't answer. She was dead on the floor in the living room. The man in black hadn't gotten any more information out of her than he'd gotten from the pretty little pot dealer he'd shot the night before, and he was beginning to feel a little irritated at the lack of progress he was making in finding this Blackwell kid. Now that the money was gone, and it would be a small miracle to try and find it again, his only shot at salvaging the loss was finding the boy. Frustration was setting in, but the man in black knew that would only make him sloppy, so he took a minute to breathe. He took a cold bottle from the cardboard six-pack holder and used the buckle on his belt to pop the top. He walked back into the living room and sat down in a chair at the desk. He drank nearly half the beer in his first swig before he eased open the doctor's laptop and stared at the log-in screen. He wasn't quite sure what he expected to find on the computer even if he was able to crack the password, but he considered taking it with him anyway. He let his mind wander for a moment as he tried to figure out his next move. He knew that he and the good doctor bleeding out on the floor were the only two people in the house, so he wasn't concerned about getting caught there. He let himself relax a little. It didn't last long. He flinched when his cell phone buzzed against his leg. He slid the chair back away from the desk and pulled the phone out of his pocket to look at the display. He tapped the green button.

"Agent Dahmer here."

A frantic voice came over the line, so loud that Dahmer needed to back the phone away from his ear to understand. When the yelling was over, he simply said "Okay" and ended the call. He tucked his phone back in his pocket. Apparently the local PD was on the way. So much for taking a minute to himself. He slapped the laptop closed with his elbow and finished the beer. He shoved the empty bottle into another pocket of the tactical pants he was wearing and then searched the kitchen floor for the small aluminum lid. He found it and tucked that away, too. He wanted to do another search through the filing cabinet, but he supposed that would have to wait. He'd still need to change his clothes, too. He left through the back door and eased it shut behind him before melting into the shadows of the backyard. He hopped the privacy fence into the narrow ditch that divided the house he was just in from the one behind it. He walked leisurely back to his car and took off his balaclava before getting in and turning the key. He pulled the black SUV out of the neighborhood and drove about a half mile up the road to a small Baptist church parking lot, where he changed back into the dark suit he had hanging from a hook above the back seat. Once he'd changed his clothes and used a little pomade from the glove box to slick back his hair, he tapped the doctor's address into his GPS. It wasn't that he needed it, but he was covering all his bases. At this point in the game, it was the little things that were necessary. If anyone were to check the device in Dahmer's SUV, they'd see he clearly had no prior knowledge of where he was going. When he heard the sirens, he eased the Tahoe over to the edge of the parking lot and waited just a minute longer. He didn't want to be the first one on the scene. He looked at himself in the rearview mirror, then rubbed at his hair to mess it up a little. Maybe he didn't need to appear so raring and ready—it was the small details. He was only supposed to have become aware of this situation during his off time, and he was supposed to be in a rush. He needed to look the part. Once he was confident that Decatur's finest were at least in the neighborhood, and closing in on the split-level house on Neville Court, he pointed his big Chevy back toward the very place he'd just come from. He smiled. At least now he'd get a chance to look through that computer.

CHAPTER TWENTY-ONE

Dane got the call from August less than an hour later. They'd gotten to the teacher's house too late. Another body had been added to the list. Dane also had to counter that news by telling his boss that the prisoner he'd convinced him to have released had eluded custody before he could return him to the McFalls County sheriff. Dane sat in his truck outside the trailer park he grew up in and tried to pack it all away for a few hours. Dane had sold the trailer to Misty's sister a few months ago, but it still filled him with a feeling of coming home every time he turned in the gate and saw that wooden sign with the arrowhead carved in it and mounted to the gate. ARROWOOD: A MOBILE HOME COMMUNITY. Dane had kept the place even after his mother passed away, and he let Misty convince him to let her sister move in, despite his best efforts to cut all ties to McFalls County. This place may have been home once, but it was still another gut-check reminder of his other life. Dane could hear Misty and her sister talking inside when he pulled up. He couldn't hear what they were saying, but neither of them sounded happy. He got out of the truck and heard the water running in the kitchen. He gave a quick knock on the door before walking in, and the conversation the two women were having came to a dead stop. Jenn sat on the kitchen counter watching Misty wash dishes. It was a little late to be cleaning anything, but that was Misty's way. It always had been. Whenever she was pissed off about something, she cleaned the house. In this instance, Jenn had benefited from that particular quirk. It was a win/win situation. She got to see the sister *and* she got her house cleaned.

"Hey, girls, what's the word?"

"Hey, Dane," Jenn said. Her voice was flat and cold as she hopped off the kitchen counter. Jenn wasn't much to look at, a younger, less attractive version of Misty. Her hair was thinner and years of smoking and tanning beds had leathered her skin. Dane looked around at the freshly vacuumed carpet and the newly dusted secondhand furniture—some of which had belonged to Dane's parents when it was firsthand and hadn't been moved from where it sat since he was a boy. The trailer was normally cluttered with gun magazines and newspapers, children's toys, and all sorts of thrift-store shit that Jenn could never bring herself to throw out, but now the place had been Misty'd, so it actually resembled the home he used to know except for Jenn's shitty attitude, which filled the place like the smog from a paper mill.

"Where are the boys, Jenn?"

She didn't look at him as she stuffed her keys and a pack of Salem 100's in her purse from the end table. "Jackson's in his room on the PlayStation and Jake's at his piece-of-shit father's house. It's his weekend to have him. He'll be home tomorrow." She slung her purse over her shoulder and grabbed a beer from the fridge. She held it against the edge of the counter top and banged the cap off with her palm. She whispered something to Misty before passing Dane to get to the front door. "There's two more Blue Moons in the fridge if you want one."

"Thanks, Jenn, but I don't drink, remember?"

"Maybe that's your problem, Dane." She turned the bottle up and pushed open the screen door. "I'll be over at Granny's if you need me, sis. Good luck."

Dane stopped the door from slapping shut and walked into the kitchen, where Misty was scrubbing a frying pan that had been burnt black weeks ago. "Good luck with what?" he asked. "We're not fighting, are we?"

Misty stopped scrubbing and turned off the faucet. She dried her hands on a dish towel and opened up the fridge to get one of the last two beers. She was cleaning and she was drinking. That told Dane what he needed to know. They weren't fighting yet, but they soon would be. She held her beer against the counter and tried to smack it open the way her sister had, but only ended up hurting her hand.

"Ouch. Goddamnit." She shook the injured palm in the air as if she could shake the pain out.

"Here, give me that." Dane took the beer bottle, twisted the top off, and set it on the counter. "She's going to tear up the counters in here doing that. Dad spent weeks cutting all these countertops." He rubbed his hand over the area of small nicks in the granite. "And for twist-top beers. Misty, I love your sister, but damn, she doesn't have respect for nothing."

"That's pretty funny coming from you." Misty picked up her beer and walked into the den.

Dane leaned against the sink. "Okay, so I guess we are fighting."

Misty sipped at the beer. It was clear she didn't even want it. She stood in the den looking out the screen door into the dim purple light of the bug zapper hanging above the porch. The fluorescent light brought out the tense muscles in her face. She wasn't wearing any makeup, or she'd cried it off. Either way, she was angry, and it dawned on Dane that she hadn't even made eye contact with him since he'd been there. He scanned the interior of the trailer looking for his envelope—for those goddamn lab results—but he didn't see anything. Maybe they were still in his pants on the floor back home. Just because he didn't see them didn't mean she hadn't found them or knew what they said. Still, it was possible. He wasn't about to volunteer anything—not yet. Maybe he'd been way off about the whole thing. Maybe this was just something silly—about money—or something he forgot and should've remembered. Misty had anniversaries for everything—first date—first movie—first kiss—first fucking trip to the grocery store. It was exhausting and hard to keep up with. He came up behind her and put his hands on her hips, and she let him. She was wearing a pair of black and orange spandex leggings and a loose-fitting tank top over a sports bra. Dane loved it when she dressed like that. A lot of women went for the workout look, but Misty had the body to pull it off. She actually made it to the gym every day.

Her granny only lived three lots over, so he could hear Jenn talking from where they were standing. "Your sister is loud as hell." Dane moved his hands off her hips and up her back.

"Stop it. I'm sweaty."

"I like you sweaty." He leaned his head forward and kissed her neck. She let the first kiss go, but pulled away from the second. He slid his hands back down to her hips. He wasn't ready to let go. He needed something to go right tonight after everything else had gone off the rails.

"I'm serious, Dane. I'm sweaty and I'm not in the mood. It's nine thirty. I talked to you at two o'clock this afternoon. I thought you'd be here long before now."

"So did I, but Ned—"

"But Ned," Misty repeated, not giving him a chance to finish.

"He's in a lot of trouble, Misty."

"Does *he* know?"

Dane's heart dropped. "Know what? What are you talking about?" He took his hands off her and sank them into his pockets. She walked into the den, set the beer down on the coffee table, and pulled the tattered envelope out of her purse.

Shit.

"About this, Dane. Does Ned know about this?" She slapped the envelope down on the coffee table and there it was. She finally looked him in the eye. "These are dated over a week ago."

Dane walked back into the kitchen. "Misty . . ."

"You've known about this for a week?" She was yelling now. "A fucking week. When were you going to tell me?"

"I don't know. I—didn't know how."

"You didn't know how to tell the woman you share your bed with every night you have a tumor in your lung? You didn't know how to tell me you're sick?" She started crying immediately.

Dane moved in and tried to hold her, but she pushed him away. She circled the den and then barreled back at him and banged her fists into his chest. He took the first few hits before grabbing her by the wrists. "Calm down, Misty."

"How can I calm down? Do you even know what this means? Do you even know how serious this is?"

"Yes, I know how serious it is. It's happening to me, remember. I haven't even been able to process it myself. I didn't want to admit it to myself, much less you. Listen, I told you about the weak spells I've been having— the dizziness. I played it down but it started worrying me a little, so I went and had some tests done. I thought McKenzie was going to tell me I had high blood pressure or something, not that I had stage-two lung cancer. I was scared. I'm still scared. I didn't know how to tell you, so I waited, and then I waited so long that I was afraid this would be how you'd act."

The slap surprised him—and it hurt. Misty must've hurt herself, too, because she started waving her hand in the air again. Dane touched his face. It was raw and pink even under the fresh new beard. "Jesus Christ, Misty. What the hell was that for?"

She lowered her voice and Dane saw something in her face—something he hadn't seen before. "You went fishing, you son of a bitch. You found out you were sick and not only did you ignore what the doctor said—I found your prescriptions, I know you didn't fill them—but you decided not to tell me of all people, and then you went fishing."

"It's not like that, Misty."

"The hell it isn't. Does Charles know? Did you tell him that was the reason for taking the time off?"

Dane didn't have to answer her. He had told Charles and she knew it by looking at his face. "I can't believe you would do this to me—to us." She picked up the envelope from the table and pointed it at him like a weapon. "This isn't just happening to you, Dane—it's happening to us. We are supposed to be partners, remember? I guess you were just going to wait until you dropped dead in the creek somewhere—or out with your high-school buddies—and leave me to sort it out on my own. It's almost like you want it to happen. Is that why you let me move in? Because you knew it wouldn't matter in a year or two anyway?"

"That's ridiculous, Misty."

"Is it, Dane? Is it ridiculous?"

Dane understood exactly where her anger came from. She was right. They were supposed to be partners. She had every right to know about his health and what was happening to him, but he'd been selfish and he knew it. He took the envelope out of her hand and she let him. He unfolded the paperwork and spread it out on the coffee table. He sat on the sofa, and after a long moment, Misty sat next to him. She let a few more tears escape before she wiped her face clean. "Okay," she said. "Okay. What do we do now? We need to get you on these meds."

"Misty."

"And then what comes next. Radiation? Tell me how it works. Tell me how we're going to beat this."

"Misty."

"What?"

"I'm not taking any meds or any radiation."

Misty sat and stared at him with a blank expression. Dane kept her eyes and nodded. After an awkward moment, Misty slowly stood up and grabbed her purse.

"Please, babe. Don't leave. You don't understand. Hear me out."

"You want me to hear you out? No, you're right, Dane. I don't understand. You're sick. It's treatable but you're telling me you're not going to do anything about it?"

A toilet flushed down the hallway, and Misty stood quietly in the middle of the den, holding her purse as if she'd forgotten where she was. She stared at Dane, waiting for an answer as he watched Jackson come up the hall and plop down on the sofa.

"Are you going to die, Uncle Dane?"

The boy's casual question snapped Misty out of her trance and she stormed out of the trailer sobbing. The screen door slammed shut behind her. Dane knew she wasn't going anywhere. Just to find her sister. She wanted him to follow her and he knew he should, but her nephew sat down next to him on the sofa and put his arm around him. Jackson pushed his glasses up on his nose and asked Dane again. "Are you going to die?"

"Everybody dies, Jackson."

"Like the dinosaurs?"

Dane laughed. "Yeah, buddy. Like the dinosaurs."

"I don't like that."

He pulled the kid into him and hugged his neck. "I don't, either, kid. I don't, either."

Dane could hear Jenn coming all the way up to the front stoop, so he straightened himself out and got ready for another ass chewing. Sisters—piss off one, piss off them all. He hoped Jenn wouldn't hit him, too. His face still burned from Misty's slap. Jenn opened the door and poked her head inside. "Dane, she's a mess. I'm going to take her down McDowell Road for a while, maybe stop at the Food Lion and get some ice cream if they ain't closed—if that's all right with you."

Dane exchanged looks with Jackson. That wasn't what either of them expected. "Of course, Jenn. Thank you. I'm sorry about all this. Is there anything I can do?"

"That one there needs a bath, if you're up for it? If not, don't worry about it."

Dane looked at the digital clock on the microwave hanging over the range and then down at Jackson. "I can do that."

"Thanks. Be back soon."

"Okay."

Jenn almost let the door shut but turned and poked her head back in the trailer. "Dane, I'm sorry."

He was used to the twinge of sympathy that came hand in hand with talk of his dead wife and daughter, but that was the first time he'd heard it from someone talking about him. He hated it just as much.

"I am, too. Thanks."

This time she let the door close all the way, and a few minutes later the girls were off running down McDowell Road.

Dane squirted a little shampoo from the bottle on the ledge into the stream of water from the faucet and watched it form a heavy layer of bubbles across the surface. Jackson stripped out of his little boxers and got in. The boy was thin as a rail. Dane could see every rib. He smiled. He looked just like that when he was kid. He stayed that lanky until the day he turned thirty. That's when shit starts to fall apart. He looked at himself in the mirror and pinched at the soft flesh above his belt. Getting old was a bitch. At least now he wouldn't have to see it happen. That shit in his lung would kill him long before he'd be old enough to wear dentures or shit his pants.

Cancer jokes. You're making cancer jokes. Maybe Misty is right. Maybe you are welcoming it. One happy dead-family reunion, right? You selfish prick.

He looked deeper into the mirror at Misty's handprint on his left cheek. Thank God he hadn't shaved in the past few days—domestic camouflage. He took a seat on the commode and watched Jackson make a Santa beard out of a heap of bubbles. Dane leaned over and gave himself one. They both made faces at each other before shaking them off. They spent the next few minutes cycling through variations of bubble beards before Dane grabbed the shampoo bottle again and got to washing the boy's hair. Jackson was specific and bossy about how it needed to be done, the way mama did it, and Dane thought about some of the things that Clem Richland had said about William Blackwell's condition. She called it Asperger's. He wondered how many people he grew up with were bullied for having something no one even knew was a thing. A kid like William or Jackson would just be labeled a spaz or a freak and that was it, a lifetime of being treated like shit, especially out here in the country. Dane leaned in and turned Jackson's head around under the running water to rinse out the shampoo. He finished rinsing the suds out of the boy's hair and dried his hands on the towel.

"I love you, Uncle Dane."

"I love you, too, Jack."

The boy went back to building new and more elaborate structures out of the dissipating bubbles. Dane smiled and out of the blue decided to drink that last beer. "Hang on a second, Jackson. I'll be right back."

"Where are you going? The water is going to get cold. It wasn't that hot to begin with."

"I'm only going to the kitchen. Wait right there, okay? I'll be right back." Dane went and got the last beer, twisted the top, and drank about half of it standing in front of the fridge. He was headed back down the hall when his phone rang.

"Agent Kirby," he answered.

"Kirby!"

Dane closed his eyes. "Hello, Agent Talbott."

"It's Eric, bro. Call me Eric. Where you at? Come meet me at the Vortex. I've got a tallboy and a shot of Fireball with your name on it."

"I can't, but you sound a touch past lit. Are you all right?"

"Hell yeah, I'm all right. I'm better than all right. Come on down. You know the place? The beer's on me, brother."

"Not gonna happen, Eric. I'm in Waymore Valley about two hours away. No late-night beers in my immediate future. Sorry, man. Maybe next time."

"Hell, Kirby, I thought that's why you were calling me."

"What are you talking about? You just called me." Dane switched the phone to his other ear. The reception was bad.

"Kirby—I had two missed calls from you in the past hour."

Dane looked at his phone and thought about the number Talbott had written on the Walmart receipt. He rifled through the paperwork on the counter and there it was. "Goddamn," he said. "Sorry, man, I've got a girlfriend who doesn't like to find phone numbers in my pockets when she does the laundry. She must've called you, man. Sorry about that."

"Damn, son. Sounds like you got woman problems, too. I hope she don't turn out like mine. Bitch is takin' me to the cleaners, man."

"I hear you, man." Dane sipped at the beer and stood in front of the screen door. He couldn't believe Misty blind-called a number she found in his pocket like they were in high school.

No. Scratch that.

Yes, he could.

He wanted to be angry with her for not trusting him, but he knew how ridiculous that was. She had every reason not to trust him. "Well, I'm sorry to bother you this late, Eric."

"Hell, it ain't no bother. I'm just disappointed you can't make it out. I could use a wingman."

Dane looked down the hall through the open door of the bathroom, and Jackson scooped up an armful of depleting bubbles and made himself a big, sparkly Afro. Dane held up a finger and mouthed the words, "Wait a minute. I'm on the phone." Jackson pushed the suds off his head and stared down at his reflection in the cloudy water as Dane sat down on the sofa. "After an entire day of getting kicked in the nuts with this case, I could use the time out, but maybe next time."

"I thought you were working the airport homicide with Velasquez and them. Ain't that shit figured out?"

"Sorta. August—Director O'Barr—put us on a missing kid. The dead guy at the airport has a little brother. We followed a lead up here to a farm owned by someone I know. It's a long story."

"A farm?" Talbott said, as if he'd never heard of such a thing. "How did it turn out? You find anything?"

"Not what I was looking for. At least, not yet."

"Well, I can't believe you got Roselita Velasquez to go out to a farm. That woman breaks a fingernail and goes ballistic. I can't see her stepping a foot into a place that might get shit on her heels. She's particular that way."

Dane laughed. Eric was right. "It's funny you say that, Eric." He took another sip of his beer and pushed the screen door open. "But to tell you the truth, I like her. She puts up a pretty good front, and I guess she has to working around all us humps, but she's good police."

"I didn't say I didn't like her. I said she was uptight, that's all. You know she plays for the other team, right?" A pause on the line. "Kirby, you know what I mean?"

"She's a lesbian, Eric."

"Right."

"So wouldn't that make her a member of *our* team?"

Another pause on the line. "Huh?"

"Never mind, man. Yeah, I know what you mean."

"Right. Anyway, I ain't talking shit about her or nothing. I like gay people. Chicks or whatever, I'm just saying, I can't picture that one out in the pastures, milking cows and shit, wearing those thousand-dollar suits of hers. That chick is all about presentation."

Dane was done with this conversation. He felt the breeze come in through the screen door. The night was going to be cold, he thought. He saw Misty's jacket lying over the arm of the sofa and suddenly regretted everything he'd said to her. He'd told her so, but he hadn't actually felt it until just then. If the roles had been reversed—if he'd found out she was sick and had kept it from him—he would've reacted exactly the same way. He hoped Jenn didn't have her out all night. They needed to talk this out. Dane missed a little of what Eric was saying on the phone, but he didn't care. He sipped his beer and waited for a break in whatever story he was telling to cut him off and let him go.

"Shit, Kirby, I'm just running off at the mouth, so I'm gonna shut up and get back into the game over here. And hey, you want to fuck with Rosey? Do me a favor."

"What's that?" Dane said as a courtesy. He had no intention of "fucking with Rosey."

"Before you roll out of there, take her over to Black Mountain. There's a drive-through Safari Park over there where the llamas and zebras and shit eat right out of your car window. If you think getting her to go to a farm was something, I'm telling you she will have a coronary if she gets llama slobber on one of those silk shirts of hers. That, my friend, would be awesome."

Dane froze on the porch. "Hold up. What? A what kind of drive-through?"

"It's a zoo—right off the interstate. The place is awesome, but Velasquez will—"

"No, I mean, what did you call it?"

"The Safari? That's what it's called. The Black Mountain."

"Do they have birds?"

"I guess so. It's a zoo."

"Son of a bitch."

"What? What's happening right now?"

"Nothing. Listen, I've got to go. I appreciate the call, Eric, really."

"Whatever you say, Kirby. Last chance, and this is my final offer, beers and blondes, on me. This place stays open twenty-four seven."

Dane leaned back more on the doorframe. "Thanks, but no thanks, Eric. I'm happy with what I've got at home."

"Until she fucks a dentist."

Dane laughed. He knew he shouldn't have. It wasn't funny. "Have fun, man, and be safe—don't drive."

"Scout's honor, Kirby. I couldn't if I wanted to. The ex took the Malibu."

Dane ended the call and leaned his forearms down on his knees. He sat there for a second alone on the ramshackle steps and took one last pull from the Blue Moon.

"You know, you shouldn't be so hard on her," Gwen said. She sat next to him on the porch, her yellow dress perfect and unsullied by the dirty stoop, her dark honey-streaked hair hanging loose over her shoulders.

"Not now, Gwen," Dane said.

"Don't get snippy with me. I'm not the one keeping me here, Dane. You are."

Dane closed his eyes and pinched the bridge of his nose. "No, uh-uh. Don't do that," Gwen said. "You've got to stop seeing only what you want to see. That girl loves you. How many people find that twice in their life?"

"She's not you," Dane said, his eyes still closed. He wasn't sure, if he opened them, if she would vanish or steal his breath. He also wasn't sure which he'd prefer.

"Of course she's not me, silly. I'm a supernova. No one can be me—

but I'm also dead. You're not. She's not. So why don't you wake up and see what's right in front of your face?"

"I don't want to see it," Dane nearly yelled at the empty stoop as he opened his eyes and realized he'd just wished her away. "Fuck," he said into his beer bottle before turning it up. He took a hard swallow and nearly choked on it when Misty walked out of the shadows beside the trailer.

"Let me guess. You're talking to her again, right?"

"Jesus, Misty, you scared the hell out of me. I thought you were going to the store with Jenn."

"I did, but I thought I'd come back and see if we could talk like adults."

"Where's Jenn?"

"She's at Granny's." She pointed at the empty bottle in his hand. "That's new."

Dane held the bottle out in front of him. When he stood, he realized the damn thing had given him a buzz. "Yeah, well, it's been a shitty day."

"I know the feeling. You gonna tell me who that was?"

He looked at the phone in his other hand. "That? Nobody. Just someone from work. You could've just asked me whose number it was instead of calling it, by the way. What were you going to say when he answered?"

"Someone from work?"

"Yeah, a kid. I barely know the guy. He's the agent that flew me home the other night. He thinks we've bonded or something."

"It sounded to me like you did."

"He called. I answered. Why is everything so raw with you?"

"I don't know. Maybe the same reason nothing is raw for you." She stepped past him through the door. "It was a mistake coming back. I thought we could talk and try to figure out how to deal with this, you know, as partners." She was crying now. "But apparently you've already got enough people to talk to—living and dead. I'm just going to get my jacket."

Dane dropped his head and poured the backwash from the bottle into the dirt. "I don't want you to leave. I do want to talk to you. I just answered the damn phone. That's all."

Misty had already walked inside and left Dane talking to himself. He stepped up on the stoop and got a head rush. He stood and waited it out before following Misty into the house. She was standing in front of the open freezer looking at nothing. She didn't want to leave, either. She wiped at her face. Her voice was softer now—less angry. "Did you tuck Jackson in?" she asked, and Dane's heart sank for the second time. "What?"

Misty recognized the panic on his face. "Where is he, Dane?"

"He was in the tub. I gave him a bath like Jenn asked me to, and then Eric called."

She was already passing him on her way to the bathroom. "Take it easy, babe. I gave him a bath. He's clean. I'm sure he's got himself out by now."

"He doesn't just *get himself out*, Dane." Misty pushed open the bathroom door and Jackson was still sitting in the middle of the tub. He held his tiny knees close to his chest and was shivering. He looked up at Misty and his thin lips were tinted pale blue. "Hi, Aunt Misty." His voice quivered.

Misty rushed to the tub and snatched a towel from above the toilet. Dane stood in the doorway behind her and watched her lift the skinny little boy out of the water and wrap him in a bundle. She spun around, holding her nephew to her chest. In the entire time Dane had known this woman, he'd never seen her look the way she did now, as if something behind her eyes could explode into splinters. Her tan face was a hot pink and her light green eyes were piercing. Dane's own vision blurred from his beer buzz and he felt a crushing wave of guilt seize his gut.

"Damnit, Dane, you left him in here by himself?"

"Yeah, but just for a few minutes. He was playing. He was fine."

Misty was practically growling. "Does he look fine to you? He's freezing."

"He's not freezing, Misty." Dane went to touch the boy's face, but Misty smacked his hand away. She'd never done anything like that before, either. "What the hell, Misty?"

"You really don't care about anyone else but yourself, do you?"

"Misty. C'mon, I—"

"Get out of my way," she said, and bulldozed past him out of the bathroom. Dane had to balance and pivot on one leg to let her by. He grabbed the wall to keep himself upright and stood there confused, watching

Misty storm across the trailer into the boy's bedroom. Dane walked behind her. "Why didn't he just get out?"

"Leave us alone, Dane. Seriously. Go find your friend *from work* or do whatever it is you do when you're not here."

"No. I seriously want to know." Dane looked at the boy as Misty dried him off and dressed him in his pajamas. "Jackson, tell me, if you were done in there, then why didn't you just get out?"

Jackson didn't answer.

Dane's temper rose, although he knew he was wrong. "I asked you a question, buddy. If you were cold, why didn't you just get out on your own?"

"Just leave him alone," Misty said as she tucked the boy under the covers. Jackson still said nothing. "I'm sorry, Jackson. We shouldn't have left you. We won't do it again."

"Jesus, will someone please tell me what the hell just happened?" Dane was getting loud. He heard the front door open and Jenn's voice call out. "Everyone okay in here?"

"We're fine," Misty answered, before standing up and shoving her face just inches from Dane's. "I said leave him alone, and get out of my way."

"I'm not going anywhere, and I just asked a question, Misty, and I should be able to do that without being ignored. I was only on the phone for ten minutes tops. Look for yourself."

"I don't want to look at your stupid phone."

"And I want an answer."

"I was waiting for you, Uncle Dane," Jackson said, and sat up in the bed. "You told me to wait. I thought you might've died. I didn't know what you wanted me to do."

Misty burst into a full sob and pressed past her man. She made her way to the other side of the trailer—to Jenn's room—and slammed the door. Jenn stood in the middle of the den. She didn't even ask what had happened. She didn't have to. Misty was her sister. Sympathy for her sister's boyfriend had run out. She glared at Dane with the same anger Misty had directed at him, then joined her in the bedroom. She slammed the door, too. Dane stood alone in the den, baffled for a full minute before he sat down on the sofa. He figured that was where he'd be sleeping tonight. He leaned his head back and stared at the whirling ceiling fan. A few minutes later, his head popped up straight, and he tried to remember where he'd put his phone. He remembered what Eric had said. "Son of a bitch." He spotted his phone in the kitchen and stood up to get it. He ran a hand through his dirty hair and thought about the last time he'd showered as the phone rang. He could barely contain himself. The damn thing seemed to ring forever.

"Velasquez," Roselita said when she finally came on the line.

"He's not hiding, Rose."

"What? Kirby? It's nearly midnight."

Dane looked at the clock on the microwave. It was late. Neither of them had gotten any decent sleep in two days. He didn't care. "My girlfriend's nephew," he said more to himself than Roselita.

"You're what?"

"Nothing. Listen. Arnold didn't stash William away somewhere so no one could find him."

"What are you talking about, Kirby?"

"He told him to wait. Arnold thought he'd gotten away with it. There was no reason to hide him, so he just told his brother to wait—and he's still waiting—right now—the kid is still waiting for Arnold to show up."

"Okay, great. He's not hiding. He's waiting. How does that help us?"

Dane snatched his ball cap off the coffee table and pulled it down low on his brow. He saw it all playing out in his head at once. William's fascination with animals. The Safari that Richland mentioned. The Farm. Eddie. He pictured Jackson sitting in that nasty tub of cold water—and knew William was sitting somewhere the same way. It all made sense in his head, but it was coming out like gibberish through the phone. Dane pushed open the screen door and headed toward his truck.

"I know where he is, Rose. I know where William Blackwell is—and I'm going to get him."

CHAPTER TWENTY-TWO

"I swear to God and all the saints, I ain't never had nobody call me out of bed to open this place in the middle of the damn night. Not once—not in all my years—not even the fire department."

"Well, there's a first time for everything, Mr. Edwin." Dane looked like he'd just inhaled a full pot of black coffee. Roselita looked like she was doing her best not to let anyone know she was still running out a vodka-martini buzz. James Edwin, though, the key holder for the Black Mountain Safari Zoo, just looked irritated. The obese man in sweatpants and house shoes fumbled around in the large pocket of his canvas jacket the way a woman would rifle through the insides of a purse until he pulled out a set of keys that allowed entry to the front gate. Dane had been the first to arrive and had already introduced himself, but took a moment to introduce the man to Roselita. He didn't give her the head-to-toe once-over that she normally invoked from men. Edwin was either a decent man or too old and tired to bother.

"I appreciate you meeting us out here like this, Mr. Edwin," she said. "I know it's late."

"Yeah, well, I was gonna be getting up soon to come here anyway, so it's not that big a deal. Just keep in mind that I haven't even looked at a cup of coffee yet."

"We understand," Dane said. "But if we find what we're looking for in here, the extra-large latte from Dunkin' Donuts is on me. I'll even throw in a dozen glazed."

"I'm gonna hold you to that, Agent Kirby." James Edwin looked to be in his midsixties and about a hundred pounds heavier than his wife or doctor would like. The whitish-gray scruff on his face matched the length and color of the thinning circle of hair that covered the bottom half of his head. For his size, he carried himself well, but with the ease and pace of someone who rarely found himself in a hurry. For once, it was Dane rushing someone else. He anxiously waited with Roselita for the big man to find the right key. "You say y'all are with the government?"

"That's right." Dane had already shown the big man his wallet ID when he got there. Roselita brandished hers and held it out for Edwin to see. He barely looked at it. He didn't really care. He'd gotten too old to give a shit about folks and their titles. If this wasn't on the up and up, so be it. He'd just go home. "A lady FBI agent?"

"Yes, sir. Is that a problem?"

"No. No. I think it's great. It's great. I just thought, the other guy's ID said GBI."

"It does," Dane said.

"Huh. I didn't even know you guys still existed. What does the GBI actually do, anyway?"

"They wake people up in the middle of the night and ask them to do cryptic shit," Roselita said, and smirked at Dane. "That's what they do."

Edwin glanced over at Roselita, smiled a warm smile, and continued to cycle through the keys on the massive steel ring. Roselita shrugged at Dane, who nervously gnawed his lip. He wasn't the slightest bit bothered by his partner's snark. He just watched as the old man finally found the right color-coded key and opened the first and then the second lock on the gate. He pushed the gate open and waited for Dane and Roselita to go through before he followed and locked it behind them.

"Wait here a minute." Edwin tapped a five-digit numeric code into a keypad on the wall just inside the gate, and a small LED light turned from red to green. "The security system is off now, so you two can do whatever you need to do."

"Can we get a little light in here?" Dane asked, and Edwin nodded. "Sure, hold on." He swiped a plastic card through the reader on the end of a row of turnstiles and pushed his way through. Dane and Roselita followed him as he made his way to an unmarked door behind the ticket office. He searched the key ring again and then unlocked and opened that door as well. He went in and a few seconds later, the main lights illuminating the treetops, walkways, and map signage began to pop on, one section at a time. Once the entire park was lit up, Edwin came back out of the office and tucked the key ring back in the pocket of his coat.

"I thought this was a drive-through type of place," Roselita said. "You know, with free roaming animals. This looks more like a regular zoo."

"That's the back end of the park," Dane answered. "You get to that entrance by SR seventeen, but that's not where we want to be. Trust me on this."

Roselita reached in her purse and put on some ChapStick. It had gotten cold. Dane turned to the big key holder.

"Are you the only security on the premises?"

"At one in the morning I am," Edwin said. "We used to have a night watchman, but the county cut the budget a few years back." Edwin held his arms out and then let them flop back down to his sides. "So I'm all you get."

"No one else should be here then?"

"Nope. Just us and the residents."

"The residents?"

"The animals. They're the residents."

Dane looked around, unsure which direction he needed to head in. Edwin stuffed his hands in his pockets. "I know you guys like your secret-agent stuff and all, but this is a big place. I might be able to help out if you told me what it is we're looking for."

"Right. Okay. We're looking for a stowaway, Mr. Edwin. A kid holed up here. And to be completely honest with you, I'm not positive that we're going to find him. It's just a hunch."

"Well, we don't get that many stowaways, but would this hunch of yours be a fan of Paydays?"

"Paydays? I don't follow."

"You know. The candy bar?"

"I'm sorry, Mr. Edwin, I still don't follow."

"Why do you ask?" Roselita said.

"Well." Edwin hiked his pants up by the sides of his belt. "Night before last, I took out all the trash on this side of the Safari myself. All of it. The next morning when I come in around five in the AM, I found about

a half dozen Payday wrappers in the fresh can liners. I figured it was
employees, but I asked around, and it ain't. It's the weirdest thing, too.
Just Paydays. Nothing else. Cleaned out the vending machine of them.
Nobody likes Paydays."

Dane thought about what Clem Richland had told them in her office,
about William and the M&M's. "Our boy isn't a fan of chocolate."

Roselita was awake now and looked excited. "Dane, Payday bars don't
have any chocolate on them. It's probably the only candy bar in existence
that doesn't. That's why nobody eats the damn things."

"Well, somebody does," Edwin said.

Dane smiled. "And where did you find these candy-bar wrappers?"

"Over by the flamingos."

Dane smiled even wider. "Could you please take us there, Mr. Edwin."

"Sure thing. Right this way."

Dane convinced Roselita and the caretaker to keep their distance as he
sat down on the bench next to a pond filled with bright pink birds. His
presence and possibly the lighting had them in a tizzy as they marched
back and forth in shallow water. The bench was damp with dew, and he
eased himself down onto its wooden planks. He looked to his left toward
the vending machine Edwin had pointed out as they walked over—the
one with the empty row in the center where the Paydays had been. To his
right was a wooded area that, even with the park lights turned on, stayed
pitch black at night. Down on the bench by his left hand he saw the last
thing he needed to see to know he was in the right place. The letters *W*
and *B* were carved into the treated pine. Not by a knife or any kind of
blade, but by something dull like a small twig or a thumbnail. Something
that had been rubbed and pressed into the wood over and over again,
repeated over time, to make the indentation. Dane looked around at his
feet until he found a small piece of wood that had splintered off the side of
the old bench itself. He picked it up and dragged it lightly over the letters
carved into the bench. It was a perfect fit.

Dane set the piece of wood down next to him and kept both hands between his knees. He leaned back on the bench. "It's okay, William. You

can come out." He didn't yell. He just spoke loudly enough to be heard in the woods behind him. He didn't even turn around to look. "I'm not here to hurt you." Dane heard nothing—no response—no movement. "My name is Dane—like a Great Dane—you know—like the dog? I'm a police officer and I'm here to take you home." Still nothing. Not a sound. Dane leaned forward a little and pushed some leaves around on the sidewalk with his foot. "I know your brother told you to wait here for him, William. I know you don't know me, and you're just doing what your brother asked you to do, but you can come out now. You did good, William. Arnold would be proud of you for waiting this long— real proud—but you don't have to wait anymore. He's not coming, son." Dane took out the photo of William and his parents. He held it over his head so it could be seen by anyone looking and then set it down next to him on the bench. "William, I know you lost your folks last year. I know how much that hurts. I also know you're scared of letting Arnie down because he's all you've got, but you're not going to let anyone down. I promise. You know if he was coming he'd be here by now, but he's not, so you're gonna have to trust me. I only want to get you home safe."

This time Dane thought he heard something rustling around in the woods. He looked but didn't see anything. It might have been just the wind or a squirrel, but he directed his attention toward it. "I can protect you, son. I can—"

"Is he dead?" William said from the side of the bench opposite the way Dane was looking. For the second time that night, Dane about jumped out of his skin. William stood next to the bench with his hands buried in the front pocket of a gray hoodie. He was just skin and bones. The hood of William's sweatshirt was down, and Dane saw in person for the first time the face of the boy he'd been looking at in that photo. He was thinner and taller now, and his cheeks were hollow and sunken, but they were still covered in freckles like the younger, happier version of the kid in the picture. He eyes were still just as gray and distant. Dane felt the need to reach out and hug the boy. He was just a few years older than Joy. He fought the urge and instead just answered the boy's question honestly. "Yes, William, your brother is dead. I'm sorry."

If William was surprised, he didn't act like it. "Did you kill him?"

Dane was surprised by the question. "What? No. No, William, I didn't kill him. I work for the people who are trying to find out who did. I've been trying to find you ever since it happened."

"Was it because we won the money?" The boy's abnormal sense of calm was unnerving, but Dane continued to sit and clutch at the bench wood between his knees. He kept his answers short and honest.

"Yes, William, it was because of the money, but it's not your fault. You have to understand that. None of this is your fault. But right now we should get you somewhere safe."

William stood there with his hands buried deep in his pockets and studied Dane's face. Maybe he was looking for a lie, but Dane thought he was most likely looking for a friend.

"What do you say, kid? Can we get out of here? You've got to be starving. We can go and get something to eat first. Does that sound good? We can go anywhere you want."

William picked up the photograph from the bench and sat down next to Dane. "I miss my mom."

"I imagine you do, son. Why don't we get you out of here, and we can talk about it?"

William stuck the picture in the pocket of his hoodie and said nothing.

Dane grabbed his phone from his jacket. "I need to let some people know I found you, okay?" He began to lift himself off the bench.

"Do you see that flamingo over there?"

Dane eased back down and looked over at the wading pond. "I see a bunch of them, William."

"Seven over from the right. The really tall one with the yellow dots by his beak. See him?"

Dane counted seven over from the right. "Yeah, I see him."

"That one," William said, "has been bothering that female next to him for hours, but she already has a partner. Any second now he's going to make his move and—wait, watch."

Dane watched the taller bird close in on an identical-looking pink bird to its right, if closing in meant taking a single step. But just as it took that step, a third identical-looking bird flapped its wings and cawed in protest. The rest of them followed suit and the taller bird backed away to the edge of the pond. William shifted on the bench. "Did you know that flamingos mate for life? Once they find a partner, it's them two until the very end. They never leave each other. And if one of them dies, the other one lives alone until it dies, too."

Dane stared at the birds. "No. I didn't know that."

William looked up at Dane but didn't look him directly in the eye. "That's pretty cool, right?"

Dane's heart felt as if it doubled in size and no longer fit in his chest. "Yeah, it is. It's very cool."

William stood up and motioned for Dane to do the same. "We can go now," he said.

Dane nodded and stood. He let William lead the way.

Dane and Roselita stood in the parking lot of the Black Mountain Safari Zoo as James Edwin locked it back down. William sat in the back of Roselita's car looking at the photo of his family. There were still no tears. They shook Edwin's hand and thanked him, and then watched the big man get into his truck and leave the parking lot. When he was gone, Dane pulled out his phone. "I'll call August and let him know we found the kid and we're bringing him in."

Roselita looked at William in the back of the car and, for the first time, she didn't argue with Dane. She just stood and watched him tap in a number and turn his back to her.

"I'm sorry about this, Kirby."

"Sorry about what, Rose? Hold on a sec—"

Roselita brought the handle of her gun down hard on the back of Dane's head and he went sprawling to the pavement. The phone flew from his hand and spun like a top on the asphalt. Roselita walked over and picked it up. "For that," she said, and began to drag Dane's unconscious body toward the Infiniti. It took some work, but she managed to get him in the car. William watched from the back seat but made no attempt to get out. He just watched—expressionless, as if he'd always known it was going to go this way. When Roselita loaded Dane into the car, William simply moved over.

CHAPTER TWENTY-THREE

Dane came to in a room he didn't recognize. There was a lot of red—the walls, the plush chair in the corner, the shag rug, all red. His head was killing him and he didn't need to touch it to know there was a goose egg on the back of his skull rising like a biscuit in the oven. He tried to touch it anyway. He couldn't. His hands were bound. He tried wriggling free, but his hands were zip-tied behind his back and he'd been sitting on them long enough in an awkward position that they'd both fallen asleep. It was starting to come back to him. He got hit—hard—who—"Rose?"

"I'm sorry about clocking you like that, Kirby, but I didn't think you'd have given him up on your own."

"Given who up, Roselita? What's going on? What are you doing?" The blur at the edges of Dane's vision began to clear and he could make out more details of the room he was in. It was a nice room. He was on a sofa—real leather. Long red curtains ran all the way from ornate brass rods to the floor, filling the room with filtered sunlight—explaining all the red. A large antique china cabinet took up almost a full wall filled with old metallic-rimmed dishes. He'd been in here before, but it had been a long time ago. He knew for sure when he saw the oval-shaped window cut out of the center of the front door. He could make out the huge letter *H* etched in the glass, but from the inside this time. He was in Eddie Rockdale's house. "Roselita, why are we here? Why the hell did you hit me? Where's the boy?"

"I'm just doing what I'm told, Kirby. You should've just left it alone back at the motel like you wanted to. Now look how fucked-up it's gotten. I didn't have a choice."

"A choice about what? Where the hell is William and why are we here?" Dane pulled at the zip ties. His head hurt like a son of a bitch.

"She's here because I asked her to meet me here. She's my guest." Eddie turned the corner and entered the living room from the kitchen. He was holding two glasses of whiskey—no ice. He handed one to Roselita. "Damn, Kirby, you got some shitty luck. First that shit with your family, ouch, killing your own wife and daughter? That shit right there would make a lesser man eat a bullet, but not you. You stuck it out and was working on a new life but now look at you, all tied up in my living room involved in something else that is gonna leave a bullet in you. It's sad, really. I mean, I was just going to take you out back and shoot you before you woke up, let Tater toss you in the incinerator, but your girl Roselita here asked me not to. Not that it matters. There isn't a way this goes down that lets you live, and she knows that. I don't know what she's waiting for." Eddie took a seat on the leather sofa and slapped a gold ring–covered hand down on Dane's knee. He licked his teeth. "Maybe Mamacita is sweet on you, Kirby."

"Killing him isn't your decision to make, Rockdale."

"Whatever you say, Velasquez, but you know your boy is going to kill him no matter how sweet on him you are. He has to." Eddie stood up and tossed back the whiskey, but Roselita set her glass on the table. "He's not my boy. He's my partner. And this is only business, so why don't you shut the fuck up until he gets here." Roselita was holding her gun. The same gun she'd hit Dane with at the zoo. Eddie licked his teeth again. It was strange to see him keep his temper under control. No one spoke to him like that if they knew him, much less a woman or a stranger.

Unless they aren't strangers.

Dane's head was swimming. "What's with the gun, Roselita? What's he talking about? Did you two already know each other before last night? Was all this one big act? And where the hell is William Blackwell?"

Roselita nodded to a closed set of French doors leading to another part of the house. "He's fine, Dane. He's in there. And no, I didn't know this gold-mouthed asshole before yesterday, but apparently plans changed. I didn't want anything to do with this, but it is what it is."

"Why don't you tell him everything, Velasquez? He's going to find out soon enough anyway." Eddie crouched down in front of Dane again. He was still groggy and the sound of Eddie sucking his teeth made his stomach roll.

"Listen, Rose, whatever is going on here, I know you're not okay with it. I know you're not one of these—these—"

"These what?" Eddie asked and stared directly into Dane's eyes.

"These killers."

Eddie looked offended. "I ain't killed nobody, Kirby. Not yet, any-way." He stood up to refill his glass and Dane could feel the warped piece of metal in his pocket—the high-caliber slug that had been with him every day for the past twelve years. It pressed against his leg, and the feel of it made him struggle even harder against his restraints. He stopped when Lydia came into the room through the French doors. She held an empty plastic cup and walked into the kitchen as if there wasn't another woman in the room with her husband holding a gun and a man she knew tied and bound on her sofa. She turned a corner where Dane couldn't see her, but he could hear her open the fridge and refill the tumbler. When she came back into the room the cup was full. She stayed quiet and returned to the other room. Dane caught a glimpse of William sitting on a loveseat when she opened the door. She tried not to look, but Dane caught her eyes before she closed the door. Her face was pink, and her eyes were red. She'd been crying. She mouthed the words "I'm sorry," and then she was gone.

"So what now, Eddie? You plan on doing what Arnie did? You gonna use the boy to get yourself killed next?"

"I'm gonna use that boy to get myself rich, Kirby. You and I both know I've got a little more up here than his idiot brother." Eddie tapped at the side of his head. "As soon as Uncle Casper gets back here with the money, he belongs to me—lock, stock, and barrel." He picked up a bottle of bourbon and poured it in his glass.

Dane squirmed. "C'mon, Roselita. You don't really think these guys are going to pay you for something they already have, do you? You can still turn this around."

"Just stop talking, Kirby."

"Yeah. Easy, Kirby, I ain't the bad guy here. Your people came to me. They set all this up. I just happened to be in the right place at the right time. Too bad I can't say the same thing about you. You see, this was all supposed to go down real easy. My boy Bobby, my main man who is always bringing me the kush—well, he was supposed to bring me the boy once that dipshit Arnold was airborne. See, Bobby hated that guy, used to bang his girl or some shit back in the day, so he made a deal with me way before the Slasher even went down—but dumbass Bobby got a little money-drunk and went home first instead to do a little partying. That little decision got hisself and all his buddies killed. Damn shame, too. He had the best weed in the motherfucking state. And since dead men tell no tales and shit, nobody knew where the kid was—until you, Kirby. I gotta say, you one hella detective. Almost makes me sad to see you go, you know? All that wasted potential and whatnot." Eddies mouth gleamed with spit-slickened gold.

Roselita stuck her gun into the holster on her hip. "Where's the money, Rockdale? Your man's been gone a long time. If you're thinking of fucking us over, you're going to end up worse than your good pal Bobby Turo."

Eddie picked up a walkie-talkie from the table and mashed the button. "Tater, pick up. Where the hell is Casper? He should've been back already." He waited but didn't get a reply. "Tater, pick up."

Still nothing.

He set the radio back down and pulled a rifle off a rack on the wall. He chambered a round and downed the fresh shot of whiskey in his glass. "I'm going out to the barn. You watch this one and remember your place in all this, girlie. Remember what you've got to lose if you do anything to jeopardize this deal."

"I got this. Just find out what the hell is taking so long."

Eddie left through the back door and Roselita took a seat at the table. She stared at the untouched glass of whiskey. "I'm sorry, Kirby."

"I don't even know what's happening here, Rose, so maybe you should start filling me in so I can help you unfuck whatever this is."

Roselita kept looking at the glass.

"C'mon, Rose, why are you doing this?"

"The money," she said, and it exhausted her as if the word itself weighed fifty pounds. "The money we were trying to retrieve from Arnie Blackwell, before August shut us down and brought you in. We knew who he was ten minutes after we found his body. We knew there was over a million at play, and that whoever had killed him hadn't gotten their hands on it yet. At least not all of it." Roselita walked over and squatted down to face Dane. "I found the joint on the floor, Dane, long before you got there. It was in my damn pocket the whole time you were giving me my *big break* in the case. We already had a good idea who and where his partner was and hopefully his half of the winnings from the Slasher. We'd put everything together and were about to move on Turo—and then, well, then there was you—and everything went up in smoke. Those flip fuckers got to the money first while we were catching you up and acting like we didn't already know. It could've been over in hours, but you came along and fucked everything up. We lost every dime to those evil bastards, so our only option was to try and find the kid and sell him off to somebody who would be willing to pay for him as a reimbursement."

"Reimbursement," Dane repeated. "For a bag of money that wasn't yours to begin with?"

Roselita looked as if she would be sick. "It was the only option."

"That's not your only option now, Rose. You can cut me loose and we can get the hell out of here. We can get William somewhere safe. This can't be about money anymore. That's not who you are."

"You have no idea who I am, Kirby."

"I know you're not someone who would sell a child to these assholes. For a payday? You've got a kid of your own on the way. Is this the way you want to start off being a mother?"

Roselita stood up. Dane expected the punch she was going to throw at him to hurt, but Roselita just looked more sickened than anything else. "Props for finding him, Kirby, and ending all this shit. Truthfully, I hoped you'd figure it all out before we did. I hoped you'd feel in your gut that you were being played. Then you would've stayed away from me—from all this. You wouldn't have called me to go walk into the lion's den with you. I mean, you handed the kid right over to us. I told you. I had no choice."

"Yes, you did, and I didn't get played, Rose. I trusted you. Big difference."

Roselita walked back over to the table and finally drank the bourbon. She picked up the radio, set it back down, and stared into the empty glass.

"Roselita, listen to me, you're not a murderer. And you're not someone who would do this to a child."

"I told you, you don't know shit about me, Kirby. I am a murderer. I killed a pregnant woman. We killed her." Roselita picked up the glass and threw it. It shattered on the far wall, glass raining down all over the hardwood flooring. Dane flinched but felt more confused than frightened.

"You were with me when the Sellers woman was killed. How can you say we killed—" Dane stopped. He understood. "You're not talking about you and me. You keep saying we—you're talking about you and Dahmer, aren't you?"

Roselita didn't answer.

"That's why you were so tore up when you found out the Sellers woman was pregnant—because your partner is the one that killed her? And you're blaming yourself?"

"Shut up, Kirby."

"That wasn't supposed to happen, was it? Did she survive the attack from the Filipinos? Did Dahmer go finish the job? I saw your face when you found out. Why didn't you tell me? What does he have on you? I know this isn't who you are."

"He doesn't have anything on me. He's my partner. He's saved my life too many times to count."

"And he's a killer, Rose—a cold-blooded murderer. Cut me loose and let me help you out of this. We can put a stop to all of it—together."

"There's no stopping it, Kirby." Roselita sat back down at the table and sank her head into her hands. "When Gold Mouth's uncle gets back with the cash, they are taking the kid and I'm going to have to live with what I did. I'm sorry it played out like this."

"Tell me then, why haven't you killed me already?"

"Shut up, Kirby."

"Because you can't, Rose. Because you're not Dahmer. You're waiting on him to get here so he can do it, aren't you?"

"I said, shut up, Kirby."

"You can still stop this, Rose."

Roselita jumped out of her seat and pulled her gun from her hip. She pressed it into Dane's forehead. "Stop calling me Rose."

"Stop letting a man who would kill a woman with a baby in her belly and sell another child like property make your decisions for you."

Roselita closed her eyes tight and stood quietly before lowering her gun and looking at her watch.

"We're running out of time, Roselita. And just so you know, that piece of shit out there in the barn right now has no intention of paying you anything. He's waiting for your partner to get here so he can take us all out at once. Believe that."

"That guy out there may be stupid, Kirby, but he's not stupid enough to kill federal agents. Not if he wants to continue to live his life above ground. Nobody is that stupid."

Dane actually laughed at that. "You still don't have any idea where you are. Do you, Rose? The only reason he hasn't put a bullet in both of us already is because he needs to make sure Dahmer eats one, too. Loose ends matter up here, Rose, not federal agents. Jesus, wake up."

Roselita shook her head frantically, but it looked to Dane like she was listening. She took a breath and settled herself. She spoke smoothly and calmly. "I'm not going to tell you again to shut up, Kirby. This is happening, and there's nothing you or I can do about it. It's done."

Dane stopped squirming. He sat up as straight as he could, ignoring the pain in his neck and skull. "There is no honor in that man out there, Rose. Trust me on that. I know."

Roselita stayed quiet. She just wanted all of this to go away.

Dane's voice took on a more conversational tone, as if he wasn't being held against his will. "Rooster was there when my wife and daughter died."

Roselita snapped back to the moment. The words wife and daughter punched her in the chest and her shoulders sagged back. Her voice had lost all its bravado as well. "Sorry, Dane. After I talked to your friend Keith, I did my research on you. What happened to your wife and daughter was an accident. I read the report."

Dane spoke from a faraway place, as if he could feel himself out in those woods again. "If you read the report, then you know I hit a deer, right? That's what caused the truck to flip."

"Yeah, and what does that have to do with Eddie Rockdale?"

"He shot that deer. He was hunting land that wasn't his. He was hunting out of season. Maybe if that bastard hadn't shot that deer, it wouldn't have taken to the road. Or maybe not. Maybe it all would have played out the same. But one thing I know for a fact, Rose, is that man let me lay there on the side of the road holding my wife's hand as it turned cold for almost an hour." Dane's voice seized in the middle and he choked on the story. "He just watched, Rose. Or he ran away. Either way. He did nothing." Dane's eyes went distant. "He let my baby girl hang in a tree for a hour—before someone eventually came along and found us."

Roselita was nearly in tears listening to this man who'd lost everything and still tried to believe there was good in the world. He stared directly into her dark brown eyes. "That's how I know he's not just going to give you what you want. Hell, Rose, it sounds to me like you don't even want it, but I can guarantee you he's not going to own up to his end of this deal he's made. I promise you, they are planning how to kill us all in that barn right now, and if what you said about your partner is true, Dahmer isn't going to care who dies because of Rockdale's decision to cut him out. That means Lydia, William, anyone."

Roselita stood up and walked over to the sofa. "How do you know any of that really happened when you wrecked the truck? How do you know he was there?"

"I heard a shot right before I lost control. Right before that deer ran out in front of me."

"It could've been anything—anyone."

"It was a .30-30. The same caliber that Rooster pulled out of the gun cabinet just now."

"A .30-30 is common. It could've belonged to anyone."

Dane shifted on the sofa. "My left pocket." He shoved his hip into position for Roselita to reach in. She did. Roselita pulled out the warped slug. "What is this?"

"Ned Lemon pulled that out of the animal remains after the accident. He knew Eddie hunted that land. He knew Eddie was out that day. Ned took his time, but eventually matched the ballistics on that bullet to one of Eddie's rifles. Most likely the one in his hands right now."

"How the hell could Lemon have access to ballistic records?"

"Remember Sheriff Burroughs? There was no love lost between him and Rockdale, so he helped Ned on the down-low. They gave me that information and that bullet to do with as I pleased. I've been carrying both around with me ever since. So I know Eddie was there when my family died—and did nothing. Just like I know he's going to kill all of us as soon as your partner walks through that door."

Roselita squeezed her eyes shut again, opened them, and stuck the slug back in Dane's pocket. "Why didn't you ever do anything about it?"

"Because I couldn't bring myself to cross a line that there is no coming back from. Just like I'm trying to stop you from doing right now."

The whole house stayed quiet for almost a full minute before they heard the gunfire from the barn.

Fenn set the rifle down on the plywood table. "I'll never understand you Americans and your love for guns. They are loud and cumbersome and, most importantly, ineffective in close quarters." Tater sat against the wall of the barn, his head tilted forward on his chest, both hands holding his guts in. He might still have been breathing, but death had breached the room. The tips of Tater's boots twitched in the dirt, but by the time Fenn had finished disassembling the long gun, Tater was gone. His hands dropped and blood pooled out underneath him like the shadow of an inflating black balloon. Fenn turned and wiped the sharp end of his baston on the shoulder of Tater's shirt. It was a much better weapon—a cleaner weapon—more of a natural extension of the man holding it than any machined piece of metal with too many moving parts that increased the odds of failure. Fenn admired his weapon and his handiwork. He was pleased that he'd been able to dispense with the lackey without allowing him to get any shots off. Fenn wasn't ready to alert anyone in the main house. Especially the black one. He seemed to be in charge and could prove to be formidable, but size alone did not bring skill. The black man, the one called Rockdale, relied too heavily on guns as well, and that would be his downfall. Fenn came very close to going inside and killing them all at his leisure. He had thought about spending time with the cinnamon woman, too, but he was glad he'd waited through the night. The female FBI agent had brought the boy right to him. She'd also brought the other policeman, the one with the baseball hat, but it seemed they were no longer on the same side. Americans didn't believe in loyalty, either. This would also be their downfall. Regardless, the money was in the car, and the boy was within his grasp. Fenn's mission in the US was almost at completion. He would soon be home. He would be celebrated. He felt good despite his throbbing shoulder. He turned toward the house. His intention was to wait in the shadows behind the barn door by the blackout boxes. He would wait until the men inside turned on each other. When the time was right, he would kill the last one standing and take the boy—maybe the cinnamon woman, too. He turned from the dead man and was surprised to see Eddie Rockdale standing in the wide-open doorway of the barn sighting a rifle right at Fenn's head. He thought about the dead lackey's radio. Maybe it had been a mistake to turn it off. So be it. It was what it was.

"Wow," Eddie said. "You are one big ugly son of a bitch."

Fenn said nothing. He slowed his breathing and gripped the length of bamboo with both hands.

"Is my boy Tater dead?"

Fenn still said nothing. Eddie inched forward and moved Fenn slowly backward into the barn. Eddie saw the remains of Tater in his peripheral vision but never took his eye off of the big intruder. "You know I've known that fella my whole life? He was my friend. You kill him with that stick? You must've snuck up on him." Eddie nodded at his own summation and licked his teeth. "Yeah, you must've snuck up on him 'cause you can't expect me to think you got a shot in hell against a man holding one of these—unless you got the drop on 'em." Eddie kept the rifle on the big man in his barn and smiled. "See, 'cause that ain't possible. Watch." His teeth gleamed in the sun as he fired.

"Get up," Roselita said after the shot rang out, and nudged Dane with the barrel of her Glock.

"Just cut me loose, and we—"

"Just get up, damnit." She yanked on Dane's arm with enough force to pull him to his feet and used her gun to nudge him toward the double doors. Dane bumped them open with his shoulder. William still sat on the loveseat holding the plastic cup Lydia had filled up earlier. It was empty again. William didn't look frightened or bewildered. He didn't look anything the way an eleven-year-old boy should look in a situation like the one he was in. He looked dismal and sad. He didn't even flinch when Roselita used her gun again to push Dane farther into the room. "Are you okay, William?" Dane asked.

"Yes, sir."

Roselita moved deeper into the room and peeked through the heavy drapes out toward the back of the house. "Wait," she said, and spun around to scan the room. There was a bathroom, but its door was wide-open, so it was easy to see it was empty. The doors they had come through were the only ones leading in or out. "Where's the woman?" Roselita said. "Where's Lydia?"

William pointed to the window on the other side of the fireplace. It was open and the screen had been pushed out. Roselita pushed the curtains out of the way with the pistol and cussed under her breath. She swung the gun around. "Where did she go?"

"Take it easy, Roselita. Don't hurt him."

"I'm not going to hurt him, Dane. Find something for me to use to cut you free." She looked at William and tried to sound calm. "Where did she go, William? She may be the only one who can get us out of here safe."

William didn't look frightened. He didn't look anything. He shrugged. "I don't know," he said. "She said she'd be back. She told me to come with her but I didn't want to."

"You didn't—" That confused Roselita and Dane both. The kid had had a chance to escape but didn't? "Why?" Dane asked.

"Because you're the good guys. That's what you said."

Roselita laughed, but it was dry and humorless. She motioned for William. "Let's go. C'mon. Get up." The boy was compliant. He stood and walked to the door. Roselita followed Dane back through the main living room, past the massive china cabinet, and out the front door. She grabbed William by his sleeve and guided him out onto the porch as well. "Where the hell is she?"

"I'm right here, bitch." Ned brought the hardwood grip of Dane's Red-hawk .44 down on Roselita's neck like a sledgehammer. She dropped her own gun and collapsed as it spun off the porch into the azaleas. Again, William didn't move or act surprised.

"She probably wasn't talking about me, was she?" Ned flipped open a pocket knife and cut the zip tie off Dane's wrists.

"Jesus Christ." Dane looked down at Roselita out cold on the porch. "Where have you been, Ned?"

"I'm sorry, Dane. I freaked. I should never have called you. All this shit is my fault. I never—"

"Not the time to talk about it." Dane narrowed his eyes at the gun Ned was holding. "Is that mine?"

Ned looked down at the Redhawk. "Yeah, I took it out of your glove box. That okay?"

Dane swiveled around and saw his truck parked out past the clearing. "Well, fuck me. Are the keys in it?"

"No."

"Shit."

"They're right here." He reached into his pocket and handed Dane the keys. "They were gonna dump it in the quarry. I'm glad you had a piece in there, or I would've showed up empty-handed."

Dane squeezed the keys and almost laughed. "C'mon." He grabbed William's arm and headed toward the steps.

"Go, I got this piece of shit." Ned pointed the Redhawk down at Roselita's head and held his other hand in front of his face to block the spatter of blood.

"No," Dane yelled and snatched the gun. "Leave her be."

"Are you kidding? This bitch sold you out, Dane. She was going to kill you."

"But she didn't. Leave her for now and let's get William somewhere safe. I'll come back for her."

Ned looked confused. "Back for her? What?"

"No time to explain. Come on." By the time Dane got to the driver's door he was seeing white bursts in his vision. He had a concussion, maybe. His head hurt like hell. He swung the door open and motioned for William to get in. The boy began to crawl in when Ned called out for Lydia.

"Where is she?"

"I left her here in the truck," Ned said, and yelled her name again. He was frantic. He screamed her name a third time.

"She's right here, Mr. Lemon. Now all of you slowly back away from the truck." Dahmer stood at the tree line, holding Lydia by her neck. He used her body to block his and held a pistol to her head.

"I'm sorry," she said. She tried to say something else, but Dahmer squeezed the words from her throat.

"Come on out, you big ugly motherfucker," Eddie said, and racked another cartridge into the rifle and walked slowly through the barn. He'd shot the big man full on, center mass. The bastard should be lying on the ground with a hole in him, but he wasn't. The back end of the barn, where all the fighting pens were, was blacked out and there were a thousand places for him to hide, but no one knew the barn better than the man who built it, so Eddie carefully cased each pen. He kicked open each cedar door one by one and swung the rifle in. Each time he came up empty. The third door he kicked open allowed him to see his uncle. Casper had left earlier—to gather a few more men from up the mountain. They were supposed to wait until the other Fed showed up and then swarm the house and take them all out, but he never even made it off the property. Casper lay in the dirt in an unnatural position. His arms broken, his throat carved open. His glass eye missing, leaving a black hole in the left side of his face. Flies had already begun to gather and buzzed around the body like it was three-day-old roadkill. His blood had already dried into the dirt and congealed into pools of strawberry jelly. Eddie's stomach roiled before the anger took over. "I'm going to kill you slow, you gook motherfucker." He turned and felt the baston as Fenn shoved it through his abdomen.

"You will do nothing," Fenn said. He pulled Eddie close to him and twisted the length of bamboo in a way that made him slide slowly to his knees. Fenn pulled the baston out and Eddie dropped backward, next to his uncle. Fenn crouched down and looked in his eyes. It hurt him to move. It was the second time the vest had saved his life, but it still hurt like hell. Watching the light fading from Eddie's eyes eased the big man's pain. "At least you die with your family. You have that to take with you." He waited a minute longer as Eddie began to spew up large bursts of blood. "I'm gonna—kill—you—" he managed to say between coughs.

"In another life, my friend." Fenn stood. He wiped the baston off on Eddie's jeans, and then walked out of the barn toward the house.

"Let her go," Ned yelled as Dahmer stepped cautiously out of the woods. Dahmer was careful to keep Lydia positioned between him and Dane, the only one carrying a gun—the only threat he needed to worry about.

"Give me the boy and I will let her go. A simple exchange. There's no reason for anyone else to die. This wasn't supposed to happen, Kirby." Lydia struggled against him, but Dahmer only tightened his grip. He was so tall, so thin, that he practically had to hold her on the tips of her toes to shield him.

"You have my word, Kirby. The woman for the boy."

Dane had already dropped to his knees behind the fender well. He hoisted the Redhawk over the hood. "Go fuck yourself, Dahmer. You don't have a play here. You hurt her and you die next. So the only real trade is you let her go and I don't blow your head off."

Dahmer took another carefully placed step. "That's one possible outcome. Another one is I kill her and then I kill him." He nodded at Ned, who stood with his hands in the air in front of the truck. "You'll lose two people you care about to protect someone you just met. It's been a while since you've had to fire that cannon. Are you sure you want to take that chance?"

"Just let her go, Dahmer."

Dahmer sighed. "I want you to remember that this is on you, Kirby. I gave you a choice."

He pushed the barrel of the gun into Lydia's temple. She tried to scream but no sound came out. Ned's scream was loud enough for them both. The shot echoed over the clearing and Dane could hear himself screaming, too, but it wasn't just him and Ned. Lydia had found her voice and she screamed as she ran toward Ned, who grabbed her and sank to the ground. He ran his hands over the sides of her head and felt no wound. She was whole. He kissed her eyes, her nose, her whole face. When he looked up, Dahmer had taken to the woods holding his shoulder. Ned was crying and confused. He looked at Dane, who was sitting on the ground behind the truck staring past him back at the house. Ned turned to see Roselita Velasquez lying in front of the porch on her stomach. Her face was scratched up by the azalea bushes she'd had to fish her pistol out of. She dropped the gun she'd just shot Dahmer with in front of her and laid her face in the cool grass. She had no cover. She was best off hugging the ground. Ned pushed Lydia behind the truck and covered her the best he could. Another shot came from the woods and then another one pinged off the truck's hood. Everyone was on the ground now, no one knowing who or where the shots were coming from.

"Dahmer's still out there. Get in the truck. Now. Go." Dane sheltered Lydia as he helped her into the truck. She joined William on the floorboards. Dane's arms were made out of taffy and the pain in his head nearly caused him to black out. More shots hit the ground behind them and on the hood of the truck. Dane crouched down behind the driver's-side door and pushed Ned down closer to the ground. Lydia covered William with her body, and her face with her hands. Dane fired two quick shots from the Redhawk over the hood of the truck. He didn't even know which direction to fire in.

"Give me the boy, and you can go home, Agent Kirby."

Dane tried to gauge where Dahmer's voice was coming from and fired another two rounds in that direction. "I said go fuck yourself, Dahmer."

Dahmer fired on the truck, busting out most of the glass. The shots were explosive, but they were coming from the wrong direction. He knew Dahmer was in the woods, but they were being fired on from the house. He couldn't see a damn thing. William eased his way into the floorboards on the driver's side. He reached out and tugged on Dane's shirt. "Not now, William. Don't worry. I'm not going to leave you." Dane fired blind into the woods again. William pulled at Dane's shirt again as Dahmer returned fire. The shots hit the dirt by Dane's leg and kicked up pea gravel all over him. "Jesus Christ, Dane," Ned yelled and covered his face. "Just shoot him already."

Dane glared at Ned. "I'm trying, asshole."

William pulled at Dane's shirt again. Dane turned to face the boy, finally. "Look, we're in trouble here, but I will not leave you, okay? I will not let this man take you from me. So just let me do this, okay?"

"Okay," William said. "But that's not what I wanted to say."

"Well, what then?"

"I can see him. There in the mirror."

Dane looked into the side mirror mounted on the door. He couldn't see anything but blue sky. "Well, I can't, and if I lift my head to look I'll get it shot off."

"He's standing between the trees in the middle of the moon."

"What?" Another shot took out the grille of the truck. Ned yelled again and Lydia screamed.

"I said he's standing in the moon. Can you see it?"

"Kirby, I don't want to kill you or your people but I'm starting to get pissed off. I just want the boy. We can work together on how to spin it. If I shoot Rose right now, then she can be our patsy."

Dane rolled over and looked under the truck toward the woods. There was a crescent shape of sky between a cluster of sweet gums and a big yellow pine. He thought he could see the shadow of another tree between them, but the tree was moving.

Son of a bitch. The kid is right. He's the man in the moon. Please keep talking, asshole. Please.

Dane got his wish.

"We can figure something out, Kirby, but you know as well as I do that doing it this way is going to kill everyone in that truck. You don't want to be responsible for the death of another family, do you?"

The moon and the stars. Thank you, Gwen.

Dane rolled over on his belly and aimed the Redhawk at the shadow between the trees.

"This is the only feasible option, Kirby, and my last attempt to reason with you."

Dane narrowed his eyes, let out a slow breath, and squeezed the trigger. He knew he'd hit his target even before he heard Dahmer yell out. Dane watched the shadow in the moon sway, become half as tall, and then finally fall. "How's that, buddy? Is that feasible?" He waited for the lump of shadow to answer or to get up or move. It didn't. Dane felt the urge to sit up, and he almost did, but another blast came from the other direction—from the house—and blew out the passenger-side window. Rough beads of broken glass showered the front seat, pelting Lydia as she tried to keep William covered.

"Goddamnit, Eddie. Stop," Dane shouted. "It's over. Velasquez's partner is down and I'm calling it in. This place is going to be covered in cops any minute now." Another shot ricocheted off the hood. "Jesus Christ, Eddie. Give it up before you shoot your own wife." Dane thought that did it. He was listening. The farm went quiet. For a moment the whole world went quiet. No gunfire. No breaking glass. No shredding metal. No birds or leaves rustling in the breeze. Just the sweet silence of time frozen to a stop. Ned lifted himself out of the dirt and gravel and slid closer to the wheel well. He reached in through the bottom of the open door and grabbed blindly for Lydia. When he found her hand, he squeezed it tight three times. *I-love-you*. She did the same and added an extra one. *I-love-you-too*. They'd been doing that since high school. It kept them from having to say it out loud. Afterward, he didn't let go. He couldn't.

"I think he's giving it up, man."

"Eddie doesn't give anything up, Dane." Ned held tight to Lydia's hand. "He'll die first. You know that. He's probably just reloading."

"Then we need to get out of here before he does. Climb over me and get in the truck." Ned started to move although his arm was bent awkwardly under the door. Lydia wasn't letting go.

"The black man you call Eddie is dead," a strange, high-pitched voice said.

Ned stopped moving. "Who the hell is that, now?"

"I don't know," Dane said. The strange new voice just added another layer of confusion to the chaos. The man spoke again. "All of his people are dead, too—the one-eyed man—the one they called Potato. They are all dead."

Dane's brain raced as he tried to understand what was happening—who was talking—who would kill Eddie if not Dahmer. He struggled to recognize the voice. It sounded foreign.

"I have need of the young one. The Blackwell boy."

"Goddamnit," Dane said as it clicked in his head. He slid up against the rim of the front tire.

"I must kill you, too," Fenn said. "But know that I will take no pleasure in it. I will not enjoy killing the woman, either, but you have my word it will be swift and painless."

"Who the fuck *is* that?" Ned said.

"My best guess is that's the same psycho that killed William's big brother, Arnold." Dane wiggled his way across the quarter panel to see if he could get a look at the new problem. He did, and it didn't inspire hope. When Fenn stepped out into the sunlight from the side of the main house, Dane knew he'd used the right word to describe him back at the motel. He was a monster. Even from that distance, Dane could tell that Fenn was the biggest human being he'd ever seen. The man was a beast. His shirt was white and dirty, ripped at the shoulder and the sternum, and Dane could tell he was wearing Kevlar underneath. He was also covered in blood, but Dane assumed most of it belonged to other people. He moved stiffly and slowly, as though he'd been hurt but not enough to retreat, and he still felt confident enough to stand out in the open. He tossed Eddie's rifle into the grass. Dane banged his head back on the tire, lifted himself to his knees, and fired at the house. Fenn didn't even bother to duck or take cover. He'd been watching. He knew Dane's Redhawk wasn't a threat. Firing on him with a handgun of that size from that distance would be pissing in the wind.

"Did you hit him?" Ned asked.

"I can't. He's wearing a vest so I need a head shot and that's a hundred to one shot. I can't do it, not from here and not with this, and he knows it."

"That's because you're shooting wrong," William said.

Dane stared at the boy for a second. The freckles on William's face were lit up in the sunlight, and the bits of glass from the broken windows reflected light all over the inside of the truck like stars. If they weren't all about to die, Dane would've thought it was beautiful. "Listen, William. I know you're smart, but I know the limitations of my own skill and my own gun, and I know that right now it's about as useless as tits on a boar. So hush and let me figure this out. Okay?"

William shrugged. "Okay."

Dane dropped the Redhawk into his lap and clicked open the cylinder, but William had already taken count. "You have two bullets left."

"Yeah, thanks for that." He locked the cylinder back in place.

"I am going to hurt this woman now," Fenn said, and held up the blood-covered baston. He had one huge boot buried in Roselita's back, pressing her into the grass. "She will suffer. She will scream. But you can make it stop by releasing the boy to me." Fenn pressed his foot down harder, leaned over, and shoved the razor-sharp bamboo straight through Roselita's shoulder. She did scream, too, just like Fenn said she would. Fenn twisted the baston and Roselita shrieked.

"Jesus Christ," Dane said, and crushed his eyes shut. He needed to do something. He pushed the door open. "Listen, kid, I'm going to try and get behind the wheel and crank this truck. If we get lucky, the engine is still intact and we can run this bastard over. I want you and Lydia to crawl over the floorboard and—"

"No," William said, and shook his head. He beat his hands at his ears as if he were shooing off a swarm of bees.

"Okay, okay. Stop it. Tell me what to do. What do I do?"

"I already told you. You're shooting wrong."

"That woman out there on the ground doesn't have the time for me to take a lesson in firearm technique from an eleven-year-old, okay? Just get out of the way and let me try to crank the truck."

"No," William shouted, and hung himself out of the door. He pointed. "Just look."

Dane inched over to look through the door hinges at what William already knew was there. He dropped his head to his chest. "Son of a bitch." Dane looked again. "Wait—no—I can't do that. It will kill Rose, too."

"I don't think it will."

"I can't take that chance."

"Mr. Kirby." William held his face inches from Dane's, and he looked in his eyes for the very first time. It was unsettling. Dane knew William's eyes were brown from the file he had on him, but it must've been wrong. Looking at them up close like that, he could see they were more of a deep blue with green and specks of gold in them. Dane knew immediately why it bothered him. The boy had eyes like Joy. Dane couldn't speak.

"It won't kill your friend if she stays low," William said. "Just shoot."

Dane hung his head. He couldn't take the boy's stare a second longer. Roselita screamed again. Dane wiped at his face and then made William and Lydia crawl onto the floorboards of the truck's cab. He let Ned climb inside before falling flat on the ground under the front bumper.

"Hey, asshole. Okay, I'm ready to play ball. Stop doing that and tell me what you want me to do."

Fenn answered, but Dane didn't give a shit what he said. He just wanted Roselita to stop screaming while he took aim at the LPG tank less than twenty feet away from where Fenn was standing. "Rose, hug the dirt. Hard! Now!"

Roselita pressed herself down into the grass with every muscle in her body and Dane fired.

The explosion rocked the truck from across the yard. Dane felt enough heat on his face to think he was on fire. He was afraid to open his eyes. He yelled out above him to make sure William and Lydia were okay. They all sounded off, one by one. Dane rolled onto his back in the dirt and then forced himself up to survey the damage. The LPG tank had gone from a smooth oblong cylinder to a warped and jagged tower of blackened scrap metal. Pieces of it covered the yard and the clearing. The grass had burned out in an almost perfect circle surrounding the tank, and spot fires were everywhere. A cloud of black smoke mushroomed out and spread across the property. Dane's ears were ringing, but he could see Fenn. He was down and he wasn't moving. Dane stood up completely and spotted Roselita lying on her side in a U shape with the lower half of Fenn's broken baston still sticking out of her shoulder. She wasn't moving, either.

"Ned," he yelled. "Ned—" He felt a hand on his shoulder. Ned was already out of the truck and standing behind him, but Dane couldn't hear him. "Take this." He handed the Redhawk to Ned. "There are more shells in the toolbox, make sure that big bastard is dead—the one in the woods, too."

"He's dead, Dane. Goddamn, you blew him half to hell."

"Just do it." Dane yelled to hear his own voice.

Some of Roselita's hair had been burned off above her left ear and her eyebrows were singed. The first and possibly second layers of skin on the tops of her arms and back of her neck had been burned away and were peeling, but the heat seemed to have cauterized the wound around the broken piece of bamboo sticking out of her shoulder. She was in bad shape, but she was breathing. Dane motioned for Ned. "Try to get her inside," he yelled. His ears were still ringing.

"Why?" Ned yelled back. "Let's just go."

"Goddamnit, Ned. Just do it."

The yard was smoking with several grass fires as Dane reached the barn. The smoke hadn't entered the building, but it was dark in there, so he moved in slowly. He walked past a disemboweled Tater, slowly, holding his nose, zigzagging from pen to pen until he found what he was looking for. The smell of blood and other bodily fluids was ripe in the third set of pens. Dane looked down at the two bodies. Casper had been dead for a while, but Eddie's body still hadn't gone cold yet. Dane entered the pen and held his fingers to Eddie Rockdale's neck. He could see the fatal wound to his belly. He was gone. Dane straightened out and stared down at Eddie's body.

"You were there, weren't you, you son of a bitch. Did you watch? Did you watch me pull my wife out of the woods? Did you watch them use a ladder truck to get my daughter's body out of the tree?" Dane spit in the dirt by Eddie's still head. "She loved the stars, my wife. Did you know that? She talked about them every day. And you know what else? I can't see them anymore. I can't look up anymore. I can't look at a night sky without seeing her—all broken—and cold. Like you are now." Dane laughed and kicked the corpse at his feet. "I just wanted you to know. One dead man to another." Dane stopped talking, as if he had suddenly understood that Eddie couldn't hear him. He backed away from the body, reached into his pocket, and took out the .30-30 slug. He tossed it into the dirt where he'd spit. He didn't need it anymore.

When Dane turned to leave, he saw Ned standing in the doorway of the pen. Something cold passed between them.

"How much of that did you hear?"

"Enough."

Dane walked through the gate. Ned took his arm and helped him. "What did you mean 'one dead man to another'?"

"Now ain't the time, Ned. I'm asking if you heard what Eddie said."

Ned looked back and then at Dane. "Um, Eddie didn't say shit. He's dead."

Dane spit in the dirt again. "No, no. He wasn't when I first came out here so I was able to get his confession."

Ned stopped walking. "His confession. Confession for what?"

Dane stopped walking, too, and motioned for Ned to come on. "For killing Tom Clifford. For setting you up. Because he knew you and Lydia were—you know."

Ned didn't say anything. He just stared at Dane with confusion and maybe the hint of a smile.

"C'mon," Dane said. "Let's go."

As soon as the two men passed through the barn door, back into the smoky haze of the yard, it was Ned that took the brunt of the hit.

Fenn landed the punch right between his shoulder blades, sending Ned into Dane and both men sprawling down into the grass. Fenn had been burned so badly he barely looked human anymore. Ned turned onto his back and reached for Dane's Redhawk. It wasn't in his waistband anymore. He hadn't checked Fenn's body as Dane had asked him to, and now he'd lost his gun, too. The huge mass of pink and black curling skin reached down and grabbed Dane by his throat. Ned tried to stop him, but Fenn swung his fist and easily knocked Ned back to the ground. He got back up and grabbed at the creature, but his skin peeled right off in Ned's hands. Ned pounded on his back as pieces of him fell away exposing raw pink flesh and muscle. "Jesus, how are you still alive?"

Dane struggled on the ground but had begun to turn blue in Fenn's grip. Drool dripped onto his face in wet clumps from the big man's ruined mouth. Dane closed his eyes. He was about to black out when he heard the shot. Fenn's grip released and Dane opened his eyes. The blackened man was missing the right half of his face. Ned rushed him again and knocked him over before his huge body fell on Dane. Fenn collapsed again into the yard. Dane wiped at his face and looked around. The blood in his eyes made them sting like hell, but he could see. Lydia stood a few feet away from them, still in a practiced shooter's stance and still pointing Dane's Redhawk with both hands. Ned approached her carefully and took the gun. Dane sat in the grass and wiped the blood from his face with his sleeve. That's when William came out of the house and crossed in front of Lydia and Ned and extended a hand to help Dane up. Dane took his hand, but before he got to his knees, Dane noticed William's eyes again. They were brown. There wasn't a hint of green in them at all.

Lydia held a wet rag against Roselita's face. She'd lost a lot of blood and needed medical attention. The baston still stuck out of her shoulder because no one thought it was a good idea to remove it. Ned forced two tabs of oxy from the kitchen into Roselita's mouth and held the glass of water to her lips. She drank and faded in and out of consciousness as Dane pulled a chair up close to the sofa. He took his time sitting down and balanced himself with both hands. "Roselita, are you with me?" He snapped his fingers in front of her face and Roselita did her best to focus. "I'm—sorry, Kirby. It was—never—"

"I need you to listen to me. I'm about to call for help. You're going to be okay. Do you understand me?"

Roselita nodded.

"I need you to say it, Rose. Do you understand what I'm saying?"

"Yes."

Ned held the glass to Roselita's lips and she drank more of the water. Lydia's pacing back and forth behind Dane was making her dizzy, but Dane snapped his fingers again and brought her back to the moment. "I need you to tell me all of it. Everything."

"I—don't—"

"Start with Dahmer and tell me everything, Rose. I need you to tell me the truth, and I need you to trust me. You still with me?"

"Yes."

"Good, and when you're done, I'm going to call this in." He looked around the room at everyone. "And then all of you need to do and say exactly what I tell you to."

When the conversation was over, Dane got out of the chair and went out on the porch. Ned and Lydia followed him but took the steps into the yard.

"You sure about this, Dane?"

"Yeah, Ned. I'm sure."

"Okay." There was no need to discuss any further what had to be done. Dane had already taken his phone from the top drawer of the china cabinet. Roselita had told him where he could find it. He tapped in a number and held it to his ear.

"O'Barr."

"August, it's Dane."

"Give me something good, Kirby. Tell me why the hell some hillbilly sheriff is blowing up my phone about a prisoner he hasn't been able to locate and tell me why I've been dodging his damn calls because I haven't been able to locate you."

"August."

"And before you start, just know that your answer better be worth hearing if you plan on remaining actively employed by the Bureau. I am not dicking around here, Dane."

"I found the boy, August. I found William Blackwell."

"Well, I'll be damned. That's a good start. Where are you? I'll send people to help you bring him in."

"August, there's more."

"Christ. What *more?*"

"It's a warzone out here."

"What are you talking about?"

"Special Agent Geoff Dahmer and one big Filipino bastard with a bamboo stick just tried to kill me, Agent Velasquez, and several other people. There are multiple casualties, including those two assailants, and Velasquez is in bad shape."

"Are you fucking with me right now?"

"No, August, I'm not. I'll explain when you get here."

"Is the boy all right?"

Dane reached over and ran his hand through William's hair. "He's a little shook up, but otherwise he's fine."

"Kirby, where are you? Tell me now."

"Hard Cash Valley. Rockdale's farm."

"I'm on my way. We'll figure all this out. Your priority right now is keeping the boy safe. Don't you move."

"Copy that."

CHAPTER TWENTY-FOUR

Within minutes of the first helicopter arriving at the farm, the valley began to look like an anthill kicked in by a size-eleven boot. There were suits everywhere. State police arrived next and there wasn't enough yellow tape created to wrap off everything that needed it at the Rockdale Farm. Fire crews had arrived due to the explosion and were still stomping at small grass fires with shovels and rakes as the Rabun County Coroner's Office carried away the bodies of Eddie Rockdale and his uncle Casper, John "Tater" Hopkins, Special Agent Geoff Dahmer, and a big, burned-up Asian killing machine missing a significant portion of his face and skull. Over the next few hours, Dane informed Assistant Director O'Barr of what had occurred. He and Special Agent Velasquez found the boy, William, where his brother had told him to wait at Black Mountain Safari Park, but were attacked, bound, and brought here to the Farm by Eddie Rockdale, who had a deal in place with Special Agent Geoff Dahmer to exchange an unknown sum of money for the boy. Dane and Special Agent Velasquez both tried to reason with Rockdale but failed, right before Rockdale and his people were attacked and killed by the now headless and barbecued Filipino mobster. This allowed Dane and Velasquez to escape with the boy, when they were engaged in a firefight with Dahmer, who had taken Mrs. Rockdale as a hostage. Roselita heroically held a low ground position and fired the shot that freed Lydia Rockdale, allowing Dane to shoot Dahmer dead. Dane also shot the LPG tank, causing the massive explosion that burned the Asian man and accidentally injured Roselita Velasquez. He also informed August that it was

Lydia Rockdale who had saved his life by putting the fatal bullet in the assassin.

The story was a mouthful, and Dane wondered how many times he was going to have to tell it over the next few days. It was going to be a lot, he was sure. Roselita was stabilized and taken to McFalls Memorial to be treated for her injuries, while EMTs examined the newly widowed Lydia Rockdale and a very tight-lipped Ned Lemon, who was ready to be taken back into custody by the McFalls County SO. Dane sat on the front porch with William and they watched August O'Barr approach again as key players of Dane's story were taken away and the federal and state manpower was dismissed.

"Well, this is one big shit show, Kirby."

"Yeah. I know."

August extended a hand to William, who didn't look at it, much less shake it. "I'm August. I'm happy to see you came through all this okay, William. We have some people from child services on their way here right now."

William said nothing and kept his eyes on some fixed point in the distance.

"I'm really sorry for your loss, son." August shot Dane a "what gives" look.

Dane shrugged. "He doesn't talk much. Hasn't said more than two words since I found him."

"Is that right?"

"That's right."

August lowered his hand and they stayed like that for a minute, enveloped by an uncomfortable silence, until it was broken by McFalls County Sheriff Darby Ellis. He'd already cuffed Ned, who had apparently been hiding out in the woods and had nothing at all to do with the events at the farm, and had him in the back of his car.

"Assistant Director O'Barr?" Darby said, and removed his hat.

August pursed his lips and nodded to the Sheriff.

"Do you reckon I can be on my way with my prisoner now, or do your people need to talk to him any more?"

August ran a hand over his bristle-brush head. "You can take him, Sheriff. I know where to find him if I need him. Oh, and thank you for your help on this, son. It won't go unnoticed." O'Barr shook Darby's hand, and Dane thought he saw the old man wink at him when he let go. "Yes, sir. Thank you, sir." The sheriff reseated his hat and walked toward his car. Not long after Darby's taillights disappeared into the trees, another vehicle showed up from DFCS for William. He went with a big, solemn-faced woman with a clipboard without a word spoken, but nodded at Dane as he got in the van. Dane nodded back.

August sat down on the porch next to him. It took him a few beats to speak, and he lit up a long menthol cigarette in the meantime. He inhaled and spoke through a big mouthful of smoke. "My boys found a compact car about a half mile away from here stashed in the woods. They think it belongs to that big dead Asian fella."

"Oh yeah?" Dane said, doing his best to sound surprised. "Why do they think that?"

"Oh, blood and bandages, that kind of thing. It just doesn't belong here, you know? Like him." August nodded to the biggest of the body bags laid out by the last remaining ambulance.

Dane nodded. "Makes sense."

"Yeah. Didn't find any money, though."

"No?" Dane said.

August shook his head. "Nope. They sure did not." He sucked in another big drag of smoke. "Kirby, can I be honest with you?"

"Sure, August."

"I don't give a fuck about you. Not one. Not one single fuck. Not since the beginning of all this."

"Well, okay," Dane said.

"From what I hear you got one foot in the grave anyway, so giving a fuck would be a wasted fuck, you tracking?"

"I think so."

"It true you got the cancer?"

"Yes, sir."

"In the lungs?"

"Yes, sir."

August looked at his cigarette and then stomped it out under his loafer. "Bad shake."

"Yes, sir."

O'Barr removed a toothpick from his shirt pocket and began to gnaw at it as he swished it from side to side in his mouth. "But my point is, you and what happens to you ain't something I'm going to lose a wink of sleep over—but—the boy is safe—so good on you. And everybody I can tell that ended up dead here today pretty much needed to be so. My casebook is lighter for it, and I'll be damned if that deathbed confession you got from Rockdale about your hometown unsolved wasn't one hell of a masterstroke. That's even going to make that goofy-ass teenage sheriff of yours happy—not to mention clear your buddy, Lemon, of the murder charge. I mean, it's like the whole scenario is wrapped up all nice with a bow and everyone comes out peachy, smelling like a fresh-cut rose." August took the toothpick out of his mouth and held it between index finger and thumb. Dane said nothing. "You know who gets fucked here, Kirby? You know who comes out looking like a chump?"

"I couldn't tell you, August. I'm just laying out what happened."

August let a slow laugh build in his belly and then turned to lock eyes with Dane. His stare was cold, gray, and hard, and his face wasn't so much old to Dane now as it was wise. Dane knew the old-guard policeman could see right through him. "Me," he said. "Me. I'm the one who leaves here looking like an ass-clown. I have less than a year until I retire without a single blemish on my jacket and you—you just dropped a psychotic rogue agent operating under my charge into my lap with me none the wiser. That makes me look incompetent. Not to mention not a nickel of the money that got everybody so hot and bothered in the first place was recovered, and you deliver me a story so full of holes it looks worse than that old Ford over there." August pointed the toothpick at Dane's destroyed pickup.

"It's what happened, August."

"It's Assistant Director O'Barr," August said as he stood up. He jabbed the toothpick into something imaginary in the air between them. "Holes," he said. "You know the funny thing about holes. When you pick at them, they get wider and wider and wider until you know what?"

"What's that?" Dane said.

"The truth falls out. And the best way to wipe the shit of a dirty agent off my shoe is to be the first to expose another one."

Dane said nothing but kept O'Barr's cold stare. "You can't expect me to believe Special Agent Velasquez was not aware of her partner's actions, Kirby." He let that suspicion hang between them for a moment. "So here's what I'm going to do. I'm going to go down to that Podunk hospital of yours and sit my tired ass in a chair and wait until *Rosey's* sweet little ass wakes up, and then I'm gonna start poking." He jabbed the toothpick in the air again before turning to walk away. "Oh," he said, turning back. "And if I can find even the smallest whiff of bullshit about what happened out here, how much credibility do you think that deathbed confession you witnessed is gonna hold? One lie—one itty-bitty lie compromises the integrity of the whole, and then it's off to the pokey for your buddy, Lemon. And I understand he's a two-time loser as well. Damn, Kirby. That's got to suck. But fuck it, right? I mean, you ain't gonna be around to see it anyway." He turned to walk off again.

"O'Barr," Dane said and pulled himself upright using the porch railing. "Wait."

August stopped again and faced Dane. He put the toothpick back in his mouth. "Wait for what?" he said.

"They're good people, August. Ned is good people. Rose—she's good police. One of the best detectives I've ever worked with. We saved the kid and closed the case. Everybody wins."

"Not everybody. I thought I was pretty clear about that."

"You were, but setting out to ruin good people because of bad press? C'mon, August. There has to be a better way."

August looked down into the grass and pulled the toothpick from his mouth. "Sorry, Kirby. Bad press ruins careers. I'm not about to let it ruin mine."

Dane took a step off the porch. He lowered his voice. "I'm not about to believe you were unaware of the atrocities your agent was committing right under your nose, August."

O'Barr's eyes sunk back and he turned into the darker, harder man Dane had witnessed days ago in the motel room Arnie Blackwell was killed in. "You have no idea what you're talking about, Kirby."

"Oh, yeah? So if I did a little bullshit sniffing of my own, you'd come out of that smelling like an Irish spring?"

O'Barr took a quick step back toward Dane and then looked around the yard and calmed himself. "Are you in too big a hurry to die instead of waiting on the cancer to kill you, Kirby?"

"No, sir. I can wait."

"Then watch your mouth and stay out of my way."

"I can do that, sir. If you take my eyewitness account and leave the people involved alone."

O'Barr smiled, but it was venomous. He took another step toward Dane. "I could end you right now, Kirby. Not one of the men out here would question me."

"I believe that, sir."

"Then give me one good reason why I shouldn't."

It was Dane's turn to look at the ground. He rubbed a hand through his hair and then sunk both hands into the pockets of his filthy cargo pants. He met August's eyes and held them. "What if I gave you one point two million reasons?"

August sucked on his toothpick for what seemed to Dane like a lifetime before the smile came. "Did I tell you I'm retiring soon?"

A day later, when Roselita woke up, it wasn't August O'Barr sitting next to her hospital bed. It was Dane. Roselita was practically mummified and drunk with painkillers, but her round face was mostly clear and she could understand what was happening around her. Dane stood when she turned her head to look at him and he saw her eyes were open. "Hey, partner."

"Where am I?"

"You're at McFalls Memorial Hospital, but I believe they are going to send you down to Augusta to the Burn Center. It sounds scary, but you're okay. You're going to be okay."

"The kid?"

"Is fine. He's under the protection of Clementine Richland and her people down in Cobb. He's going to be okay, too."

Roselita closed her eyes again.

"Your fiancée is out there talking to the doctors now," Dane said and Roselita's eyes popped back open.

"Kelly is here?"

"Yeah. I called her on your phone. Used your finger to unlock it while you were sleeping. I hope that's okay. She got here about an hour after I hung up. She must drive like you."

Roselita let out a small smile that seemed to hurt her. "Dane—did he—did—"

Dane leaned down closer to the bed. "He did. Just like you said he would. All August wanted was the money. Now that he has access to it, he can't get this case wrapped up quick enough. You're coming out of this clean."

Roselita jetted a bandage-wrapped hand out and grabbed Dane's shirt. "Why? Why did you do this—for me? After what I did. After what I—" Roselita stopped talking and let go of Dane's shirt when the door opened behind them and a beautiful but tired and obviously pregnant blond woman, in jeans and a pink flannel shirt, with tear-streaked mascara lining her cheeks, burst in. Dane moved as Kelly rushed in to be at her woman's side. She kissed her cheeks and mouth before leaning down to hug her. Roselita winced but kept her eyes wide on Dane. Dane slipped his ball cap on and put one hand on his stomach. He made the shape of a half circle—the universal sign for pregnant—and nodded at Kelly. He mouthed the words "Don't waste it." Roselita didn't have enough time to say thank you before Dane left the room.

CHAPTER TWENTY-FIVE

The fluorescent light of the southern diner didn't stand a chance against the bright afternoon sun that flooded the Waffle House through the huge plate-glass windows. The light warmed everything it touched, the laminated menus, the coffee cups and spoons, the napkin caddie, the black and white checkerboard tile in the table, and Dane's skin. It felt good on his face. He'd taken off his hat, put the keys to his rental car inside it, and set it next to him on the booth. It had taken a few months for Ned to be completely exonerated of all charges for the death of Tom Clifford, and this was the first time Dane had seen him in weeks. He sat with Lydia, the back of her hand absently rubbing his leg, at the table across from Dane.

"I like the haircut," Dane said. Ned pushed nonexistent bangs back over his ear.

"I don't think I've seen it that short since fifth grade."

"The lawyer said it would play better in court," Lydia said, and ran her hand over Ned's ear. He pulled away slightly and his face showed the disdain he held for his new clean-cut look. "It will also help with the foster-family application we're filling out to get custody of William," Lydia said. "I don't know, Dane. They ask a lot of questions about Ned's past, and we're not married. I don't know if we're going to be able to do it."

Dane reached into his shirt pocket and pulled out a business card. "I've been thinking about that. Call this woman. She's a friend and she may be able to help." He slid Clementine Richland's card across the table and Lydia took it. She looked at it briefly and then put it in her purse. They sat in silence as Dane sipped his coffee and Ned let his get cold. Lydia took another stab at conversation.

"I'm sorry to hear about Misty, Dane."

"Don't be. She had every right to leave. She deserves better, anyway."

Ned shook his head and broke his silence. He was angry, too—and hurt. Dane understood that as well. Ned leaned across the table and spoke softer than normal.

"I'm not okay with this, Dane. I mean, look at you. You're skinny as a rail and you look like shit, and what? I'm supposed to do nothing?"

Dane had dropped a lot of weight. It was the cancer chewing him up from the inside. He knew he looked bad but he felt good. Today was a good day. He laced his fingers together and sat his hands on the sun-warmed table.

"You're doing something right now, Ned. Your being here is what I need."

"Fuck that." Ned's voice got louder and Lydia rubbed his leg harder to soothe him back down. He lowered his voice again. "How am I supposed to let you walk out that door, knowing I'm never going to see you again? How can you ask that of me—of us. It's bullshit."

"It's part of the deal, Ned. We talked about this."

"The deal ain't fair, man."

"Life ain't fair, brother. But it is what it is. I'm a loose end. O'Barr has nothing to fear from the two of you. He doesn't even see y'all as real people, but me? I'm a cop who can bend the ear of bigger cops. I can destroy the man. He knows it. This—this is a better way."

Ned leaned back. "And what about Velasquez? Isn't she a loose end, too?"

"Rose can take care of herself. Worst case scenario, my way gives her an out, too. Someone to pin any blowback on, if she needs to."

Ned flared up again. "No one is pinning shit on you, Dane. I won't—"

"Ned," Lydia said sternly, in order to calm him down. He did. He took a sip of his cold coffee and pushed it away. "I just don't see how you expect me to just let this happen."

"Ned, listen to me. You're my brother. That isn't going to change. But you aren't letting anything happen. This is my decision. I'm a grown man. This is my call. And it's the only way I know of to protect Lydia."

Both Lydia and Ned looked confused. Dane leaned back in his seat. "What? C'mon, y'all. I'm a detective, remember? Ned, you were tested for GSR. It was negative. But more importantly, I know you. You can't shoot for shit. Never could. You couldn't hit the side of a barn with bird-shot. But I was willing to believe what you told me until . . ." Dane caught Lydia's eyes, and her face was stone strong. "Until I saw you shoot that big bastard at the Farm. You've been training. It was easy to see. The way you were standing. The way you held the gun. The aim from that distance. Not too many people I know could've pulled off that shot. I know Ned here couldn't. And Tom was shot center mast—twice—by someone who could shoot."

"It's not what—"

Dane waved a hand to keep Ned from spinning another pointless lie. "Ned, it's okay. I understand why you protected her. I understand why you did it, Lydia. Y'all have to live with what happened. My role in this is to make sure you two are never found out. That's why this has to be handled my way."

Ned said nothing. His eyes were wet but he held it together. A few uncomfortable minutes later they heard a horn blare outside and they all turned and looked out the window. Dane smiled wide when he saw his father's old Ford truck ease into the parking lot. It was completely restored and painted thunderbird blue. The damn thing looked as if it had just been wheeled off the showroom floor. Ned sank his head to his chest as Keith Bell opened the driver's-side door of the classic pickup and stepped out into the lot. He waved. Lydia picked up a yellow slip of paper from the table and offered to pay the check while the boys talked outside. Ned stood up and helped Dane out of the booth, although he didn't need it. Dane grabbed his hat, now warm from the flood of Georgia sun, and sat it low on his head. Ned held the door and the two of them walked out to meet Keith.

"I cannot believe you got her looking this good," Dane said. Keith scratched at himself under a black *I, Zombie* T-shirt and gave Dane a half smile before meeting Ned's angry eyes. He immediately looked back at the truck. "She runs even better than she looks," he said. "It took me a while and I maxed out one of Dad's credit cards finding the parts, but she's as good as new, if not better."

Dane walked around the truck dragging a hand over the fresh paint, with a genuine ear-to-ear smile, flooded with memories of his father, of childhood rides over back roads, and Gwen, and steamed windows. It was hard to believe this was the same vehicle that had taken such a pummeling at the Farm just a few months back. Dane hugged Keith and for the first time he realized how frail he'd become. He felt like a paper doll in the arms of his muscular friend. He whispered in Keith's ear. "And the other thing?"

Keith nodded and tightened his grip on Dane. "Yeah, Dane, it's in the glove box." They stayed that way, locked in their embrace until Dane let go and thanked him. Keith just nodded again. Dane turned to Ned, who was now standing with Lydia, and he held out his hand. Ned looked at it for a couple seconds before taking it and pulling Dane in for another short brotherly hug. Ned let go quickly and ran both hands back over his new haircut. Dane handed the rental-car keys to Lydia and asked her if she would still handle bringing it back to town for him. She gripped the keys in her hand and lurched at him. She held him so tight he thought he might snap in half. She was openly crying now, but Dane held her there until she regained control. When he let her go, she couldn't look at him. She turned and walked to the rented Celica, hit the key fob, and unlocked the door.

Dane raised an imaginary shot glass. "Here's to swimmin' with bow-legged women, boys." No one laughed. Keith handed him the keys to the truck. Ned and Keith both remained silent when Dane got in and cranked the engine. They moved back and out of the way as he dropped the shifter into reverse and than punched it into first. He didn't look back at his friends although he knew they were there watching him go. Instead he pointed his father's truck toward the highway and disappeared into the afternoon.

Lydia backed the rented Celica out of its parking space a minute later and pulled up next to Ned. She asked him if he was okay. He mumbled something she couldn't understand. He wasn't okay. But he had to be. The two men watched the Celica leave the lot next and stood there in the sun.

"Nice haircut, Ned."

"Fuck you, Keith."

Dane rolled his window down and reached for the stereo when Gwen stopped him. She put her hand on his. Her fingers were long and delicate like a piano player's—the diamond in her wedding ring shiny in the sun. "Are you sure this is what you want?" she said. He looked over at her sitting on the passenger side in that yellow dress he loved. Her molasses-and-honey hair streaming out the window. Her high cheekbones accenting a look of concern. Dane ignored the question. "You look amazing, Mrs. Kirby."

"Well, of course I do, Mr. Kirby." She removed her hand from his and he clicked on the stereo. He turned the dial and the red needle behind the glass searched for a signal through the static. Steve Miller began to blare through the speakers—that big old jet airliner. Dane drove and sang along and listened to Gwen's tonally challenged voice wisp in and out of every song to play, one after another. It was one of the most beautiful sounds he'd ever heard. Every now and then he took his eye off the road and soaked her in. "I love you, woman," he said before he took a random exit. She smiled that smile that broke him and owned him at the same time. "I know," she said.

Dane wheeled the truck to a stop at the end of the off ramp and turned left. He saw the black Chevy Tahoe in the rearview follow him onto the exit and he shook his head. He'd seen the truck a few times. August's people were either getting sloppy these days or just didn't care anymore. Dane looked around. He'd never been to this part of Fannin before, so he just drove the two-lane blacktop for a few hours, watching as the needle on the gas gauge dropped. Overhead, crisscrossing turkey vultures flew in patterns and moved with a hive-mind fluid grace. The greens and browns and golds of the trees blurred and swirled, and Dane held one arm out the window, forever trying to catch the wind. He passed over bridges and over waterways that were too low to catch any good fish in and drove slowly through small communities with wooden stop signs, antique stores, and old men at picnic tables. He waved. Most of them waved back. When he saw the wide-open field of wildflowers and saw grass coming up on his right, he slowed the truck and pulled over to the red clay shoulder. Gwen would've made them stop here if she were alive. This would be as good a place as any. He turned off the engine and ran his fingers over the soft fabric of the empty bench seat. Of course Gwen was gone now. She wouldn't be here to see this. She would be a million miles away from here with Joy, singing out of tune. Anywhere but here, not now, not for this.

Dane opened the glove box and took out a blue envelope. He removed the title to the truck and used a BIC pen to sign over ownership to Jackson Gordon. He addressed the envelope to Jenn Gordon and wrote a short note. *For the coolest kid I know, when he's ready.* He signed his name with a flourish and returned the envelope to the glove box.

Next he removed the Colt revolver Keith had left for him. Dane's Redhawk had been confiscated during the federal investigation of the Farm and was never given back, so Keith had procured a proper and untraceable replacement. He held the gun and let the heft of it fill both hands. After a time, he laid the gun in his lap, reached back inside the glove box, and removed a pack of Camel Blues and a Zippo lighter that Keith had also left there at Dane's request. That's when he saw the postcard. It looked old and yellowed, so he didn't think it was part of Keith's care package. No, this was something else. This had been in here a while—for years. This was from Gwen.

It was one of her surprise notes. Like the ones she'd put in his lunch or left taped to the bathroom mirror in the mornings when she was alive. He didn't know how he'd missed it after all this time. Maybe Keith found it under the seat or something when he'd had it cleaned out and just tucked it in here. Maybe he'd left it in here instead of throwing it out, thinking it mattered in some way. Dane slid it out of the glove box and read the poem printed there. Pablo something was the author and the gist of it was typical Gwen, Roman numerals, stars, and lines about love that Dane almost never understood. But this time he didn't have to understand the words. He just needed to understand the timing. He read it over and over, flipped it over and over in his shaking hands, and then for the first time in months—since the bathroom fight with Misty a few months ago—he cried. He laughed and cried again until it became a combination of both.

After a while, he tucked the postcard in his shirt pocket and peeled the cellophane off the pack of smokes. He pulled one out, lit it up, and tossed the pack and lighter onto the seat of the old Ford. Dane let the cigarette hang from his lips as he popped the cylinder on the revolver and inspected the load. He flipped it back into place, took a long drag of Turkish tobacco, and got out of the truck. He waved at the black Tahoe looming just over the hill behind the main road. He held the Colt across his forehead to block the sun from his eyes as he waited to see if it would move. The black SUV only simmered and blurred in the heat like a distant mirage, and Dane began to wonder if it was even real or if it was just a figment of his sickness. At this point in the game, he didn't care.

So, after giving the truck the bird and waving his cell phone at the occupants, he lowered the gun and walked toward the field, feeling the sun on his face and the tall grass whip at his shins and knees. The gun was heavy and so the idea of weight occurred to him—weight and strength. He'd carried so much of it—so much weight for so long—he'd felt defined by it. Defined by the strength it took to bear the load. Now, despite the heavy gun in his hand, standing in that open field, Dane felt weightless, like a floating ash from a long-extinguished fire, and there he realized that the real burden he'd been bearing hadn't been carrying the weight on his back, but finding the strength to set it down—to let it go.

He'd smoked the cigarette down to the filter, pinched it out, and tucked the yellow cotton nub in his pocket. He dropped to his knees and pressed the gun into the soft flesh under his jaw and looked straight forward. He waited, his thumb frozen on the hammer, his body frozen in time, before finally dropping the gun in the grass by his knees. He waited a little longer for the inevitable, for the sound of someone behind him. He knew he'd hear it eventually, and finally it came, along with the pressure of another gun being pressed into the back of his head. Dane didn't flinch or try to look back.

"We were over there waiting. We thought you were going to off yourself out here and save us all the trouble."

"Sorry to let you down."

"Yeah, well," the unfamiliar voice behind Dane said. "O'Barr is done waiting, too."

Dane stayed facing forward, still and calm. His voice was relaxed. "Can you at least listen to something before you pull the trigger?"

The gunman hesitated but didn't seem to be in any rush. "And what would that be?"

Dane slowly moved his hand to his pocket. He felt the gun barrel on his skull press in tighter. "Take it easy," he said. "I'm just getting out my phone."

"Slow and easy," the voice said.

Dane eased his cell phone out of his pocket, swiped it open, and tapped the voice memo app. He held it up backwards for the gunman to hear. The recording of August O'Barr accepting the million-dollar bribe along with Dane's story of the events at the farm rang out over the field. After a minute or so, he felt the pressure of the gun at his head ease up and he lowered the phone. "I have it all. And so do a few other people I trust," he said. "Every word of the deal I made that your boss wants to renege on now. O'Barr will go down in flames over this."

The voice behind him took a few beats but answered exactly the way Dane expected him to. "That recording incriminates you, too, Kirby. O'Barr goes down, then so do you."

Dane shrugged and his shoulders sagged. "You think I give a shit? Look at me. I'm already dead. You idiots oughta know that better than anyone. You've been watching me get closer for months. But here's the thing. I don't give a damn about me. Like I said, I most likely won't see the end of the year, but if anything happens to me right now, or to Roselita Velasquez, or to anyone you assholes were staring at back at that diner, or to the boy, William Blackwell—I mean, if any of them even stubs a toe in a way that looks shady, this recording goes viral. It starts showing up on desks everywhere. Starting with the office of Charles Finnegan at the GBI. So yeah, I go down as a collaborating witness in a nice comfy hospital bed, but O'Barr goes down on a big boy named Bubba in a prison cell. How's that for a retirement plan."

A full minute of silence followed before one of the two men standing behind Dane made a call to his boss. Dane couldn't hear the conversation, but he already knew the outcome. The gun came completely off his head. He smiled but still didn't move. Within a few more minutes, his would-be executioners were gone. He stayed on his knees a while longer before dropping down on his haunches in the grass completely. He didn't look behind him. He didn't have to. He knew August had called them off. He stared down at the Colt in the grass and then picked it up. He clicked out the cylinder and let all the slugs fall into the field. He tossed the gun far enough away that he couldn't see it and picked up his phone from his side where he'd laid it. He scrolled the contacts, found the right name, and tapped the number. It only rang once.

"Dane?"

"Misty?"

"What do you want, Dane?"

Dane could feel his eyes swell up with water again. "Well, for starters, I could use some company."

"I'm not going to hold your hand while you die, Dane. Told you, I can't—"

"I meant some company at Dr. McKenzie's office. I'm scared and I don't want to go alone."

Silence flooded the line before Misty finally blurted out, "Dane, where are you? I'll come and get you right now."

"How about I meet you there?"

"How long?"

Dane looked around the field. "About an hour?" he said. He could tell she was already crying and asked her to stop. He'd grown so tired of making this woman cry. That stopped today.

"I'm on my way," she said.

"Okay—and Misty?"

"Yes?"

"I'm sorry I waited so long."

"Just get there," she said through a broken sob, and ended the call.

Dane stared at the phone and then looked up at Gwen. He knew she would be there and he knew she'd have that "I told you so" look on her face. How he loved her face.

"Now was that so hard?" she said.

Dane wiped the tears from his own face. "Yes," he said. "It was."

"Well," Gwen said as she helped him to his feet. "Nothing worth having is easy. And that phone call you just made was the smartest thing you've done since the day you married me." She wiped at his face, too, and helped clear away his tears. "Now, go," she said. "Go, Dane Kirby. Go—and live."

Dane nodded and tried to hold on to her hand as she backed away, turned, and disappeared into the sunlight and the wheat and the straw. This time he didn't close his eyes. He watched her go, maybe for the last time. When he couldn't make out the shape of her anymore, he looked up. He looked up at the stars he couldn't see, at the constellations hidden behind the blue. The clouds were thick and white and the sky was as bright as he'd ever seen it. He kept his eyes open for the first time in over a decade. He wanted to see the sky. He needed to see it. He missed it. He took the postcard from his shirt pocket and read it one more time before letting the wind carry it to the ground. It served its purpose. He didn't need it anymore. He took a deep breath and the air tasted sweet. Maybe the sweetest he'd ever known. He took one last glance at the sky before leaving. "Goddamn," he said. "It's a beautiful day."

LOVE SONNET XVI

I love the piece of earth you are
because in all the planetary prairies
I do not have another star. You repeat
the multiplication of the universe.
Your wide eyes are the light I have
of the vanquished constellations,
your skin pulses like the roads
the meteor follows in the rain.
Of so much <u>moon</u> were your hips to me,
of all the sun your deep mouth and its delight,
of so much burning light like honey in the shade
your heart burnt by long red rays,
and this is how I follow your fire—kissing you,
small and planetary, dove and geography.

—Pablo Neruda

Acknowledgments

As always, I'd to thank Nat Sobel and Judith Weber, along with everyone at Sobel/Weber that work so hard for me on a nearly everyday basis. Also huge thanks to my editor, Kelley Ragland, who consistently makes me look better than I am, and the entire team at St. Martin's Publishing Group and Minotaur Books. They are a class act from the ground up and without them, no one would be holding this novel. I'd like to thank Jordan Desarrio and Isaac Kirkman, who both influenced my life in many different ways. You deserve a better memorial than just your names in the back of this book, but it's a start. I miss you both and hopefully I'll see you when I get there.

This novel, at its heart, is about love and loss and how frequently those two things walk hand in hand. The sonnet entitled "Love Sonnet XVI" by Pablo Neruda is written on the postcard that Dane finds at the end of the story. It was left there by the great love of his life who also happened to be his greatest loss. The words on that postcard are what kept Dane alive, proving that at least for me, love truly does conquer all. I know that's cheesy to say out loud, but I'm one of those guys that still believes it when Lennon sings "All You Need Is Love." I still believe my Dad's advice to always love hard and never be afraid to shout it from the rooftops. So that leads me to the last person I'd like to acknowledge here. For my son, Wyatt James Panowich, a third-generation outlaw, I can give you this: You're going to grow up and get your heart broke. There is no avoiding it and there's no cure for it either. But don't let it stop you from getting back up and falling in love just as hard the next time until you find the great love of your life. And when you do, hold on with both hands and never let go. And if you ever feel like it's all too much to deal with, you can always call your old man, because there is no shortage of love for you here.

Brian Panowich
March 2020